8117

27/8/19

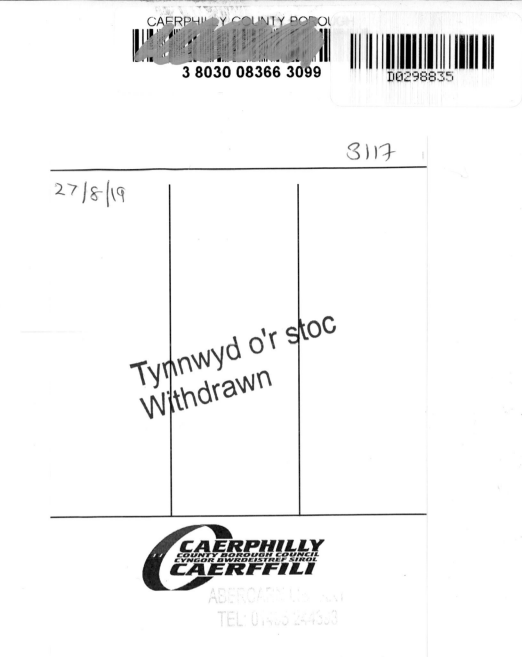

Tynnwyd o'r stoc
Withdrawn

CAERPHILLY
COUNTY BOROUGH COUNCIL
CYNGOR BWRDEISTREF SIROL
CAERFFILI

ABERGAER LIBRARY
TEL: 01495 244333

Please return / renew this item by the last date shown above
Dychwelwch / Adnewyddwch erbyn y dyddiad olaf y nodir yma

A
MIGHTY
DAWN

Theodore Brun studied Dark Age archaeology at Cambridge, where he graduated with a BA in Archaeology and Anthropology and an MPhil in History. Professionally, Theodore qualified and worked as an arbitration lawyer, in London, Moscow, Paris and finally Hong Kong. In 2010, he quit his job in Hong Kong and cycled 10,000 miles across the whole of Asia and Europe to his home in Norfolk. Theodore is a third generation Viking immigrant – his Danish grandfather having settled in England in 1932. He is married and divides his time between London and Norfolk. *A Mighty Dawn* is his first novel.

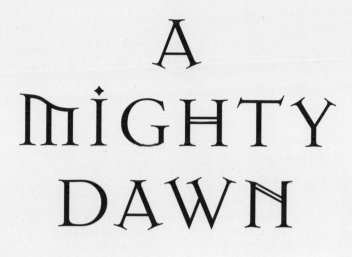

A
MIGHTY
DAWN

Theodore Brun

CORVUS

First published in hardback in Great Britain in 2017 by Corvus,
an imprint of Atlantic Books Ltd.

10 9 8 7 6 5 4 3 2 1

A CIP catalogue record for this book is available from the British Library.

Hardback ISBN: 978 1 78239 994 0
Trade paperback ISBN: 978 1 78239 995 7
E-book ISBN: 978 1 78239 996 4

Printed in Great Britain by Bell and Bain Ltd, Glasgow

Corvus
An imprint of Atlantic Books Ltd
Ormond House
26–27 Boswell Street
London
WC1N 3JZ

www.corvus-books.co.uk

For Cousin Henry

N

HALOGALAND

Site of
Norsk Battle

RAUMERIKA

HEDAMARK

RINGARIKA

Nislagard

SVEÄLAND

Uppsala

FINLAND

WESTERN
GOTARLAND

EASTERN
GOTARLAND

EAST SEA

ESTLAND

Vendlagard

Vitullsuven

JUTLAND

JUTENBELT

Freyhamen

WESTERN
OCEAN

DENMARK

Leithra

Rerik

GAUDARIKI

Southern Scandinavia
in
Early 8th Century

– – – Voyage of the Vendlings
· · · · · · Journeys of the Stranger

PROLOGUE

The laugh rose in his throat, joyous and wild.

Around him, dusk dew sprayed in silver showers, his legs pumping through the bracken.

He glanced back.

Far behind languished the fastest of his companions. He'd left them all dead-footed. Now they were no more than pinprick shadows darting through the trees.

He surged on, thighs burning. He felt alive. Beside him ran his beloved hound. The dog had only one eye – half the sight of other dogs maybe, but twice the heart.

So far the sport had been thin: a pair of foxes and a red deer were all they had to show for a long day. But this was going to make it a day to remember.

Ahead of him, the beast fled through the undergrowth. A magnificent hart, crowned with towering antlers of a dozen proud points.

King of the forest.

And a prize worthy of the son of a king, thought the young man, breathless. The gods knew a feast was long overdue at his father's table. If he could only get a line on it. One chance was all he needed.

Suddenly, there it was.

He pulled up. His dog stopped beside him.

The wind had dropped, the air now still as death. The deer stood, not fifty paces away, blowing panicked breath into the dirt. The prince sniffed with satisfaction. He'd guessed he would get his chance. With those antlers, it was never going to run far.

The dog's one eye stared faithfully up at him, patient as ever. The prince shot him a wink for luck.

Noiselessly, he nocked an arrow, inching right for a clearer shot. The dog shadowed him, stealthy as a ghost. Up ahead, the stag had found a few old blueberries and was picking at them. The light was fading. This would be his last shot of the day. His last, and his best.

He stilled the beat of his heart, drew back the bowstring, sucking in a breath, locking it away.

Just. . . one. . . more. . .

Suddenly the deer's head snapped up. For a heartbeat, its eyes pierced the gloom. The prince's arrow tip wavered. And just for a second his blood ran cold.

The deer had the eyes of a man.

Surely he was mistaken. But before he could look again, the beast sprang towards him.

He backed away. Only a step, but enough to break his concentration. He could shoot a moving target, but deer should run away from their pursuers, not towards them.

The dog growled as his master's mind flirted with his sword

hilt. But there was no time. The deer was heading straight for him, muscles rippling under its hide.

He raised the arrow tip again, took aim, felt the power in the bow. One shot.

Suddenly, the deer swerved across his line of sight. He glimpsed its flank, swung the arrowhead giving the animal a lead.

And loosed.

The arrow flew like a comet. But at the last instant, the deer chinked left. The point raked its haunch, but didn't bite, and the arrow skittered away into the dusk. The animal bellowed in protest and charged. His bow felt sickeningly empty. He backed away, panic rising like bile, then his foot snared and he was falling.

A dull thud of bone on wood. His head exploded in pain and he slumped against the trunk, only to see the stag drop its thicket of antlers. He had hardly time to whimper before they slammed into his body. He screamed, pain surging through his torso like a burning tide. He tasted blood. The dog was barking.

Do something, he begged in his mind. But for once his faithful friend failed him. He lay stupefied. Bleeding.

Dying.

The stag backed away slowly, as if measuring a second blow. But for the moment, it held off. Instead, its head peered closer, snorting hot breath into his face.

He groaned. His body was aflame. And then he saw those eyes again. The same terror gripped him, and as he watched through a fog of pain, the animal seemed to change. The bulging haunches shrank, the legs grew thick and long. The fur shrivelled, became taut and smooth. The muzzle melted away.

Only those eyes stayed the same.

Noiselessly, the creature reared up. The dog let out a whine and scampered off into the gloom. The prince's heart was pounding. He couldn't believe his eyes. Yet he had to. There was no mistake.

The hart had become a man.

The figure stood over him, naked body streaked with dirt, blood streaming from his shoulder. In his hand, he clutched the fragment of an antler, tips wet with blood.

The prince's bowels turned to water. This wasn't real. Couldn't be. This was the stuff of old songs.

The stuff of nightmares.

A shiver passed over the figure, and then, slowly, he leaned closer. The prince stiffened with the horror of recognition. 'You!'

A glimmer of a smile passed over the cold, white lips.

Then a hand closed around his throat. He coughed, felt blood spatter his lips. This wasn't how it was supposed to be. He was the son of a king, heir to the realm. But the shape-shifter only snarled and stabbed the antler into his stomach, sinking it deep.

He felt the bone twist. Caught the foul smell of his own innards. Tried to push the man away, but his arms wouldn't respond.

He heard voices, undergrowth cracking. He tried to cry out, but all that came was a crumpled moan.

'Hush.' The voice was cold as winter. A hand covered his mouth. His heart was kicking like a mule at his ribs. The noises grew fainter. His eyes fell shut.

And then, he heard nothing at all.

PART ONE

CHOSEN SON

CHAPTER ONE

Four months earlier, in the faraway land of the Jutes, the farmstead of Vendlagard was a whirl of excitement. These were the last busy days before the Feast of Oaths.

Geese flapped, chickens squawked as hairy-chinned thralls chased them round the yard. The womenfolk, up to their armpits in bubbling tubs, scrubbed their finery: bright dresses of tight-woven wool, silken ribbons for their hair or costly shawls to adorn themselves for the revelry. Sunlight danced off blades burnished like mirrors by warriors' servants. Every man was to look his best.

The boys and girls were sent to gather flowers and ivy from the woods, and heather growing wild on the heath to the west. The little ones shrieked around the yard in delight, strewing foliage in their wake.

Before long, the hall of Vendlagard was a burst of colour, its dark pillars decked in red and blue and white and yellow flowers, the carved faces in the gable still grousing away, in spite of the colours playing about their ears.

This day had been a while coming. In nineteen years of service, Tolla had seen many a young man stand before his lord and swear his oaths, kin looking on. No more than boys, every one. Some of them still lived; many had fallen. That was the way of things. The All-Father made his choosing, and nothing anyone could do about it.

But tonight was special. Tonight it was Hakan's turn to bind himself, blood and iron, to his lord father. She felt a glow of pride. After all, didn't she love him like he was her own? Perhaps better even than that.

And now all the Vendling kinsfolk would come, and many others from the Jutish families, to see him sealed a man. Word had gone out to every corner of Jutland. Lord Haldan's hall would be full to the rafters with merriment. No seat left empty.

And it's past noon already.

The thought suddenly made her feel sick. There was precious little time before the first guests arrived and still much to do.

Now where was Inga? Hakan's younger cousin was flighty as a swallow. Always getting under your feet when you wanted her out the way, and never to be found when there was any work needed doing.

'Einna!' she yelled at the scrawny maid toting a pail of milk across the yard in a hurry. 'You seen that dratted girl Inga?'

'Like to get my hands on her myself,' returned the girl, her cheeks flushed. 'She promised she'd split half my chores and I haven't seen a hair of her all morning.'

Lord Haldan's spear-master loped by. 'You haven't seen Inga have you, Garik?'

'Check the stables. I'd lay my hand she's off on Sorvind. And Hakan with her.'

Most days, that was a fair bet, but Tolla had just come from the stables and Inga's beloved stallion was tethered.

'Thinks she's too grand for hard work, that one,' said Einna, setting down her milk and pushing her feathery hair out of her face.

'Just needs taming by the right fella,' grinned Garik, licking at a crooked tooth. 'High blood or low – it's the same for all you wenches.'

'You just keep a-walking, you leery brute,' snapped Tolla, shooing him away. 'And mind you don't talk like that about Lord Haldan's kin. Especially not today.'

Garik gave her a wink. 'They all gotta learn it sometime, sister,' he laughed, and stalked off.

Maybe, Tolla thought. *But not Inga. Not yet.*

Now where the blazes *was* that girl?

'They're going to find out,' giggled Inga, still making half-hearted efforts to fend off his wandering hands.

'Never!' Hakan laughed. 'They wouldn't know a nail if it poked 'em in the eye.' He pushed her back against the tree. The sweet, sticky smell of pine mingled with the sea air. This time she gave in, looking up at him. He shook his head, marvelling at those doe eyes. In them he saw a girl and a goddess both. Everything he ever wanted.

'You need a leash,' she smiled, biting her lip. 'And that Tolla – she's got her beady eye on everything. We must be careful.'

'Bah! Hel take the careful! Come here.' He slipped his hand round her and drew her close, catching a whiff of the sea in her hair. Her lips met his and parted. She tasted salty. Her tongue flickered against his teeth – a trick they had discovered together that summer.

They had discovered many.

'The best kisses are after a swim,' she murmured.

'Aye – and more than just kisses,' growled Hakan, tugging hungrily at her girdle.

'Not here! Not now. Someone might come.' She glanced anxiously over his shoulder towards the farmstead.

'You didn't seem to care the other night.'

'That was different.' She smiled, remembering. 'Besides, they're expecting me in the yard. Tolla's probably already marked me for a birching as it is.'

'Just a while longer,' he murmured into her dark curls.

'I can't,' she insisted, pushing him away. 'There's too much to do.'

'Horse shit.'

'Well, you can hardly complain, cousin. It's all for you, isn't it?' She broke free and began strutting up and down. 'Tonight, you must become a man, Hakan,' she boomed, aping his father's voice.

'I'm a man already.' The joke irritated him. Hadn't she made him that?

Was it only two months since the morning they had set out for the Skaw, the northernmost tip of Jutland? It seemed like a lifetime ago. They had been two different people then, riding north to the point. To the place where seas collide. That day, they had been cousins – the closest of childhood companions. Hers was the first face he could remember, the last he would ever forget. But that day, under the shadow of the swaying

10

grass, he had tasted her for the first time. Had been able to show her the love he had always felt for her.

When they rode back to Vendlagard, to the ancient hall of their fathers, as they had done so many times before, they both knew. The world would never be the same again.

'Don't be angry.' She brushed her fingertips against his cheek. 'Come on.' Taking his hand, she led him back to their things.

'Are you nervous?' she asked, as he pulled his tunic over his wet hair.

'Nervous?'

'About tonight,' she replied, fussing at the brooches that held her work dress in place.

'Maybe. A little.' He shrugged. 'Everyone'll be looking at me. But it's all pointless, don't you think?'

'Why?'

'Hardly takes a ceremony to make me loyal to my own father. Or serve him. It's not as if I have a choice.'

'Maybe. But an oath makes all the difference. Your life becomes bound to his in a deeper way. In life. And in death.'

'Gods – you sound like Garik!'

'Well?' she laughed. 'Isn't it true?' Her face clouded. 'Now you'll have to fight.'

'I would fight anyway,' he said, bristling at the reminder that he had never stood in the shieldwall.

'Yes, but you would be sworn to it.' He saw a glimmer of sadness in her hazel eyes.

'Inga,' he said, squeezing her hand. 'You know I'd never leave you alone.'

She forced a brave smile. 'That's for the Spear-God to decide.'

'Listen, my fate is joined as tight to yours as any oath can tie me to my father.'

'Do you promise?'

'Haven't I a thousand times?'

She made a teasing pout. 'Just once more then.'

'I promise.'

Inga smiled, and the breath caught in Hakan's throat. Her beauty was fresh as the first morning of the world. Suddenly she pulled him close and kissed him.

'Come on – I'll race you back to the yard!'

'Bitch,' he grinned. 'You know you'll win.'

'Every time,' she winked, and took off down the slope, laughing.

He set out after her, pain shooting up his leg with every stride.

When they stumbled breathless back into the yard, the air was rich with aromas wafting from the cookhouse – hogs turning on spits, cauldrons filled with bubbling fish soups, garlic sauces and freshly baked bread. And of course the malty smell of ale.

When they spotted Tolla, she was talking with a woman neither recognized. From a distance, it didn't seem the friendliest conversation.

'I've told you once,' snapped the nurse, her usually warm features looking decidedly cold. 'We don't want your kind here.'

'But on such an occasion,' insisted the stranger. 'And such a noble family. The Lord of Vendlagard would be delighted to have a telling. Tonight of all nights.'

'Don't you presume to know Lord Haldan's mind. He don't want bothering with the likes of you!'

The stranger had quick, darting eyes. She couldn't have seen more than thirty summers, though her skin was hard and tanned. 'I'll take my leave from him and none less,' returned the woman. 'So you'd better go and fetch him.'

She was leaning on a staff, for all the world looking like she owned the place. Tolla had a job on her hands.

Inga tapped Tolla on the shoulder. 'Did you miss me?'

The nurse rounded on her. 'You little pest! I'll say I missed you. Where have you been?'

'A girl needs to bathe,' offered Inga.

'Does she just? And while you're splashing about, the rest of us do your work, is that it?'

'I'm sorry.' Inga was doing her best to look contrite. Not one of her more obvious qualities.

The fraught lines in Tolla's face showed a woman in an unforgiving mood. Sensing his cousin was in for a tongue-lashing, Hakan decided to intervene.

'Who's this then?' He jerked his head at the stranger.

'A *spakona*!' Tolla spat the word like a curse. Hakan didn't see why Tolla was all riled up about a teller of fortunes. They were common enough in those parts.

'My name is Heitha,' said the woman, unruffled by Tolla's hostility. 'I am a *vala*.'

'*Vala*? *Spakona*?' exclaimed Tolla. 'They're all one. Leeches are leeches, I say.'

'Oh, Tolla,' said Inga. 'Don't be such a grouse. Why – this is perfect! You couldn't have come on a better day.'

'So I heard, little sister,' nodded the *vala*. 'Them folks at Hildagard told me of a feasting here tonight.'

'Hildagard? My – that's a long way!'

13

'Not for these old legs,' Heitha smiled. 'They've carried me many leagues over the years, and they'll carry me a lot further yet.'

'Did you give the Hildagard folks a telling?'

'Indeed, I did. Happens a fine one. A newling in the spring, and a good harvest before the leaves fall. Some other trifles. What I saw pleased them well enough.'

'And I'll warrant there's gold in your pocket to prove it,' said Tolla.

'Happens there is, sister. I'm bound to say I found the lord of Hildagard an open-handed host.'

'You'll not find my uncle any the less,' promised Inga.

'Hush, you silly girl!' snapped Tolla. 'We need no foretellings here.'

'What harm can it do?' asked Hakan, amused.

'These folk trade in curses,' said Tolla. 'They rob a man's purse and put his feet on the road to Hel.'

'Tolla!' protested Inga. 'She's our guest.'

'Not yet, she ain't.'

'Seems you have a dim view of a *vala*'s talents,' smiled Heitha.

'Talents? Is that what you call it? You meddle with darkness. I've seen it. Your touch is death.'

'Come, sister. These are lies.' And for the first time, a little heat crept into Heitha's cheeks. 'A *vala* sees what will be, that's all. I meddle with nothing. The Norns have woven all our fates. I only tell where the thread must run.'

Hakan's mother had said the same. She would often sing of the three Norns – three sisters dwelling in the shadows among the roots of the Tree of Worlds, spinning and weaving the destiny of men. Each thread unbreakable as iron. Unchangeable as granite.

Tolla gave an indignant grunt. 'That's how it *should* be. But there's none love gold more than a *vala*. None who'll curse so black to get it.'

Heitha was peering at Tolla. Seeming curious at first, but then harder and harder, like she was looking right inside her. And then, unexpectedly, she gave a brittle laugh. 'Now I begin to understand! I see what's sown in your face.' Tolla shifted uncomfortably. The *vala* cackled. 'How much of the past is in the masks we wear!'

'Never mind about my past.' For a heartbeat, Tolla looked as though a shadow had crossed her soul.

'It's not for me to mind. But perhaps for others . . .'

'Are you threatening me?'

'Oh Tolla!' broke in Inga. 'Enough of this. You're so serious! Let her stay. It could be exciting.' She clapped. 'Perhaps Heitha has brought us a great blessing.' She looked around for Hakan. 'Cousin – it's your day. What say you? Wouldn't a telling be fun?'

Hakan wasn't sure. It might be amusing to know the course his life must take. But to have that knowledge . . . to be bound by it. Did he want that?

Before he could answer, a familiar voice called his name.

They all turned to see his father crossing the yard.

Haldan Haldorsen – Lord of Vendlagard, headman of the Vendling blood and ruler over the Northern Jutes. He was taller than his son with shoulders broad as a bear, but the rest of him lean and hard as a knife. Folk often said Hakan was his father come again. Certainly they shared the same tousled black hair, same sharp nose, same square stance. But Hakan's face was still young, while his father's beard grew thick as tar, and twenty years of steel and slaughter leave their mark upon a face.

'You should be getting ready, so you still have time to visit your mother before things get under way.'

'All the way up there?' Hakan's mother was nothing now but bones, drying to dust in a barrow-grave on the hill where his father had laid her eight years before.

'Just get it done. It's what she would have wanted.'

'If you say so.' His father seemed to care a lot more what his mother wanted now that she was dead.

'Who's this?' Haldan nodded at Heitha.

Inga started tugging excitedly at his hand. 'Uncle, you have to help us. This is Heitha. She's a *vala*, offering us a telling tonight. Please say she can.'

Haldan looked Heitha up and down.

'All she wants is your gold, my lord,' said Tolla. 'Did you ever meet a *vala* wasn't grasping as a dwarf when it came to gold?'

'A woman has to live, my lord.' Heitha smiled at Haldan.

The Vendling lord considered her. 'A good *vala* speaks truthfully what she sees. An evil one what she thinks will please whoever's paying her. Which are you?'

Heitha opened her palms. 'I cannot speak for myself.'

'Aren't you curious, Uncle?' asked Inga, excitedly.

'I've known many folk regret learning too much about what will be,' Haldan answered.

Hakan shrugged. 'Surely it's useful to know what good or evil is coming our way.'

16

His father's mouth tilted in an ironic smile. 'So you want to become all-wise, do you, my son?'

'The *vala*'s word binds, my lord,' pleaded Tolla. 'It brings no good.'

Hakan saw the *vala* was staring at him intensely, and then at Inga, apparently heedless of the outcome of the talk. There was something discomfiting about those far-seeing eyes.

'Then she can bless as well as foretell!' cried Inga. 'It's simple. Give her gold to speak the truth of what she sees, and gold to speak a blessing over each of us.'

The *vala* smiled. 'There is much love in this one. She'll bring a man a good deal of luck one day.' She turned to Hakan and for an unsettling moment, those darting eyes seemed to know his every secret. 'Aye – and a good deal of trouble.'

'You can stay,' said Haldan.

'But, my lord—' began Tolla.

'I said, she stays.' Inga clapped her hands in triumph. Tolla bristled, but held her tongue. 'You'll get your gold.' Haldan nodded to Heitha. 'Only be sure you speak the truth. Now get along, all of you. Our first guests will arrive within the hour.'

Hakan was about to leave when his father beckoned him closer. 'Are you ready?' He took hold of Hakan's shoulders, digging his thumbs in deep. Hakan nodded. 'You know the oaths you will make?'

'I do, Father.' Hakan had known every word of the ritual for five summers past. *Longer.* Every boy knew them. Every boy dreamed of the day he would get to utter them – in fire, in iron, in blood.

'The time is on you now, Hakan.' A smile ghosted over his father's lips. 'My Chosen Son.'

CHAPTER TWO

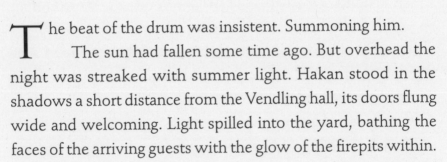

The beat of the drum was insistent. Summoning him.

The sun had fallen some time ago. But overhead the night was streaked with summer light. Hakan stood in the shadows a short distance from the Vendling hall, its doors flung wide and welcoming. Light spilled into the yard, bathing the faces of the arriving guests with the glow of the firepits within.

He'd watched them come a while now. Kinsfolk, near and far; his father's oathmen with their wives and younglings; house-karls with bonny maids.

The men strutted like stags, though most were ruffians and drunkards. But tonight they had their finest daggers on display, tunics brightly trimmed, mail glinting under newly dyed cloaks. Their womenfolk glided on their arms, long hair brushed till it gleamed, bound in braids of every style, threaded with ribbons and flowers. The air danced with their gossip and laughter.

Hakan watched, trying not to think about the hollow in his belly, or that soon the eyes of everyone who'd passed would be on him.

He heard footsteps running towards the thinning stream of people. It was his friend Leif, late as usual, tugging at the buckle on his belt.

Hakan whistled. Leif pulled up, peering into the shadows. 'Oh, it's you!' he cried. 'The man of the hour.' He poked a finger into his jug-ear and grinned. 'So I'm not late?'

'Not yet. Any tips?'

'Stand up tall. Don't scream.' He shrugged. 'And if you drink too much, try not to piss yourself. Never looks good in front of the girls.'

'Sage words.'

He snorted. 'I learn by experience – same as the next fool.'

'Well, that's me.'

'Exactly.' Leif winked, scratching at the star-shaped scar above his eye. Leif had been a wild boy. Their battles went back as far as he could remember. But he'd also been the closest thing Hakan had had to a brother.

'Better get in there.' Leif slapped his shoulder. 'Good luck.'

The scar had been a gift from Hakan. Revenge for calling him a cripple after the accident. He'd only been five winters old, but he'd got him a sweet shot with a stone all the same. In the end, it hadn't been worth it – his mother gave him the beating of his life. 'You're to be a man,' she'd said, 'not a monster.'

She'd said that a lot.

Still, Leif never called him a cripple again. Not to his face, anyway.

You're to be a man . . .

He still wondered what she meant by that. Now he would never know. The dead kept their secrets close.

19

The last of the guests crossed the threshold; the drum beat on.

Hakan stepped from the shadows.

Inga was in an ecstasy of anticipation. She couldn't remember a feast so grand. The women were beautiful, ornaments glinting, robes cinched with gilded girdles, their lovely figures whispering through the cloth.

The men looked handsome. Well, as handsome as they could. Even Hadding, her aunt Tuuri's lecherous old husband, didn't look quite so like a toad as usual.

Inga wondered whether the other women were admiring her crimson dress in turn. Tolla had helped her re-cut the cloth from one of her mother's dresses. It had been left along with the small chest of things that were the only link between her and her parents. When Tolla had applied the final touches to the hem, and Inga tried it on, the nurse had gasped. She'd even shed a tear, saying Inga was her mother's blood and fresh as the spring.

Inga couldn't help but notice the glances of many of the men. She dropped her eyes demurely, as she knew she should. But inside, her heart sang. The last big feast at Vendlagard had been two summers before. She'd been thirteen then, and few men had given her a second look. Now, almost everywhere she turned, she felt their eyes, young and old, on her, which then flitted away like ghosts if she looked up.

She decided she liked it. Tolla would probably say she oughtn't to, but then Tolla was always worrying. The old goose reckoned it safer to sit among a pack of hungry wolves than on a bench of men.

Tolla doesn't know everything, Inga giggled to herself. Indeed, there was a lot that Tolla didn't know.

The drum was banging away. If it kept on like that, it would drive them all mad. But suddenly, a hush fell and all the guests turned towards the door.

All but one.

One face across the hall remained in her direction. She had to look. The face belonged to a man. Quite a young man, but she saw at once he was very handsome. He was looking straight at her, bold as Baldur. In truth, looking her all over, up and down, like he was pricing up some thrall at a market. And now, seeing she'd caught him, he still didn't look away. Far from it. His stare turned into a smile. Warm but goading.

She frowned a little. She hated to be laughed at. It was one thing for a man to admire her beauty, another to make her feel uncomfortable. She saw him snigger, and looked away sharply, annoyed when she felt her cheeks colouring. In the tail of her eye, she saw this only made him laugh the more.

Well, she wouldn't let that insolent fool spoil the moment. Because Hakan had entered the hall, and he looked splendid.

Six feet tall and straight as a spear. The firelight bounced off his leather tunic, waxed to a shine. Round his shoulders hung her gift to him – a cloak trimmed with the skin of the wolf he'd slain. Even his limp didn't seem so pronounced as he walked past their kinsfolk. It would be causing him pain, she knew, but he didn't let it show.

She clamped her lips shut, afraid she'd end up grinning like a halfwit, and she didn't want to look foolish. Hakan was close now. She wanted him to look at her. To see how beautiful she had made herself tonight, for him. But his eyes were fixed on his father at the end of the hall. She felt annoyed he could be so cold. But just as he was passing, she saw the corner of his mouth curl and tighten, and knew he was suppressing a smile.

Of course he noticed her! He loved her!

Hakan reached the platform where her uncle sat and stopped before the Lord of Vendlagard.

She sighed. This was the boring part, her uncle Haldan having first pull on the pitcher, as it were. He stood, droning on and on about honour and duty and bonds of blood, or raven's wine, as he called it. Inga never understood why men liked to talk of things with other silly names. The sea was the whale-road. Battle was the spear-din. A warrior was a feeder of ravens – an image she found especially loathsome.

Wasn't there enough poetry in the world speaking plainly?

After Haldan, it was Logmar's turn. White as a corpse from head to toe, with a nose knobbly as an old stick, Logmar was *godi* to the Vendling clan. Had been for as long as anyone could remember, since he was old as the giants, so of course the prayers and blessings fell to him. Inga rolled her eyes. The Jutes had many gods, true. But it seemed Logmar wanted to squeeze a favour out of every one of them. Odin, the All-Father, god of war and kings – of course. Frey and Freya, the twin gods of prosperity and good luck and fertility – fine, although she didn't see that fertility had much to do with swearing oaths of fealty to a warrior lord. Thor – for weather luck and strength; Njord – for luck at sea; Loki – for cunning; Tyr – for skill in weapons; Weyland – for blades forged strong. The old *godi*'s prayers croaked on and on. When he started asking Heimdall for a blessing that Hakan's horn may ever sound long and true, Inga wanted to stab herself with frustration.

At long last Logmar was done and summoned Hakan closer. Inga nearly whooped with relief.

'In the name of Odin the All-Father, are you ready to make your oath – by iron, by fire and by blood?' asked the *godi*.

Hakan nodded. 'I'm ready.'

Logmar drew a dagger, seized Hakan's wrist, and tugged him closer to a brazier. Deep in its heart, embers shimmered red and orange.

Logmar lifted the dagger for all to see.

'Iron is the mettle of your strength. Do you swear by iron that you pledge your strength wholeheartedly to the service of your lord, Haldan, son of Haldor, chieftain of the Northern Jutes?'

'I swear it,' said Hakan.

Logmar plunged the long blade into the glowing embers. 'Fire is your life spirit,' his ragged voice rang. 'Do you swear by fire that your life is now subject to the will of your lord, Haldan, son of Haldor, bane of Gotars, champion of the Vendling?'

'I swear it.' Inga snorted. As if Hakan needed to make such an oath to his own father. She found herself detesting the *godi* and everything he was saying. Perhaps because she knew what was coming.

Logmar withdrew the dagger, its blade glowing red from the heat. He turned his cold eyes on Hakan. 'Blood is the suffering and death through which all must pass – either to rise to Odin's table or to go down to the halls of Hel. Do you swear by blood that you are willing to suffer unto death in service to your lord, his land, his people and his good name?'

'I swear it.'

'Then let iron, fire and blood be joined in one solemn oath, witnessed before gods and men.'

The *godi* grabbed Hakan's wrist, raised the dagger high, and then sliced its searing edge across his palm.

Inga winced at the sound of iron cutting flesh.

Everyone was watching Hakan. To cry out would have brought shame on every Vendling. But his face was stone. Inga saw nothing but a tensing of his jaw. He squeezed his fist and blood dripped onto the dusty floorboards.

The ceremony wasn't quite complete. Hakan had sworn all to his father as his oath-lord. Now Lord Haldan had an oath to swear.

An oath of love and trust. An oath to provide grain and gold. An oath of protection. Inga felt sorrow well inside as her uncle spoke. He must have made the same oath to her own father, all those moons ago. She gazed longingly at the seat beside her uncle. Her father should have been sitting in that empty place. In his stead Wrathling – the ring-sword that had belonged to him – set there to honour his memory.

A pitiful trade: a father for a sword. What did it matter that Haldan honoured his brother so faithfully? What had his oath of protection been worth after all?

Oaths were but words. And words were weak as the breath that spoke them.

But everyone was clapping, and her bleak thoughts were swallowed up in applause.

'Drink to our newest warrior! To Hakan! To my son!'

Hakan was free to smile now, and no sooner was he than he sought out her face. She laughed when he found her, his bright eyes dispelling any disquiet in her heart. She must pull herself together. This was a great occasion and she was proud of her cousin. Of course she was.

She would show him just how proud she was.

Later . . .

But now, they must feast.

It was a while later when Hakan decided he wasn't going to piss himself. *At least, not yet.* But his head was swimming. Tomorrow he would have Thor's own hammer beating in his head. But what could he do? Every cousin, every kinsman, every karl – they all wanted to drink a toast with him. Man to man. Brother to brother. And down it all went. Horns of mead, pitchers of ale – cup after cup, drowning him in drink.

By now, the feasting was well under way. Faces swam in a fog of hot breath and steaming food and laughter. Thrall-wenches stalked up and down, serving yet more food or replenishing pitchers. Smoked-fish stews, honey-glazed shrimps, great slabs of hog flesh, roasted to a crisp. Barley pies filled with cheese and leeks, baked beets and boiled lamb; sweet blackberry patties and fruit puddings, flavoured curds and nut cakes. Hakan had never seen so much food.

The guests grew ever louder, bawling across the table, the talk moving from crops and herds to conquests over seas or under covers. Even his father, who usually could raise a lead shield easier than he could a smile, became quite merry.

'Hadding!' he cried. 'A drink to old Ottar!'

Aunt Tuuri's ogre of a husband bashed his cup against Haldan's upraised horn. 'To Ottar and his pig!'

'What about his pig?' slurred Hakan, struggling to keep the big man in focus.

'What?' roared his father. 'Don't tell me you haven't heard this one!'

Hakan shook his head and immediately regretted it when the oak pillars holding up the roof seemed to wobble alarmingly.

'You remember Ottar!' cried his father. 'Fierce as a bear, dumb as an ox. Always returned from a fight in a Hel of a lather. He'd bundle up his wife and hammer at her till the rafters shook. "Thunder-weather," they called it when he came home.' Haldan's face creased with mirth. 'Well, he saw to his wife a sight better than he saw to his house. The place was rotten through. One day he comes home and the two of them get to work, and in the thick of it, there's a cracking and a creaking, and before he knew his arse from her tit, the two of them were crashing through his bower and landed slap on his favourite pig!'

'Killed the thing stone dead!' cried Hadding, and the kinsmen bellowed with laughter.

'Best meat I ever tasted,' roared Haldan, sinking another horn of honey-wine.

'Aye – and the poor fool didn't live another year,' said Hadding. 'Left his woman all alone.'

Hakan felt a bony elbow in his ribs. 'And *she* was the best meat I ever tasted,' hissed Garik, through broken teeth. Hakan's instructor was lucky, in battle and out of it. He'd taught Hakan everything he knew about combat, ever since Hakan could hold a stick. But he'd never bothered with a wife. Instead he had a reputation for consoling lonely widows whose husbands had gone to the dust. After the summer raiding most years, that kept him busy enough.

26

'Reckon we have to see you blooded this summer.' Garik gave Hakan a thunderous slap on his back. 'One way or t'other.' He reached out and grabbed a passing thrall-wench, and hauled her into his lap. 'You've got a soft eye for our young hero, haven't you?'

The girl was one of the fleshy pieces that his father had bought the previous spring, sold on from the faraway lands of Gaudarika, beyond the great rivers across the East Sea. She had darker hair than the women of the north, a broad squat nose, and full lips.

'More than I do for you!' she giggled, slopping ale in his breeches.

'Yah!' Garik shoved her away. 'Silly bitch!'

'Serves you right. Why can't you be a good boy like him?'

The girl leaned over and refilled Hakan's cup till it was frothing over. As she did, she bent close and whispered, 'Wouldn't I like to show you how to be bad though, eh?' Hakan felt her tongue curl up the edge of his ear. He jerked away. Suddenly, all he could see were dark eyes, plump lips and a heaving bosom. Truth was the whole hall seemed to be heaving like a ship in a storm. He shoved her away, mumbling, 'Some other time.'

Weak, he thought disgustedly, hauling himself to his feet and prising his legs from the bench. He was going to be sick. And very soon.

He needed air. Needed to get out. But then he saw something that hit him like an arrow in the eye.

Inga.

She was standing on the far side near the doorway that opened into the blue and balmy night. Through the cloud of

27

ale in his head, she appeared like a crimson dream, her long auburn hair pulled over one shoulder into a single loose braid, twined through with scarlet ribbons. He would have hailed her, but just then she threw back her head and laughed, and in a heartbeat, his dream became a nightmare when he saw whom she was with.

He was older now, of course. A man, no longer a boy. But Hakan recognized the smug half-smile, the conceited tilt of his head. Konur, son of Karsten, heir to the Karlung lands and the bane of Hakan's childhood memories. He remembered Konur's taunts, the crushing humiliation of the other children's laughter, his powerlessness against his older kinsman. He had tried to fight him then, but it had availed him nothing but a black eye and another stern talk from his mother.

This time it would be different.

As he stumbled towards them, Konur leaned in and whispered something to Inga. She smiled and Hakan saw Konur's hand touch her elbow and steer her towards the door. Next moment they were gone, out into the night, and some other drunken clod was blocking his way, trying to get him to drink another toast.

'Fenrir take you, fool!' The guest looked wounded but Hakan didn't care. 'Out the way,' he snarled, staggering off towards the bright midsummer night.

Inga had been having a wonderful evening. The sights and sounds of a feast always filled her heart with warmth. How pleasing to see her hard work paid back in the happy faces and raucous laughter of her kin!

Well, at least *some* of it had been her doing. Not as much as Tolla expected, but Tolla always expected too much. Especially from her. After all, wasn't she the ward of the Lord of Vendlagard? Why should she have to do the same as a common thrall-girl?

Anyway, the main thing was it was all a grand success. Hakan had been honoured and their guests were riotous. Songs had been sung; the men were in their cups; the women were full of stories; and everyone had been most gracious to her.

Particularly the men. Whichever way she turned, there was another one wishing to speak with her. How different from the last feast when she'd been treated as little more than a nuisance! Now thanes and earls and great warriors were competing to make her laugh. As if *she* were someone to impress.

Yes – it had been a splendid night.

And one man especially had wanted to amuse her. The one laughing at her earlier. At first, when he'd come up to speak to her, she'd tried to brush him off, but he was quite determined and, it turned out, quite charming. He had sworn they had met before. When she had assured him he must be mistaken, he had insisted.

'Twelve years ago. At this very hall.'

'I can only have been three.'

'Indeed, you were very small. You kept begging to climb all over me.'

'And did you let me?'

'I hardly had a choice,' he laughed. 'Perhaps the time has come for you to return the favour.'

It took a moment for her to understand him, and when she did she felt her cheeks colour. 'This hall is full of men sworn to protect the honour of my uncle – and his household. That includes me.'

'Ha! Have no fear, Lady Inga. It's not your honour I'm interested in.'

He had levelled a gaze at her that she found discomforting. She had suddenly remembered Hakan, and glanced over to the high table where he was sitting. To her surprise, Hakan appeared to be engulfed under the flouncing curves of Kella, one of her uncle's thralls. The girl was a slattern, everyone knew, but Hakan didn't seem to be minding her attention at all.

Inga turned away, annoyed.

'There was a water butt, I remember,' her admirer had continued. 'In the end, you were being such a little pest, I threw you right into it.'

'So that was you!' Inga threw her head back and laughed. She remembered the shock of the cold water, and screaming for someone to lift her out. 'You must be Konur.'

He nodded. 'I hope you've forgiven me by now.'

'That depends.'

'On what?'

'On whether you're worth forgiving, I suppose.' The two looked at each other. He had light grey eyes, pretty as a girl's, and high sharp cheekbones. She couldn't deny he was pleasing to look at.

'This talk of water has made me thirsty,' she suddenly blurted to break the moment. But when he offered to accompany her to the water butt, she let him. She didn't know why.

Outside the sky was a rich purple. Streaks of summer light broke up the darkness, though it was long past midnight. Inga loved the world in the summer. The way it throbbed with a kind of lust for living – from the great sun in the sky down to the tiniest little beetle under the earth. Like there was no time to sleep. Like there was too much life to be lived.

The water butt was there, just as it had been twelve years before. She led Konur across the yard and took up the ladle hanging on a bit of twine. She offered him a drink, but he shook his head.

'Are you mad? A man can't quench his thirst with water! What would folk say?'

'Stupid,' she smiled, putting the ladle to her lips. The water was soothing after the heat of the revelry.

She tossed the ladle back in the water. When she turned back, Konur had stepped nearer and without any warning, his hand slid round her hips.

'What are you doing?' she gasped.

'What do you think?' he murmured, his voice thick, pulling her close. 'I've seen how you look at me. I want you too.'

'Want you?' she stammered, trying to slip from his grasp. 'No – you're so mistaken.'

'Feel here.' He grabbed her hand and forced it down. Her fingers brushed something hard. 'There's no mistaking that. I'm aching for you.'

She recoiled, disgusted, but he only pulled her tighter against him, his mouth searching for hers. She flicked her head side to side, desperate to get away, but he didn't seem to care.

'Stop – please, let me go.' She pushed him away harder, but it was no good. 'Let me go!'

All of a sudden, Konur spun away and before she knew what was happening, a fist slammed into his face. There was a sickening crunch and Konur reeled back against the water butt.

31

The barrel rocked, then crashed forward again, slewing water over Konur and his attacker.

Konur was moaning, trying to shield his bloodied nose. Inga staggered away, glad to be free of him. The attacker threw himself on Konur, and the two set to writhing in the dirt.

'Bastard! Bastard!'

'Hakan!' she cried, recognizing her cousin's voice. But he wasn't listening to her or anyone else. They rolled over and over, trying to get a hold, and even in the half-gloom she could see the anger on Hakan's face.

She'd never seen him like that. Never seen that blind rage burning in his eyes. It scared her.

Konur had recovered his wits enough to fight back, and they went at it in a blizzard of fists, fingers, knuckles and knees, butting each other like boars. Konur got his arm around Hakan's throat, twisting his head. Then Hakan seized his groin and yanked, hard. Konur shrieked and fell back, flinging out a lucky fist that cracked Hakan in the jaw. Hakan spat a shower of blood and rolled away groaning on the ground.

'You're a dead man,' yelled Konur, leaping on top of Hakan, pounding at his face.

'Stop it!' screamed Inga. 'Both of you! Stop!' But it was no use. Nothing would make Konur stop until Hakan slammed a palm into his face. Konur squealed, blood streaming from his nose, while Hakan's lips frothed scarlet spittle.

She had to do something. This was no drunken brawl. One of them would do murder before much longer. She ran back into the hall. 'They're killing each other! Uncle Haldan! You must come at once!'

She waited long enough to see her uncle turn to see what

was the commotion and get up from his seat. Then back she went.

The two of them were a tangle of limbs and mud and blood and curses, neither able to gain the advantage over the other. She heard voices behind her; at last people were coming. The first just gaped. Others circled around the fight, laughing and jeering drunkenly. And then, thank the gods, her uncle was there.

He didn't even break stride. Just went in, took hold of Hakan's collar and yanked him off. Inga marvelled at how absurdly easy her uncle made it look.

'What the Hel are you two about?' Haldan slung his son down in a heap away from Konur, who was propped on an elbow, wiping his blood-smeared face on his sleeve.

'Why don't you ask your son? He's a fucking animal.'

Hakan was gulping down great lungfuls of air, his face still black with hatred.

'Well?' demanded Haldan.

'He was attacking Inga!' shouted Hakan.

'I wasn't attacking anyone!' protested Konur. 'Your idiot son was trying to murder me.'

'Watch your tongue, boy,' warned Haldan. 'It's unwise for a guest to insult his host.'

'Aye – and a host his guest,' returned Konur, picking himself out of the mud. 'Is this the kind of hospitality a man should expect under your roof?'

Inga was at Hakan's side. He was spitting splinters of tooth into the mud. 'It was a misunderstanding,' she said.

'What kind of misunderstanding?' her uncle demanded, eyes as fierce at her as at the others.

Inga wasn't sure how to answer. Konur had thrown himself at her. But had he *attacked* her? 'He . . . he was . . . forcing himself on me.'

Konur scoffed at this. 'Bah! I hardly laid a finger on her. Next thing I know, your cripple broke my fucking nose.' He screwed up his eyes and tilted back his head.

'He was hurting her. She was screaming. Father, believe me.' There was no hiding Hakan's slurred speech. 'He's nothing but contempt for us all.'

'Go to Hel, cripple! Your son's a madman, Haldan. You should keep him tied up.'

'I suggest you tie that tongue of yours before your quarrel is with me and not my son.'

'I had no quarrel with your son.'

'He would have dishonoured Inga, Father.' Hakan was picking himself up. Inga reached to help him, but he knocked her hand away. 'She's your ward. You're sworn to protect her.'

'I don't need reminding what I must do. Inga, tell me what happened.'

Inga always felt thrown when her uncle demanded she speak up; now worse than ever. Her mouth flopped open, but she had no notion what to say. Maybe this was her fault. She tried to think. What *had* happened? It seemed only moments ago she was a confident woman, yet now she was a naughty girl again. But before she could answer, another man appeared from the crowd.

'I see your son has your father's hot blood,' the man said in a strangely whispery voice. She recognized him as a distant kinsman, of the Karlung clan, though with all the guests that night, she couldn't recall his name. But she remembered that one dead eye. As a child, it always terrified her. It unnerved her still.

'Just a squabble between boys, Karsten.'

Karsten – that was it. Which made him Konur's father and earl of the Karlung lands.

'Let me guess. Injured Vendling pride?' Karsten gave an easy chuckle. 'Your father was the same. There's many a man around the East Sea dead, thanks to his thin skin.'

'His honour was precious to him.'

'A good deal more than the lives of other men's sons. Or his oaths. Or his loyalty.'

'It was he who was betrayed.'

Karsten snorted. 'That's not how the Wartooth sees it.'

Inga was trying to keep up. The Wartooth, she knew, was Harald Wartooth, the old king of the Danish Mark, once overlord of their lands. But she knew the story of her grandfather, Haldor the Black, breaking faith with the Danish king. 'I can't help the stories that old boar tells himself,' her uncle replied. 'Men weave the truth as it suits them.'

'Perhaps. But you can ill afford to let your son lose the few friends left you. Whatever his grievance.'

'The insult was with your son.'

'The insult is there,' hissed Karsten, pointing at Konur. 'In his bloody nose. A guest; a kinsman come in peace. An insult and provocation, I say.'

'A scrap between boys. Nothing more.' Haldan's tone left no room for argument. That was obvious to everyone. Except, apparently, Karsten.

'Boys who are heirs to both our lands. We share blood, you and I, even if it is five fathers back. But if our lines must feud,

35

so be it. You'll find the loss of the Karlungs' friendship goes ill for you. And I have powerful friends—'

'There will be no feuding. Whatever was traded between these two has been repaid. A bloody nose for a bloody mouth. There's an end to it.'

'So long as you tighten your son's leash.' Karsten's dead eye glinted, pale as the moon.

'And you the same,' Haldan returned. 'There's more than one way to cause trouble.' He nodded at Inga and she suddenly felt foolish. Like some stupid sheep to be bartered over.

Gradually the hard lines of Karsten's face softened into a languid laugh. 'Truly said. Very well.'

'Come – shake hands and make your peace.' Haldan beckoned the two sons together. Hakan began to protest. 'You will do as I command!' Haldan bellowed.

Inga watched them, half-expecting them to be at each other's throats any moment. But they accepted each other's hand, and shook. Yet all the while, Hakan's gaze seethed hot with anger; and in Konur's pale eyes was hatred cold as ice. *There's no peace here. Not a scrap.*

They separated.

Seeing the climax had passed, the crowd was dispersing, distracted by something else. A loud thumping was resounding from inside: fists banging on oak tables; a murmur, growing ever louder.

'*A telling! A telling!*'

Her uncle had already gone in with Karsten, an arm round him as they shared a joke. Her uncle knew when to fight, and when to talk.

She turned back. Hakan was staring at her. She could see the

36

drink in his eyes, but he said nothing. Just stood there, staring. Then, slowly, he turned and spat blood into the dirt.

'Hakan, I—'

He cut her off with a shake of his head and stalked after his father.

'A telling – a telling!' The chant grew louder still.

Inga frowned, tears prickling her eyes. Konur was on his feet, his face a lascivious grin. Perhaps he expected one in return, even after what he had done. She turned her back on him. She was mad at him. Mad at everyone. Mad at herself most of all. But she wasn't going to cry, she told herself, bunching her fists, swallowing down her tears. Suddenly, she wanted to yell a curse on all men. Confusing, infuriating, pitiful, frightening and wonderful all at once.

'A telling! A telling!' The very pillars of Vendlagard seemed to shake with the cry.

Curiosity getting the better of her, she followed the others inside.

Hakan was confused, angry and thoroughly drunk. He'd never been able to take much in the way of strong drink. Tonight only proved the point. Still, Konur had had it coming for ten years, and whatever he had tried with Inga only made it worse.

His head hurt from too much ale, too many punches. But it didn't bother him half so much as the pain in his heart. Why was Inga out there with that greasy son of a whore to begin with?

He resumed his seat opposite his father when the chant of a hundred voices reached its climax.

'A telling!' they yelled. 'A telling!'

At last, the *vala* had made them wait long enough. She rose; a cheer erupted around the hall. She smiled, waving down the revellers, her bronze staff glinting in the firelight.

'A telling you shall have,' she cried, bowing her sharp-lined face to his father. 'If it pleases our Vendling lord. And the lord has gold,' she added.

A knowing jeer slewed around the drunken faces.

His father slipped a ring from his finger and tossed it to her. She plucked it expertly from the air. 'There's gold to make a start. Speak nothing falsely just to please us, sister.'

'Never,' she said, scraping low; the ring vanished into the fathomless folds of her cloak. 'Those who speak lies to gain gold mock the True One. Scabby hags – and fools! They curse their own heads. Fear no deceit from me, noble host. As the Lord of the Hanged shows me, I will tell.'

She backed closer to the firepit. So close Hakan thought her cloak must catch fire, but the heat seemed to bother her none. Her silhouette darkened before the dancing flames, her face shrouded in shadow.

'The road to the World Tree is reached by *galdra* song. Will any sisters stand and sing to the Slain-God?' She looked about, a crooked grin creeping over her mouth. 'Perhaps you, sister?' Her gaze fell on Tolla.

The nurse blanched. Tight-lipped, she shook her head.

'Sing,' his father said. Tolla's eyes darted to him, but still she didn't move. 'Must I tell you twice?'

Slowly, Tolla rose. 'My thanks, sweet sister,' cried the *vala*. 'I need three more.'

Another thrall stood. Then a distant kinswoman, come from the shores of the Western Ocean. Last of all, Inga

38

rose, dark and lovely in her crimson robe. Hakan's heart quickened.

'Sing out, sisters,' the *vala* cried. 'Sing to Odin, the Ancient One. Sing so he gives me sight, far into things yet hidden.'

Tolla was first to sing, the others soon weaving their voices with her sweet and wandering melody:

The Brown-Eyed God hangs on a tree
Screaming he sees of Was and Will Be

The song meandered on, the four voices rising with the tendrils of smoke to the rafters.

When fire burns the Masked One calls
The slain about him all will fall.

The *vala* began to sway, face tilted, eyes closed, staff weaving back and forth, fingers rattling the bones at her belt. The song reached its end and the women stood, silent. But the *vala* went on dancing, as if to some other music, unheard by the hushed revellers. Eyelids flickering, she began to utter a guttural moan. She stretched on her toes, arms swaying higher and higher. Suddenly her eyes snapped open, half-maddened with heat, searching, scanning, far above Lord Haldan's seat.

'The High One speaks,' she wailed. 'The High One sees. This land is favoured – fortune and wealth, for this generation and many.' A cheer rose around the hall, some beating the table with approval. But they were soon hushed. 'Sons and daughters of Jutland will carry their blood far, over wave and vale. The Jutes will live long in the songs of men.'

Hakan scanned the grinning faces, flushed with mead, as his own must have been. By the gods, he could speak as well as this damned *vala*. Fortune and wealth? It was easy enough to promise that and get his father's gold for it.

'From your sisters' wombs, fame and gold shall come,' she continued. Another cheer. But then she paused, a frown wrinkling her brow. 'And yet...' Her stare grew wide. The hall-folk leaned in, hushed in a moment. 'This land knows fire and death,' she murmured. 'Ere long, blood will run in its furrows. Tears will run like rivers.'

The listening faces darkened. This was less pleasing.

'And you! Lord of the Vendling blood! Neither man nor beast will cut you down.' The band around her head glittered silver, her eyes grown suddenly fierce. 'Yet you will take a wound. A wound so *horrible*! Pierced through your heart with a blade that cannot be stopped. Your days will be long and bitter. The All-Father will never grant you rest.'

All eyes sped to their lord, waiting for the eruption of anger many knew only too well. But his father only sat, listening, face hard as flint.

Suddenly, the *vala* gave a shriek that split the air. 'Quail, you men – tremble, you women! The Slain-God thunders here! The final destruction shakes these walls from the ends of time. The kindling that will burn the World Tree to ashes is lain here – bonds of kin are cut; beauty and love are slaughtered like swine. You must drink the cup of sorrow to its dregs.' Her body was shaking; at last her legs faltered and she fell to her knees.

The last words of her telling died away and the company sat stunned. Was no one going to say anything? Hakan lurched to his feet, indignation boiling his head.

'This is all you tell?' He slammed down his cup, sending it bouncing away. 'You speak good fortune on our folk, then curse this household?'

The *vala*'s head turned to him, eyes aflame, and immediately he wished he had stayed in his seat. She glared at him a while, as if seeing something that was strange, even to her.

'Who speaks?' she said at last, her voice shrunk to a whisper.

'I am Hakan, son of Haldan. Chosen Son of the Lord of the Northern Jutes. This you well know.' Flush with ale and still angry from the business with Konur, Hakan spoke far louder than he meant. He suddenly felt foolish.

At first, the *vala* made no reply. Instead, slowly she pulled her hood over her head, and bowed down to him. Once . . . twice . . . a third time. Each bow, she lay down flat, pressing her head to the ground and stretching out her arms. His kinsfolk gaped on, making no sense of this strange prostration or what it might portend.

Hakan held his tongue, puzzled as anyone.

The *vala* got to her feet. 'Hail to you, you Chosen Son. I bow because your road will be one of suffering. You are marked for a path beyond even the All-Father's sight. A greater hand is on you – deeper magic, outside my telling. You will bear much pain, but you will never break. You will fall and rise again.'

'Enough – wretch!' Haldan's roar broke like a thunderclap. 'Black whore of Hel! We give you gold and you repay us with curses!'

The *vala* was ready for this, returning his outrage with a cool smile, her face a dance of shadows. 'For gold, I spoke – aye. Yet it scarce matters whether Odin has me tell what will be or not.

41

The fate of all men is graven on the World Tree. It cannot be undone.'

Lord Haldan looked on her a long moment before he answered, eyes dark as a storm. 'You see the fate of other men clear enough. I wonder, have you seen your own?'

A flicker of doubt crossed her face. Haldan gestured to a nearby thrall. 'Fetch a rope.' The servant hesitated, eyes flitting between them. 'Now!' The man scurried off.

The *vala*'s face greyed to ash. 'Lord, I spoke only the truth – just as you asked.'

'And for that you have your gold. But speaking truth bears fruit. Both sweet and bitter.'

'But, Lord, this is not just!'

'With this hand, I hold justice,' he replied, holding out his left; and then offering his right. 'And with this, I protect my people. True or not, your tellings are a cancer in this land. One I intend to cut out.'

The *vala* scrabbled to dig Haldan's gold from the depths of her cloak. 'Lord, keep your gold. It is nothing to me. Please. Take it.'

'Nay – keep it. It was fairly earned. Along with this.' The rope had arrived. Haldan took it and began tying a knot. 'You should be pleased. Odin has spoken tonight. We show our gratitude with a sacrifice to his honour.'

The fear on the *vala*'s face twisted into a sneer. 'You cannot turn what must be.'

'Nor can you. Take her.'

Two men flanking her rose without question and seized her. She wrestled uselessly as they shoved her up on to the dais.

Haldan flung the rope up into the shadows of the rafters. A moment later, the noose dropped to the floor. He snatched it up and slipped it over her writhing head. The *vala* was babbling a flood of prayers and pleas and curses. But his ear was iron to them all.

Every eye was on him as he pulled the rope tight. Hakan's heart was thundering like a stallion's hooves.

'The Lord of the Hanged awaits you.'

The *vala* screamed.

The rope whined, and the scream was cut short.

Yet the *vala*'s words still echoed in Hakan's mind. *You will bear much pain, but you will never break.*

Above him, her feet, calloused and black, capered to Odin's dance of death.

You will fall and rise again.

CHAPTER THREE

N ext morning, a breeze was blowing from the southwest. Hakan decided this was the only good thing about the day since, instead of sleeping off the ill-effects of the night before, he was astride his horse.

His father had woken him with a kick, and told him to get dressed. When he'd shaken the sleep from his head and appeared in Haldan's chamber, his father said he was sending him to Vindhaven, the small market harbour half a day's ride south.

Officially, he was to report on the provisioning there: how trade had gone over the summer, what stores they had laid aside from harvest, the state of their flocks and herds, how they would fare through the coming winter, what levies in skins, amber and such like they meant to send north to Vendlagard.

Unofficially, his father ordered him south to cool his heels. 'I don't want to see you for a week,' he growled. 'Preferably two.' After Vindhaven, Hakan was to head to Vestberg and then cut north to Hallstorp, before he came home. It wasn't the first time he'd taken the brunt of his father's wrath. But that morning, Hakan had to admit, Haldan was in a rare fury.

'You and your bloody temper!' Hakan had put at risk everything he had been building for fifteen years, he railed. Hakan knew a feud with the Karlungs wasn't in their interest, and his scuffle with Konur had given Earl Karsten leverage against his father.

But he also suspected his father had woken with a few regrets of his own. He had gone too far last night with that business with the *vala*. Perhaps it had been the drink. That and Haldan's steel-edged certainty of always knowing right from wrong. But Hakan suspected this time his father had acted without thinking. That was a rare thing. Whatever came of it, his father's deed would win no one's praise.

So Haldan was taking out his disgruntlement on his son. And here he was, under a sweltering sun, sweating through breeches too thick, with a stomach leaping about like a herring on a hook.

It was just before noon. Already he had stopped to nap in the shade of a wood to avoid tumbling from his saddle asleep and breaking his neck. He'd tried sticking his head in a stream a league back. Bliss while it lasted, but not enough to stop the pounding in his temples nor the sick feeling in his belly.

Sick and angry.

It was all well for his father to berate him for his short temper but it didn't take a *vala* to know where that came from. Almost as long as he could remember, Hakan had had to answer the taunts of other boys. Cripple, they called him. And a cripple he was, thanks to his father.

He'd hardly been five winters old when Haldan took him for a walk down by the shores of the Juten Belt. There he had helped him climb to the top of a rock, as high as he'd ever climbed. Hakan thought they were playing a game. His father stood below, arms outstretched. 'Jump!' he'd said. 'Jump and I'll catch you. Come on, don't you trust me?' Of course, he had trusted him. Hakan had swallowed down his terror and jumped. And at the last moment, his father stepped aside. He meant for his son to land in the sand and take a tumble. But there had been another rock hidden under the sand. Hakan had landed right on it and cracked his ankle. After that he could walk only with a limp; run hardly at all. Not like the other boys anyway.

His mother had been furious. 'What the Hel do you think you were doing?' she had screamed.

'Teaching him a lesson,' replied Haldan.

She had sworn and asked what possible lesson that could be.

'That you can't trust anyone in this world,' Haldan had replied. 'The sooner he learns that the better.'

Well, Hakan had remembered the lesson. His ankle would hardly let him forget it. Of course, his father had been sorry. He hadn't meant for him to be hurt. It was no honour to Haldan to have a son with a limp, after all. But in a twisted way, it had served Hakan. If you can't run, you have to stand and fight.

He'd learned how to do that, and right well.

When the thumping in his head allowed, he spent the journey trying not to dwell on the words the *vala* had spoken over him. Easier said than done. They kept returning to his mind like the refrain in some unending song. With each repetition, they pushed further into his brain, roots burrowing deeper, never to be dislodged.

He tried to dispel them with happier daydreams of Inga. But these seemed to slew from sun-bathed visions of them as man and wife, an absurdly pretty child running about their feet, to recollections of their sweaty couplings, up against a barn or rolling around in the dry dirt of some wood. Neither of these achieved much besides leaving him simmering with frustration. And then he remembered seeing her across the feast, laughing at something Konur had said, the way he touched her elbow. And instead of his own body, writhing with hers in a slick of sweat, he pictured Konur's, and jealousy bubbled bitter in his guts.

And yet, this was Inga. Maddening as she was, he had never been able to stay angry with her for long.

When the sun reached its highest, he came to the top of a hill and saw for the first time the inlet where Vindhaven lay. The settlement had grown up along the northern edge of Odd's Sound, a shallow fjord that opened into the grey rollers of the Juten Belt. A small beech wood ran along the ridgeline, obscuring the village from view, but over the treetops he could see skeins of rising smoke.

He kicked his horse on towards the wood. But as he did, he sensed something was wrong.

On a summer's morning, there would be fires. People had to cook; the smiths' forges must keep burning. But so many? With smoke so black? Instead of a few wisps, dark billows stained the sky.

Reaching the wood, he slipped from his horse and guided it through the undergrowth. Suddenly he stopped. Some instinct told him to go on alone. Tethering the mare, he crept forward the last few yards.

At the treeline, he froze.

Vindhaven was burning.

Below, the ground fell away into meadows; beyond that, along the shoreline, were the barns and dwellings of Vindhaven. Every one was on fire.

Thatching snapped and cracked. The village was chaos. Men stalked about bristling with war-gear, menacing in their iron helms and mailshirts. Some went bare-chested, others wore wolf-skins. All of them carried evil-looking axes or crude butcher's knives. Even from there, Hakan saw they were stained red with blood.

He shrank behind a blood-beech, fear drying his mouth. Screams and wails spiralled towards him on the breeze. The roof of the meet-hall, the heart of the little harbour, suddenly caved with a gush of soot and sparks.

He saw heaps of discarded clothing. *Not heaps, but bodies*, he realized. Vindhaven was not well defended. They had spears, axes, a few swords, and a handful of men who knew how to use them. But nothing to withstand these killers. The butchery must have hit them like a sea-squall.

There was worse to see.

In front of the meet-hall, a furnace was blazing. A few yards away was a line of villagers on their knees. Some sobbed; some writhed on the ground. Others pleaded with the big warriors. A few waited meek as lambs.

Within the furnace, darker shapes broiled. The stench of burning flesh floated like demon's breath to his hiding place. And then the biggest of the wolf-warriors began his grisly work.

Schuck, schuck, schuck. The noise of his axe carried with the stench. Hakan watched, eyes riveted to the sight of head after head rolling on the ground like gaming-bones, painting the mud crimson. From that distance they might be rag dolls, heads plucked and tossed away – one child taunting another. Except dolls didn't scream like that.

Suddenly, from one of the nearby houses, a boy appeared, not ten winters old, screaming like Hel's own hound. He ran at the nearest raider – a squat killer, half-naked, face black with tattoos. The boy had a butcher's knife.

Brave little bastard.

There was a streak of steel, and the killer's axe opened him up from rib to spine. He crumpled into a shuddering heap of rag and bone.

Hakan tasted bile.

Something caught the tail of his eye and he looked east. An old woman broke from the lee of a smithy and ran for the slope. She was coming straight for him. He clenched his teeth, willing her on; but she was desperately slow.

She'd put maybe forty yards between her and the village before one of the wolf-warriors saw her. He sprang after her, and was on her in moments, knocking her down without even breaking stride. She rolled over, trying to fend him off, but he just ignored her puny fists, threw her on her face, and shoved up her skirts. Her wails faded to pitiful moans. When he was done, he pulled up his breeches, and, almost as an afterthought, pinioned her with his spear.

By now, most of his comrades were carrying chests or trestles loaded with pots and barrels and other goods. They wouldn't find much of value among the meagre homes of Vindhaven. A little gold or silver hidden away if they were lucky. Bronze or glassware maybe, what they could carry of the harvest yields, a few weapons.

They wouldn't leave empty handed, but it was hardly rich spoils.

Then Hakan looked further east, and through the drifting smoke he made out the lines of a ship. Even from there, he could see it was a true wolf of the sea: hull sleek and black, maybe thirty paces end to end; with a single mast, its sail furled out of the wind; a fierce prow. In the hold, lashed together and wretched as beggars, Hakan spied women – a dozen of them, heads drooped in fear.

Perhaps the raiders had done better than he thought. Thralls were valuable anywhere; thrall-girls more than most.

He was suddenly filled with fury. These were his people. They looked to his father for their protection. One day it would be him they looked to. Yet how these folk had been failed!

He felt ashamed and full of vengeance.

But what could he do? An unblooded warrior – against a whole raiding party? There must be forty, if a man.

He looked at them more closely. One nearest to him had a rusty beard; another, white-blond hair poking out from his helm. Many others had the same colouring. Most were of a hefty build. They weren't Jutes. Nor even Danes. Truth was they could have come from anywhere around the East Sea. To Hakan, they looked like northerners, but then many lands lay to the north. Gotars or Finns. Estlanders perhaps, or Norskmen?

Whoever, the raid must be avenged if possible.

If he brought word to his father now, what use would that be with no clue as to where they went? So, settling down in the shadow of the wood, he decided to wait and see which course they set.

It was mid-afternoon before the raiders had loaded all they could, readied their ship and took up their oars to follow Odd's Sound out to the open sea.

He swung into his saddle and rode for the shore. The wind was up, having wheeled to the west. Men were moving on deck, and then the great russet sail unfurled and caught the wind.

The ship leaned over, planks kicking up spray as they cut the waves. At first, the ship headed east, away from the land. *Straight across the Juten Belt*. Towards Gotarland.

But some way offshore, the prow swung north.

The course was set.

Northwards.

He rode up the beach, staying with them best he could until the ship built momentum and began to slip away.

'Norskmen,' he muttered. He thought he heard laughter chattering across the waves. 'Laugh, if you will. But you'd better flee like the wind.' The arm of his father's vengeance was long, swift and crueller than Hel. He watched the stern of the Norskmen's ship rise and fall with the swell.

'We're coming for you,' he whispered, putting his heels to his horse's flank. The mare took off in a spray of sand.

'We're coming for you!'

CHAPTER FOUR

'Ale or honey-wine?' Probably the twentieth time Inga had asked the question.

'Mead, thanks, my lady.' Same as every other. Mead was the brew of Odin – the Spear-God. The Chooser. What else would a superstitious warrior drink before a fight?

She filled the cup and moved down the bench.

It was a different mood in the hall that night. Gloomy as thunder.

A lull was to be expected, as guests pulled themselves together, head-sore and dry-tongued, before setting off for their halls and farmsteads. Sometimes folk lingered, squeezing the last drop from Haldan's hospitality, but today the guests had cleared off early, with a sour taste in their mouths in more ways than one.

Wanting to keep out of her uncle's way, Inga had spent the day making something for Hakan. It wasn't much. A token really: a silver amulet in the shape of a hammer. Not that Hakan had a particular fondness for the Thunder God, but Thor's hammer was simple to make. Even so, Brok the smith had helped her, and it took her most of the afternoon to engrave the elaborate weavings into the metal.

But she liked having to concentrate. It gave her time to think. And there was plenty to think about.

Mostly about Hakan. She was annoyed, but also relieved, when she found her uncle had sent him on one of his silly errands. Annoyed that Hakan hadn't bothered to say goodbye; relieved to put off their unavoidably awkward conversation. But when she discovered he was away for at least a week, she realized how much she would miss him.

Still, if she was honest, Konur popped into her thoughts more than once. Quite a few times, in truth. And every time, she tried to squash his image like a roach, only for it to come scuttling back a little while later.

It was because she was angry with Hakan, she told herself. Even so, she was ready to forgive him for being such a brute. He was only trying to protect her after all, albeit in typically blunt fashion. Sometimes, she wished he were a bit quicker with his words than his fists.

She debated a good deal whether she, in turn, should be asking his forgiveness. After all, what had she done but talk to Konur? Laugh with him, maybe. But wasn't she allowed to laugh if someone said something funny?

By the time she was applying the finishing touches to the amulet and polishing it to a shine, she had decided that, if she must, she was ready to ask his forgiveness when he returned. Anyway, he wouldn't be back for a few days. Perhaps he would have calmed down and there would be nothing to say.

So she had thought.

Hence her shock when, just around sunfall, Hakan came clattering into the yard, his horse a lather of sweat, raising all Hel about raiders at Vindhaven.

After that, everything moved fast.

Her uncle appeared and listened to the grim tidings.

'Blood will run in its furrows,' he whispered when Hakan was done. And in an eye-blink, he was changed, his black mood forgotten, shooting orders like arrows.

He took his horn and blew it so long and loud she thought his head might split. Its echo had hardly died than other horns on neighbouring farms took up the call. And soon, Haldan's summoning was racing away in every direction.

Many kinsfolk were still close when his summoning reached them. Many turned back, though not all. Inga had watched anxiously as riders came in, but Konur and his father were not among them.

As evening turned to night, the men sworn to Haldan's sword and honour assembled one by one, and with them what vassals they could muster from the nearest farmsteads. In all, enough to fill two longboats – close to eighty men.

Haldan gave the grizzled twins Eskel and Esbjorn a dozen thralls to make ready the boats, waiting on the strand. Each had helmed since boyhood. Each could make a sea-wolf fly.

Eskel said they'd have a favourable tide two hours before dawn, if all was ready.

'Good. We leave then. Meanwhile, let every man eat and sleep as he can.'

Word came from the eastern lookout. A sail had been seen tracking north just before dusk: rust-coloured, heading for the Skaw. It was a long lead, but Haldan was undeterred.

Of course, Tolla had collared Inga into helping feed the men.

'For some, the next hot food they taste will be in the halls of Valhalla,' Tolla had said. The thought made Inga's stomach tighten. *Some*, she prayed to the Spear-God. *But not my Hakan.* A shameful prayer for a warrior, but she didn't care.

Meanwhile, sparks flew into the gloom as whetstones worked, till each man was satisfied his killing edge was ready. Thralls hurried to fill barrels with bread and beer, packing salt casks with dried pork and fish, and carrying them to the boats. Tents of hemp and woollen blankets were loaded. Oars were checked, ropes lashed, sails made ready.

Everything had been too frantic to snatch even a few moments with Hakan. And foreboding gnawed at her belly. She had known this moment must come. One day. Just not so soon. Now, thanks to those stupid oaths, Hakan must sail too.

Along the benches, men shared jokes, or sang bawdy songs to amuse the thrall-girls, or sea-shanties in anticipation of the voyage. Over the womenfolk, she noticed a darker mood. For them, it was no joke. Some of these benches would be empty when Haldan and his men returned.

If they returned . . .

She filled another cup, and moved to the next man. 'Ale or honey-wine?'

'Ale for me. I'm sweet enough already, my lady,' said Garik, with a friendly leer.

'But your breath is still sour,' she teased, happy to empty some of her ale. Garik chuckled grudgingly, and when a few others laughed too, he disappeared into his cup.

But he soon reappeared, wiping his beard. 'You're a hard one to please, my lady. Still, there's plenty girls round here don't seem to mind. Then it's not my mouth they're usually interested in.'

'Leave her alone,' said Gunnar, a fair-haired man with serious eyes, and the best bowman sworn to her uncle. 'High-born ladies like her shouldn't have to hear about your sordid exploits.'

'What? There's nothing sordid about it! What I've got is a thing of beauty, so I've been told!' He laughed heartily.

'Gaaah – you know all women are liars,' returned Gunnar, sparing an apologetic wink for Inga.

'Well, I've had no complaints.' Garik called down the table, 'Here, Hakan! You seen them girls they took. Any beauties among 'em?'

Hakan looked up from his food to see everyone waiting for his answer. He shrugged. 'I was pretty far away. And they weren't exactly looking their best.'

'Hmm – well, there'd better be one or two worth going after, otherwise what the Hel are we doing?' Garik gave another roar of laughter. A few laughed with him, but Inga noticed his question left a couple of younger ones stony-faced.

'Don't you ever take a rest from thinking with your cock?' drawled a voice up the bench. They all turned to see who spoke. Sat apart from the others where the torchlight was dimmer was a man with a long sharp nose and dark sunken eyes. Inga knew him. His name was Dag. His reputation as a killer was enough to curdle anyone's blood.

'And why the Hel should I?' Garik snorted. 'Whatever gets you up in the morning, I reckon. Or whoever!' he yelled, to more laughter.

Dag drew deep on his cup and, without looking up, said, 'It's just you sound – so – fucking – boring.'

'You reckon?' sniffed Garik. 'Well, we know you're a heartless son of a bitch, Dag, but I never knew you had nothing between your legs neither!' But the others weren't so keen to laugh at a joke about Dag. 'Anyway, a man's got to have some reason to fight.'

'Why can't he just fight?' Dag's voice sounded cold as the northern snows.

'You telling me you care nothing for getting back what those Norsk bastards took?'

'If a man steals a horse from me, I'll go after him. I'll kill him. But not because I care two shits about the horse. I'll do it 'cause he thought he could steal from me. 'Cause he took me for a fool.'

'Suit yourself.'

'There's one other thing,' said Dag. 'If you make it home and I don't – you even think about going near my old woman, I swear I'll come back from the dead and scare you fucking shitless.'

'Don't worry yourself, friend,' grinned Garik. 'A man's got to have some standards.' He dropped his voice. 'Besides, he scares the shit out of me already!'

They broke into gales of laughter. Garik raised his cup to Dag who gave him a wink back, his mouth curling in a wolfish smile.

Inga, seeing Hakan only a couple of seats on, took advantage of the laughter and went to refill his cup. 'I need to see you before you go,' she whispered.

He looked up. 'And I you.'

'Outside. Soon as you can.'

He gave a quick nod.

'All gone,' she lied to the next man, shaking her far-from-empty pitchers. Leaving behind half-hearted groans of disappointment, she heard Hakan announce he was going out for a piss. She hurried back to the kitchen, abandoned her pitchers and slipped away unnoticed through the back, out into the night.

Outside the air was cool. She crept along the edge of the hall, one hand brushing the wall, hugging the shadows. In the two months of their secret love, they had learned to make darkness their friend. Her fingers slid into her apron pocket, feeling for the hundredth time the squat arms of the amulet nestled there.

She saw a silhouette appear at the end of the hall, then melt into the shadows of the buttresses.

Suddenly Hakan's face appeared, pale in the gloom. She stopped, startled. Opened her mouth, but nothing came out. For all her thinking that day, she didn't know how to begin.

Instead, they eyed each other warily in the half-light.

'You went without saying goodbye,' she said finally.

'I had no choice. The old man wanted me away as soon as possible.' He sniffed. 'Besides . . . didn't think you cared.'

'And you proved you don't.'

'You should be glad. I'm sure it gave you more time to say farewell to your new friend.'

'Don't be such a child.'

'Oh, but you're so ready to be a woman, aren't you? All grown up, ready to impress fine men like Konur.'

'You become very horrid when you're jealous!'

'Whose fault is that?'

'I did nothing wrong.' She'd spent all day protesting as much to herself. 'We were just talking.'

'That's not what I saw.'

'Then he forced himself on me! You said so yourself.'

''Course I said that last night! I had to have some reason for flattening his face. Whether he did or not, I don't know or care. I just wanted him off you.'

'You didn't seem so keen to get that fat little slattern off you!'

'What?' He seemed genuinely mystified.

'Kella! She was all over you.'

He shook his head. 'I don't remember that.'

'I'm not surprised – you were drunk as a Dane!' She felt her hands bunching into fists. 'Oh, you were such a beast last night!'

'We're all of us beasts,' he snapped back. 'You're no better than the rest of us, you slut!'

She slapped him then. Hard as she could. The sound cracked the darkness. Both froze; each shocked as the other. His hand went to his cheek.

'I'm sorry – that was too much,' he said. 'I . . . I didn't mean it.'

'Why are you being like this?' She felt tears welling. 'Why?'

No answer.

She leaned forward, searching his face for some sign of softness. At last a little shame leaked into his eyes. 'Before the sun rises, you'll be gone,' she sobbed. 'The gods only know when you'll come back. I'm frightened for you – don't you understand?'

She waited, weeping. And then he reached out, brushing away a tear with his thumb. His fingers had always been more eloquent than his tongue. Neither said a word. More tears fell, warm rivulets tickling her cheeks. His fingertip traced her temple, down her jawline, then his hand slid around her neck under her hair.

'My love.' He pulled her close. She felt his warm breath on her lips mingled with the taste of her tears. 'Forgive me.' He kissed her again.

After a few moments, she pulled away. 'I'm sorry too.' She dabbed her cheeks with her sleeve. 'I wasn't thinking last night. Maybe I was jealous of the attention you were getting. But there could never be anyone but you. Our lives are bound as one.'

Hakan gazed down. He didn't need to say anything. His thoughts were her thoughts. No one knew her like he knew her. No one had done as much for her. She saw love burning in his eyes like a madness. And then he clasped her tight against him. She heard the urgency in his quickening breath. Felt it rising in herself.

Her hand closed around his in the darkness, guiding it downwards until his fingers touched the heat between her thighs. She shut her eyes and moaned. The wool felt coarse against her secret parts, the motion of his fingers stirring up sweet agony.

Hakan pushed her against the hall. She watched him drop to lift her skirts, glimpsed her own thighs, white and slender in the night. She slid her hands around his neck as he picked her up, his hands rough against her buttocks, pushing her harder still against the wall. Her thighs closed around his hips. There was a fumbling, and then she felt him, hard and hot as firestone, against her. She was wet with wanting him, and suddenly he was inside her. They groaned together.

Inga giggled. 'Someone might come.'

'Let them come – damn them!' gasped Hakan, biting at her ear. The muscles in his shoulders were taut as a stallion's. Once this hunger took him, there was no turning him aside. His chest pressed against her, smothering her, squashing the soft heat of her breasts, chaffing her hard nipples inside her dress. The murmur of many voices seeped through the cracks in the wall. But no one came.

A moan rose from faraway in the depths of her throat. She licked her lips, still tasting his there. Their movements grew faster and faster.

Her mind was a storm of pleasure, but she still remembered one thought.

Be careful, she meant to murmur. But never did. Perhaps she was beyond caring. Now it was too late. She felt his body stiffen, felt his seed inside her, and then they slumped against the hall.

'If that isn't a good reason to come back alive, I don't know what is,' Hakan gasped, chest heaving.

Inga laughed. She felt invincible, like her world could never end. But then, too quickly, her ecstasy subsided. What seemed so shatteringly real vanished like the dew. She held him tight. 'Come back,' she murmured. 'You must come back.'

'I know.'

'I keep thinking about what the *vala* said.'

'You mustn't.'

'I can't help it. I have a kind of dread about it.'

He passed a tender thumb over her ruffled brow. 'You must put it from your mind. Promise me.'

'I promise.'

'I will live. And we will be happy. Together.' She saw his eyes shining in the gloom. He seemed so confident. But how could he be so sure?

She nodded. 'I have something for you.' She felt in her pocket and produced the amulet on its leathern cord. 'I made it for you.'

She slid the cord over his head. The little hammer fell into place around his neck. He took it, turning it in his fingers. The metal glinted in the moonlight. 'For luck,' she added.

'And love?'

'Yes. For love too. Keep it safe for me.'

'I will.'

She pressed it against his chest. 'Now you must sleep.' She sighed. 'And I must send you out, my love – into the wild winds of the All-Father's will.'

CHAPTER FIVE

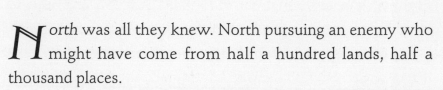

*N*orth was all they knew. North pursuing an enemy who might have come from half a hundred lands, half a thousand places.

Some croaked the judgement of a lad wasn't much to go on. But Hakan was sure: the raiders were Norskmen. North, they would find them.

And with the last light of that first day, Njord, god of the seas, tossed them some luck. A sail on the horizon, no bigger than a rivet on a shield. The men cheered, sniffing their quarry.

The wind carried them west around the Skaw and then north, leaving far behind the lands of many enemies. Raumarika, Horthaland, Hedamark, Ringarika.

Then the wind turned. Grey rollers bore down from the north. Haldan ordered every man to an oar, and stroke by wind-whipped stroke the rusty dot on the horizon grew bigger.

Two days and nights the two longboats went on like that. An arse-skinning, stomach-sucking nightmare of lurching seas and freezing spray. Wind-lashed, caked in salt, hair stiff as straw, Hakan endured. His back a river of pain, his palms rubbed bloody, stopping only to eat morsels of dried cod, which he spewed straight up in a sour stream of spittle.

He had never known such misery. But the men around him rowed, so he rowed with them, while the lookout called that the fugitive ship was still there.

He overheard Eskel tell his father that the only land further north was Halogaland. Beyond that was only ice. The world of unending winter. The world where the giants dwelt.

To the east, the land rose in glowering towers of rock, stabbing at the sky like colossal spears. Now and then, deep fjords cut gashes through the mountains. It was a land beyond anything he had imagined. Beautiful, strange and frightening.

As dusk fell on the fourth day, the raiders were a bare half league ahead. His father cried, 'Lift yourselves till daybreak, and tomorrow you will have blood!'

The men cheered, then fell back to their work. The night passed softly, disturbed only by the rush of bubbles under them, the grunts at the oars, and the breathing of the ocean.

Dawn revealed that the raiders were headed inland. The Jutes went hard, oars hammering at the water to catch their quarry before they could reach land to pick their ground. They were soon close enough to hear the raiders' shouts. Around them the land rose up in towering shadows.

'They're heading for that island,' Eskel yelled, stabbing his finger ahead.

Hakan glanced over his shoulder, sweat stinging his eyes. He glimpsed the shape of a treeless fell, blistering out of the dark waters, dead ahead.

An island was a good place for a fight, his father once said.

A place of land and sea. A place between worlds. A place of the living and the dead.

The raiders beached, so the Jute longboats swung north, landing on the island's other side. Men stank of sweat and sea and stale vomit. Five days at the oar had shredded Hakan's hands. Now, at least, they were back on solid ground.

A crimson dawn bled back the darkness into the Western Ocean.

'We'll meet them on the fell,' shouted his father, pointing to the saddle of land above them, while his men poured from the ship.

Hakan landed with a crunch. The grit felt good underfoot. He hated the sea. Always had. Five days of salt-flayed Hel were over. A new Hel awaited him.

His stomach retched one last time, from fear and nausea both. He wiped his mouth. The weight of his axe felt reassuring. The letters carved into its blade would be tested today – rune magic to bind arms or blunt edges. Overhead the wind sighed, and for the thousandth time, he fingered the amulet around his neck.

I send you out, my love. Into the wild winds of the All-Father's will. He traced the shape of the hammer, remembering her warm sweet breath.

'Here you are, lad.' Garik jammed the skin of mead into his chest. 'Drink deep.' The spear-master grinned at him, greasy hair blowing across his laughing eyes. 'Now we'll see whether what I taught you was worth a thrall's fart.'

Hakan put the skin to his lips and drank, gulping once, twice, before the heat hit him. The brew burned hot as Loki's fire. He coughed hard, then passed it on, expecting men to laugh.

But no one did. Instead their eyes grew bright, intent only on their lord.

Hakan watched him too, feeling the blood swell in his veins. Ears humming, heart quickening, his aching back and buttocks forgotten. The brew worked fast.

His father drew his sword, pointing at the crimson clouds above them. His eyes shone blue under the shadow of his helm. His beard, wet from the salt-spray, glistened red in the morning light.

'A red sky over us, brothers! A day of death! The *valkyries* are done choosing. They ride this way, screaming for Odin's marked men. If you're among them, luck is with you.' A few of the older men laughed. 'As for the rest of you – it's been told from the shadow-lands: the Victory-Father favours us. Ride to the Slain-Hall, if you must! Or stay, and have victory over these blood-drinkers.'

His men cheered, mouths ragged, full of terror.

'Do you feel it, brothers?' Haldan grinned, gazing up at the wind. 'Gondul's gale stirs. Let the ravens feast on their bodies. Fight and never falter, till every one of them eats the black earth!'

The fell loomed behind him. *Death awaits at its summit.* Hakan gaped up at the saddle of land bulging high above them. *But not for me.*

Valhalla's delights awaited the chosen. Feasting, fighting and fucking until the Ragnarok came, the final battle when all would burn. All men knew this.

But he wanted none of it. He had something better in this world.

To Hel with the All-Father's favour.

Let the others perish if they wanted. He must live to come back to her. He must live because she told him to.

He must live.

Inga found it quiet with them gone.

Deathly quiet.

The thatched byres and water troughs had a strange emptiness now. Even the hall seemed sinister, still as a barrow-grave, doorway gaping, inviting the dead into its embrace.

How can anyone stand this awful waiting?

She was glad of the sound of Einna's loom. Inga glanced over. The *clack-clack* of the shafts, Einna's thin hair flicking in the wind. Somehow, the sight calmed her.

The long face whickered, nudging her.

'You're so impatient.' She went on rubbing down the horse's neck.

It had been a few days. They might be gone many more. What if days became weeks, or, worse, months? How long before she must accept they weren't coming back – ever?

No. I won't think that. I mustn't.

Her gaze drifted to the place where she had bid Hakan farewell, a smile rising in her heart as she remembered the warm shadows, the rough planks, his hands sliding her dress over her thighs.

'Keep on like that the poor horse'll have no neck left at all.' Inga spun around, spilling curls over her shoulder.

'Oh, Tolla – it's you.' Inga felt silly, realizing she'd been rubbing the same spot for ages. She nuzzled the stallion's cheek. 'My mind was a thousand leagues away.'

'I know you're worried,' Tolla smiled, setting down her bucket. 'It's always this way. It has to be. They still come back.'

'My father didn't.'

'Aye,' Tolla admitted, 'your father fell. But you won't change a thing worrying about them. They'll come home. I feel it in my old bones.'

Tolla wasn't *that* old. She hadn't seen more than thirty-eight summers, but if she felt it in her bones. . . well, they were right more than most.

'What if they don't?'

Tolla squeezed Inga's arm. 'We'll go on.'

As if it were that simple. How could Tolla understand? She doesn't know. No one knows. Inga tried to shake her doubts, forcing a smile instead.

But Tolla's gaze had drifted beyond her, out of the yard. 'What we got here then?'

Inga turned to look. Beyond the gate, a rider was coming down the track. A tall man on a tall horse. He entered the yard, chickens fleeing from his hooves.

Inga knew him only too well.

Konur.

'What's *he* doing here?'

Tolla didn't answer. She was eyeing him suspiciously.

He looked fine enough, clad all in black, his cloak pinned with a silver brooch, his brown hair streaked blond from the long summer. The loom stopped its clacking. Inga wasn't surprised. Einna's stomach would be turning cartwheels at this one's pretty face.

Though without the bruise across his nose he would have been prettier.

'A fine day, ladies!'

'What are you doing here?' Inga tried to sound especially cold. That was the right thing to do.

'Hardly a welcome for blood kin,' he smiled, unruffled. 'You can't have forgotten me so soon.'

'I remember you. As much as I care to.' It sounded proud enough, and there was no power in the world would get her to admit he'd been in her thoughts more than he ought since the feast. 'Back to start a feud with my cousin?'

'That was a drunken misunderstanding.' *A vicious hate-filled fight, tearing at each other's faces, is what he means.* 'I'm sure Hakan wouldn't begrudge me a lost tooth,' he added, chuckling.

'Hakan has many other teeth. I'm sorry you only have one nose.'

'Fairly said!' he laughed, prodding at the swollen bridge of his nose. When she didn't laugh, he tried contrition. 'If I caused offence, let me make amends.'

'You did. And I don't know that you can.'

He snorted, growing impatient. 'I would have liked to let your uncle be the judge of that. But we had word that he's been taken away on urgent business. Is it true?'

Inga and Tolla exchanged uneasy glances. 'It is. My lord uncle has gone,' said Inga. 'Along with all his fighting men.'

'Hakan as well?'

'Of course, Hakan,' retorted Inga. Did he take Hakan for some kind of stay-at-home coward?

'Where to?'

'How in the Nine Worlds should we know?' said Tolla.

Konur shrugged, as if it were merely of passing interest.

69

Inga threaded her arm through Tolla's, giving it a comforting pat. 'There was a raid.'

'I heard that much. Not much else.'

Inga told him as much as anyone knew – of the killers dressed in wolf-skins, of the slaughtered folk of Vindhaven, of the women taken.

Konur listened, smoothing his beard to a point. 'So your uncle went after them, hey?'

'They sailed north four days ago in two ships. Eighty men in all.'

'All a bit hasty.'

'Hardly. My uncle cares about his womenfolk. He's determined to get them back.'

'Doesn't seem so careful to me.' Konur raised a cynical eyebrow. 'After all, here you are, the lady of the hall. All alone.'

'She's not alone,' said Tolla. 'We have men to protect us.' She nodded at an old thrall labouring his way across the yard under a sheaf of hay. The man had a short axe hitched at his belt. 'Old Rapp. And others besides.'

'Terrifying.'

Inga didn't care for his tone. 'What is it you want here, Konur?'

'I came to bring word from my father to your uncle.' He flashed his pretty grey eyes at her. 'And to see you.'

'Me!' she exclaimed. No one had ever come to Vendlagard to see her. 'What do you want with me?'

'Nothing. . . in particular. I just wanted to see you again. Your cousin interrupted us last time. With his fist in my face.'

'You deserved it.'

'You don't think he's a little. . . over-protective?'

'You were both drunk, and he had every right to be – it was a feast in *his* honour. You were the one in the wrong.'

'Is it my fault if I can't resist a face as beautiful as yours?' His mouth tilted into something between a smile and a leer.

'You're very free with your words where they're not needed. Anyway, my uncle isn't here. If you've nothing *in particular* to say to me, I've nothing to say to you.'

'We'll tell him you called when he comes back,' added Tolla.

'*If* he comes back.'

'When,' insisted Inga. 'Sorry, but you can't stay.' She saw he was losing patience, but she didn't care. She enjoyed annoying him.

'You can't be serious! We're *blood* kin. Understand what that means? I've ridden twenty bloody leagues from Karlsted. And now you're going to turn me away?' The cords in his neck stuck out when he got angry. And his ears went red. But she quite liked how fiery his eyes became.

She shrugged. 'Well?'

'And without so much as a bowl of gruel?' He shook his head. 'I wonder what my father will make of this? Another insult to his son and heir? He'll take that ill. To say nothing of hosting custom.'

She watched his beard bristle. He really was irritatingly handsome.

'You can't turn away blood kin *and* a traveller on the road,' he continued.

'Why not?'

'What – and bring the Wanderer's curse down on this place?'

Behind them, Einna dropped something. The girl was like to have a fit any time curses were mentioned. And there had

71

been too much talk of them in the last few days. Inga and Tolla looked at one another, uncertain.

Konur saw his chance. 'One night,' he said, softer. 'Let my horse rest. Bread, meat, ale. A little talk. I'll be gone in the morning.'

Inga could sense every sinew in Tolla ready to pounce on Konur. But he was right. In her uncle's absence, she had charge of Vendlagard. The laws of hospitality couldn't be ignored. She couldn't turn away a wanderer on the road asking for shelter. Much less her own kin. And her uncle wouldn't thank her for stirring up bad blood with the Karlungs.

'One night.'

'Haha!' he laughed. 'A thousand thanks, cousin! You never know – it may be more pleasant than you think.'

That's what I'm afraid of.

The spear soared over the raiders like a comet cutting the scarlet sky.

The Norskmen gaped upwards. Some wore wolf-skins, some leather byrnies or mail, others went half-naked. The spear skewered the turf behind their battle-line.

Now the gift was sealed. Odin would have his reaping.

And the killing could begin.

Screams rent the sky. The wind howled back, blasting the bleak summit. Hakan yelled, mad with terror.

The Norskmen's shields banged together in a wall.

Haldan screamed a command. Javelins lanced the air. Round shields, white and black, clattered. Shrieks climbed the wind as iron found flesh, the first blood spilled.

Strike hard and watch for their mistakes, Garik had said. Seemed like the first time the randy bastard hadn't tried to make a joke.

Strike hard.

'Bowmen, ready!' bellowed Haldan through the din of screams and battle-cries. Arrows hissed, Norsk spears slit the sky, thudding into wood and mud and flesh. A bowman beside Hakan nocked an arrow, then flopped on his backside, five feet of ash in his belly. He clawed at it, shuddered, then fell back, dying.

A spear whispered past Hakan's ear. He stared at the thing, quivering in the turf.

'Go on, lad – let the bastards have their stick back.' Garik's wolf-grin snapped him into action. He yanked out the javelin and flung it back, watching it disappear behind the shieldwall. A Jute arrow struck a raider's face, spewing dark blood. The Norsk lord screamed something and their shieldwall ran howling at the wall of Jutes. The morning light flashed red on their weapons.

Valkyries' flames. Now we'll see how hot they burn.

Hakan had time to suck a breath, then the wall hit. There was a ripping sound of oak on iron. Hakan glimpsed a hate-filled face, a gaping mouth, an arc of steel. He raised his shield; a sword smashed against its rim. He ducked low, sweeping his axe. The Norskman screamed, the axe biting into his knee, blood spilling in the dirt. Hakan stood over him.

For a second, he glared down at his enemy. Young eyes full of fear, a grimy beard flecked with spittle. Then Hakan drove down his axe, cleaving the man from shoulder to breastbone. He tore it clear. The man fell, flapping like a herring, a weird hiss in his throat. And then he was still.

I've killed a man. Fire burned in his brain. *Killer.* 'Killer!' he screamed, half-mad.

All around, it seemed Hel had ripped open the earth, spewing out death into the world of men. He saw twisted bodies, a severed arm, dead faces, white as chalk, spattered with mud and gore. Others, still alive, jaws gurning. *Slaughter-mad*, he thought. *Only madness makes sense here.*

Arrows and spears peppered the mud, gear strewn like jetsam on the black earth. The battle-din roared – grunts and screams, the thud of flesh, strange bestial cries. The stink of blood and piss and open guts rank in his nostrils.

And through Odin's storm, he spied a bronze helm, glinting red in the dawn: his father, cloak flying about him, going blade to blade with the northern lord.

Not you, Hakan prayed. *Not today.*

Closer to him was Leif, his boyhood friend, his scrub of a beard smeared muddy. A towering man launched at him with the biggest axe Hakan had ever seen. Leif cut, the big man stepped aside, rolled his shoulders, whipping round the double-headed axe. Leif didn't even see it. The metal tore through his arm. Leif screamed, falling to his knees, arm gone. The axe swung again. This time his body crumpled – an eye-blink and his oldest friend was dead. The giant bellowed triumph.

Fury flashed through Hakan's mind; fury, fear, half-formed curses and whining prayers. There was only one way out of this briar of men and steel and blood and death: that was to cut his way free.

The only way back to *her*.

Men were dying all around, both shieldwalls splintered into savagery. But the Norskmen were few and growing fewer. And then his father's voice rang across the fell. 'Their king is dead! Now, brothers, finish it!'

The Norsk king was dead. The rest must die with him.

Someone screamed Hakan's name. He turned, seeing Gunnar, a sword in one hand and a long-knife in the other. Nearby the huge axe-man spewed a stream of curses. Hakan leaped forward, trying to land a cut, ankle burning with the old pain. Instead he took a colossal blow to his shield. Wood and iron shattered, splinters pricking his arm.

He fell face down, but kept rolling, dreading the bite of the massive blade in his back any moment. He flopped over to see the bloodstained blade looming high above him. There was a sudden flash of metal and Gunnar slammed into the axe-man, sending them both crashing to the ground in a tangle of limbs.

Suddenly Beri, one of the white-haired *aeldrener*, was standing over the pair writhing in the mud. The old warrior lifted his sword and then plunged it into the Norskman's back.

He reared up, bellowing like a bull, mouth stained red. Beri twisted the hilt, and Gunnar squirmed free, face oozing blood. The axe-man screamed, then flopped flat on his face. Gunnar spat, stooped over him, and with one quick motion of his knife, the screaming stopped.

Hakan scrambled to his feet. The last beleaguered Norskmen stood nearby. Some of them bare-bodied berserkers smeared red with the blood of his kinsmen, others hard-looking killers in mail and leather. Many lay around them. Magni the Ox, a spear through his neck, dead. Ran, his cousin, chest splayed – dead. Aevar the White, sword shattered – dead.

A fine day's reaping for Odin's hall, he thought bitterly.

The Norskmen formed shields and the Jutes went for them again, relentless, wanting the dying to be done.

Gunnar took a hard cut to his arm and fell back. Hakan took up a spear, lunging with the last of his strength, glimpsed an axe, lurched backwards, and felt his helm ring and the kiss of steel. A heartbeat slower, his head would have been split.

'Stand back!'

The Jutes looked round. Haldan was with them, the bronze mask of his helm menacing and cold.

'We lose no more. Do you wish for quarter?' he shouted at the huddle of Norskmen. Only four were left, eyes yellow as wolves, full of hate.

'Walk the Hel road, Jute,' one of them spat. 'We die with our kin.'

Haldan gave a grim nod. 'So be it. Stone them.'

His men hesitated, uncertain.

'You heard me – stone them!'

They looked at each other, and then at the ground. The fell was strewn with rocks. The northerners snarled curses, seeing what was coming.

The rocks found their mark, and in a few moments the last of them crumpled. The Jutes swarmed in, stabbing out any last signs of life.

At last the fell was still, the only sounds the gasps of the living and the groans of the dying.

Hakan sank down, bone weary.

'Victory!'

He looked up at his father, standing with his sword pointing at the sky.

A weary cheer went up. Gunnar slumped to the ground, face

pale under smears of blood. His arm hung limp, his side a slick of blood. Garik was no better. His breeches glistened darkly where his hand pressed down on his thigh.

Hakan's ankle throbbed. He was a killer now. A proven man. As he sat on the grass, gasping for breath, out of nowhere his mother's words came to him. *You're to be a man, not a monster.* He remembered the piss-yellow terror in that lad's eyes, the whistling sound when he pulled the axe free.

A monster. Aye – what was that?

His father stood looking up at the clouds still aglow with the rising sun. 'A red sky for a red day.' Sheathing his sword, he looked around him at the remnants of his shieldband.

'You – Dag.' The shadow-faced killer stepped forward. 'Take Hakan and check on their ship. And the women.' He gave Dag a hard look. 'If they're still alive.' Dag licked his lips, nodding.

'We need an archer. Where's Eskel?' The helmsman pushed his way through.

'You go too.' Haldan pointed west where the land dropped to the sea. 'Be careful. I want the women alive, but if there's more than one guard, come back here. I want no more men killed.'

The three moved off wordlessly across the fell. Above them crows and gulls were gathering for their feast. At the crest of the slope, Hakan spied the Norskmen's ship far below, beached, its hull half-rolled and black as tar.

Everything was quiet.

'Come on,' he said, striding on, 'there's no one there.' But he hadn't gone two steps when fingers, hard as iron, bit his shoulder.

'Slowly, lad, slowly.' Dag grinned yellow teeth. 'No need to be too hasty, eh? Let's sit here a while. Have a watch.'

He shoved Hakan down into a hollow, out of sight from the beach. He and Eskel dropped down next to him.

They watched in silence. They didn't have long to wait. A lick of wind ruffled the sail and a rusty head appeared under it. A Norskman came hopping from bench to bench to the bows.

'Is he all there is?' scowled Dag, unimpressed. 'Reckon you can take him from here?'

'Tha's a pig of a shot,' grimaced Eskel, already nocking an arrow. 'Still, might be you won't forget this in a hurry.'

'Just don't fucking miss,' hissed Dag.

The guard was hanging off the prow, shading his eyes to the hill.

'He can't see us,' whispered Hakan.

''Course he can't fucking see us.' Dag spat into the mud. 'He might feel us soon enough though, eh?' A chuckle rattled in his throat and he patted the haft of his knife.

Eskel drew back his bow, the string creaking in protest, then – *thrum* – the arrow shot into the sky. It arced high. For a second, Hakan lost it, hoping it would reappear in the Norskman's chest.

Instead there was a thud, and the arrow was quivering two feet wide of the mark.

'You dozy bastard.' Dag was already climbing to his feet. 'So much for the easy life. Right, here we go.'

The guard didn't wait for a second shot. He was over the benches and under the sail before they were even out of the hollow.

'He's gonna kill 'em,' yelled Eskel.

'Best fucking run then, ain't we?' Dag tore off down the slope and Eskel after him. Hakan lurched on behind, best as his ankle would allow.

They were still a way off, running hard, when the first scream shattered the quiet.

A woman's scream.

Then another. Wails that were like to make the sky weep. Almost as quickly, they grew less and less. Until, abruptly, they ceased.

'Shit on it!' cried Eskel. 'Move!'

They reached the beach, the soft sand slowing their pace.

'Easy now, fellas,' called Dag, slowing to a menacing stalk.

The sail billowed. What it revealed hit Hakan like a stone wall.

There was the redhead Norskman, and behind him, a miserable sight.

Lashed tight around the mast were the women from Vindhaven. Most were still; for some the spasms of death weren't yet done. Some were naked, others in rags, their bodies slumped forward, filthy hair hanging down. And daubed down the front of each of them, an ugly scarlet smear: blood, still welling in lazy pulses, their throats cut to the bone.

'Bastard!' shouted Hakan. But it was too late. The guard leaped languidly over the gunwale. He was clad in dirty breeches and a loose mailshirt, and underneath nothing but bones. He couldn't have been many winters older than Hakan, with a few dirty wisps of stubble around a crooked mouth.

'What you been up to, fella?' Dag's eyes glinted cruel in their hollow sockets.

The guard only laughed. 'Long way to come for nothing, pig-fuckers.'

'Pig-fuckers, is it?' chuckled Eskel. 'And there was I thinking that was your mother.'

'They're all of them dead,' the guard sneered.

'You think we care a soft turd about them,' said Dag, nodding his head at the dead women. The scars on his face twisted into a dark smile. 'No – it's you we came to hear scream, boy.'

The guard's grin faltered. 'I'm ready to die.' He shifted the weight of a short sword in one hand, and rolled an axe round his wrist in the other.

'Oh, you'll be begging for death by the time I'm done with you.' Dag licked his lips.

Without warning, the redhead thrust at Dag, who knocked it aside casually with his shield.

'You'll have to do better than that.'

The Norskman fell back on his guard, but Hakan had seen his eyes were on the others. He lurched in and struck right. The guard saw it late, parrying with his axe. He tried to retire, but couldn't: the axe-heads were locked tight. Hakan yanked hard, pulling his arm out straight. Steel streaked down, and the Norskman's axe flew loose.

With it, his hand.

'Gaaaaaaaaah!' he screamed, falling to his knees, blood leaking all over the sand. Dag smashed away his sword, Eskel put a boot in his chest. The guard went sprawling, clutching for the hand that wasn't there.

Dag was astride him in a heartbeat, punching him with the pommel of his sword – once, twice. The redhead slumped back, unconscious.

'There you are,' said Dag, grinning up at them, dried blood flaking off the twisted scars on his face. The guard's wrist was squirting blood. Dag undid the man's belt and wound it tight around his arm.

'What are you going to do to him?' asked Hakan.

'Hang about, lad, and you'll see. Might learn something.'

Hakan didn't reply. Hadn't he seen enough for one day?

'Come on, lad,' said Eskel. 'He works best without an audience.'

'Suit yourselves.' Dag shook the redhead's chops. The man started to come round, all groggy. 'You leave him with me. I'll soon make him real comfortable.' There was a raking sound as Dag drew out his long-knife. 'Won't I, boy?' The lad only whimpered, eyes wide with fear. The wind caught the sour smell of urine.

Hakan turned away. Eskel was already striding up the beach towards the fell. The first scream sounded when Hakan caught him up.

'Scream once, and they never stop.' Eskel quickened his pace.

'Doesn't everyone scream?'

'Some never utter a sound. Others squeal like hogs. You can't tell which a man'll be just from the look of him.'

'This one's a screamer anyhow,' Hakan murmured. He thought of the women. The blood in their hair would be clotting, their bodies stiffening with the chill of death. 'I guess he deserved it.'

Eskel gave him a slantwise look. 'Guess he did. Might be we all do one way or another.'

The guard screamed again, a sound so savage Hakan had to look back. He saw Dag sit up and fling something small and red over his shoulder.

'Seems a waste now.'

'What's that?'

'The women. That's why we came here, isn't it?'

'So it is,' Eskel nodded grimly. 'Hel's got 'em now, I guess. Still – you can't change what the Norns have woven.'

Can you not?

He'd often pictured those three ancient sisters in their gloomy dwelling, far below the woods and fields of his homeland, sat at the foot of the World Tree, spinning their thread, weaving the fates of men. Each sister had a name: *What Was, What Is* and *What Will Be.* They would sit till the Ragnarok, working their loom of destiny in the shadowy depths.

'We did what we could,' sniffed Eskel. 'That's it.'

Hakan nodded. Aye, they had done what they could. And now they could go home.

To Inga.

High on the wind, the gulls swooped, each shriek shrill and taunting.

They're laughing at us, he thought, looking up. They must be. *Laughing at the bloody strife of men.*

His face twisted into a grimace. *Let them laugh. Or scream in rage at the ceaseless wind.* The dead were riding for the Hall of the Slain now.

But he was still alive.

He pushed on up the hill, pain twinging each step. Behind him, the screams grew fainter.

CHAPTER SIX

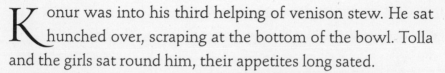

Konur was into his third helping of venison stew. He sat hunched over, scraping at the bottom of the bowl. Tolla and the girls sat round him, their appetites long sated.

Inga had told the thralls they could go to bed. Old Rapp was doing his best to snore a hole right through the roof at the end of the hall. Flames rippled in the firepit, smoke curling up into the summer sky. On the wall, torches burned, sending shadows dancing over the tapestries hanging there.

Einna giggled. Inga shot her a reproachful look.

'What?' Einna frowned. 'He's a good strong eater, tha's all.'

'You have to be under my father's roof.' Konur shoved away the bowl, satisfied at last. 'With four brothers, it's bed with an empty belly if you can't eat fast as a hungry pig.'

'You've certainly took that lesson to heart,' said Tolla.

'Four more.' Einna's eyes widened. 'And all of 'em pretty as you?'

'Stop bothering him,' said Inga.

'No bother.' He flashed Einna a smile.

They fell silent a while.

'You like the food then?' asked Einna, eventually.

'Very fine.'

She squealed, and clapped her hands. 'I knew you'd like it. I told Inga so. Even though it was her taught me, and Tolla taught her. Isn't that right, Tolla?'

'Do you have to make such a fool of yourself, girl?' said Tolla.

'It's grand hospitality. Worthy of Thor himself.' Konur stretched and gave his belly a pat. 'Not much talk though. . . Except from you.'

Einna giggled. 'Oh, I prattle away all the livelong day!' *She wasn't wrong there*, thought Inga.

Tolla rolled her eyes. 'Just *stop* talking, you little halfwit.'

'Oh, leave her,' said Inga, putting a protective arm round Einna. 'She can't help it. Can you, silly goose? Besides, he's used to women turning gooey on him. Isn't that right?'

Konur cocked an eyebrow.

'Don't be bashful.' Inga decided she liked teasing him. 'You know, Nussa told me he's kissed every thrall-girl within five leagues of Karlsted.'

'And more 'n kissed besides,' sniggered Einna.

'I didn't know you took such an interest in my kisses.'

'Me? You flatter yourself. *I* don't care. I guess when folks haven't got enough to say, they talk any old nonsense.'

'You shouldn't believe everything you hear over an ale-cup.' He took a long, steady swallow, never taking his gaze from hers. Inga shifted. *He sure loves staring with those big grey eyes of his.* 'Still,' he conceded. 'They're right about one thing. I do like women.'

84

Tolla's scoff into her cup could have been heard at the other end of the hall.

Konur laughed. 'Well – what man doesn't?'

Tolla thumped down her cup. 'Plenty! Wanting to bed a thrall-girl or three, and liking women isn't the same thing. A man can hate a woman and fondle her teats just the same.'

'Tolla!' cried Inga. Einna was a fountain of giggles, evidently enjoying herself.

'Can't a man like a woman both ways? To me, you're all fascinating.'

'Sure, sure,' said Inga. 'Maybe you've forgotten what you said to me at the feast. You seemed a lot more fascinated by teats then than anything else.' She knew she should still be angry about what happened. But just then, it all seemed faintly ridiculous.

He looked suddenly abashed. 'Well – perhaps I didn't know what I was saying.'

'I don't make you *ache* for me, then?' She feigned a grimace, enjoying his discomfort.

'No – I. . .' He snorted. 'You're laughing at me.'

'No one ever done that before?'

'Not so much.'

'Well then – welcome to the lesson. All part of our hospitality here at Vendlagard.'

'I'm glad for it,' he smiled. 'If you're the teacher. Still, will you accept an apology?'

'Hah!' scoffed Tolla. 'You think it's all dealt with that easy?'

Inga bristled. She didn't like Tolla telling her what to do. Konur hadn't asked Tolla, after all. 'I suppose I will.'

Tolla gave her a sharp look, but she didn't mind. It was all best forgotten anyway. Hakan would have to bear the grudge for both of them.

'Excellent!' he cried. 'Will you drink to it?'

'Why not?' she shrugged. Then, clapping her hands, 'Come on, we all will!'

They pushed in their cups. Konur poured the amber liquid. The cups clattered in a toast and they all drained them. Konur snatched the pitcher again.

'Another.'

Tolla shook her head. 'Not for the girls. It's not for womenfolk—'

'—to make ale-soaked sluts of themselves,' chanted the two girls together, bursting into laughter.

'Darling Tolla, we know!' Inga planted a kiss on Tolla's cheek. 'Come – it's not too strong. We'll only sip it.'

'Your uncle wouldn't let you.'

'If he's so worried about a second cup of ale, he can come back and stop me!'

The girls took another sip. Einna spilled hers, setting off more giggles.

Inga wiped her mouth. 'So, Konur, son of Karsten, heir to the Karlung lands – tell us. We're all ears. What is *so* fascinating about us then?'

He leaned closer. 'You're all a mystery.'

'A mystery, eh? Hear that, Einna?'

'So you are. You're a comfort and a terror. Unfathomable as the ocean, wild as the north winds, beautiful as the autumn sun. Bitterness and sweetness in one bite.' He snapped his teeth shut.

Inga glanced at Einna. *The silly thing's eyes are big as platters.* 'My – don't you sound like a skald-singer, just? I suppose you scatter a few pretty words like that and a girl is ready to lift her skirts for you, is that it?'

'I'll not deny it,' he smiled. 'Doesn't mean I don't believe them.'

'And that makes it so much better, I suppose! Well, we're not all so beautiful as you say. I've seen swine licking shit off a stick prettier than my aunts.'

'Inga!' scolded Tolla.

'I'm right, aren't I?' she laughed.

'They ha'n't been kissed by Freya, and that's the truth.' Einna nodded earnestly, as though that were a point worth considering.

'Not like you.' Konur was trying to hold Inga's gaze, but she wouldn't let him. It was very flattering and all, but she wasn't going to play this game with him. Meanwhile, Tolla's scowl was growing ever deeper.

'Do your brothers' lips drip as much honey, I wonder?'

'Hardly. Karni's too busy thinking up his next wisecrack, and Kufri singing songs with his mother.'

'And the others?'

'The littl'uns? They've barely stopped pissing their breeches.'

'Doesn't sound like you like them much.' Inga sighed. 'I always thought it would be nice to have a brother.'

'Brothers bring their own trouble,' said Konur, knocking back his ale. 'You know the tales. Of Brani and Brusi. Gerdrik and Arnulf. Feng and Horvand. My father's lands will be mine. Brothers have killed each other for less.'

'Do you know how stupid that sounds?'

'Don't you trust them?' asked Einna.

'They're no trouble now. But we all grow older. I just make sure they know their place.'

'Oh, I bet you're good at that,' said Inga.

He leaned back, considering her. 'You like laughing at me, hey?'

'That's because you're ridiculous. You take yourself so seriously.'

'Well, it's a serious business. . . Being me.'

They stared at each other, and this time she let him. Suddenly they burst out laughing. Konur threw his head back and laughed long and hard.

'What's so funny?' asked Einna.

Inga shook her head. She hardly knew.

'Now, your cousin Hakan.' Konur reached for the pitcher again. 'That one's serious as the pox.'

The mention of his name suddenly jarred in her head. How could she have forgotten him this whole time they were sitting there? 'You don't know him,' she said, suddenly serious. *No one knows him like I do.*

'Don't think I care to know him much.'

'Well, you should. He's. . .' She checked herself. *He's beautiful. Gentle, wild, strong. . . He's. . . mine.* She wanted to shout it. But no one must know. 'Ask Einna – she's been in love with him for years. Haven't you, little goose?'

'Shut up, you!' snapped Einna, colouring scarlet.

'It's very sad,' teased Inga, laying her hand against Einna's cheek. 'Like one of the old songs. He doesn't love poor little Einnaling back.'

'I can't think why,' offered Konur.

'There you are, little goose,' smiled Inga. Einna was blushing something fierce. 'We should send you to Karlsted. You can pick yourself a husband from this one's brothers.' Einna squirmed. 'How about the one that wets his pants?' Inga clapped in delight.

'Didn't I tell you to shut your big hole? I'll be fourteen this winter. I'll soon marry a proven man. Not some wetpants baby. A man like. . . well, like you.' Einna gazed adoringly at Konur.

'You can't have forgotten Hakan so quickly, little goose!' Although hadn't she just done that very thing?

'Like Hakan then,' added Einna. 'Yes – certainly like him.' She sighed, going all dreamy.

'Hakan's hardly a proven man,' sniffed Konur.

'Didn't your father ever teach you only a fool insults a man under his own roof?'

'I don't see him here, do you? Besides, this isn't his roof.'

'It will be.'

'You get nothing but folly from a fool,' threw in Tolla, before disappearing back into her ale-cup.

'Truly spoken,' agreed Inga.

'That right? Well, just to prove you both wrong, here – another toast. Come on.' Konur poured again till their cups were brim-full. 'To Hakan! Son of the *great* Lord Haldan – may he return here safe. And whole.'

His words suddenly brought back the gnawing dread of the afternoon. It crushed her heart, cold and cruel. *Yes – mighty Frey*, she prayed, *bring him back to me.* Inga squeezed the cup in hope.

Konur tapped each cup. 'There – you have to drink to that now.' Tolla looked doubtful. 'All of you.'

They all drank. 'You've my sympathies anyway, Einna,' he said, wiping his lips. 'I've been thinking of marriage a little myself.'

Inga nearly bit her cup. 'You?'

'Why not?'

'And break the hearts of all those ass-headed thrall-girls?' scoffed Tolla. 'I don't believe it.'

'No?' he grinned. 'I'm of an age. I have lands – or will have. I need a wife.' Inga didn't like the way he was looking at her. 'I *want* a wife.'

'And who's the girl fated to have this *good* fortune?' asked Tolla. Inga had to admire her. In one word, Tolla could make marrying Konur sound worse than a winter bath in cold piss.

'No one,' said Konur, ignoring the jibe. 'Least, not yet. But she'll be a worthy woman.'

'Worthy?' Inga hit the table with merriment. 'As if you know what a worthy woman might be, after all those hay-turning sluts.'

'I mean a woman of beauty. Strong in body, straight in mind. Noble, loyal, obedient—'

'Docile, dumb, dull and dead! Boring, boring. What is it about mooning fools like you? You don't want a wife – you want an obliging goat!' Inga didn't know why, but she was getting riled.

'I think she sounds wonderful,' mused Einna.

'You would,' snapped Inga. 'She's straight out of some stupid song he's heard. Come to think on it, maybe you *should* marry Einna. The two of you could float around with your heads in the sky like two little clouds.' She gave a sharp laugh, feeling her cheeks flush. The ale was making her louder.

'I suppose you don't want a man then.'

Inga snorted. She didn't like his tone. Besides, she had a man already. 'I have no need of a husband yet. I'm not even of age.'

90

'You will be soon,' chirped Einna. 'Then your uncle will start looking for a match.'

'He'll do no such thing!'

It was Konur's turn to laugh. 'That'll be news to him, no doubt. You're dreaming if you think he'll let you pick a man for yourself.'

'You don't know my uncle.'

'I know he's a man who knows the world. A man of good sense, at least by reputation. And it's good sense to see you married with some advantage to your kin.'

'The world's a foolish place to treat women no better than cattle.' Now she *was* angry. 'Trussing them up and carting them off to market. Well, my uncle can try all he likes. It won't happen to me. I'm free – like my mother was free. Folk tried to make her do whatever they wanted, but she never gave up. Isn't that right, Tolla?'

'Just so, my kitten,' soothed the nurse, smoothing down Inga's errant curls.

'She married for love. My father married her for love, not for any advantage, as you call it. I'll do the same. I'll not be bound by any silly custom, just because someone says it *must* be. The world can go drown itself in the sea before I'd do that.'

'But that *is* the world,' he chuckled. 'You can't escape it. You'd have to drown yourself in the sea before that changed.' He shook his head, amused. 'And you say I'm the one with my head in the songs.'

'You *do* sound like one, when you talk like that,' agreed Einna.

Inga could have kicked the table. *They don't understand. Life is a song. If only Hakan would return.*

91

'I've got it!' Einna's face lit up. 'You're Guldis! Why, you're *just* like her. Shut up in her snowy hall. Have you heard this song, Konur?'

'Here, you can't sing with a dry throat.' He raised his cup. Einna knocked hers against his, excitedly.

'You're trying to get us drunk.' Already, Inga's words felt clumsy in her mouth. 'We're not as stupid as your bondsmen's daughters.' Her cheeks felt hot. 'Are we, Tolla?' She gave Tolla's hand a squeeze. The nurse gave an affectionate smile in return. *Did he think it was so easy? After what he did the last time?* Suddenly she wanted the song more than anything.

'Go on then, Einna. Sing! Sing, my Einnaling!'

And Einna sang, her voice pure as a ray of sun, her pale fingers drumming the rhythm on the table. Inga closed her eyes.

Black were the berries and green the leaf,
When stole away the Asgard thief.
With Freya's dust and the pelt of Frey,
Loki flew beyond night and day.

He knew a maid in a high-rock hall,
Where eagles nest and falcons call.
Long she'd wept as the wind did wail,
For no man rode that stony trail.

Winters came and winters fled,
The lonely maid with lips so red,
Sang of a love that once she knew,
Of kisses soft as morning dew.

Loki slipped on Ingvi's pelt,
A wolf he came to where she dwelt.
Alone, afraid, the maid—

Einna stopped, then shook her head. 'Alone, afraid, the maid was . . .' Suddenly, she knuckled her brow. 'Pig *shit!*' she swore, looking dismayed. 'I've forgotten how it goes.' So Inga took up the song instead.

Alone, afraid, the maiden screamed.
The wolf she'd feared from darkest dream.

She sang on as the torches burned low. Her voice was a shade darker than Einna's, singing of Loki's beguiling love, of the monstrous sons Guldis bore: werewolves, shape-shifters. Of terror and blood, of a hero's coming and slaying her wicked offspring, of their passionate love. The song ended.

'You have a sweet voice,' murmured Konur.

Inga smiled. 'So sweet it has put Tolla to sleep.' She looked affectionately at her nurse, whose head was in her arms, the silver threads in her hair flickering gold in the firelight.

Einna's eyes were still bright. 'You sing one, Konur. If you can.'

'If I can?' He raised a dark eyebrow. 'Judge for yourself. But first, another drink.' He poured out more ale. 'While your watchdog sleeps.'

Konur put down his cup. His voice was deep. He sang almost in a whisper, and soon Inga found herself swept up in his tale. The tale was sadder than hers, the melody mixing bitter with sweet. He wove his story well: of distant lands and cruel kings, of faithful love, of loss and triumph, of wisdom and, finally, of death.

As the song went on, Inga's mind floated on its currents. Konur could sing, no question. And by the end, her heart had fallen a little captive to his voice.

The last note died, leaving only the crackle of the fire. His song had been long, and now only she was awake. Einna was snuggled close, fast asleep, breathing deep, dream-filled sighs.

'They must be glad to hear you round the fires of Karlsted.'

'Every fire loves a song.' This time he didn't look at her. His pale eyes were gazing far away into the flames. 'Did you know it?'

'I've heard it before, long ago. Or one like it.'

He turned away from the fire and his sweet eyes settled on hers. But he said nothing. Instead they sat like that, the silence seeming to linger for ever. Inwardly, she groaned. What was she doing? *The air smells rank with trouble.* But instead of groaning, a laugh eventually escaped her lips; a tinkling, nervous laugh, not like hers at all.

'I'll grant you this, Konur – I can see why all those girls fall on their backs.' She laughed. She felt stronger when she laughed at him. 'It may work on them.' She leaned forward and tapped his cheek. 'But it won't on me.'

Suddenly he caught her wrist. She tried to pull away, but he gripped tight. A flicker of fear shot through her. She pulled again, insistent this time, and her hand came away. 'It's late.'

Konur glared on, those girlish eyes of his intent; and for a heartbeat, she thought she saw something cruel lurking in their beauty.

She stirred Einna. Her friend blinked drowsily and stretched. Inga got to her feet, feeling suddenly unsteady. 'Ooh – too much of that stuff.' She pushed away the cup. *Much too much.*

She went to Tolla and gently roused her. Einna was already stretching out again, sinking back into sleep, but Tolla rose and lifted her to her feet, pushing her up the ladder to the sleeping-bower on one side of the hall. 'You too,' the nurse called, before climbing wearily after Einna.

Inga disappeared into the shadows and returned with a homespun blanket.

'Men up there.' She gave a tired nod towards the bower on the other side of the hall.

'Well then.' She pressed the blanket into his chest. 'Goodnight.' He glanced up into the shadows. The others were now quiet as the dead.

'Inga, when I spoke of a wife, I meant you,' he suddenly whispered. 'That's why I'm here.'

'Shhhh! Don't be so ridiculous.'

'Why is that ridiculous?' His voice sounded all whiny. Stupid.

'Because—' she began. 'Because. . .' *Because of a thousand reasons, surely?. . . Or is it only one?* 'Because I'm not of age. Because I don't even want to think about marriage. Not with you. Not with anyone,' she lied. Seemed there was a lot of lying to be done.

'But you'll be old enough soon. Next spring. And. . . and I love you.'

'No, you don't!' she hissed, angry that he was being so clumsy. Worried he would do something that would make it even worse.

But he already had an arm round her, mouth lurching at hers. She snatched up her hand between them to prise him away.

'Stop it, Konur!' But his eager face kept pressing in. 'Stop it!' She wriggled and wrestled, at last getting free. 'You mustn't do that.'

'But . . . but I—'

'You *don't* love me. Stop saying that! How can you? You don't even know me!'

'How do you know how I feel?'

She backed away. He was right; she didn't know how he felt. Truth was she didn't even know how she felt just then. 'Just go to sleep.' And when there was enough distance between them, she fled to the ladder.

'Inga!' he called after her. Her hands were already on the rails. 'Is there any hope?'

She looked back over her shoulder. 'No,' she insisted, but his expression was expectant as ever, like some stupid dog who knows he'll get what he wants if only he'll sit still and wait. *Well, he can wait till the Ragnarok!* 'No!' she hissed again, wanting to scream it.

Instead, she put her foot to the first rung. But by the time she reached the top, she was wondering why her 'no' sounded so much like 'yes'.

Many leagues north, Hakan watched white tops on dark waves swell about the hull, a thin wind whistling off the sail, the old fear of the sea gnawing at his guts.

The hull lurched, a scuff of spray made him shiver. Two ships had sailed north; one was returning. The other, filled with their dead, was set on a course for the setting sun, flames licking at rope and mast. The fire road would carry their comrades on to Odin's hall.

They had taken back all the Norskmen stole, leaving behind only the dead women. His father ordered the ship burned on the beach, deaf to Eskel's protests that it was a fine vessel. Hakan had watched the women's skin char black before the smoke had swallowed them. The dead Norskmen they left on the fell.

Food for the ravens.

The slaughter was over. But death still lingered.

The two men beside him were slumped against the strakes, dying. Gunnar's face was haggard, his cheek torn, gobbets of black blood stuck to his pale beard. But it was the wound in his arm that was killing him. Garik was little better. At first, he'd hid the wound in his thigh. But eventually he'd been forced to show it. It was deep. By the second day, his jokes had dried up, and his breeches and leggings were sodden with blood.

What do you say to a man who's already dead?

The wind gusted. Gunnar shuddered.

'You need another cloak?'

Gunnar grimaced. 'Bring me another ten – it'd make no difference.'

Hakan sank back against the planking. His hand went to his own wound above his eye. It smarted from the salt-air, lumpy and tender to touch. His head ached. But he had come through Skogul's storm. Somehow. And if Njord, the god who ruled this miserable wet wasteland, wasn't an utter whoreson, his feet would touch the strand of Vendlagard again. He would touch *her* again.

He would live. These men would not.

'Are you afraid to die?'

'No. Just sorry to.' Gunnar's shoulders heaved a weary sigh. 'You ever love anyone?'

Hakan fingered his amulet. 'No,' he lied. He heard Garik snicker in the gloom. He wanted to tell him to go fuck himself, but then he remembered he was dying.

Gunnar tried to shift his weight. 'I'm sorry I won't see my Freya again.'

'You'll forget her soon enough, once you cross the rainbow bridge,' growled Garik.

'What do you know of it?'

'Reckon I took my fill of women. I've no regrets.'

'At least she can be proud of you,' said Hakan. As soon as he said it, he felt stupid.

'For dying?' Gunnar shook his head. 'She'd scold me for a fool, more like.'

'But the slain will live with honour in the All-Father's hall.'

'So they will,' nodded Gunnar. 'Are we still the slain if we die in this stinking slop? I guess this lanky bastard and me'll find out.'

'No doubt,' agreed Garik, voice hoarse.

'We go on a journey from which none come back.'

'I'll be sure to ask how much you want to come back when you've got a *valkyrie*'s tongue down your throat.' Garik chuckled, thin and dry.

Gunnar gestured for the skin. Hakan crouched down and gave him a swig. 'It's a well of riches and riddles.'

'Valhalla?'

Gunnar gave a weak snort and shook his head. 'The heart of a woman. You could live a hundred lives and never fathom the heart of one woman.'

'You sound like a bloody woman, talking like that,' hissed Garik.

'Maybe love makes men talk so. Love – and death.'

'We all end up in the same place. If you carry steel. . .'

Hakan saw Gunnar shudder in the darkness. He felt suddenly sad listening to these men, talking like two spirits already dead. 'Why must we die like that?'

'We die because we must fight,' said Gunnar. 'We fight because we must live.'

'Live for what?'

'We live so that one day we die well.'

It makes no sense. But he kept his thoughts to himself.

'The cold is right through me,' muttered Gunnar, voice a guttering flame. 'Keep our names well, boy.'

'I will,' he whispered.

'The blood-river carry me then. Wherever it will.' Gunnar rolled away, pulling the cloak tighter.

'Reckon I'll leave them maids to your fumbling hands.' Garik's mouth twitched with the last of his grins. 'May luck keep you longer than she did me.'

Garik closed his eyes, slipping down the hull till he lay flat and still. Hakan watched the outline of his comrades, shivering with the cold, until at last he fell asleep.

When he awoke, it was light and he knew they were dead.

He reached out and touched Garik's shoulder. Hard as rock. A tide of blood had congealed around the two comrades, the last of their life mingling in death.

He heard a footfall. He looked up to see his father's silhouette against the grey sky.

'They're gone.'

His father smiled wanly.

'So many. Gone, I mean.'

Haldan nodded and held out his hand. Hakan let himself be pulled to his feet. 'Come.' His father picked his way to the prow.

The wind flicked Haldan's tar-black hair around his ugly stub of an ear: gift of an Amunding axe twenty years before.

Old scars.

Hakan fingered the clusters of gristle under his hair. He had old scars of his own. *If they don't kill you, they bring you luck.* So his father said. He should know. But there was something about his father's shoulders that spoke of more than luck, something unshakeable. A challenge to the world: *Cut me down if you dare.*

So far, it hadn't.

For a while, Haldan stared out over the grey waves. His father never wasted words, but they weren't always quick in coming. 'The Spear-God taught me something new back there.'

'What?'

'A new kind of fear.' Haldan looked down at his son, an awkward flicker of tenderness in his eyes. 'That I was going to lose you.'

'Not this time.'

'No, not this time.' He gazed off to the horizon. 'The blood of our line rests with you, Hakan.'

'I know, Father.' He'd known it since he was soiling his breeches and his father was never like to let him forget it.

'I thought of this day. A long time, I've thought of it – the day you would stand in line with me. To fight.' He turned to his son. 'I can't say I wasn't tempted to keep you clear away from it. Many times.' He chuckled. 'But the truth is – you did well.'

Hakan's heart swelled with pride. Hadn't every drop of sweat he'd ever shed, every bruise he'd ever taken, been to hear those words from his father?

'I survived,' was all he answered.

'Aye, you survived! And that's *bloody* well!' cried Haldan. 'This world is red with blood. It's a killing world. One man takes whatever he can from another. Even if that's only a glorious death.'

'Like your father?'

'Your grandsire was a man made for this world, sure. A killer. He left it far bloodier than he found it.' He scowled. 'Stirred up a heap of trouble for all of us.' He took Hakan by the shoulder. 'But that's not the only way to live. You understand?'

'I think so.'

His father's bright blue eyes wandered out onto the ocean. 'Your mother taught me the truth of that.'

'You still mourn her?'

Haldan shook his head. 'A man cannot mourn for ever. But he can remember.'

Hakan watched him askance. He wanted to reach out, to lay his hand on those broad shoulders that seemed like they must bear the world. To say something that could fill the silence. But what words could answer his father's long-dead love?

'I'm sorry,' said Haldan, eventually. 'I wasn't ready for the risk of losing you. It was suddenly so close. So. . . *possible.*

Everything I've done these eighteen years has been for you. To see you secure. . . ready to lead our people.'

'I've done all I can to be ready.' It felt like his life had been meant for little else.

'In the midst of that slaughter, all I could think was: if you were killed, it was all worth nothing. My life. Your life. Your mother's. . . Nothing.'

Once again, his father's expectations weighed on him, heavy as iron. The weight was long familiar, but now *he* felt different. Felt strong enough to bear the load. He was a man now. He had Inga. Yet his father was talking like everything was about to end. For him, everything was just beginning.

The Vendlings would live on, as his father had always wanted. Perhaps he *could* tell his father about Inga. Perhaps he would even be pleased. Sure, according to the old ways, his father would give Inga to another man in some dreary exchange for an acre or two, or a few marks of silver. But it didn't have to be that way. He was his father's sworn man now. He had killed for him. Didn't he deserve the woman he wanted? This way, the Vendling blood would be secure. Better than that, it would be strong.

'Father.'

Haldan turned to him, but as Hakan was about to speak a cry came from the stern. 'My lord!' They both turned.

Eskel hung over the tiller, pointing northeast. 'The wind's come around some. Won't be long before that lot is on us.'

A wall of darkness was fast approaching under roiling skies. Lightning suddenly crackled to the water, the storm sweeping towards them, engulfing everything in gloom. The wind rose in pitch.

'Tie everything down,' his father bellowed. Around the ship, heaps of furs and cloaks stirred into life. But not Garik and Gunnar. They lay stiff and still.

The Spear-God had let Hakan go. Perhaps the father of the seas wanted him instead. He took his place, gripping the gunwale as the rollers turned white.

CHAPTER SEVEN

Inga shivered.

She loved the Juten Belt's cool waters, but getting in was always a shock.

This morning, a shock was just what she needed.

Her mouth still tasted sour with ale, and her eyes felt bulgy – too big for her head.

They'll feel better underwater. . . Everything will.

It was early. The morning light sparkled off the sea to the east. She could never sleep long after daybreak, even in late summer. She had slipped out without stirring a soul. The others would sleep a while yet.

The water lapped at her thighs. Most days she felt fresh, breathing in the wild smell of the sea, shading her eyes from the dawn light. But now she felt sick. She hadn't drunk *that* much last night, had she? And she wasn't like some girls who could barely take a few cups of ale. Besides, she'd been ale-sick before. This was different.

The wind was gentle, the waves little more than humps of

green water gliding past, almost courteously, before flattening onto the strand. She let the next swell rise over her head, taking a few strokes underwater until the blood began to warm her limbs.

She emerged in a burst of spray. Her head felt better already. Her stomach, not at all.

Had she said too much last night? Did it even matter? Konur seemed determined to like her, whatever she said. If she had somehow encouraged him, she hadn't meant to.

Had she been disloyal to Hakan? Certainly, he wouldn't have been happy that Konur had tried to kiss her. *Again!* But was that her fault?

Suddenly she felt annoyed, hitting the water with a splash. *Why did Konur come here, the love-struck fool?* If he *was* in love. More likely, he'd come to make another conquest. Well, that wasn't going to happen. He would have to leave today – this very morning. Then she could stop worrying.

Everything will be fine when they return, she assured herself, then realized she had stumbled into the same awful dread. The same question: *will* they return?

What would happen to her if they didn't come back? Would she have to give herself up to Konur then? Or someone like him?

She shook her head. *NEVER!* Anyway, Konur was stupid. What was he thinking, declaring himself like that? And with no encouragement from her at all! Or hardly any. . . She'd only been friendly. Shouldn't a host be friendly to a guest? She remembered his imploring face, the childish desperation in his voice.

Her stomach suddenly tightened. She touched her belly, a bitter taste in her throat. *What is this?*

105

She groaned and took a gulp of air, then slid under the surface. It felt good sitting underwater like that. Safe. Her mind was always running too fast. Galloping this way, then that. Here, it was calm.

She came up for a breath, ready to sink below again. But she stopped, something catching her eye.

A figure had appeared from the trees beyond the dunes. In an instant, she recognized Konur, making his way down to the beach.

How did he know I would be here?

It irritated her that anyone should interrupt her solitary time, let alone him. She watched him approach, wondering if he could see her, suddenly very aware of her nudity. Pulling out the long pin holding her hair, she slicked back her curls, coiled them up, then re-fastened the pin.

Of course he can see me.

He stood over her dress and other things, dumped in a heap on the sand. 'Good morning!' he called.

She didn't reply. She had nothing to say to him. She only peered at him, standing there with his hands on his hips, looking like he owned the wide world. He couldn't have been awake long – he hadn't even bothered with his shoes, or anything more than breeches and a tunic.

She wished he'd just go away. This was *her* secret time. She slid sullenly under the surface again, blowing out tiny bubbles, one by one. If she stayed under long enough, perhaps he would have vanished when she came up – caught by the wind and carried far beyond the farthest horizon.

She waited till her lungs were near bursting, but when she bobbed up he was still there.

'There you are!' he laughed. 'I thought you'd turned into a seal and swum away. How's the water?'

'Cold.' *As cold as my voice. Can't you hear it, stupid?*

'Good – I like it fresh.' He tugged his tunic out of his belt.

'No – don't!' She sounded a little too anxious. 'I mean, wait – I'm coming out.'

But she didn't move. He stood watching her, grinning. 'Well? I thought you were getting out.'

'Turn your back. Didn't your father teach you *any* manners?'

'He taught me exactly what I need to know.' His voice sounded different from last night. A trace of conceit seemed to have crept into it. She didn't like it. 'Still, if it makes you feel better. . .' He looked north along the strand.

'Promise you won't look?'

'Of course!'

She didn't know whether she trusted him. But she had to get out sometime, and her clothes were twenty strides up the beach. Covering herself, she rose out of the water. Her skin prickled in the brisk air as she waded the last yards to dry sand.

'I couldn't sleep.' He was still looking away. 'Too many thoughts in my head.'

'Ale troubles a simple mind,' she said, skipping through the shallows. 'If you can't take it, you shouldn't drink so much.'

'It wasn't the ale.' He turned around. 'It was you.'

'Hey!' she squealed, covering the dark triangle between her legs. 'You promised!'

But he seemed oblivious to any promise. Instead he came at her, all eager. 'I was going crazy – imagining what it'd be like to kiss you.'

Abashed, she made a scramble for her clothes, desperate to cover up.

But he sprang into her path. She stopped, clutching herself, looking everywhere but his face. 'Let me past!' She hated that she sounded more afraid than angry. He was smirking, but made no move out of her way. 'Please! Just let me by.'

'I will. In return for a kiss.'

'That's ridiculous!'

'Just one. I promise I'll let you pass.' His eyes sparkled with mischief. He had already broken one promise. But despite everything, Inga couldn't deny he looked handsome in a wicked kind of a way.

Perhaps seeing something in her soften, he took a tentative step towards her. 'It'll be over in a moment. You may even like it.'

'One. That's it.' Maybe then he would leave her alone.

He reached out and took her head in his hands, delicate as if she were a sparrow. She watched him come closer, saw the little curls of triumph on his mouth, smelled the musk of his body. And then his lips were on hers, light as the dew.

But then he slipped his tongue in her mouth. She started, trying to pull away, but he only held her tighter, his hand closing over her breast. His touch was cold, alien. The effect was like a lightning bolt. What was she doing? What a fool! *Hakan!*

Panic flooded her brain and she shoved Konur hard, twisting her head away. 'There's your kiss. Now let me go!'

But he only growled something incoherent, tightening his grip, thumbs digging into her flesh. She screeched in pain and, hardly knowing what she was doing, lashed out at his face. She felt her knuckles crunch against his temple, saw the surprise in his eyes. He reeled away, staggering.

'Bitch!'

But she didn't waste a moment, tearing loose and slipping past him, feeling a thrill of elation that she was free.

Hel take my clothes!

She was fast, and was sure she'd reach the hall before he could catch her. But she hadn't gone two yards when something tripped her. She fell sprawling, sand filling her mouth.

Konur dived for her. She twisted, frantic, but strong hands held her, clawing their way up her legs. She tried to kick him off, screaming a wretched sound like a gull's cry, but it was lost in the empty sky. He was crawling up her, horribly relentless. She wriggled desperately, punching at his leering face, but her blows wouldn't tell. A hand closed round her throat, squeezing so tight she feared he'd crush her neck like a dry reed.

'Time for more than a kiss now, sweetling.' Konur laughed in her face and his breath was foul. He squeezed tighter, pinning her body to the ground, while he shoved down his breeches. She couldn't breathe. Panic filled her chest. Her vision was fading. She had a dim sense of Konur's member, swollen, grotesque, slapping against her belly. She kicked her thighs, muscles burning, but he was determined to get between them.

Suddenly he had them apart. She sobbed, frantically sucking in air, still thrashing, but he was too powerful. Her secret parts exploded in pain, as his monstrous shaft bashed against them. She heaved her hips, refusing to give up.

'Hold still, you little whore,' he snarled, jamming back her head even harder. Something pricked her scalp. Something sharp

109

and hard. Through fading vision, she remembered the hairpin.

Grabbing the handle, ignoring the pain, she tore it free from her tangled hair, and with all the savagery she had in her, brought it down over his head. The spike plunged deep into his back. He screamed.

She ripped the pin free and stabbed again, still harder, half-burying it under his shoulder blade. Konur reeled off her, squealing like a swine, scrabbling for the spike sticking out of his back.

Inga gulped at the air flooding back into her lungs, rolled onto her belly and staggered up, lurching towards her clothes. Her belt was there. And on it, her knife.

Reaching them, she flung aside her dress, tugging the knife from its sheath. It was no match for a sword, or any kind of battle-blade. But it was still six inches long with an edge cruel as winter.

She'd gutted many wild animals with the thing. *I'll gut this one too if I must.*

Konur was writhing about spitting curses, trying to lay hold of the spike. Inga steadied herself. Hakan called her brave once. That time, she'd faced a grey-whiskered killer with cruel, yellow eyes in the forest. She must be as brave now.

'Gaaaaaaah!' yelled Konur, pulling the spike free finally.

'You pig-fucking son of a whore!' she screamed, brandishing her blade, her beautiful features twisted in rage. Konur got to his feet, stooped, pawing at his wound. His face was white, but he still mustered a sneer.

'What do you imagine you'll do with that, slut?'

'I'll shred that pretty face into a thousand bloody ribbons if you come near me.'

His expression soured. 'You couldn't cut me.' A rash challenge from a man with no blade and his cock hanging out.

'You want to find out?' She shook the knife, oblivious to the hair plastered about her face, her naked body taut as a bowstring. Wasn't she the blood of the Vendling, like her warrior forefathers? *Perhaps I'm already the last of them!* 'Go back to the shitheap you crawled off of – else I'll gut you like a hog!'

With a sudden snort, he held up his hands. 'All right then. I'll leave. I was tiring of your hospitality anyhow. Fucking shrew.' He spat. 'But mark this: you *will* be my wife. And when you are, I'll enjoy whipping some sense into you.'

'I swear to you – if the gods are ever that cruel, you'll wake on your marriage morn with that fucking thing shoved down your throat.'

She jabbed the knife at his crotch. Konur looked down at his now-limp manhood and began putting himself away. 'You'll learn, sweet Inga.' His grin seemed so greasy now. She wondered how she'd ever thought otherwise. 'Soon, you'll learn.'

'Just go.'

He gave her a last bitter look, and left her.

She watched him clamber up the dunes, still nursing his wound. Only when he had disappeared under the trees did her heart begin to beat slower.

CHAPTER EIGHT

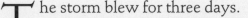

The storm blew for three days.

They ran before it on waves high as halls. Most were sick. All were miserable; each man fingering amber charms, carving runes into the gunwales, or muttering prayers to gods whose ears seemed far off through those shrieking winds.

Hakan clung on, his fear of the deep a stone in the pit of his stomach. Sleep came in scraps and his dream was always the same: the wave engulfing him, the sudden terror, his childish hands losing their grip, his scream smothered by cold salt water filling his lungs. His father had saved him then. Who would save him now?

The abyss writhed around them, as if far below the World Serpent was stirring in the bowels of the earth. But eventually the storm abated. They came about and began the long pull to the east and home.

Four days later, someone cried 'Land!'

'Horthaland,' Eskel declared. 'Know it like my old woman's tits.' He must have known them well, for two days after turning south, they were passing the familiar spit they called the Skaw, where the Western Ocean joined the East Sea in a never-ending kiss.

Hakan gazed at the sliver of sand. The water was grey and lifeless now. When he and Inga had ridden there in early summer, it had sparkled. That was another world.

'Aren't you coming in?' she'd said. He remembered her eyes, suddenly serious, mouth half-open with a hunger he'd never seen before.

That night, they had made love for the first time, her skin glowing orange and gold by the fire. She sat astride him, guiding him into her, timid but intent. Her body soon lost its shyness, trembling under his fingers, her voice urgent, her delicious heat engulfing him, her eyelids flickering in ecstasy.

What had become of that little girl? The bothersome heap of curls always getting in his way, irritating as a stone in his shoe. That girl was gone for ever. Instead, a goddess had awoken him with teasing kisses.

'You have all of me now,' she'd whispered. 'You'd better take good care of me.'

'I will. I promise.'

A promise he meant to keep.

On an evening breeze, the battered ship glided to shore. The headland watchman had spread the word: many women and children were waiting on the sand.

Men jumped into the shallows in search of wives. Children called for their fathers, mothers for warrior sons. Hakan watched Dag wade through the water and gather up his little wife. Her small face beamed, as she pecked kisses over his scarred cheeks.

Would she smile so wide to see him cut pieces off that boy?

Wails of mourning rose as women saw their man wasn't among the living. *Didn't you know? They're drinking in the Hall of the Slain. You should be happy.* But they didn't understand. Their youngsters stood clutching their skirts, confused by their tears.

He saw her before she saw him. Her face looked careworn, dread and hope warring in her soft brown eyes.

He called her name.

She started running, as he vaulted the gunwale and splashed his way towards her.

They had said they shouldn't show too much affection. But who was watching amid all that grief and joy?

He flung his arms around her, burying his face in her hair. It smelled so clean after the stench of the sea and fear and death.

She looked up. 'You stink like a sow.' Her eyes were bright and earnest, welling tears. He laughed. And suddenly a dam had broken. Laughter came harder and harder, flooding out of him in mad relief.

'Now you know,' said a craggy voice. Releasing each other, they saw his father smiling like a tender-hearted bear. 'Odin sent this one back.'

'Uncle!' Inga threw her arms around his father. He stiffened, looking awkward as she burrowed into the folds of his cloak. Just for a moment, he hugged her back, then pushed her away. She hardly seemed to notice, already scolding them for making her worry, wanting to know everything that happened. When she heard of the fate of the women, she wept.

Of course. There isn't a creature under the sky that Inga wouldn't weep for.

'Will you feast tonight, Uncle?' she asked, drying her cheeks.

'No. This voyage was bitter.' He wanted only meat, fire and mead, and the sleep of the dead.

'I'll see it done.' She stretched up and kissed his cheek. When she tried for another, he pushed her away.

'That's enough, child. Run along. These men need feeding. I'm relying on you.'

She gave an earnest nod, looking disappointed, and was about to go. But then, abruptly, she turned to Hakan and hugged him. 'I'm glad you're safe, cousin,' she said, loud enough for his father to hear. Then close to his ear, 'I must see you later.'

She pulled away, wearing a smile. But behind it, Hakan saw something else – some disquiet. He squeezed her hands, with a nod of assurance.

Satisfied, she left them, hurrying away through the throng.

There was little merriment in Vendlagard that night. The warriors' faces were lined and weary. Toasts were raised to their dead, but talk was thin and the benches half-empty.

Inga waited on them dutifully, watching them shovel down honeyed duck, black bread and cheese, brooding over their bloodstained memories. The women were subdued, knowing to bridle their chatter on such a night.

'Let them drink themselves to oblivion and an early bed,' Tolla told the thrall-girls. 'In a day or two, they'll come up smiling.'

Shouldn't she be smiling? They had come back. *Hakan has come back*. And she *was* glad. But somehow it didn't feel as it should. After relief, the weight lingered. A heaviness that had come upon her since Konur rode away. A heaviness within, that grew like thickening air before the break of a summer storm. A month ago, everything was bright: the world seemed made for those who loved. Now, some nameless dread stalked in her heart.

She looked at Hakan, hunched low over his bowl, tousled hair shading his eyes. Under it, his brow, usually so plain and honest, was furrowed.

Where have his thoughts taken him?

He looked up and saw her, and his face changed into the secret smile kept for her alone. She smiled back and turned away, telling herself someone might see. But in truth, she was shy. *What will he think when I tell him? Will he still smile then?*

Her gaze moved along the table, settling on her uncle. *Would things be different now?* She cared for him deeply. Always had. She remembered his strong arms throwing her in the air, his pale eyes watching over her in the dark. But now. . .

What will he do when he finds out?

If only he'd taken another wife. . . A woman might have understood, might have spoken up for her. But folk had stopped wondering when Haldan would remarry long ago.

She watched him push away his platter, his eye wandering to one of the servants: Tandra, a Danish thrall. The girl had fire, for sure, and she moved gracefully enough. Haldan caught her by the elbow to speak a word. Inga watched her listen, nodding obediently, before he released her.

Her uncle would satisfy other appetites tonight. Tandra was pleasing enough, but the girl was dreaming if she thought he'd ever take her to wife. Or any woman. The only woman he'd ever loved lay half a league away, in the belly of a barrow-grave. Dust and bones.

Would Hakan be so faithful. . . if I were to die?

Suddenly the question scared her. She tried to think of something else. They were home now. All would be well.

It was still early when most folk had drifted to bed. Haldan had retired to his chamber, Tandra slipping after him. Hakan had left a while before. She would find him once her work was done. Taking a bucket, she went out for some water.

The path followed the stream down to the washing pool. The night sky sparkled in its surface, wide and wonderful. She stopped, admiring the reflected stars. Then, with a sigh, plunged the bucket, scattering the silver pinpricks. After she'd hefted it out, she stood a while, listening to the night.

'How long have you been there?'

A chuckle came from the shadows. 'Not long. How did you know?'

She turned with a wistful shrug. 'You still need a bath.'

'That bad?' Hakan laughed, appearing from behind the old alder tree growing nearby. 'Come here anyway.'

She could see his shadow, sharp in the moonlight. The outline of his shoulders – so unmistakably his. Dropping the bucket, she ran to him. His lips were dry and warm. She felt him already, hard against her belly. Excited, she tugged free his tunic, running fingers up his back. A groan of desire filled his throat.

'I'd forgotten how good you taste.'

'You said you never would.' She meant to tease, but it sounded like a reproach. She wanted him, but something stronger was coursing through her, something out of control. She began to shiver as he bit at her neck. Suddenly, she was sobbing, fat tears rolling down her cheeks.

'It's all right. I'm here now.'

She wiped her nose. 'It's stupid. I haven't cried once while you were away. I told myself I would be strong. That I would see you again.'

'So here I am,' he smiled. 'I swore I would live. Hel take the choosing of the gods.'

'You shouldn't say that.' She put a finger to his lips. 'It's bad luck.' She dropped her hand, toying with the amulet she'd given him. The engraving in the silver was crusted with blood. Her fingers strayed to his face. 'You're wounded.' She pulled him closer, examining the cut above his eye. The skin was swollen, but already there were signs of healing. She passed her thumb over it, ever so lightly. Still he jerked his head away, catching her wrist.

'Sorry.'

He lifted her hand, placing a kiss in her palm. 'Wounded. But alive.'

'What was it like?'

'It's hard to tell. . . Confusing. Terrifying. Bloody.' He grimaced. 'I don't think I want to tell.' She listened, trying to understand. 'Leif is dead. And Garik.'

'I know. And many others.' She gathered up his hand. The knuckles were bruised. 'Did you kill?'

He nodded.

'So you're a warrior now.' She let out a long sigh. *Just as he was always marked to become.* She swallowed hard, staring through his chest. 'You're going to be a father, too.'

Even in the gloom, she saw the shock on his face. 'A father! But how?'

'How do you think? You lie together as many times as we have—'

'But didn't we—?'

'What?' She felt herself getting angry.

'Well. . . we kept the seed from the furrow, as it were.' He looked confused. 'Didn't we?'

'Clearly not,' she snapped. 'Why are you being like this?'

'Like what?'

'So. . . difficult.'

'I'm not. I just. . . How can you be sure?'

'A woman knows, Hakan.' Since Konur had left, her suspicions had become a certainty. She'd often dreamed what it would be like to know a child was in her, imagining the joy at the discovery. Instead, all she'd felt was fear.

But even in the dim moonlight, she saw his brow softening, his mouth sloping into a grin. 'A father, eh? And you, a mother!' Suddenly he pulled her close, laughing, and gave her a long kiss. She kissed him back. This was better. Her heart felt lighter. *At last.* It seemed he was taking *this* news well.

Did she have to tell him what else had happened?

She had turned the question over many times. *But whom does it serve to tell anyone what that snake tried to do?* Konur had gone by the time she had returned to the hall. Gone even before the others were awake. She had explained away his early departure easily enough. And once he had left, his words seemed empty threats. He'd have to be mad to want her as a wife after that. And she had meant what she said: she would kill before she gave herself to him. But if she told Hakan, there would be a feud, and that meant more killing. *Hakan might die.* And for what? For revenge? It seemed a stiff price to pay for her naivety, and that worm Konur wasn't worth the blood that would be spilt. Enough had been spilt already.

All she wanted was Hakan.

She broke the kiss. 'We must tell your father.'

'Haldan?'

'You have another? We have to tell him about us.' She had to know everything would be all right.

'We can't tell him,' he said, face blanching. 'Not yet. Hel, finding out his ward had lost her maidenhead would be bad enough. But to discover she is carrying his son's bastard—'

'The child will be true-born if we're married.'

'It isn't that simple. He's more like to hide you away till it's born, then drown the thing.'

'That's horrible!'

'You know how it goes with the ones that aren't wanted.'

'*I* want it.' *Why was he scaring her like that?* 'If we tell him we love each other, that we want to be married—'

'Do you know him at all? You know how it works. The old man's got two marriages to see done. Love doesn't come into it. For him, it's about wealth. Or sealing loyalty, or getting an heir.'

'I'm giving him an heir. It's already in my belly.'

He laughed, and it sounded cruel. 'He'll want to see you married to someone else.' Her stomach twisted; 'someone else' might mean Konur. 'For me, the same. He's hardly going to waste *two* chances to make a good match.'

She knew what he said was true, but hated that he'd said it. 'Why should it be that way? We make each other happy. Isn't that enough?'

'It's not about us. It's about this land. It's about the Vendling blood. My whole life I've been raised to succeed him as lord over our folk,' he said, bitterly. 'I am who I am because of him.'

'Sometimes you sound so spoiled, Hakan. Everything is about you and your stupid future.'

'It's *him* that's obsessed. He's not going to toss away his expectations of me just because we say this is how it is. He'll have plans for you too.'

The image of Konur invaded her mind again. She suddenly felt so angry. *What if it were Konur? Or someone worse, if that were possible?*

'You should be on my side!' She shoved him away. 'You don't want me, do you? This is *your* child in my belly. You put it there! It was easy enough to do that, wasn't it?' Suddenly she went wild with fury, beating his chest.

He let her hit him till the worst of her anger had passed. 'Of course I want you. It's not easy, is all.' He stroked her cheek. 'I'm sorry, my love. I'm just . . . at a loss.' He shook his head. 'It's a mess. I nearly told him about us before. But this changes things. Now, I don't. . .'

'What?'

'Look, I'm just trying to figure out what's best now.'

'What's best is just to tell him.'

'We have to pick the right time.'

'There'll never be a right time. I need to know now it'll be all right.' She screwed up her eyes against the pressure swelling behind them. Her thoughts were multiplying and multiplying, becoming too many for her head. 'Something's changed.' She tapped her forehead. 'In here. The summer was full of light. Now, all I see ahead is darkness. I want to run but I don't know where. I'm afraid, Hakan.'

He took her hand and kissed her forehead. His lips felt calming. 'Afraid of what?'

She looked into his dark eyes and felt tears well in her own. Did she even know? Fear seemed to have sprung out of nothing. *Or maybe it was always there. . .* 'Of losing you.'

'But I'm here.'

'. . . and more.'

She saw he didn't understand.

She'd never told anyone this, not even him, whose face was the first she could remember. She hardly knew how to begin. 'Lately, my mother keeps coming to my mind.'

'Your mother? Why?'

'Once she had to wait, like me. Her man returned. . . but dead. Tolla once told me about it. How her cries tore the sky all through that night. Tolla said it seemed the wind and the rain and the sea mourned with her. The hall-folk got scared, said it was ill-fortune to scream so long, that it served as a summoning for dark spirits from the lands of mist. From the realm of Hel and the black fires burning there.'

'Folk talk like that. What's that to you?'

'I was in her then. I was my father's seed in her belly. I should have given her hope. But she gave up on life. Gave up on me.'

'But you can't know that's why she died. No one can.'

'Maybe. I just wish I could've put some joy in her. To push out the shadow there. Tolla says it spread like a cancer, smothering her will to live. But I couldn't do anything.' She sat down on the bank circling the pool, drawing him down beside her. 'Sometimes I think that shadow has its mark on my life too.' She laid a hand on her stomach. 'On my blood.'

'Why would you think that?' he urged. 'Don't you know who you are? You're my Inga.' His smile tilted to the night. 'You shine so bright you make the stars look plain.'

She stroked his cheek, grateful for his words, but she couldn't smile. 'You know the stories of my mother. Even before Father was killed, some shadow had pursued her down the roads of her life. She outran it a while and found some happiness, only it found her again.' She grimaced. 'Her blood is in me. Speaks to me sometimes.'

'What does it say?'

'That I don't belong here.'

'But this is your home.'

'I know. But it wasn't hers, was it? She came from far away. I *want* the feeling to go. To vanish and never come back. But it persists. Calls me to some other place. A kind of nowhere place. I can't explain it. It must be her blood. Restless. It makes every drop of beauty in the world bittersweet. I don't know why. A stab of joy so intense it pricks my heart, only to fade again, leaving a pang of sorrow.' She saw his eyes intent on her, but doubted he understood. How could he when she hardly understood herself? 'Maybe it's only sorrow at the moment's passing. Or maybe it's beauty that is the illusion, and sorrow that is real. I can't tell. But I'm sure my mother felt the same. In those moments, I feel so connected to her, and yet so afraid of her at the same time. Afraid of her despair. Afraid of her pain. Afraid that she gave up on this beautiful, broken world.'

'But that's not you.' His voice was tender. 'You never give up.'

'Don't I?'

'No. Never.'

She looked away. 'Then there were the words of the *vala*.'

His face darkened. 'You shouldn't pay heed to the words of some old swindler. That's what Father says.'

'I know you don't think that, my love. You can't lie to me. I know you too well.' She kissed his cheek. 'The *vala* had the far-sight. We both know it. And there was something else in her words. A kind of beckoning.' She stared up into the night. 'Remember last autumn, when we fixed the roof of the hall?' He nodded. 'I stood right on the top and looked out to sea. It was beautiful. And that moment, I felt an impulse so strong, just to throw myself out into the air. To become part of the beauty. I didn't care about the danger or the pain – I just wanted to live that moment.'

'What has that to do with the *vala*?' he frowned. She smoothed it away.

'Her words made me feel the same. That's what we've done. We saw something beautiful and threw ourselves out into the empty air.'

Hakan said nothing. She knew he was thinking about what the *vala* had spoken over him. 'I'm afraid,' she whispered, 'of all this running together. Now I have you, Hakan, you must always be mine. I hardly dare dream of the life we could live together. It's too much happiness to hope for. And with this child. *Your* child.' She turned his face towards her. 'I have something so precious – and now, just when I have something to lose, the shadow appears. As if it has been waiting for me to have something it could take from me. Something it could destroy.'

'Just stop,' blurted Hakan. 'Stop talking!' He took her hands in his. 'You sound like a bloody *vala* yourself. This isn't you.'

'I know, but—'

He leaned in, eyes shining with passion. 'No one is going to take you from me. I don't care what the *vala* said or what anyone sees, far or near.' He squeezed her fingers so hard it hurt. 'Hel take custom and oaths of blood or kin. Hel take lordship over our people, take gold, victories, the favour of the gods. Hel take it all! But not you. No one else can have you.'

'Do you swear it?' Her voice was trembling.

'I do. I'll die before I lose you.'

She wanted to believe him. 'Because if we aren't together—'

'We will be,' he said, final as death. 'Besides,' he grinned. 'I'm lucky. A Chosen Son, remember? The Norns love me.'

She was glad to be able to giggle. 'Not half as much as you love yourself.'

He pulled her towards him and burrowed under her chin, tickling her neck with kisses. But her smile quickly faded. 'Please, Hakan. Let's know now.'

He sat up, with a sigh. 'Then let's think. At winter's end, you're old enough to be wed.'

'A month before Freya's Feast.'

'Can you conceal this till then?' He touched her belly. 'Folk wear more clothes during the white months anyway.'

'I suppose.' Then more boldly, 'Yes. I can.'

'The day you can be wed, I'll tell my father I want you as my wife – that I'll have no other. Oh, he'll bellow like an ass, but I'll persuade him. He goes on how I'm his only son – well, that knife has two edges. If he's relying on me to carry on the Vendling name, he can't have it all his own way.' He smiled. 'When will the baby come?'

'Late spring, I suppose.'

'A spring baby, eh?' He winked at her. 'I shouldn't worry. Once everyone sees you blown up like a heifer, no one else'll want you!'

'Hey!' She gave him a playful punch. She felt better having him close, even if it didn't change things.

'I figure the less time he has, the easier he'll come round. I mean it's not as though anyone else has asked for you, have they?'

Nausea lurched in her stomach, something between guilt and fear and anger. She'd told Einna not to tell Hakan about Konur's visit. Said it would only stir up needless trouble, though trouble was what that snake deserved. And Tolla. She'd wanted to tell Tolla what he'd done. But the truth was she felt stupid. She knew she'd been naive. Tolla would have scolded her, cuddled her and afterwards made her tell her uncle. And then. . .

'What's wrong?' he whispered. 'You've gone so pale.'

The child. *Their* child. 'What if he makes me give up the baby? What if he does away with it?'

'I won't let him.' He gripped her hand fiercely. 'I swear it.'

'I'll run away if I think he'd do that.'

He grinned at her. 'Waddle away, more like.'

'It's not funny.'

'It's all right, my love – I'd run with you.'

'Would you?'

'Of course.'

'Wherever I go?'

'I'd follow you through all the Nine Worlds if that's where you took me.'

She took his face in her hands, kissed each eye and then his lips. Suddenly all her fears were washed away on a wave of longing. She heard herself moan as he found her breasts. They felt hot and tender in his hands.

126

She pushed him away and stood up. Leaving her eyes on his, she undid her girdle, slipped her dress off her shoulders and let it fall to the ground, soft as a lover's sigh. She watched his eyes roaming her body and felt bolder. Excited at her quickening pulse. She looked down at herself. Her skin shone smooth as soapstone under the light of the moon, her dark nipples drawn tight, anticipating his touch. When their eyes met again, his were drunk with desire.

'Then follow me now, my love.'

She went to the edge of the pool and slid into its shimmering waters. Behind her, she heard him pulling off his clothes, stumbling after her.

CHAPTER NINE

Lord Haldan rode back from the orchards enjoying the shades of autumn. Behind him, the hall-folk were gathering in the apple crop that should see them through to spring. The old oak trees standing outside the gate were a blaze of fire. On the hill, the beech wood shone golden in the sun.

Autumn's fading beauty.

Many leaves had fallen. Winter's bitter breath would soon be on them.

More than three months had passed since their return. The dead brought home were long dispatched on floating pyres, out onto the Western Ocean. With those left behind, they numbered four dozen. Many of his best.

Blood cannot go unanswered. Every lord knew it. But sometimes the answer seemed a futile cry against the wind.

Yet the line of Vendal the Grey lived on. His blood had flowed through the lords of this land for twelve generations. Haldan would see it last another twelve. Duty bound him to his fathers, as it did to his son and his sons after him. *Duty binds blood and land together.* His folk served him; he served them. The land carried them all, fates interwoven, stretching into the mists of What Will Be.

He recognized Old Rapp the smith hurrying along the track at a stumble.

'Lord Haldan,' he wheezed. 'We've 'ad a noble rider come.'

'Who?'

'None less 'n Karsten, lord of the Karlung lands.'

Haldan grunted. Karsten. The Dark Stone. Though most called him the Whisperer. He was distant kin, but that wasn't reason to ride so far from his seat at Karlsted. Haldan hadn't thought of him since that trouble with his son at the Feast of Oaths.

He found his kinsman in his chamber, sitting in his chair, feet on his table, drinking his mead. *No less than I expected.* The Karlung lords were earls, sworn to the headman of the Middle Jute clans, but had risen no higher, though many had figured they ought to. Karsten more than most.

Haldan had hardly entered than his guest was on his feet, lithe as an old cat.

'Greetings, cousin,' he said, clapping his shoulder. His cheerful manner made odd company with his whispering voice. 'You look about as happy as a corpse.' Karsten laughed, his one dark eye sparkling. The other showed nothing – milk white and dead.

Haldan gave a grudging snort. Karsten wasn't the first to see something cold in his face. 'Welcome, kinsman. Sit. Drink.'

Karsten nodded his thanks, resuming his seat, although refraining from swinging his long legs back on the table. Haldan stood six feet tall, but Karsten had some inches on him, and stood straight as a spear. Impressive for a man of fifty winters. He had been handsome once. Some might say he still was, but for his skew nose and leathery jowls running to fat, and the mottled scar in his neck. It was rumoured the arrow tip that had reduced his voice to a breathy whisper was still lodged there.

Haldan wasn't one to spin out pleasantries. After pouring another drink, he asked why he was here.

'You could say it's to our mutual profit. I wouldn't bother riding up here if it wasn't.'

'I'm listening.' There was rarely anything mutual about any proposition of Karsten's.

He smiled, sardonically. 'I'm having a little trouble with my son.'

'Don't we all? Now and then.' Haldan remembered Karsten's son from the Feast of Oaths. A good-looking lad. Tall, like his father. Arrogant. Like his father. 'What kind of trouble?'

'He's sick.'

'Sorry to hear it.' No man wanted a sickly heir, though he didn't see why it should concern him.

'It's no worse than what most men have suffered.'

'What's that?'

'Love.' Karsten raised his cup. 'Here's to it. We've all known it. Even you.'

Haldan snorted. 'Long ago.' Love and he had been strangers for many years.

'Not so long you've forgotten how it goes. My son is sick as a goat for your brother's girl. Inga – isn't that her?'

The name took him by surprise, but immediately he knew he should have seen it coming. Should have guessed it the moment he'd heard Karsten's name. *Inga*. This was a game he'd known must come one day, yet here he was, wrong-footed. Unprepared. 'She's too young to think of marriage.'

'My friend, I understand – I do.' Karsten leaned back, running fingers through his sandy hair. 'I told my son the same. Told him that would be your answer, but he wouldn't listen. No surprise, there. I remember what it's like to feel that burn. The passion soon cools once you dip your beak in other pails.' He gave a conspiratorial wink of his good eye. The dead gaze of the other was disconcerting. '"Go, drink your fill," I said. "Come back in a couple of months and tell me how you feel about this girl then."'

'And here you are.'

'Here I am.'

Haldan remembered the fight at the Feast of Oaths. It hardly boded for a propitious bond between their families. 'All this from one encounter?'

'One?' Karsten looked confused. 'Two – so far as I know. He was so taken with her he rode straight back here after your son's feast. I believe you were off fighting.'

Did he just? The gall rose in Haldan's throat. He didn't like surprises. Least of all from a man like the Whisperer. His ignorance must have been plain to see.

'This was news to you?' Karsten rapped the table with amusement. 'You see! Young love must have its secrets.'

'Young love and old power – they have secrets both. Some might call them lies.'

'That's a little hard-hearted, cousin.' Karsten turned out his hands. 'So you see, I've come a-begging. Begging you to save me from my lovesick son. I swear I'll go mad if I have to listen to his bleatings all winter.' His shoulders shook with breathy laughter. But when Haldan didn't laugh with him, he added, 'You *do* understand me?'

'It would be simpler if you spoke plain.'

'As you wish, kinsman. I ask for your niece's hand for my son. Consider this a formal offer.'

There it was. Haldan nodded stiffly. 'Come – let's drink.' He stood and held out his cup.

'Gladly,' returned Karsten, rising with him.

'To the blood we share.'

'To the blood.' The cups clattered and they drained them.

'You honour me to ask this. I know you don't ask lightly. But I must refuse you.'

Karsten nodded, wiping delicately at his lips. 'I honour you, yet you dishonour me, is that it?' His mouth screwed into a smile, but his dark eye glinted, hard and mirthless. 'The girl may be too young now, but that is hardly a reason. She will be of age soon, as I understand—'

'My answer now is no.' Haldan heard the edge in his own voice. Sharper than was wise. A man's honour was bruised easier than an apple in this kind of business. 'If your lad is so moonstruck, let's see if his passion outlasts the winter. Meantime, I shall speak with her.'

Of that, dear Inga may be certain.

'Listen, *Lord* Haldan.' Karsten weighed heavy on the word.

As you should. Karsten was an earl, who answered to his overlord. Haldan answered to no man.

'I know you're a man who won't be swayed once he's picked his course. But perhaps you'd take a word from an elder kinsman. I don't say wiser, but one you can trust.'

132

Haldan trusted no one. It mattered little whether he was kinsman or foe.

'It's better to agree to this now,' Karsten went on. 'The match would serve both our families. A union between Karlung and Vendling blood would bring you power. And. . .' He barely concealed a smirk. 'Power, you certainly need.'

'The Vendlings have power enough.'

'Is it so? Tell me, kinsman – who are allies to the Northern Jutes?'

'A people's power doesn't rest on its allies. I could call on a thousand spears if it came to that.'

'As many as a thousand?' Karsten's eyebrow rose in feigned admiration. 'And all of them bog-farmers and rabbit-skinners. Truly, a fearsome host.'

'The Amundings found us fearsome enough.'

Karsten snorted. 'A heap of corpses was your father's legacy. Don't be as blind as he was. You need friends of steel.'

'My father left the world bloodier than he found it, true. But men followed him. That's legacy enough for me.'

'Your father had a talent for making enemies at every turn, that much I grant you. Difficult to keep faith with a man who so loved the stench of death.'

'It was his allies who broke faith.' Haldan felt his temper fraying. He'd been a young man then, not much older than Hakan, but he still remembered the taste of bile when they realized Koldir, son of Kelling, had betrayed them. *Never trust a Dane.* Koldir had promised them twelve warships, and sent them two. Rotten skiffs filled with rotten men – all of them spears that fell cheaply. The Vendlings could have finished the war that day, could have ended the feud with the Amundings once and for all, if Koldir had but kept his word. Instead, there was a deal more blood before the killing was done. 'My father never forgave the Danes their betrayal. Afterwards, we never doubted it was best to stand alone.'

'You had little choice.'

'*You* had a choice though,' returned Haldan. 'You Jutes of the Middle Lands have plenty of kin among my people. But I don't recall one of you raising so much as a fart to help your kinsmen.'

'You do me wrong, cousin. I tried to persuade Lord Arve to raise our spears. But he said he wouldn't help a folk who'd broken faith with King Harald Wartooth.'

'Piss on the Wartooth! Piss on the rest of you – whipping boys to that old boar.' Haldan slugged back his mead, and poured himself another. 'Baah,' he growled. 'It's all past now. The web is woven. One thing my father did right: he freed us from any overlord.'

'And how long will that last?' For once, the sardonic expression was gone, and Karsten's jowls were flushed with sincerity. 'Listen, cousin. I stood before King Harald's high seat at Leithra, not one month ago. Listened to him railing about the Skaw, that it should be his. Heard him spit poison about you pitiful Northern Jutes.'

'Harald speaks of us?'

Fifteen years, Haldan had been lord of the Northern Jutes, subordinate to no other. He had long since stopped fearing King Harald Wartooth, the Danish overlord, would come to force fealty on him once more. Was that time coming to an end? *Blood will run in the furrows.* The *vala*'s words boded ill. 'We're no enemies of his. Neither are we allies, nor vassals. We're nothing to him. If ever we have need to raid again, it won't be Danish lands or Danish harbours. How do you think we have managed this long? When the wolf sleeps in his lair, only a fool goes in to wake him.'

'If you're not his vassal, then by his reckoning, you *are* his enemy,' urged Karsten. 'I know you're not as blind as your father. You can't sit up here with your head in the sand.' His dark eye flared. 'The world is coming to you, cousin! Don't you see that? Maybe not this year, maybe not next. But it's coming – like it or not.'

Haldan's wintry eyes were staring right through his kinsman, already far away, lost in slaughter.

Was there always more?

'Let them come. We will fight. Fight like a bull-bear raised from Hel, if we must.'

'Now you sound like your father. He was always too quick to fight. Look where that got him.'

Haldan scowled. 'What would you do?'

'Why fight when you can get what you want by talk?'

'You mean like you? With a honeyed tongue in every lord's ear?'

'I'd have it in every lord's arse if it would get what I want.'

Haldan laughed. 'Shouldn't an earl have more honour?'

'Don't speak to me of honour, cousin.' He tapped beside his dead eye. 'I've seen enough of blood and honour and oaths and all the rest. They got me no closer to what I want.'

'What do you want?'

He held up his palms and smiled. 'I have five sons. I want silver, and I want land.'

'You think I can bring you those?'

He shook his head. 'You misunderstand me. Listen. You cause the Wartooth no trouble – so you say. But you *could*.'

'Go on.'

'His gold chests grow heavy from the trade up and down the East Sea and through the Juten Belt. If you wanted to, how much do you think you could disrupt that?'

'We don't want to. I give them no cause for quarrel.'

'Maybe. Now. But if you don't, another could. Your son. Or his. The Danes have overlooked you till now, but they will come for your lands one day. I'd wager my head on it. Sooner or later, the Skaw must come under oath to the Danish Mark.'

'Never in my lifetime. I swore it.' *That was a black night. And a black oath.* The rain had whipped their faces as they fled the shores of Raumarika, his father's blood dripping dark from his fingers, leaking from the wound Arnalf Crow-King cut in his chest. That was when his father had cursed Koldir to the blackest chasms of Hel, had sworn not another grain, not a ring of gold, not a sliver of silver would ever go to King Harald's hall again. He swore enmity with the Danes, and made him do the same. 'It was the last thing I ever promised my father. I can never kneel, even if they do come.'

'And what if they do?'

'I suppose you're going to tell me.'

'Friendship with the Karlungs cannot harm you. Indeed, it could do you much good. I have the ear of Lord Arve. Add to this that Harald favours me even over his Danish earls. I am sworn to him, but a war between the Jutes of the North and the Danes gains me nothing. The Karlungs could prove your surety against the Danes.'

'Our surety? You mean you would stand with us against the Danes?'

Karsten gave a rueful shake of his head. 'It need never come to that, kinsman. But I would put the full weight of my words at your back.'

Haldan considered this. The weight of Karsten's words. *What good are they?*

'If war *were* to come,' Karsten went on, 'how do you think your thousand spears would fare against the Wartooth's ten thousand?'

Haldan's jaw tightened. It was a grim thought.

'Fight him and you condemn your people. Where will the blood of Vendal the Grey be then?' He snorted. 'Nothing more than a stain in the dirt.'

Haldan peered into his kinsman's cold, dead eye. 'And friendship with you would stop that?'

'Listen, oath or not, one day you may have to kneel.' Haldan could almost hear his father's growl of protest. 'But better you've a friend who can persuade Harald kneeling is enough. Without that, he's like to take your head, together with your son's, and grind his boot on the neck of your people till they choke.'

Must it come to this? There was truth in Karsten's whisperings. How long would the world leave his lands in peace? Raiders would come – those choosing the Viking way. Vikings would always come. But a king? A forger of realms? A greater lord to make him kneel? Sometimes steel and shield were not enough to throw back the grasping hands of greedy men.

'And the price of your friendship is Inga.'

Karsten threw back his head and laughed. 'For my son to

stop his moaning – aye, *that* means a good deal to me. For that, I would offer friendship.'

'Inga is beautiful,' Haldan mused. *Worthy of a lord. Worthy even of a king.* Yet, with Inga, it was never simple. He was very fond of her. . . more than fond of her, but. . . *No – no good would come from dwelling on that.* 'I owe it to my brother to make the best match I can.'

'Your ward has her charms, I'll grant you. But when all's said, she is nothing but the daughter of a dead younger brother. She brings no lands.'

Haldan smiled to himself. The Whisperer was bargaining now, and he was crafty as a Wendish fishmonger when it came to striking a deal. 'Why so easily swayed by your son's whining then? What do you really want?'

'Something of value to us both. Vindhaven.'

It was Haldan's turn to laugh. 'Vindhaven! Friend, Vindhaven is destroyed. Surely word reached you? We burned forty good men avenging the blood those Vikings shed.'

'We heard.' Karsten sniffed. 'May the Spear-God be grateful for the gift.' Instinctively, his hand went to his dead eye at mention of the god. 'Vindhaven may be destroyed, but it can be rebuilt.'

'Its people were slaughtered to the last child. The harbour is burned. Only ashes and blood remain. If it can be rebuilt, work certainly won't begin till spring.'

Karsten leaned closer. So close Haldan could smell the mead on his breath. 'And what if I offer to seal my son's pledge to your ward with timber and turf enough to rebuild it all, and the men to do it? Now. Quickly. Before the first snows.'

'Why would you do that? Vindhaven isn't on Karlung lands.'

'Maybe not. But it lies not far to our north.' His dark eye shone. 'Think on it. A restored market harbour could bring you much prosperity. Great wealth even. Vindhaven could become a name to rival Rerik. Or even great Riba in the south.'

Haldan stroked the knotted remains of his ear.

Vindhaven was certainly a wreck. Its destruction had weighed heavy on his mind, he had to admit. They needed a market harbour. Without it, there might be trade along the long, empty strands skirting his realm, but it would be scattered, haphazard. Without it, it would be a hard winter on meagre provisions. They would cope – they always did – but come the spring, it would take time to rebuild Vindhaven. Time his folk could ill afford when they should be sowing their crops and looking to their flocks. And time before the traders came back.

What if they rebuilt it now – and bigger than it was – in time for the first trading in the spring? *What if it flourished?* His folk would prosper, might even grow rich, and a rich folk was secure. A rich folk could raise more spears to keep their lands safe. Safe even from King Harald if he ever came. The Vendling blood would be stronger.

And when I'm gone, Hakan will be secure.

'This is your bride price?'

'If it's agreeable to you.'

'What would you have in return?'

'Half the market rights.'

'Half?' exclaimed Haldan. Why was he surprised?

'A small return,' smiled Karsten. 'Given the investment we would be making.'

'Your memory must be failing, kinsman. Did you forget this isn't your land? And you expect half the market revenues?'

'Half seems fair. Vindhaven is not ours, but it lies not far from our lands. A word from me, and every skinner, every smith, every craftsman in Middle Jutland would bring their wares to your markets. That's a lot of trade.'

Haldan pulled at his beard, considering. 'A place that prosperous would have to be well defended. I would have to provide the men.'

'Come – these are details. I offer you friendship against the Wartooth, a new market harbour that will make what stood there before seem a piss-sodden pig pen, *and* the goods to fill it.' He snorted. 'Take your head out of your sandhill, cousin! It's only fair the Karlungs have something worth our while in return. And all this sealed by a marriage bond. Your brother's beautiful daughter, and my son and heir.' He suddenly laughed. 'Why, I would even be in your debt for shutting up Konur's whining.'

All this, and yet a shadow of doubt remained in Haldan's heart. That scrap between their sons at the Feast of Oaths. To others, it might have been nothing but a drunken brawl, but he'd seen something else in it. Seeds of hatred. Who knew how those seeds would grow? *Hakan must have the best chance I can give him.* He would have battles enough without a feud brewing with the Karlung blood. Inga would grow into a woman of calm counsel, he was sure. She could be the ice to cool the heat between their sons. *It were better she were there.*

'Settle for a third. And I will provide half the men to build.'

Karsten's good eye flitted between his own. 'So it is,' he nodded at last. Then chuckled. 'For a third, it's you who should be asking for a daughter of mine, if only I had one to give. *Ha!* A third then – and Karlung and Vendling will be joined together by new blood.'

'And one thing more.' Haldan fixed his gaze on Karsten's dead eye.

'Well?'

'If the Wartooth ever makes war on us, you forsake your oath to him and stand with your kin.'

For a long time, Karsten didn't answer. But at last, he seemed to make up his mind, and held out his hand.

Haldan took it.

And the match was made.

The place was a mess.

A row of pits, half-filled with foetid water and charred stumps – the wreckage of the dwellings that had stood there before.

Vindhaven. . . what was left of it.

The smell of embers lingered, together with the tang of rotten flesh. In front of the wreckage of the meet-hall was a circle of rain-soaked ashes. The fire had blazed high that day. Hakan remembered the stench of burning bodies, drifting on the wind to where he lay hidden. Drizzle settled on the bristles of his beard. He kicked at a potsherd in the mud.

'A fine fucking shithole they left this place,' said Dag to no one in particular, sifting through the blackened remains of a smithy with the butt of his spear. Something caught his eye. He bent and picked it up, turning it over. After a moment, he flung it away.

'Bloody magpies. They haven't left much. Won't be nothing worth a toss in all this mess.'

'What do you expect?' Hakan answered. 'It's three months since this was done.' Though it felt like a lifetime. Burned, flattened, finished. But that hadn't stopped the mud-folk living along the Sound from salvaging anything useful that the raiders had left behind. Down to the last rivet. They were welcome to it. They were alive.

The raiders were dead.

'Those boys knew their business, all right.' Dag had done his share of raiding down the years, so he should know. The other men were wandering among the burned-out dwellings clustered along the Sound's northern shore. Dag leaned on his spear, eyeing the ruins of the gangway collapsed in the water. He snorted and spat a gobbet of phlegm in a well-practised arc. It landed on a patch of ground, stained darker than the rest.

Hakan recalled the line of villagers kneeling just there; the noise of the blade carrying with the stench. *Schuck. . .*

'This is going to be one bastard job,' sighed Gunnrek, a burly bondsman from south of Vendlagard, with a beard so thick up his cheeks Hakan mused whether an ancestor had rutted a she-bear.

'My father said the Karlungs will send men to help. It's all agreed.'

'Well, if we're here and they ain't, that makes us the dopes.' Dag scratched at a scab on the back of his neck. 'Better save 'em some shit to do.'

Hakan reckoned they would be along soon enough. The way his father told it, he wanted a close eye on the Karlung men; on everything they did and wanted to know. Apart from that, he hadn't told Hakan much – that they were rebuilding Vindhaven; that he'd accepted an offer from Karsten to partner them in the work; that he should get there at once. His father wanted as much done as possible before the snows came. When

142

Hakan had asked what was the Karlungs' upside, his father just glowered. A thriving Vindhaven would profit both their clans, he said. They both wanted it done fast, and they had reached an agreement. That was all he needed to know, and he had better bury any trouble with the Karlung lad. When he'd opened his mouth to protest, his father lost his temper. There was no talking to him then.

Still, reluctantly, Hakan had promised to bury his grievances. There were more important things at stake, Haldan said, with that solemn look of his. 'I'm trusting you, son. This could do our folk great good.'

Thus, cleaning up this wreckage was the task of a lord. *Funny how it feels more like scrabbling around in a mire of shit. . . Maybe that's often the way.*

His father had given him half a dozen men. The first day was miserable. They worked all day under a leaden sky. By nightfall, the place looked as bad as ever. After the second day, at least he could see a difference. They burned the remains of the bodies first, then threw on the debris after them, putting aside any wood worth salvaging.

The jetty was foul work: up to their waists in slime, hefting out broken shivers of half-burned timber onto shore, while a sharp easterly spat rain in their eyes and chilled their bodies to the bone. When night fell, they used what they could of the shelter that had survived, sleeping round a fire under sheepskins.

By the fourth day, Hakan could at least *hope* that if the snows didn't come early, they might soon start planning how to rebuild the place. His father had said it was to be the greatest market harbour in all the East Sea; looking at the bereft shoreline, that was hard to imagine.

Well after noon, the sun had wormed through the clouds, scattering shards of light onto the dreary waters of Odd's Sound.

He left off dragging a length of wattle towards the pile of salvaged wood and called to Dag, 'Two days and we'll have broken the back of this.'

'Maybe,' Dag grumbled. 'No thanks to those Karlung whoresons.'

'They might have to feel the prick of your knife, Dag,' said Aldi, a younger lad, fond of stirring. 'If they do ever come...'

'Baaah!' Dag growled back. 'They should send some women up here instead. Happy to give them a feel of a prick, all right.'

There were a few chuckles. Gunnrek came up, flung a slab of turf into the fire. 'You can ask 'em yourself,' he said, jutting his chin off west.

The others turned and saw a horse trotting along the path, its rider joggling on top.

'One man?' hissed Dag. 'What fucking use is that?'

The rider wore a long hooded cloak, face in shadow. But Hakan knew him at a glance. 'Earl Karsten's son.' *Aye – one man.* And the last man in the Nine Worlds he wanted to see.

He snorted, remembering his promise to his father, and called up a cheery greeting.

Wouldn't he be proud?

'Good day, Hakan,' answered Konur, pushing back his hood. He looked down at the other men's sweat-stained faces, warily. After all, he was one. Hakan had six, and Dag's glowering eyes were like to throw any man off his stride.

'Old Karsten's got giant's blood, has he?' said Dag.

'Eh?'

'You'd have to be one strong sod, tha's all.'

'Why's that?' replied Konur, puzzled.

'Why else would your father send one man to do the work of a dozen?'

Konur grunted without mirth. 'You seem to like a jape. For a miserable-looking bastard.'

'Believe me.' Dag's hand coiled around the haft of his knife. 'You don't want to find out what makes me look happy.'

True enough, thought Hakan. 'One more man isn't much use to us.'

'My father's mustering a gang. They're waiting for a man he reckons the best builder in his lands. He sent me ahead to get the lie of the place. Or leastways, to make a start of it.'

'We already made a start, case you hadn't noticed,' said Dag.

'Well, he's here now.' Hakan offered up his hand. 'Alone or not – you're welcome.' They shook, neither smiling. 'We'll put your horse with the others.'

Konur slid down. Hakan collected his cloak and beckoned Konur to follow, while the others went back to work.

'Been here before?'

'A while ago now,' Konur nodded. 'Looked a lot different back then.'

Hakan gave him a sideways glance and saw he was making a joke. 'The folk who lived here probably would have thought so too. Only there aren't none of them left to say so.'

'Aye – a bad business. Still, the way my old man talks, it could soon be back to how it was. Better even.'

Better? Tell that to the women lashed to that mast. Small comfort for them.

After tethering Konur's horse with the others, Hakan offered him something to eat. But Konur said he'd rather take a look around.

'Best place to start is up there.' Hakan pointed to the shallow ridge to the north of them.

It didn't take them long to get up there. The ridge was hardly a fine lookout, but at least they stood high enough to survey what was left of the little settlement.

Odd's Sound snaked east, widening out to the open sea, its shores bounded by reed beds. Except on the north side, a distance beyond the settlement, was a shallow sweep of dirty sand. Ideal for unloading goods from trade ships, fishing boats, skiffs. . . craft of all sizes and shapes from around the East Sea and beyond.

Naturally, the little harbour of Vindhaven had grown up close by. For generations it had sat there, happy enough. Until it turned out the beach was just as good for a ship of war, Hakan told Konur. Probably they landed pretending to be traders. Or slipped ashore under cover of night. Whichever, the scattering of corpses suggested the tradesfolk had been taken by surprise.

Hakan described where everything had been before. The forges, the smithy stalls; barns for drying skins and furs, barns for grain and hay; spinner stalls, tanning vats, butchers' slabs; cookhouses, a brewery, and small dwellings dotted at the western end of the settlement, each hardly more than a hovel sunk into the earth. Amid all these had stood the meet-hall, where feasts would roar, and visiting traders could find a roof for a night.

Konur snorted. 'Look at it now.' Blackened stumps, refuse pits, timber, charred and splintered. Spaces empty as eye sockets in a skull. 'What happened?' Hakan told him all he'd seen.

They sat there a while. Konur wanted to know how the story went on: of the pursuit and the battle on that northern fell. He listened, and afterwards he too told of his experiences in 'Skogul's Storm', as he called it. Bloody combat – skirmishes, raids. For once, he just told it how it was, best as he could remember. Hakan found himself interested, almost forgetting the hatred he'd nursed for Konur since the summer. Since their childhood, come to that. Forgotten the sharp stab of jealousy as he'd watched Konur lead Inga out of the hall.

The hour was late. Twilight shadows were falling. The others would be finishing up. They strolled back down the slope.

Suddenly, Konur laughed. 'You know, I'd pegged you for a mule-headed arse. I was sure we'd be enemies, you and I, and there was nothing doing. But. . . you're all right.'

Hakan grunted. 'Could be, you are too.' They twitched a grin at one another. *Would you look at us? My father will throw a bloody feast.*

'Makes me almost glad we're to be close kin.'

'How do you mean?'

'What do you think?' exclaimed Konur, suddenly beaming. 'My betrothal, of course! To your cousin.'

Bile suddenly soured Hakan's throat. 'My cousin? You mean Inga?'

'Of course to Inga! Don't know any other cousins of yours I'd care to marry.'

Hakan could only gape, incredulous.

Konur wasn't blind. 'By the fires!' he crowed. 'Don't tell me you didn't know.'

Hakan shook his head, dumb as an ox.

Konur laughed, long and loud. 'This is too good! The son of the great Lord Haldan, and he hasn't told you he plans to marry off his ward.'

A thousand thoughts burst like a storm in Hakan's head. 'H-how?' he stammered.

'It's all arranged, friend. What do you think all *this* is for?' He swept a hand over the burned-out dwellings below them. 'Our fathers agreed on it. Mine brought my offer to yours – this was the price they settled on. Did Haldan really not tell you?'

Hakan stared stupidly about him at the pathetic piles of refuse, the broken timber, the stinking puddles. His father couldn't have traded the most precious creature in all the Nine Worlds for *this*. *And to this son of a whore!*

'No,' he growled, anger swelling in him. 'No!'

'No?' repeated Konur, his grin faltering for a moment.

'She. Detests. You.'

'Paah! Didn't seem that way when I visited her.'

'What visit?'

'She didn't tell you that either?' crowed Konur even louder. 'Seems there's a heap of secrets up there at Vendlagard.'

Hakan shook his head, heat searing his blood.

Konur gave a curling sneer. 'I'm guessing she didn't tell you what we did, while you were taking care of your fearsome raiders, hey?' He winked, evidently enjoying himself. 'Tasty little piece, Inga.'

'You're lying,' Hakan snarled.

'Am I? Why would I lie?'

'Inga would never— not with you.'

'Why not?' he roared. 'Still, I can't say she didn't need some

148

persuading at first. But in my experience, most women enjoy a bit of a struggle. Excites 'em.'

'What did you do to her?'

'Come, you're a man of the world. You don't imagine I'm going to settle for one hive for the rest of my days if I haven't tasted the honey, do you? Still, I don't see what that's to you.'

'She's my cousin.' *She's my everything, fucker!*

'Your cousin? Hel, I couldn't give a toss of Frey's cock who stuck it in my cousins. You're welcome to 'em.'

Hakan's hand was quivering with rage.

Suddenly Konur's face lit up, his mouth twisting into a spiteful grin. 'Oh my! You're sweet on her, aren't you?'

Hakan felt his body stiffen. Suddenly their secret seemed plain as the day.

'That's it! Of course! That's why you got so mad at your stupid feast. Well, don't fret – she was quite enjoying it by the end. Nice to know your wife's a good fuck before any vows are spoken.' He made to tap his cheek, but Hakan knocked it away, grabbing his tunic.

'I'll fucking kill you before I see Inga married to you – you understand?'

'Get off me,' snarled Konur. 'Your father's already agreed. It's sealed. There's nothing you can do.'

Hakan's hand was sliding under his cloak to the haft of his knife, hate burning in his belly. The blade was halfway drawn before Konur saw the danger; he snatched desperately for his hilt.

Suddenly, another voice spoke, sharp as iron. 'Friendly little chat, is it?' They stiffened and Dag appeared out of the gloom. In the twilight, the dog-faced killer looked made of shadows

149

himself. Hakan felt a hand clamp over his knuckles, shoving the knife back in his belt.

Konur's eyes darted, fear flickering wildly on his face.

'You got some place else you need to be?' said Dag.

Konur snorted, steel scraping back into its sheath. 'I'll leave you folk to your mud pies,' he muttered, with a last resentful look.

Hakan watched Konur's silhouette dissolve into shadow, fury still hammering in his head. They stood, wordless, listening. A short while later, they heard hoofbeats thudding away west.

'Short visit,' said Dag. 'Anyone would think he didn't like our hospitality.'

'He's a cunt.'

'Yep – the world's full of 'em, boy. You better get used to it.' Dag slapped his shoulder. 'Come on, I'm bloody starving.'

CHAPTER TEN

'You've been hiding something from me,' said Haldan.

Inga levelled her gaze straight back at him, trying to blend ignorance and innocence in her face. Her uncle sat, stern as ever, in his oversized chair, behind his oversized table, in his oversized chamber. He'd summoned her direct from work. She wiped her fingers, still greasy from goat's dugs, uneasily on her apron.

She had never liked this part of the hall – the walls were covered in death: polished blades, honed edges; battered shields, splattered with rusty stains that could only be one thing.

She couldn't remember laughing in this place, and it only took the musky smell of skins and smoke to make her feel guilty. She braced herself. If her uncle had somehow learned their secret, her world was about to end.

'Well?'

'Hiding something?' Inga fiddled with her apron. *Perhaps his head will erupt like the fire mountains in Tolla's stories.*

'You had a visitor when we were away.'

'A visitor?' A bad job of feigning ignorance, but inside she was collapsing in relief. Anything was better than him discovering their secret. 'No—'

'I know the Karlung boy was here.'

Her cheeks flushed. 'How?' Einna or Tolla must have blabbed. *If it was that little Einnaling, she's going to get such a slapping!*

'From his father. What was he doing here?'

'Who?'

'Konur, of course!'

'He said he had some business with you,' she garbled. 'But when he found you weren't here, he left.'

'Why didn't you tell me?'

Inga cobbled an answer. 'I thought after the trouble between Konur and Hakan at the feast. . . I didn't want to spoil your return. We were just so relieved you'd returned.'

Haldan looked unconvinced. 'Speak truthfully, Inga. Are you in love with this boy?'

'In love with him!' she exclaimed, in disgust. 'No. Not at all.'

Haldan grunted irritably. 'Pity.'

'Pity? Why pity?'

Haldan folded his hands, eyeing her in that serious way he had. 'When the winter thaws, you will be of an age to wed.'

Please, sweet Freya, no. . .

'I have come to an agreement on a match for you.'

'No!' she blurted. 'I—'

'Konur is a man of good prospects.'

'No. . . no,' she quavered, shrinking back, clasping herself, as if retreating from a black abyss opening at her feet.

'What's wrong with him? He's fine-looking, of high blood

152

and good lands. You'd have to fare a long way to find a better match than him.'

'Please, Uncle! I don't care about his looks, or his land, or if his blood runs back through a hundred fathers. I'd rather marry a toad!'

'Don't be ridiculous.'

'I hate him. I *loathe* him.'

'Is this about the trouble with Hakan?'

'No, not that. Or not *just* that, I. . .' Her words faltered. She felt abashed; ashamed somehow to tell. She still couldn't squeeze out the splinter of doubt that she had brought what he did upon herself. But that was wrong – it *must* be wrong – and that only made her angrier. Konur was the one who should be ashamed, not her. 'I won't marry him!'

'I don't see the problem,' he said, dismissive. 'Besides, this isn't a choice. This is how it will be. More depends on this than the whimsy of a young girl.'

Suddenly she boiled with the unfairness of it. 'That's all I am to you, aren't I? Some bothersome little girl.' Hot tears of anger welled in her eyes, but she didn't care. 'That's all I've ever been! And now you want to be rid of me at the first chance you get – just like that.' She snapped her fingers in his face. He snatched her hand, quick as a snake, but his face remained cold as stone.

'You know, you're more than that.' His hand crushed hers.

'Is that supposed to be affection?' she snapped, prising her hand free. 'You're blind if you don't see how you treat me.' *He had to hear this. It was past time.* 'Your heart is ice to everyone. Everyone except your precious Chosen Son.'

'I suggest you calm down.' Warning flashed in his eyes.

'Why should I?' she cried. 'Because you don't like to hear the truth?' She leaned in, seeing it was getting to him. *Even to him.* 'Did you hate my mother so much? Did you hate that your brother loved her so much more than he loved you? Were you so resentful that she dumped her child on you? How thoughtless of her just to *die!*'

'You know nothing of—'

'I'm not finished!' she screamed. 'You don't know what it's like. You're the closest thing I have to a father and you show more love to your *dogs* than you do me.' The tears were streaming now. 'I didn't want much. I knew my place. But you've given me nothing. Nothing in there.' She pointed accusingly at the hole where his heart should have been. 'And now this!' Her fists crashed down on the table. 'You pack me off with the first fool who comes asking!'

His reply was white rage. 'You've been treated no different from my son. I've provided for you since the day you were born. You had everything you ever needed.'

'Don't you see – I needed you!' She rolled her eyes. 'Oh, you've provided – yes. Just like you throw scraps to your pigs. They're *provided* for – but do you love them? I only wanted what anyone would: a father's love. A mother's touch. Instead I have an uncle who'd rather grasp a nettle than put his arm around me.' She wiped her streaming nose, drawing breath.

For a moment, she saw a glimmer of shame pass over his face. But then it was gone, the lines round his mouth hardening once more. 'You're upset so I shall overlook the way you speak—'

'Stop being so cold!'

Without warning, he sprang from his cavernous chair, like a carving come to life, slamming his fists on the table. 'Sit down and shut your mouth!'

She cowered back, scared as if he'd been a wild bear. 'You can scream and whine all you want. The match is agreed. Each of us has duties to fulfil – we don't always like it, but we do them. This, my girl, is yours.'

She shrank back onto her stool. When she spoke again, it was very quiet, her voice stiff with sullen defiance. 'I won't be part of your squalid little agreement. And no power in the Nine Worlds will get me to marry Konur.'

'You'll do as you're—'

'He's a rapist!' This time, she sprang to her feet. The word shook the walls of the chamber. 'Do you understand? He tried to rape me.'

She watched his eyes blink – twice, three times. And then he sank back into his chair.

'Rape you?' he murmured.

'He would have succeeded. Only I stabbed him.' She pulled out the hairpin, spilling her curls about her shoulders. 'With this.' She proffered it.

He took it, turning it over, his face lost between bewilderment and admiration.

'I'll do it again if he comes near me.'

He laid the pin down and, after looking long into her tearful eyes, rose and went to her. She stood, motionless. Surprised. Gently, he folded her in his arms, her nostrils filling with the manly tang of his sweat. Her cheek pressed tight against his chest. She closed her eyes, savouring his big hands clasping her tight.

Why couldn't it be like this all the time? She felt safe there. She thought about the life inside her – the life that she, in turn, must safeguard. *Maybe I could tell him about us. About all of us. Maybe he would understand.*

'What happened?' he said softly.

And so she told him. Everything that had happened with Konur fell out of her in a tumble of words.

'Why didn't you tell me sooner?'

'I would have. . . but I knew if I did, Hakan would find out. . . and he seems to hate him so much. I couldn't risk the trouble that might come from that.' She sniffed. 'And the truth is . . . I felt ashamed.'

He tilted her face. She marvelled how tender those blue eyes could look, if only he'd let them. 'You have nothing to be ashamed of.' The lines in his face seemed softer than she ever remembered. 'Truly.'

'I know I was naive. . . I could have done more. To turn him away.' She buried her face in his chest again. 'Oh, Uncle, I wish he'd never come here.'

More tears came, and she heard him murmuring, 'It's all right. It will be all right.'

'Then I don't have to marry him?' *Please, sweet Freya, please.*

She felt his chest rise and fall. And again. But he said nothing. She felt only the beating of his heart. Abruptly, she pulled away from him. 'I don't, do I?' Her voice was shaking.

Slowly, his arms withdrew. 'It's not as simple as that.'

'Not simple?' she gaped. 'Just send word to Karlsted! Tell them your agreement is done with! That I'll have nothing to do with that rat.'

'I know he hurt you,' he tried to soothe her, but every word was grinding metal. 'I will get assurances from his father – aye, from the lad himself – that it will *never* happen again.' She backed away, heart pounding, his hulking form dissolving into a blur. 'I will make them guarantee—'

'No, no, no, NO!' she stammered, feeling like a drowning woman slipping under.

But he continued speaking. 'I gave my word. This isn't only about a husband for you. I must consider what dangers are rising against our people. This is about *all* our futures. That must come before any. . . *misunderstanding* between you and Konur.'

My ears must be lying.

'A misunderstanding? He tried to *rape* me!' Her mouth twisted into a sneer. 'You don't care, do you? Oh, I see you clear now, Uncle. Sure, you're a proud lord – don't we all know it!' Her lips were white with fury. 'But you're also a *monster* – a monster! – who would sacrifice everything to your precious honour and your precious blood.'

She nearly said it. Nearly screamed the words in his unwavering face. *Your son's bastard is growing in my belly!*

But something held her back.

Maybe it was knowing he would only trample over that, as he did over everything. Or the promise made to Hakan, to guard their secret as long as she could. Or maybe it was because their secret was the last precious thing she had left in the world. She couldn't face losing that as well.

'*Monster,*' was all she whispered.

But his mask had fallen back in place, those shadows settling on his features, dark as thunder.

If he meant to reply, she didn't wait to hear it. Instead, she turned and ran from the chamber. Yet even as she ran, she longed for him to follow, hoped that he would call her name, beg her to come back, ask for her forgiveness with tears in his eyes, tell her he loved her and that all would be well.

But there were no footsteps. No call. Only the silence. . . Only the invisible hands that coiled around her throat, squeezing the hope out of her.

The rain dripped steady over the crackling flames. Dank smells, of sodden furs and the black earth, mingled with the scent of their stew. The same as every night: rabbit with onions and marjoram, thickened with stale bread. Hardly the fare of kings but it filled a hole.

Enough for five of them at least, hunkered over their bowls. But Hakan wasn't eating. His belly was already brimful of bile, his mind with the word he couldn't shake.

Murder.

He pushed it away. And away and *away*. But back it came, unbidden, relentless, till at last he let it stay. Ugly, sinister, shameful. He glared at it. The word glared back, accusing him.

Sighing for him.

This was his father's fault. Did the old man value Inga so little that he could even imagine agreeing to this? If Konur had forced himself on her, he deserved to die. And if he hadn't. . . *No – it couldn't have been like that. . .*

Yet the doubt remained. It was *his* child in her belly, so she said. Did he have to doubt even that now? He stirred the stew in his bowl, remembering Inga's face – so urgent, so honest, tears in her eyes. Could she lie so easily? *Am I really such a fool?*

He cursed inwardly. By force or betrayal – it mattered little. If that Karlung bastard had taken what was his, he had a reckoning coming. A storm of blood, and afterwards, Hakan knew, a feud that was like to live long after he was dead and gone. His father would rage, but he would have to stand behind him.

No one else could have Inga.

No one.

The others began tossing a few words to each other – complaining about the rain and the autumn chill. Hakan hadn't taken a mouthful.

'Not touching your food?' Dag nodded at his bowl, eyes glimmering, half-amused. Hakan only grunted in reply and lifted his spoon.

'Give it over then,' piped Aldi, offering an empty bowl.

'Leave him be.' Dag shoved away the lad's eager hands. 'Hate can fuel a man a while, but he still needs to eat.'

'Who says I hate anyone?'

'It's seeping out of you.' Dag sucked in deep through sharp nostrils. 'You reek of it.'

'It's no business of yours.'

Dag sniffed. 'Hate has a way of breaking out of a man. When it does, there's like to be some killing. Reckon that's my business, don't you?'

'Killing? I hadn't even thought of it.' *Only about half a hundred times.*

'You're a bad liar. Even for the son of a lord.'

Hakan threw his spoon in his bowl with a rattle. 'So I hate the worthless prick. So what?'

'You have your reasons.'

159

'Aye – I've plenty.' He kicked at the dirt. 'But it's under control. After all, I promised my father.'

Though why the Hel I should do anything for him right now. . .

'Maybe you made the old fella a promise. But in my experience, a promise ain't worth a soft turd.' Dag picked absently at his teeth with a long, dirty fingernail. 'Under control – hah! That's a good one.' He glared at Hakan, the shadows in his eyes deepening. 'You know what hate is, boy?'

Hakan shook his head.

'Hate is chaos. Wild as a wolf, she is. Loose her on the world, and blood will run just about anywhere.'

'I guess I'll keep her fettered then. Good and tight.' Hakan went back to his food. *I'm no murderer.*

'Maybe. For now. But one day, all the fetters in the Nine Worlds will break.'

'The Ragnarok,' muttered Gunnrek.

'Aye – the Ragnarok,' echoed Dag. 'That day is coming. Maybe soon. When chaos breaks the chains that hold it back.' His throat rattled with a hollow laugh. 'You think the world's a dark and bloody place now? It's bright as the sun against what's to come.'

The fire seemed to flare at his words, and a stillness came over the company as they listened to Dag go on in his halting, jagged way. They had all heard it told before – usually on a dark night such as that one. The Ragnarok – the Final Fires. The unleashing of terror upon the world of men.

The folk of the north had long passed on the ancient foretelling of the destruction to come. When the monstrous wolf Fenrir would slip his chain, and the Great Snake would rise out of the deep, and fire would burst from the earth.

They listened as Dag poked at the embers, voice brittle as the cracking wood. He spoke of the sun splintered by spears of darkness, of *draug*-spirits returning. Of Hel's children gathering the thralls of the dead and voyaging to the final slaughter on a ship of rotting flesh. Of oceans breaking their bounds, flooding the land, and the fierce frosts of winter upon winter upon winter, withering all life to nothing. When men would tear out the hearts of their kin, and Loki's lies would fill their minds. He told of brothers and sisters rutting like swine, fathers destroying their heirs, mothers burning their offspring in fire. The justice of men would come to nothing. Laws and customs would crumble. The wisdom of the ages would be swallowed up. Only the Hall of the Fallen Heroes would stand. Valhalla.

Aldi clapped his hands in excitement, earning himself a scowl from Gunnrek.

Dag went on, gazing into the flames. 'The Father of All will call them out.' Odin's host of heroes. Heimdall's horn would summon them to the field of blood. The dead would swarm under Hel's banner, and every hero would meet his bane. And then, only then, would the Final Fires burn, consuming all. Darkness, light, the turning of time, the halls of thunder, the vaults of lightning, the roaring oceans. The shining stars would fall, Ymir's skull would shatter, and then. . . There would be nothing.

'Just as it was,' he growled. 'All will be nothing once more.'

For a long time, no one said a word. There was only the rain, and the fire, and the rasping in Dag's nostrils.

'The Ragnarok,' said one, at last.

They all nodded.

161

'It starts in here, boy.' Dag pointed to his heart. 'Chaos waits in here, dreaming of the time it'll break free.' He nodded. 'Aye – the spark of those final flames burns in us. It's been spoken. So it'll be.'

Silence again, till Dag suddenly cleared his throat and spat into the fire. 'One thing to say for it on a night like this. At least it'll be fucking warm.'

'And dry,' added Aldi, with a snigger.

Dag gave a languorous yawn. 'On that cheery thought, my friends, I bid you goodnight.'

The others turned in soon after. Their makeshift canopy kept off the worst of the drizzle, but the ground was wet and the air damp.

Hakan lay nursing dark thoughts. Hate. Chaos. Killing. The Ragnarok. Had Dag meant to goad him on or halt him in his course? Somehow, his words did both. Black deeds danced in his heart.

Perhaps the only way to be rid of them is to see them done. . .

Again and again, he asked himself why Inga hadn't told him of Konur's visit. *Had* she betrayed him? And worse, was his father truly going to give her away? What would happen to the child? *His* child? These and a thousand other questions whirled through his mind. All the while, in the darkness he saw Konur's sneering face.

And then, all at once, an answer. The only answer to all these unanswerable questions.

I just. Want him. Dead.

CHAPTER ELEVEN

The tips of Inga's fingers were white and wrinkled.

Like old snowberries. Dry and dead. Perhaps they would look like that when she was old. Withering to dust. . . *Is that all life is? A slow and steady rot into death. . . and shadow.*

She rubbed together thumb and forefinger to smooth the wrinkles, but the little folds persisted, as in her mind.

'You've been staring at your hands for ages.' Inga blinked and looked up. Einna's narrow face stared back. 'What are you thinking about?'

'Nothing,' she replied hazily. *Or was it nothingness?*

'Well, while you're thinking about nothing, keep washing! Just look at all this.' Einna threw up her hands in dismay and splashed them in her washtub.

Inga gazed about her as if she'd just awoken, a little frightened that it took some moments to remember where she was. The shingle-wood tiles, the smoky beams, the gnarled pillars, and beside them two huge piles, one of unwashed linen, one of coarse-spun blankets. Some were hanging from the rafters of the washhouse, dripping wet but clean.

They would take for ever to dry in this damp weather. Perhaps they should make a fire. She imagined flames dancing, higher and higher; then the wool catching light, the fire devouring the cloth until it was burned to nothing.

She groaned inwardly. Why did her thoughts spiral so often into nothingness these days? She shifted her weight on her haunches and went back to wringing out the linen. Turning, squeezing.

Inside my head, it's the same. Turning, squeezing. She felt so far from herself. She was used to her mind galloping free, swift as a stallion, soaring like a swallow. Life was a dance she could do with her eyes shut, a song she knew by heart. Gossip and japes and stories – quick wits and quick words – she was used to weaving them all into a bright and beautiful pattern, not a stitch out of place. But now. . . now, everything in her head was moving too fast. Confusing. A thousand thoughts writhing and twisting together like a nest of serpents.

Hakan had been gone days; probably he'd be away days more. She needed him back. But what would she tell him? She used to know what to say about everything. Now, nothing made sense.

No, that's not true. Hakan still makes sense.

With him, she could find her way through a forest of fears. And yet, when she tried to lay hands on each fear to face it down, it proved ephemeral as a mist.

She had started to believe that strange powers must be moving against her. How else could all this have arisen? And now her uncle's will was against her, intent on this horrible arrangement. She remembered how one of the battle-names they called him was Stoneside. *Stoneheart is nearer the mark.* She had to find the will to fight – now more than ever. For the life inside her.

So why did she feel so weak just when she needed to be strong?

She had prayed to the good gods. The high god of the Vanir, Ingvi-Frey, her namesake. Her life had been bound to his since she'd come into the world. He must protect them, because their love was pure and good. And the high god's beautiful twin Freya, too. Wasn't it the goddess of love who gave passions of the heart, and the secret ecstasies between man and woman? Inga had lived to please both these gods. They *must* defend her.

Yet somehow, the shadow remained. Inescapable.

She felt so tired.

Maybe the shadow knows. My blood is marked. Her father's death, her mother's sorrow. The shadow only laughed, knowing her turn would come.

Einna was prattling away about one of the Birlung boys whom she had met over at Hildagard, her shock of hair bobbing back and forth with ever more enthusiasm.

Time wasn't long past when Inga would have teased Einna without mercy. And together, they would have laughed and laughed. But instead Inga said nothing. Einna's words confused her. She tried to concentrate, but none of her thoughts held together.

Eventually, Einna trailed into silence, and there was a splash of sodden linen. 'What's wrong with you, huh?'

Inga started.

'Where's my darling Ingaling?'

'Hey?'

165

'You're not here!'

Inga shook her head, forcing a smile. 'I'm sorry. I must have been daydreaming.'

'Can't have been a very nice dream, judging from your face.'

Inga only sighed.

'You've hardly said a word in days. Tell me what's wrong, little dove?'

'Just leave it, Einna.'

'Come, you can tell.' Inga wished she would just stop. 'Why are you being so stubborn, silly?'

'Maybe I'm tired of listening to your endless jabber!' Inga snapped. 'Can't you just. . . just be quiet for a while?'

As soon as she spoke, she regretted it. Poor Einna didn't know her secrets. *She doesn't even know me. Not any more.* Einna gave a tetchy flick of her hair and turned back to her washing.

Inga groaned. 'I'm sorry, little one.' But Einna was already lodged in one of her sulks, and there would be no prying her out of it.

Her back ached. It ached a good deal these days. She wondered how big their child was now. Under layers of clothing, the bulge in her belly was growing – unmistakable to the touch, but unseen.

For now.

How could she conceal herself till the spring? It was foolish to hope no one would notice. The only slight reassurance was that winter was coming on and no one would heed a few more layers as the days grew colder.

But truly – our plan is absurd!

She stood up, feeling the blood fizz down her legs. She would leave Einna to her sulking. She needed to breathe.

'I'm thirsty.' Einna only scowled in reply, so Inga pulled her cloak tight and stepped out of the washhouse into the yard.

She set off for the water butt, careless of her skirts dragging through the puddles. The mud was thick as pitch. She'd only gone a few steps when she missed her footing and slipped. She lurched, managed to catch herself, but her back jarred, the pain stabbing like a stick in the spine.

She wanted to yell in frustration, but clamped her mouth shut and leaned back, trying to ease the muscles in her back. Her gaze drifted up into the blanket of drab clouds overhead.

So tired.

Tired of chasing answers down the warrens of her mind. Tired of worrying for the little life she felt growing inside her. She closed her eyes and let her mind become blank as the sky, and for one sweet moment, she thought of nothing at all.

The pain leaked away until, at last, it was gone. She opened her eyes.

There was Tolla – standing in the doorway of the hall, bucket in hand, a quizzical look on her face. Inga straightened up and called a greeting.

The nurse tucked away a loose strand of hair and made her way over without a word. Inga watched her. Something was different about her.

'Come here, Einna,' called Tolla.

The younger girl looked up from her tub. Tolla held out the bucket of scraps. 'Be a good girl and take this to the pigs.'

'It's always me!' Einna slapped her apron, exasperated. 'Why can't *she* do it? She's done nothing all morning.'

'Just do as you're told. I need to talk with Inga.'

Hearing this, Einna conceded, with a glimmer of satisfaction.

They both knew Tolla only spoke like that when someone was in trouble. Inga's neck prickled with foreboding as Einna squelched off with the bucket of scraps. A few other farm-thralls came and went about their work nearby. Tolla beckoned Inga to the back of the washhouse, her face giving nothing away. Inga followed, apprehensive.

'I've been watching you, Inga.'

'You have?'

'More than you reckon.' When Inga didn't answer, Tolla gave a flick of her head. 'What's with your back then? Giving you trouble, is it?'

'Nothing. Just slept funny, is all.'

'That a fact?'

'I guess.'

'That's an awful shame.' But Tolla's weathered face didn't look very sympathetic. 'Only it's not just your back, is it?'

Inga tried to play baffled. But inwardly, she gathered her wits.

'Something's up with you. You're not yourself.'

Inga shrugged. 'Whatever do you mean?'

'Lately, every time I see you you're moping around.'

'Maybe it's the rain,' murmured Inga. 'I hate this time of year. Everything is dying.'

'It's not the rain. No, I've been asking myself why. And the only thing I can think, I don't like at all.'

'Well?'

'You haven't fallen for that silk-tongued weasel, have you?'

'Who?'

'Konur, of course. You've not been the same since he came by. And when he left, you wanted to be all secretive.'

'I told you why.'

'Part of the reason, maybe. Now tell me the truth.'

'You've got it so wrong, Tolla. I hate Konur.' Inga took a strange pleasure in saying the words out loud. 'Really. I hate him.'

Tolla peered closer, exploring her eyes. Inga felt naked as a babe under Tolla's scrutiny. Always did. At least this time, she was telling the truth. Tolla drew away, apparently satisfied. 'Well, I'm glad there's still some sense left in that pretty head of yours. I don't trust that boy. Haven't from the start.'

'He's a bully,' blurted Inga. 'Worse than a bully.'

But Tolla seemed occupied with her own ponderings. 'So if it's not him, then what's the matter with you? You're awful distracted. And so low. Like the spark's gone out of you. Are you sick?' She stepped forward and put the back of her hand to Inga's brow.

Inga recoiled like a startled deer. 'No!'

'No?'

'I mean there's nothing wrong with me. Or there is. . . I'm. . .' She dried up with despair.

'Just say whatever it is, honey,' said Tolla, seeing her distress.

Inga considered telling her. Wanted to tell her everything. But could she trust her? Would Tolla help them? Perhaps if she gave her one piece of the truth, it would be enough. 'It is to do with Konur,' she admitted, at last.

'Go on.'

'My uncle wants me to marry him.'

'What?' exclaimed Tolla. 'Marry him? Since when?'

Inga felt tears sting her eyes. 'He told me a few days ago. Said it was part of some agreement with Konur's father.'

169

'No, no, no,' said Tolla, shaking her head. 'What happened? Tell me quickly.'

So she told her everything that had passed between them, their argument and how they had left it, saying how she detested Konur and how she had railed against Haldan's plan, but leaving out why.

Even as she was speaking, she didn't know why she couldn't tell Tolla what Konur had tried to do. Was she so ashamed? How could there ever be room for shame with Tolla? She had nursed her from her mother's dead nipple, knew the worst of her, and still loved her. Maybe it would have to come to that.

'Can you help me?' she asked. 'Can't you talk to him?'

'I'll try, sweetling. But I can't promise anything. You know how stubborn he is.'

'But you're stubborn too, aren't you?'

Tolla smiled. 'Aye. But once your uncle has an idea in his head, he's like a dog with a bone. Especially when it comes to land and bloodlines and such.'

The old jealousy surged inside Inga. 'Our bloodline,' she said, bitterly. 'The mean old fool is obsessed. Why does he treat me like dirt, yet Hakan is so precious? His "Chosen Son". . . Chosen for what! It's not fair.'

'He loves Hakan. And you. In his way.'

'He's incapable of love! Everything is sacrificed for the good of his land or his people. But you can't hold land in your arms, can you? You can't hold a people.'

'Once he loved very deeply. Too deeply maybe.'

'I can scarce believe it. Anyway, how can you love too deeply?' She was weeping openly now, but she was beyond caring.

Tolla's face mirrored hers, pained by her pain. 'I've never told anyone this,' she said. 'Lord Haldan made me promise never to tell what I'd witnessed. But I think somehow you need to know. And one day, long after he and I are gone, you must tell Hakan as well.'

'Hakan? Why?'

'You never wondered why he was called the "Chosen Son"?'

'I thought it was just a stupid name to show he was special.'

'He is special. But he was also chosen.' The nurse sighed. 'You were only little when his mother died so you won't remember her well. But Lord Haldan loved Guthrun deeply. You never saw a man prouder of his wife when she fell pregnant. Nor more protective. She was huge! The womenfolk round here agreed they never saw a woman so big. One of the older women said it was twins, and sure enough, she gave birth to a pair of boys, as alike as two grains of barley. But it was a hard, hard birth, and left her weak as a lamb.' Tolla went on, telling how Guthrun came to the threshold of death, and there she stayed a long while.

Haldan couldn't bear to lose her. She caught a chill that burrowed deep into her lungs, and every day they thought it would be her last. While his wife languished, Haldan charged Tolla, a girl of twenty summers back then, to watch over the two boys. And all the while, Haldan grew mad with the thought of losing his wife, until one day, a *seidman* came peddling his black craft. Tolla figured he had heard of Guthrun's sickness and the Vendling lord's distress, because he came with a promise. He could cure his wife, he said, but it would come at a cost that was perhaps more than Haldan was willing to pay. He had pointed at the boys in their twin

171

cradle. *A life for a life.* One of them for his wife to live. When Tolla heard it, the horror of it was almost too much to bear.

Inga listened as Tolla told how she pleaded with Haldan to run the *seidman* off the land, but the shaman was nimble with his words. And the idea he'd planted gnawed at Haldan's mind. He believed Guthrun would live, and he would be spared losing the thing most precious to him in all the world.

Guthrun heard of the *seidman*'s offer, but wanted nothing of it. In the moments when her sickness abated, she begged Haldan not to do it; tried to persuade him to accept her time had come. But he would not. And one night, he came to Tolla and told her he had decided.

Inga watched a shadow settle on Tolla's face as she described how Haldan had stood over their cradle a long while. The boys lay side by side, arms wrapped around one another, as was their habit. Guthrun lay weeping nearby, pleading with him, but his ears were stone. Finally, he just picked up one of them, prising off the other's little fingers, took the baby outside and gave him to the *seidman*.

'What did the *seidman* do?'

'He took him away. Gave him up to the sea. To the—' Tolla's voice choked with sadness. It was some moments before she could speak. 'To the sea-god.' She shook her head. 'That's all you need to know.'

'How horrible,' murmured Inga.

'So it is. I've never forgotten the *seidman* and his kind for what he did, nor forgiven them. Nor will I ever. Their practice is wickedness.'

'And what about my uncle? You must hate him.'

Tolla sighed, wearily. 'I didn't blame him. It was the choice

172

he was given that maddened him. What he did, he did out of love for Guthrun.'

'And she lived.'

'She did. But whether from his sacrifice or not, who can say? Soon afterwards the sickness broke, her strength returned. By then, Haldan had made his choice. And he named the boy he kept, "Hakan". His "Chosen Son".'

'Poor little wretch,' murmured Inga, thinking of Hakan's twin.

'Aye.' Tolla's face clouded. 'The irony was Haldan made the sacrifice to keep his love. His punishment was to lose even that.'

'Why?'

''Cause though Guthrun lived another ten years, she stopped loving him the night he gave away their little boy. And though he loved her till her last breath, by the end she despised him.' She gave Inga a thin smile. 'You were too young to remember, but there was a frost hung over this hall all those years that never quite thawed.'

Inga didn't know what to make of all this. She thought of her uncle, his brooding features, his implacable will. She knew those ice-blue eyes had seen terrible things, but never could have guessed at this.

'So you see why his heart is hard to anything but his Chosen Son?'

'I still don't believe it. Don't believe after all these years he could cast me away like Hakan's brother.'

'I respect your uncle. He's wise and strong. But tender, he is not. The sooner you understand why, the easier you might accept it.'

Inga's heart sank. The chance of finding a way through seemed more remote than ever. 'But you will speak to him.'

'I'll try.'

'Then there's hope.' She looked pleadingly into Tolla's eyes. 'Tell me there's hope.'

Tolla, usually so quick to reassure her about anything, furrowed her brow. But then she nodded, forcing a smile. 'There's always hope.'

But Inga could see the lie in her eyes and felt sick.

'Are you quite well? You look so pale.' Tolla reached out and touched her cheek. 'So hot.'

'I'm fine.'

'What's the matter with you, girl? You're burning up. Whatever are you doing with so many clothes on? You're going to give yourself a fever. Come, let me take that off you.'

'Tolla, I'm fine!' screeched Inga, snatching back the hem of her cloak and folding it round herself.

Tolla let her hands fall. 'As you wish.'

'Look, here's Einna!' Relief washed over her at her friend's return. Tolla was eyeing her curiously. 'I should get on with all this.' Inga motioned at the piles of washing. But Tolla was only half-listening, stroking at her long nose thoughtfully. 'You will speak with my uncle, won't you?'

Tolla nodded slowly.

'Thank you.' Inga dropped down by her tub and took up her washing. But all the while she felt Tolla's eyes on her. And it was a long time before her footsteps squelched away in the mud.

· · · · · · ·

Smoke billowed from damp firewood. Hakan crouched, waiting. Listening. Watching the outline of furs beside the dying fire.

Three leagues away, his companions slept on, oblivious to the empty blankets beside them. He had risen without a whisper and followed the path west, fording the stream that emptied into Odd's Sound, before turning southwest towards Karlsted.

He'd wondered whether Konur would ride through the night. In summer, he might. But now? Only madmen and shape-shifters and sheep-thieves rode through a night like this one.

And murderers.

The rain had moved on, leaving a silver sheen over everything. He hadn't ridden far when a solitary orange light had winked at him out of the darkness. He had tethered his horse and crept forward, stealthy as a shadow, his mind numb to the pain in his ankle.

Now he waited, the tang of horseflesh sharp over the rotting leaves. The wind was blown out. Stillness hovered in the treetops, but he couldn't shake the feeling he was surrounded by shadows. *Draug* spirits – the souls of the unquiet dead. Curious. Impatient.

He listened to Konur's heavy breathing, in and out like waves on a shingle shore. And suddenly his long-knife was in his hand. *Just like that. Without thinking.*

It wasn't too late to go back. But then the madness would linger. If only the poison in his head could be drawn, once and for all. *Just by doing this thing. Such a little thing*, he thought, looking down at his knife. *Better the poison is drawn.* Anything was better.

175

Creeping the last few paces was a child's game. No one ever heard him. *Shadow-sneak*, Leif used to tease him, and get a bloody nose for it. But Leif had done all the bleeding he would ever do. Now he was nothing but ashes on a cold ocean. And Hakan was here.

The horse whickered. Hakan stopped, knife in hand. But Konur never stirred.

Now was the moment. Two steps and he could sink the blade into his neck. Two steps and Konur would never wake again. Two steps. . . and he would be a murderer.

'Get up.'

Konur rolled over. 'Get up,' Hakan repeated. 'You sack of shit.' Hakan slid his knife in its sheath, relieved it wouldn't be that way, instead pulling his shield over his shoulder and unhitching his axe.

Konur was blundering to his feet, rubbing sleep from his eyes, sword belt clutched to his chest. 'Who are you?'

Hakan didn't reply. Only pushed back his hood, feeling the firelight touch his face.

Konur's eyes grew wide. 'You!' And in a moment his sword was in his hand, the sheath flung in the dirt. 'What do you want?'

Konur's shield lay on the ground. Hakan hooked a boot under it and kicked it towards him.

'Blood.'

The shield landed at Konur's feet. He scrabbled for it. But there was no rush. He could take all the time he wanted.

'Is this about your slut of a cousin?'

'You're going to die for what you did to her.' Hakan flexed his grip, fingers cramping with anticipation. Axe against sword was no easy contest. But what else had all those hours sweating in the training circle been for? *An axe can beat a sword*, Garik had promised. He was about to find out what that promise was worth.

'You're a bigger fool than I took you for.'

'She's carrying my child.' Somehow, it felt good to have said it, even if it was to this grinning bastard.

Konur gave a hollow laugh. 'So that stuck-up bitch opened her legs to her own cousin, hey?' He flicked his sword around his wrist, ready. 'After all that, she's a kin-fucker. Why doesn't that surprise me?'

'One more word and I'll cut out your tongue.'

'That'll be hard to do after I've gutted you like a pig. And I promise you this, cripple. When this is done, I'll drown your Hel-spawned brat and fuck your darling cousin up her tight little—'

Hakan sprang at him.

Konur yelped like a kicked dog, wrenching up his shield. Steel cracked against pine and the blow glanced away. Hakan moved fast, driving his shield-rim at Konur's teeth, but his opponent had gathered his wits. He ducked, flinging out his shield, cutting down. The sword flashed, murderous; Hakan dodged, the blow juddering against his shield.

The two backed off, circling each other like wolves.

'You should've brought a sword, cripple.'

'Give me a fucking spoon and I'd find a way to kill you.'

They went at each other again, wheeling round, looking for an opening, blows probing against wood and iron. In reach, Konur had the better of Hakan. His sword cut, lunged, wound around Hakan's axe, arcing in overhead.

177

Karsten had him well trained. But Hakan blocked every stroke, his axe gouging chunks from Konur's shield while he strained to remember what Garik had taught him. *Look for a weakness – a man loses a fight more often than he wins it.*

Konur's shield was fast. Maybe too fast. Hakan feigned low; Konur's arm jerked down. Hakan kicked the rim, hard. Bone crunched against metal, pain ripped up his leg, but Konur wasn't ready. The shield smashed into his face, jerking back his head.

'Gaaaaaah!' he squawked, blood bursting from his forehead. Seeing him dazed for a moment, Hakan hooked his axe over Konur's shield-rim, yanking hard as he could. The shield flipped away.

Konur saw the danger and went on the attack, a slashing, hacking wind of steel. Hakan parried each blow, giving ground till he could feel the flame-heat on his back. Any further and he'd be in the fire. Suddenly Konur snatched his cloak from the ground. Hakan struck at him, but the cloak whirled, tangling his axe. Konur's sword fell; Hakan wrenched up his arm. There was a splintering sound and his shield flopped down like a broken wing.

He threw himself forward, heard a crack as his head butted Konur's face, felt teeth splinter on his crown. Konur wailed, clawing at his face, but Hakan clung on, tight as ivy.

They wrestled, scuffing up ash, Konur gouging at Hakan's mouth and eyes. Hakan bit down hard through wet wool, tasted blood. Konur screamed, gave ground, then slammed his knee in Hakan's groin.

Hakan buckled in agony.

Next thing he knew his legs were kicked away. Konur yelled in triumph, then vanished in a fog of smoke and cinder and flame. Hakan screamed, fire scorching his back, as he fell into its midst. He smelled burning hair, saw Konur's bloody mouth grinning like a devil above him, sword raised for the killing blow.

Without thinking, Hakan plunged his hand into the embers. He shrieked, fingers burning, and flung a cloud of sparks at Konur.

The Karlunger howled, dropped his sword, pawing at his scorched face. With his last strength, Hakan rolled away and hauled himself to his feet.

Konur was doubled over. Smoke and ash clouded everywhere. Hakan's arm swept down; he felt a dull, thick thud.

His axe was buried in Konur's spine.

Konur let out a strange sigh. Almost weary. Then reared up, hands pawing uselessly at his sides. A shiver passed through him, he dropped to his knees, and then, very slowly, toppled into the ashes.

Hakan pulled out his knife.

Konur lay twisted, eyes full of fear, yet somehow expectant. As if he wanted just one more word from this world before he went to the shadow-lands of death.

Hakan seized his tunic. Konur hung limp, eyes black with ash – swallowing and swallowing. Like he was thirsty, or had something to say. But no words came.

'See you in the High God's halls,' Hakan whispered, sinking his knife into Konur's heart. 'Or else in Hel.'

He gripped tight, until the last shudder had passed. Then he let him fall. Konur lay there, still as stone.

Hakan tore out his knife and staggered backwards, gasping.

Hate is chaos.

179

What chaos had he loosed now? His father's plans lay shattered as the body at his feet.

But in his heart, all he heard was a voice. Quiet. Insistent.

She's mine. Mine.

CHAPTER TWELVE

Vomit tasted sharp and sour in her throat.

Inga closed her eyes, took a deep breath, but another wave of nausea swept through her, bending her double.

The last dregs in her stomach splattered into the dirt.

She straightened up, hoping that was the end of it. *For now*. This was the worst it had been. So far she had managed to conceal how ill she had been feeling from any watchful eyes, but these last days had been unbearable.

Her whole body felt hollowed out, like some loathsome worm had sucked every scrap of strength from her limbs. Her breasts were swollen and sore.

She walked back towards Vendlagard, hoping it would be over soon. She knew the days of sickness didn't last for ever. But once they passed, the baby would start growing in earnest, and she'd have far more trouble hiding her belly than her nausea.

How foolish she had been, harbouring moon-headed notions of what it would be like to carry a child: that she would feel so connected to the wonderful fabric of life; that she would know the ageless wisdom of motherhood, the gods' special gift to her sex; that she would overflow with joy at the little life being knit together inside her.

Instead she felt sick, stupid and miserable.

The morning had begun with an ugly grey smear creeping across the sky, overtaking the darkness with a sullen gloom. The smell of wet grass filled her nostrils.

Perhaps Hakan would return today, if the gods were kind – though lately they had given little enough proof of that. Too many words were filling her mind. If he didn't come soon, the dam must break and it would all come flooding out. Somewhere.

Onto someone.

She had left the wood behind her and was picking her way down the meadow towards the farmstead gate when she heard a voice call her name.

She turned to see Tolla trotting down to her from the treeline. Her heart sank into her shoes.

'Come here, you!'

She'd been followed! Inga was incensed. She turned and hurried on down the slope.

'I saw you,' Tolla called, running after her.

There was nowhere to go. She spun on her heel. 'So you're spying on me now, is that it? How dare you!'

'Believe it or not,' cried Tolla, catching up with her, 'I'm worried about you.'

'Is that what you call sneaking around trying to catch me out? All you want is to get me into trouble!'

'You silly creature – you're quite capable of doing that yourself.' For a moment, they glared at one another, a cloud of anger between them. 'Well? I saw you being sick.'

'I must've eaten something bad.' She hardly cared whether Tolla believed her or not. 'I can't help it if your cooking is rotten!'

'You're pale as a ghost.'

'You would be too if you'd just emptied your stomach!'

Tolla circled round her, a she-wolf studying its prey. Fear twinged at Inga's belly. 'Tell me straight. Are you carrying a child?'

'A child! Are you mad?' She tried to laugh away the suggestion, but it sounded hollow as a reed.

'Mad I may be, but my eyes don't lie. I've seen you, sick as a sow, and this isn't the first time. Then there's your stiff back, your cheeks pale as milk and you're wrapped up like it's Yuletide. I'm no fool, Inga. Now are you going to tell me the truth?'

'I'm not carrying a baby! How could I be? I've no husband.'

Tolla snorted. 'The two needn't go together, as you well know.'

Suddenly Inga wanted to shout the truth. Scream it to the wind and collapse into Tolla's arms, sobbing. But some part of her refused to let go; some obstinate, unfathomable part of herself, that wouldn't let her give up her secret.

'I tell you, I have no child! So my back is sore – so I've been sick? So what!'

But Tolla wasn't listening. 'I still can't figure who the father is. You've been too sly for that.'

'Now you're dreaming up secrets where there aren't any.'

'Am I though?'

'I can't help it if your head's full of stupid notions. I don't have to stay and listen to this.'

183

Inga shoved past Tolla, but as she did, the nurse thrust her hand under her cloak. Inga felt strong fingers press hard against the taut swell of her belly. Even under layers of wool and linen, the bulge was unmistakable.

'You are!' Tolla gaped, in astonishment.

Inga tried to recoil, tried to think of some retort, but she was crumbling. 'Oh Tolla – you mustn't tell! No one can know.'

'Who's the father? Just tell me, whose is it?'

'I can't. Please.'

'It *was* Konur, wasn't it? It must have been.' Suddenly, she took up Inga's hands, her face all earnest. 'You lay with him when he was here.'

'No!' cried Inga. 'No! I never would. I never will. I don't care what my uncle's plans are.' The shock of discovery was being rinsed away by cold, surging anger.

'Why didn't you tell me?'

'I don't know! What could you do about it anyway? I can't think any more. I can't. . . see.' She clutched at her head. 'Everything ahead is so dark.'

Tolla slid an arm around her. 'My poor little pigeon.' For some moments, she held Inga, but her sympathy was too late. *Too late and too weak.* 'Come, sweetling. Let's think what's best done now.'

'There's nothing doing,' wailed Inga. 'Not now. Nothing.'

'Tell me, who is the father? I can help you.'

It would be so easy. But we agreed. . . I promised. She looked up into Tolla's eyes. She'd been looking into those eyes since the first day she could see. They had never held anything but love. But now, she couldn't bring herself to trust them. Perhaps she could never trust anyone again.

'I can't, Tolla. Just swear you won't tell my uncle about this. Or Hakan,' she added hastily. 'Or anyone.'

'Oh, what have you done?' The nurse's eyes welled in pity. 'How can I help if you won't confide in me? Did someone force himself on you?'

'I'm not going to tell you,' sobbed Inga. 'Just promise me you'll keep it secret. If you love me, you will.'

'I can't promise that. Not if you won't tell me everything.' The nurse's face hardened, as she tried a different approach. 'Very well – I have no choice. I'll have to go to Haldan. He'd flay me alive if he found I was keeping this from him.'

'You want to save your own skin then, is that it?' cried Inga. 'But he *mustn't* know. Not yet.'

'What difference does it make? He's going to know soon enough.'

Maybe – but not now. Not while Hakan isn't here with me. I need him here. . . 'He can't know,' Inga repeated. 'Not yet.'

Softening, Tolla took her by the shoulders, looked at her straight. 'I want to help you. Do you understand? If you only trusted me. . .'

Inga said nothing. Everything was flying out of control. But why should Tolla force her into this? Resentment coiled around her throat, choking her, enraging her. If she hated one thing, it was being forced into a corner – especially by someone wearing a smile.

But if their secret came out. . . *What then?*

Tolla shook her head. 'You leave me no choice. I have to tell him.' She turned to leave, but before she could, Inga snatched her arm, spinning her around.

'Stay where you are!' Without thinking, she shoved her,

hard. Tolla staggered back. 'You're nothing and don't you forget it! My uncle took you in from nothing! You're no better than a thrall! I am the blood of the Vendlings,' she cried, beating at her breast. 'And what are you?' Tolla shrank from her. Inga saw in her kind eyes that each word struck a wound. 'You will not do this! I won't let you.'

Suddenly, Tolla surged back at her. 'Don't come the high lady with me, Inga. I've raised you since you were soiling yourself and suckling on these 'ere teats!' She slapped her chest angrily. 'You have to wake up, girl! This isn't a game. Haldan must know. I may be nothing better than a thrall, but you're my responsibility.' And then, hearing the hardness in her own voice, she relented a little, laying a hand against Inga's cheek. 'You're my child, Inga.'

'No, I am NOT!' exploded Inga. 'I'm no one's child. My parents are dead – DEAD!' Her whole body shook with anger. Anger and fear and pain. 'I'm NO – CHILD – OF YOURS.'

The two women stared at one another, stunned into silence by the venom in Inga's voice.

'Piss on it!' spat Inga. 'If you won't help me, I'll face it myself. All of it. I am a woman now, and my father's daughter. I'm not scared of my uncle. I'll do it now! And you, Tolla,' she pointed an accusing finger at the woman who had loved her since she was a mewling babe. 'You go walk the road to Hel for all I care.' She screamed the last words, cold and dark.

Tolla started weeping. But Inga had gathered up her skirts, and was flying down the slope, furious as a *valkyrie* on the high road to war. The nurse looked after her, her strong shoulders sinking with her heart.

And suddenly, she looked very old and wounded and grey.

· · · · · · · ·

Hakan looked up at the grey skies growing darker with every moment. To the east, a dreary rainstorm was on its way in from the sea.

He was starving, but Vendlagard lay barely a quarter league on. He could see slithers of smoke. Once he'd crested that last ridge, he would be there. There would be food and warmth and shelter. Aside from those, he reckoned on little in the way of comfort.

The horse walked on while he tried, for the hundredth time, to order what he would tell his father. There was no honey-coating this one. No smoothing the edges; no washing it down with a swig of ale. Haldan would have to force it down – dry, barbed and sour.

Konur is dead. War is coming.

And he was the cause. He had killed the Karlung heir, and now all the clans of the Middle Jutes would come against them. Maybe even King Harald Wartooth and his vassal lords, if the Whisperer could talk him round. A war the Northern Jutes could never hope to win.

He groaned.

All his father wanted was peace, rest, prosperity; he worked for little else. Yet for all his talk, he had never been far from another tide of blood. One was rising now.

Konur was dead.

He wondered what the men at Vindhaven had made of his empty bed. Even now, two days later, they would be ignorant unless they had ridden out and struck upon Konur's shallow grave. He felt a pang of guilt. There would be no new market harbour now. All that digging in the mud and the slime – all for nothing.

Maybe Dag at least had seen a black deed coming.

His thoughts returned to Inga.

She was his and no one else's. They both knew it. What did it matter what his father thought anymore, now he had bought Inga with another man's blood? Or whether Haldan found out now or later? Hakan scowled at the memory of how he had talked her round. *Inga was right. She's always been right.* After all, what had his little plan been but the fear to confront his father? *Pitiful.*

Well, he couldn't be afraid any more. Soon, he would have far more fearful things to face than what his father thought of their secret. They all would.

Because now they would have to fight. The Whisperer wouldn't stop until he was dead. A son for a son. An heir for an heir. He nodded to himself, grimly. The Karlung lord could try.

Inga. . .

That doubt again. That poisoned seed. Had she betrayed him? He couldn't believe it. But why hadn't she told him if Konur had forced himself on her? *Why?*

He would have an answer from her.

He sucked in deep and sat up straight as his horse trudged *slap, slop* past the weather-scarred gateposts of Vendlagard.

He was home.

He looked about the yard. He saw Einna, working her loom, as usual, under a little slanted shelter. No one else was about. She looked up from her work, without a word.

That wasn't like her. He nodded a greeting, but she went back to her weaving with a disgruntled shrug.

The quiet was uncanny.

He dismounted, tethered his horse and left it munching a clutch of hay. *If only my homecoming were as simple as yours.*

Turning back to the yard, a feeling of estrangement caught in his belly, strange and sudden.

Nerves, is all. Maybe dread was a better word. Whichever way he cut it, this talk with his father was not going to go well.

He hobbled towards Einna, who still seemed determined to ignore him. She could at least tell him where everyone was.

He was about to hail her when a figure appeared at the hall-entrance. He recognized his beloved at once, but as she turned, he saw on her beautiful features an expression he never could have conjured in his most maddening dreams.

Her eyes were wide with terror, her cheeks bloodless, streaked with tears, her mouth ragged as a witless crone. And her hands. . . Her hands were terrible to look upon: hooked like talons, clawing at her belly.

'Inga!'

She didn't answer, something inhuman staring out of her eyes like some dead spirit. Then something shifted and she seemed to recognize him.

'You!' she cried. He ran to her but she staggered away.

'Get away from me!'

'Inga – what's wrong?'

'Get away – don't you touch me!' She shoved him, reeling away.

'Come back!' But she wouldn't stop, so he had to go after her. Her steps were so wayward, he soon caught her, spinning her round. But before he could say a word, she flew at him, fists tearing at his chest, sobbing wildly.

Hakan held onto her, dogged. Where was Inga, the bright girl he'd known all his life? Who was this raving stranger?

He got hold of her fists, but she struggled harder, head writhing, frantic to get away. Bewildered, Hakan could only tighten his grip and hope for some kind of calm to settle.

At last she stopped struggling, but when she looked up, he was afraid.

He tried to speak – but the naked terror in her face stifled any words.

'Let me go.' Her voice was strangled with anguish. When he didn't, she lunged at him, screaming in his face. 'Let go of me! Don't you touch me – you mustn't touch me, you hear – NEVER!'

'What? Why? Inga—'

'You lied to me. You swore – swore an oath. We would be together, you said. All would be well, you said! You're a liar, Hakan. You lied to me! Now let me go!' Fear and hatred danced in her eyes.

Hakan could hardly grasp her words. Behind him, a woman's voice called her name. Then a deeper voice bellowed his own.

He glanced back. Tolla was emerging from the hall, and behind her the broad frame of his father, looking grim as thunder.

'I don't understand. What's going on here?'

Before anyone answered, Inga seized her chance. With a desperate wrench, she tore free and bolted out of his reach. But immediately, she stopped and turned.

She tore off her cloak, flinging it down; snatched off shawl and mantle, and threw them in the mud after it. For a moment, she stood, clad only in her crimson dress – the same she had worn the night of his feast. That night she'd had the curves of a fresh and lovely maid. Now the bulge of motherhood swelled her belly. She looked beautiful and wretched.

'You swore to me, Hakan,' she said. 'But now I am betrayed.'

Sobbing, she turned and ran out of the gate. Hakan stood there, mouth agape. As she vanished in a swirl of crimson, Hakan called after her.

'Let her go,' his father shouted.

Hakan turned. 'What's wrong with her?'

'I think you know, boy,' grabbing his son by the collar and flinging him towards the hall. 'Get inside.'

So it must be now. . . so be it.

Wordlessly, Hakan stalked ahead of his father past Tolla. They strode through the shadowy hall, sending kitchen thralls scurrying for cover.

They were soon in Haldan's chamber, the hide curtain pulled against prying ears. Torches sputtered in iron sconces as Haldan flung himself into his chair. His eyes flared bright under heavy brows.

Hakan knew that look – furious, threatened, ready to fight.

He knows our secret. That much was clear. But that didn't explain Inga's ravings.

'Sit down.'

'I won't sit – not till you tell me what's wrong with Inga.'

'Don't waste my time, Hakan. I know what's been going on.'

'Going on? What do you mean?'

'I *know*. Between you two – I know *everything*.'

He felt blood rush to his face, but he said nothing.

'Do you deny it?'

Shit on this. The Norns wove this long ago. 'No,' he said, setting his shoulders defiantly. 'Who told you?'

'She did.'

'Inga?' He could scarce believe she would betray their secret.

'She came to me just before you returned—'

'I'm going to marry her, Father. It wasn't meant to come out this way, but now you must know: I'll take no other for my wife.'

'You can't marry her,' barked his father, hard as granite. 'I told her the same.'

'You can't stop us. We love each other.' His plea sounded so weak he almost choked on it. 'It's what we both want.'

'You're not listening, boy. You cannot.'

'Why not?' snarled Hakan. *Don't say it. . . Don't say that bastard's name.*

'Because Inga is your sister.'

The word rang like a death-knell through his head.

Sister. . .

His heart stopped beating. . . Everything stopped. And then, suddenly, a black abyss tore open inside him, sucking all the breath right out of him. His father's face melted into shapeless shadow.

'*What*—?'

'Inga is my daughter. And your sister.'

Hakan's hands were shaking, his bones crumbling. He slumped forward, catching himself on the table.

'That's a lie,' he stammered. 'She's my cousin. Inga is my cousin.' *Why would he lie to me like this?*

'No, Hakan. She *is* my daughter.'

'But her parents – her father. . . was your brother. Her mother was Briga. . .'

'Briga was her mother, yes. But I am her father.' Haldan rubbed wearily at his eyes. 'Perhaps I should have told you this long ago. But I had my reasons for keeping it from you.' He raked his fingers through his dark hair. 'Sit down.'

Hakan sank onto the bench.

Inga is my sister. The words rang again and again.

When his father spoke, his words seeped into Hakan's mind through some black dream of another world.

He spoke of a time long ago, when he and his brother Halmarr were young men. Hard days for the Vendlings: the years of the Amunding wars. They had lost many.

After the last battle was won and Arnalf Crow-King slain at last, they sailed back across the Belt from Raumarika. With them, alas, they carried Halmarr's body.

Despite their hard-won victory, Haldan was bitter at his loss. Sorrow suffocated him, and though he had wife and folk around him, that night he felt utterly alone.

And the grief of Halmarr's wife, Briga, was terrible to witness. When she saw his body, she raved like one out of her mind. They gave him a warrior's funeral, and as his body burned, her cries at last dwindled.

All went to their beds. But Haldan's bed was a cold one and had been for some years. Sleep was impossible. The night was filled with terrors: ghosts of men he had slain, fallen comrades, his father and now his brother. Haldan had risen, and after hours of aimless wandering, his steps led him near his brother's dwelling.

A light flickered inside.

Opening the door, there she was, sitting alone, carving a groove back and forth in her table. He went in, figuring each might find solace in the other's words. Or even the other's silence.

'But it wasn't like that,' Haldan murmured. 'Instead I saw something I'd never seen before. A beauty kept only for my brother's eyes.'

She had talked a great deal. Of her past. . . Of the long drifting summers in her mountain home, far to the south. She had talked of loneliness, of longing. . . for something. Just one good thing that would last. She thought Halmarr was that. But everything was taken from her. Only she remained in this world. And now, she didn't want to.

Haldan remembered her talking low in the guttering light. Her soul torn yet soaring; her face so sad yet so lovely. 'A sight no man could resist. I saw the sun, and I was blinded. I wanted to feel its heat.'

He had reached out and stopped her knife. She had looked into his eyes, taken his hand and put it to her lips, already wet with tears. And without another word, the bench fell, and he was kissing her.

The darkness bade them forget their sorrows for a time. 'And all the while,' he added bitterly, 'your mother slept in my bed.'

He shook his head, remembering. 'Briga was like no other woman. She was pleasing enough to burn a hole in any man's soul.' He had slipped away before dawn, ashamed, his brother's ashes not yet cold.

Haldan took a pull at his cup, as if the memory was a flame that needed dousing.

'That's it?' Hakan's head was so laden with thoughts he couldn't even look up. 'What of Inga?' He found he could hardly utter her name.

'I returned to Briga later that day. But she was changed. Her passion vanished. I had come to invite her under my protection, but she wouldn't hear of it.'

Instead, Briga was filled with shame. They had dishonoured Halmarr, she said, binding Haldan with an oath: to guard the secret of those stolen hours. 'And so I have, until this day.'

'What. Of. Inga?' Hakan repeated in a whisper. He had to know. Had to hear the story to its end.

Haldan looked up sharply. 'Not long afterwards Briga's belly started showing. Between Halmarr's departure and that night the days were few enough that no one suspected the child wasn't his. But she knew. Halmarr's seed was weak, she told me. She knew the child was mine.'

Haldan was sure this would change her mind. He told her he would talk around Guthrun, that they would look after her. But instead Briga held him to a second oath: that the only way he could make amends for his betrayal was to honour the child as Halmarr's. 'If I had any honour, she said, any love for him, I would swear to do this. And only we two should ever know the truth.'

He had promised, and the child had grown within her. But as the child grew stronger, Briga grew weaker. Sickness often laid her low, and each time, she cared less and less for living. Her time came on a sudden, earlier than it should, before the break of spring.

'The birth was dreadful. Bad as your mother's death in its way. She was already so weak. Before it was done, her spirit left her. Tolla had hold of the baby's head and arms. The rest she pulled from a dead womb.' Haldan leaned back, expelling a long sigh. 'That child was Inga.'

Hakan took a deep breath and then vomited out his rage. 'Why didn't you just *tell* us!'

'I kept my oath. I'd sworn to safeguard my brother's name and honour.'

'Hel take your fucking oath! She's your daughter! Your *daughter*! Didn't she have a right to know who her real father is? All you gave her was another ghost to haunt her all these years. Do you even care?'

His father's voice was a whisper. 'It sickens me to admit it. I was ashamed of her. I *am* ashamed of her. Every day, her very life accuses me of my betrayal. Do you know how often I've asked myself if I only went to Briga that night with some evil intent? Whether I'd always wanted what was his—'

'You're still only thinking of yourself! Open your eyes! Look what your lie has led to. . .' But when his father had no reply, the destruction of everything Hakan had hoped for suddenly broke over him like a wave. He hung his head, crushed. 'You don't understand. I love her.'

'You know you can't marry her. A brother and sister can never lie together. It is against nature. Not even the beasts do such things.'

'But I already have. . .' he groaned. 'Don't you see? It doesn't feel against nature. It feels good and true and—'

'It doesn't matter how you feel. Things cannot be as you want them. I told Inga the same. You must forget whatever you feel for each other.'

As if it were so easy. As if I could cut out the love that fills my heart like a cancer. And the child. . . 'What of our child? What of the incestuous bastard that your lie has spawned? She carries your grandchild. This is your doing!'

196

'Then let its blood be on my hands. We will keep her condition a secret until her time is come. And then. . .'

'You'll never take my child,' snarled Hakan. 'I'll kill you before I see you do that.'

But Haldan seemed to care little for his son's threat. 'You'll see the sense in it soon enough. A child would embarrass the plans I have for your sister.'

Hakan could hardly believe his father's cold heart. 'And when were you going to tell me these plans?'

'At the proper time.'

'The proper time!'

'It has all been arranged. Inga knows it, and she *will* obey.' Haldan cleared his throat. 'She is to marry Konur, heir to the Karlung lands.'

'No,' replied Hakan, a weird smile curling on his lips. 'She won't.'

Haldan lurched to his feet, slamming a fist on the table. 'You test my patience sorely, boy. I am lord of these lands as one day you will be. You'll soon learn there are greater concerns than a pair of mooning lovers. I'm sorry if your heart must suffer. But if it must, so be it. Inga will marry whomever I choose for her. It's decided. Konur shall have her.'

'No, Father – he will not.' Hakan laughed, and soon his laughter grew to fill the chamber. The rafters echoed with his mad cackle, mocking the great Lord of Vendlagard.

For a heartbeat, doubt glimmered in Haldan's eye. 'He will.'

'He's going to find that very hard.'

'What do you mean? Why?'

'Because I *killed* the bastard!'

His father gaped, eyes aflame. 'What?' he whispered.

'Stuck him in the heart.'

Haldan covered his face. 'You stupid, selfish, hot-headed fool! Do you realize what you've done?'

Hakan nodded, unable to shift his weird grin. 'You mean what *you* have done. More fruit from your honourable lie.'

Suddenly, there was a scraping of wood as Haldan shoved back his chair. The high seat toppled with a tremendous crash and Haldan was across the table in an instant. Hakan lurched backwards, surprised at his father's speed, and before he'd blinked, strong hands were around his neck, and they went sprawling to the floor.

Hakan thrashed wildly under his father's weight, but Haldan was heavier by far. Hakan writhed, eyes bulging, ears ringing.

And then, as abruptly, all was still. His father stopped. Frozen. Listening. His grip slackened, eyes darting to the doorway. Then Hakan heard it too.

A thin, whistling noise.

It was moments before he realized what it was: a woman's wail – high, piercing, desperate. Father and son looked at each other, confused. Then panic sank cold fingers into Hakan's heart.

He shoved off his father. Haldan yielded, rolling clear. Hakan jumped to his feet and rushed to the doorway, hauling aside the drape.

He ran and ran, ignoring the pain – out of the chamber, through the hall, into the yard, summoned all the while by the ever-loudening wails. He ran, horror rising in his chest.

The sound led him to the stream running down to the wash-pool. Another scream. He quickened his pace. He could see the alder tree. The memory of her body flashed through his mind – supple and white in the moonlight.

He reached the bank, dropping down onto the clearing around the pool. His eyes snatched at details: Tolla on her knees in the muddy grass, apron crumpled under her chin, the dreadful wailing spiralling from her mouth into the leaden sky. Next to her, Einna, rolling on her belly, head twisting in anguished sobs.

And beyond her. . .

He stopped.

There in the pool was Inga.

The water was smooth as silver. Only her pale fingers and the crimson bulge of her belly broke its surface. He stepped to the edge of the pool and looked down on her, unable to blink.

She was floating just under the surface, suspended in the crystal water, her eyes shut. Her fair features were calm. . . as if her mind had flown far away in a dreamless sleep. The folds of her favourite dress quavered with the current, her long dark hair fanning out about her face. Strange billows of crimson clouds swirled about her body, moving as though to some silent dance. An eddy from somewhere in the depths teased the dark tresses around her neck, drawing them aside.

And then he saw it.

A gash slashed deep across her throat. A wound like he'd never seen – ugly, gaping, livid against her delicate skin. Blood was leaking from it in weak ripples. Something glinted at the bottom of the pool. The image of Inga's knife rippled up from the silt, glittering.

No words came. No thoughts.

All he knew was that he could no longer hear Tolla's wailing, nor Einna's sobs. Some other sound was blotting them out, filling his ears, ringing in his head like the shrieks of the whole world in the Final Fires. And as he sank to his knees, he couldn't have said what the new sound was.

He didn't know that he was screaming.

CHAPTER THIRTEEN

The women would long tell of the anguish on Haldan's face when he saw Inga floating amid those red clouds.

He arrived moments after his son and dragged him screaming from the pool. But Hakan, mad with grief, tore himself free and staggered away from the horror of his beloved sister.

Blindly he ran towards the shore, dark clouds sweeping in from the sea, blanketing everything in a downpour. He ran and ran, legs screaming, heart tearing at his chest, till he collapsed, sobbing, among the dunes, the wind sweeping over him, the rain hammering his head.

He lay a long time, clothes soaked through, not caring whether he lived another day. Finally the cold began to seep through him and he took himself to the wood where they had so often made love. There, he found shelter. He squatted at its edge, his mind lost in the grey swirl of the sea and the rain.

The weight of the skies crushed his heart. No one's death could make her his now. No word, no reason. No strength, no wisdom. Nothing. She was dead. Their child was dead.

The storm swelled. Lightning lashed the sky. He cowered back, overwhelmed by the power of the gods, all courage shattered by their cruelty.

A league away, thunder stirred among the black-bellied clouds. The rumble rolled on and on. Closing his eyes, he saw Inga again. This time, there were no eddies plucking like invisible claws at her hem. This time, the crimson cloth whirled in delight. She was clapping, face bright, as a thousand fists beat upon the tables. *Rumbling. . .*

'A telling, a telling!'

He remembered. A telling they had, all right. *Beauty and love are slaughtered like swine*, the *vala* had cried. *You must drink the cup of sorrow to its dregs.*

Hakan shivered, shaking off the images of that night, his back stiff against the knotted bark of a tree, the rain running down his neck.

The fates of men are graven on the World Tree. They cannot be undone. The words echoed again. Now Inga's fate was settled. *Beauty and love are slaughtered. . .*

Rage ground his heart. Night was falling. He stood and peered into the listless banks of rain, shrouding the sea in gloom. The road he was fated to walk stretched away, bleak and murky.

But he had decided.

Walk it, he would.

When he returned, his face was dark as the night and changed. Before, some might have looked upon him and seen a youth. But now grief had wiped away all trace of boyhood.

He passed furtive figures skulking from the rain, but none dared approach him or utter a word as he stalked into the hall. He felt their eyes upon him.

The place was an open grave now. His beloved home, laced with the tang of death. He had to get away.

There was no sign of his father or Tolla. He hurried to his purpose, pulling off his wet things and finding a clean undershirt and tunic. He dug out his winter cloak from his chest of belongings, hesitating only to smell the wolf-skin trim. Inga had made him this, too. A token to remind him of the twilit dusk when he had gone back for her. A lifetime ago. . .

He shook away the memory. He'd shed enough tears for one day.

He went to the armoury, took a long-knife, his axe and shield. Another knife for good measure. 'Never be more than a pace from your weapons on the road,' his father often said. *Aye, and have plenty of them.*

He stopped, an idea coming to him. His mouth tightened. There was a kind of justice to it. His father wouldn't see it that way, but he was beyond caring.

He shouldered his weapons and hurried to his father's chamber. Waited a moment, listening. Hearing nothing, he pulled aside the drape. The chamber was empty. Fresh torches had been lit. And there, mounted on the wall, was what he sought: two ring-swords. He lifted down the lower one.

Wrathling. His uncle's sword.

He drew it and held it to the torchlight. The blade gleamed nearly white, polished to perfection, edges sharp as Loki's wits. He played with its weight: iron tempered with hard steel, so skilfully balanced it danced in his hand.

It would do.

Hastily, he sheathed the blade, bundling it up in his cloak. When it was done, he stood a moment for a last, deep breath. The smell of his father's chamber – its heady mix of wood and leather, rush smoke and tallow – filled his nostrils. He'd known it since infancy, but now it would be nothing but a memory.

Thus, the Norns had woven.

With that, he was gone.

He strode down the hall, wanting to be away. A couple of thralls gaped, but he paid them no heed, hurtling through the doorway and into the night.

The first lick of rain had fallen on his face when he stopped. His father appeared out of the shadows and moved hesitantly to the light.

He was almost unrecognizable, his thick dark hair plastered across his face, his ice-blue eyes soft with sorrow. Rain dripped from his sodden clothes.

'I couldn't find you.'

'I've nothing to say to you,' Hakan scowled.

'Where are you going?' said Haldan, noticing his attire.

'Away from here. Far away as I can.'

'I understand you're upset, my son. It's been a terrible day.'

'Save your words! They're too late. It all comes too late.'

Haldan shook his head wretchedly. 'I didn't foresee this. How could I?'

'If you had just told the truth. . . I never would've loved her. Not like I do. But you kept us ignorant.' He leaned in, menacing. 'It was you – *you* who brought death on your own daughter!'

'If you'd but told me of this passion,' pleaded Haldan. 'But you kept it from me. Both of you kept it—'

'You're a liar! A liar! And now she's dead.' Hakan wanted his words to stab like steel.

When his father spoke, his voice was unnatural, pained, the words unfamiliar. 'Can you. . . forgive me?'

'Forgive you! How could I forgive you? Inga is dead!' he cried. 'Our child is dead. You might as well have ripped my heart out. Your lie, your lie . . . !' He tried to steady himself, bridling his anger. 'Without her, this place is death. Without her, I cannot stay.' He levelled his eyes at his father. 'I'm leaving Vendlagard for ever.'

'Leaving? You can't leave!'

'You chose a lie. Now I must choose.' Hakan dropped his voice, hardly able to form the words. 'I renounce my birthright as your son. I am your Chosen Son no more.'

'Don't be such a fool—'

'I'll not be silenced!' He had to be heard. Had to say it. 'You betrayed us both – son and daughter. I swore an oath to you – to serve you, even to death. You swore you'd protect me as my lord. You broke your oath. So I renounce mine. Let the Norns mark me an oath-breaker if they must. I will not stay.'

'What else have you but this place? Your blood binds you to it. You're a Vendling. Your name and Vendlagard are one.'

'Then I renounce my blood! I renounce my name!'

'You don't mean that.'

'Don't I? I won't stay here. Better live a nameless wanderer than stay here with you in this open grave you've dug.'

'You selfish little fuck!' Haldan suddenly exploded. 'Shit on your wounded heart! You're a murderer now, boy. You've brought war on your own people. You can't run from your duty. You must stay and reap the slaughter you've sown.'

'It was you who sowed it long ago. When you lay with your brother's wife.' Hakan knew that would sting. 'If the Whisperer wants blood for his blood, let him take yours.'

'Honour demands you stay. Vendlagard is your home.'

'How can you speak of honour? You who couldn't tell the truth to your own children. No,' he shook his head with finality. 'I have no home now.'

His father glared at him a long time. So long, Hakan half-expected him to fly at his throat again. Instead, all of a sudden, he crumpled forward, trying to enfold his son in his arms. 'My hand bears much fault, it's true,' he groaned. 'But there were things beyond my doing that brought about her fate.'

Hakan allowed his embrace a moment, but found it sickened him. Without warning, he shoved his father so hard the Vendling lord missed his footing and fell on his backside in the dirt. 'You think you can heal this with a hug?'

'I won't beg for forgiveness. By the gods, I don't deserve it. You're right – I lived a lie, though I persuaded myself I did it for good.' He spat bitterly. 'Now I see. . . The honour of the dead is worth little against the love of the living.' He scowled. 'Bah! Was it even honour? It was pure shame that hid the truth. And it's poor Inga who suffers for it.'

'Well, she suffers no more,' said Hakan, voice flat as a windless sea. 'We suffer for her. You and I.'

His father glanced up, and Hakan watched grief suddenly engulf him. He dropped his head between his knees and uttered a long mournful moan. 'Oh my daughter, my daughter! Sweet Inga – how I should have loved you! You were so beautiful. . . Inga, my darling. . .' Tortured sobs overtook his lamenting. Even in the gloom, Hakan saw tears streaming in silver trails down his beard.

A dutiful son would have reached out, the sight of a father so distressed awakening some pity. But he felt nothing.

'Aye – go ahead and weep. Weep for your daughter. Perhaps that stone heart feels something after all.' He shifted the weight of the gear on his shoulder. 'Farewell, Father. You'll not see me again.'

Haldan's face shot up, and he fell forward on his knees, catching at Hakan's tunic. 'No – Hakan! My son. You can't go! I can't lose you as well. Not with all the others.' His eyes were wild with despair.

'You lost us all a long time ago,' said Hakan coldly, prising off his father's fingers. 'You are the last of the Vendlings. Farewell.'

With that, he turned and walked away. And though his father's cries arced into the night, he didn't look back.

PART TWO

THE STRANGER

CHAPTER FOURTEEN

Princess Aslif Sviggarsdottir tasted salt on her lips, but she refused to wipe away her tears.

No one shall think I'm ashamed to weep for my brother.

The funeral pyre flared red against the grey waters of the distant firth.

No, she was not ashamed. Just broken-hearted. In a world of heroes, none had been so fearless as her brother. She had adored Staffen since she was a little girl, and he already a young man. And he adored her adoration. But she was not blind. She knew he was proud. Too proud for all men to love him. She had forgiven him that. It was only the brittle pride of a boy, hiding behind a handsome face and a strong frame.

Still, he'd always had a tender way with her. It was he who named her 'Lilla', the name by which most folk knew her. She liked it a deal better than the name her parents chose.

Now she wept for him. Wept as the smoke engulfed his comely face for ever.

The drums beat their doleful rhythm. The *godi*'s cries grew in fervour, as the greatest lords of her father's council looked on, features hard as idols. Down the slope, a ring of spearmen cordoned back the vassals and thralls of the Uppland halls, come to watch their king's heir take the road to Hel.

She watched his beard shrivel in the heat; watched his fair skin blackening. For the first time in five years, Lilla was glad her mother was not alive. *Not to see this day.*

The *godi* wailed on at the dusk.

'Enough!' The exclamation jolted her from her grieving. Her father's voice. The *godi*'s chanting ceased. All eyes went to the king. 'You've said enough. Let him burn.'

'The words must be spoken,' insisted the *godi*, 'if Hela's gates are to welcome your son.'

'My son needs no announcing to the Queen of Hel. If there is no welcome for him in that place, theirs is the dishonour, not his.'

The *godi* shuffled about, unsure what to do. Then, making up his mind, he gave a servile bow and backed away.

Lilla felt a hand slide into hers, soft fingers threading her own.

'It's the smell I cannot abide. Like some swine-roast at a feast. How it lingers in the nostrils.' Lilla turned. Her eyes met with the emerald gaze of Saldas, her father's wife. The queen's dark beauty, suddenly so close, startled her despite her grief.

'Forgive me, I shouldn't think such things.' Saldas smiled, and then noticing Lilla's tears, her voice softened. 'Why, child, you are crying.' She pulled Lilla's head to her bosom. Lilla's nostrils filled with perfume, spicy and subtle. She tried to pull away, but Saldas held her. 'Such a sad business.' She stroked Lilla's hair. 'You two were so alike. This beautiful hair. Like honey. . .' She trailed off, fingers still caressing her. 'You must take comfort from those who love you. Your father, your brother. . .'

Lilla glanced at the only brother left her now. Sigurd was the image of their father, down to his dark curls and the brooding lines about his mouth. She felt a pang of sorrow for him. His life would change now. But was he ready for it? She wondered what he was thinking. His eyes were dry, gazing at the smoke curling high to the east.

Perhaps it's too hard to watch our brother burn.

Saldas lifted Lilla's chin and gazed deep into her eyes. '. . . And, of course, you have me.'

'I know, Lady Saldas.' Lilla's throat was tight from crying. 'I thank you for it.'

'You must call me "mother" now. Haven't I told you this?'

'Yes. Mother.' Lilla had come to hate the word. It was a betrayal. A lie. *And yet, I still say it.* She was twenty summers old, Saldas hardly twelve summers more. Whatever Saldas was to her, it was not a mother. Yet there was something about her that made Lilla feel small. Something that shrank her will. Made her obey.

She pushed away, with more resolve this time. The queen yielded.

A gust of wind goaded the pyre. The flames roared in reply.

'Where is Bodvar?' It was her father again, as if the surging fire had ignited some fresh impulse. He looked about, and Lilla saw his eyes, usually so steady, were filled with grief. And anger. 'Come – where is he?'

'Here I am, my Lord Sviggar,' croaked the voice of the Earl of Vestmanland, separating from the king's retinue. *Earl Bodvar*

213

has aged of late. His braids, usually as rusty as his voice, were showing a few threads of silver, and the lines on his face had deepened.

'I want you to find whoever did this.'

Bodvar hesitated, confused. 'Forgive me, lord. I understood this was an accident.'

'An accident?' scoffed her father. 'A king's heir is never killed by accident. Someone is responsible for Staffen's death.'

Her brother Sigurd answered in Bodvar's stead. 'Father, we scoured those woods for days. We found nothing.'

'Then scour them again! Bodvar – this was your land. You will *live* in those woods till you find whatever did this. Beast or man – whatever stole my son, you bring them to me!' His voice dropped to a mutter. 'His blood will be avenged.'

Lilla noticed the earl's face bristle. Bodvar was a stubborn one, and not afraid to speak his mind, not even before a king. But he must have thought better of it, instead bowing his head. 'I will, lord.'

'Lord, you know this isn't the only unexplained death in your realm of late,' said Finn, the amiable young warrior appointed her father's bodyguard. 'There are stories—'

'I know.' Sviggar's brooding eyes passed like a ghost over his son's body, hardly visible now beneath the hungry flames. 'I know.'

CHAPTER FIFTEEN

Darkness. Despair.

The words wrapped him like a cloak.

Ahead he could see almost nothing.

He braced himself against another heave of the boat, the murky swell rolling her salt-scarred belly. Ice-gusts from the north gnawed at the ropes. The cold in his body had dulled to a weary ache.

Dawn was some way off, perhaps another hour. Best he knew, he was still heading east. Gotarland couldn't be far off. Crossing the Juten Belt was not a long voyage, but could be ugly, even deadly, in an autumn squall.

So now he'd added thievery to his list of crimes. Esbjorn's skiff had been there for the taking. Hakan had rigged it quickly and set his course due east across the Belt. But he knew no one would come after him. Esbjorn was dead: ashes on the Western Ocean. And dead men have no need of boats. Nor of anything else.

Hakan longed for sleep. The worst of the storm had passed,

but with it the sweet distraction of fear. Fear that had choked him. Fear that had coursed through his veins like liquid metal, weighing him down, while the wind lashed his face, tore hungrily at his clothes, and the black sea threw wave after wave over his little craft. He'd clung on doggedly, knowing not east from west, nor north from south, nor even *why* he should cling to life when all he loved in the world was gone. Only that with each white-topped breaker, he surfed the line between life and death, hardly caring into which the raging sea would cast him, vomiting up every last ounce in his belly, as if the storm would only rest once the last vestige of Vendlagard was purged from his body.

At last the squall had moved on and with it the turmoil out there in the sea's darkness. But now the turmoil within him surged anew. Now he was free to think again, and every thought cut like a knife.

How? *How* had he been slung out onto these spiteful waters? *How* had he become severed from all he'd ever known?

Beauty and love are slaughtered like swine.

Not even a day had passed since. . .

He shuddered, wondering whether he could ever blot out the image of her: floating, lifeless, her warm blood swirled in those cold eddies. He opened and closed his eyes; the image was the same. He saw her clearly as if she were there in front of him. Just as she had been.

He must go far away from that place. Flee from that memory until he was free of it at last. Flee into the darkness ahead wherever it took him. That was the only course.

And yet a colossal sorrow crushed his heart. Why had she been so quick to draw the knife? *Why?* In a single stroke, she'd killed the world and him with it, and all because of their father's lie. But for that lie, Inga would be alive. Her songs, her laughter, her earnest eyes – all would be well, even now. He closed his eyes and felt the moan rise in his throat. *Why?* His happiest moments had been with her. How he had hoped to share with her even happier ones in the years to come!

No. It was all a lie. Every one of his dreams, every one of his memories – *all of it, a fucking lie.* She was his sister and every day of his life had been leading to this one. A path to an abyss. And now he was falling and falling. . . beyond love, beyond blood and honour, beyond hope.

Anger suddenly surged forward on the wave of his sorrow. If Inga was dead, why should he live? Their love was cursed. The heart that nurtured a love so foul deserved to die. Was better dead.

He gazed out over the sleek black waters. 'How easy it would be. . .' he murmured. How easy to slip into their cold embrace. Was that a sweet whisper, bidding him come – a hushed promise of peace? Was it *she* who called him? It would be but a little thing. A moment's shock as he hit the water. Life draining from his body, the cold sea enshrouding him, and then. . .

Death would come. His end in this world.

But what awaits me in the next? What if there were no end to this pain? What if the torn bonds of love, the broken promises, the blood staining his hands, the burning *rage*. . . what if these were his in any world – of the living or the dead? And whither would he go? Self-slaughter was no path to Valhalla. To some other realm of darkness then, from which there was no crossing back, where he would fester, nursing the deformity in his heart he had foolishly called love.

If death brought no relief, what was its purpose?

He scanned the horizon. A north wind licked at his bow. Dawn was coming on, bringing with it a grizzled morning and in the distance a few smudges of land. His skin prickled with the cold. In spite of all that surged in his heart, he pulled his damp cloak tighter around him and resolved to put away dark thoughts for now.

Ahead the land of the Gotars splintered into a thousand islands. He looked up at the sail that had withstood the night's winds. *Esbjorn built his boat well at least. . . Poor bastard.*

The day was still new when he spied another sail emerge from an inlet and then swing south. He decided to follow it, feeling little better than a stray dog that might trail any peddler's cart. The sail continued south until midday when it turned inland again. Hakan followed it between two shallow islands, figuring it must be headed for some kind of haven. The water grew calmer. Hakan settled beside his tiller. At least the terror of the sea was behind him. For now.

He spied a headland and on it a handful of dwellings crowding the shore, dirty twists of smoke rising from their roofs. It looked more like a trade-place than a farmstead or stronghold. A few boats came and went from a wooden jetty. Others were hauled onto the strand. He could see a few figures moving about on the shoreline.

Suddenly the thought pricked him that these were not his people. Did he even have a people any more? He was a stranger. Here. Everywhere. A man owed nothing. Trusted by no one, with no one to trust.

He tried to shake off the morbid daze that still shrouded his mind. He needed his wits sharp and the jetty was barely a stone's throw off the bow and closing fast.

Quickly he wrapped up his weapons in his cloak, hoping to avoid attention, though he saw he could hardly conceal his shield. *Maybe a stranger isn't so remarkable in this place*, he thought. It was the best he could hope for. Besides, the folk on the quayside had the look of traders, not warriors.

He pulled down the sail as the craft eased alongside the jetty.

A man passing sacks out of a small cargo-boat to an underfed boy left off what he was doing and came to grab Hakan's skiff.

'Right there, fella!' he called, catching the rope Hakan threw.

He was a small man with a face so gaunt you could see every line of his skull. Though his eyes were quick enough, darting over Hakan and the contents of his boat in a moment.

'Not often an empty hold pulls up here.' The man had a queer high-pitched voice. He frowned. 'You friend or foe?'

Hakan could only return his question with a blank stare. It was too soon to be answering another man's questions. Too soon to speak. Too soon to go on. . . As if life had not just ended in a deluge of blood and tears. As if the Tree of Worlds was not burning to ashes about their ears.

. . . *As if she wasn't dead.*

'You understanding me, lad?' the man repeated. 'Friend – or – foe?

'I. . . I need a place to harbour, is all.' Hakan spoke uncertainly, as if dredging up each word from the bottom of the ocean.

'So he does speak then!' cried the other. 'Took you for a halfwit for a second there. Or an outlander, which is worse!' He gave a high-pitched giggle and set to chewing on his bristles,

219

considering the stranger. 'Dane, is it? Or a Jute, maybe?'

Hakan shook his head and forced himself to speak again. 'I'm of no blood. No place,' he said, his voice hoarse with salt-spray.

The man picked at the hollow of his cheek. 'Well, that's one Hel of an odd answer. But I ain't one to pry into a man's business if he don't want. Wherever you're from must be a bloody miserable place anyhow.'

'Huh?' Hakan looked up.

'Your face!' he cried, merrily. But when he saw the stranger didn't much appreciate his joke, the little man shrugged and dropped it. 'Well, it's too bad you didn't bring nothing from this mysterious place of yours. I'm putting together a cargo to run south to Torsvik. There's always room for more, as I say.'

'What is this place?'

'Freyhamen.' The man set about tying off the rope.

Freyhamen? Torsvik, he'd heard of, but never this place.

'What you want here anyhow?' said the other, straightening up.

'There was a storm. I—'

''Course, that's it – so you said – needed a harbour, didn't you?' The man looked Esbjorn's boat over. 'Must be a sturdy old girl,' he said, giving the hull a kick.

'Finest skiff ever took to water,' replied Hakan, without thinking. It wasn't so far from the truth. And then a thought occurred to him. 'Say, folks round here – are they. . . rich?'

'Rich? That depends. Rich enough for what?'

'To trade this.' Hakan wrapped his knuckles on the gunwale.

'My, you are in a hurry, ain't you!' chuckled the merchant.

'Well?' It wasn't much of an idea. Hardly more than the next step into the darkness. But he'd sooner hang than risk another storm. He had always hated the sea. All sane men did, far as he reckoned.

The merchant eyed the boat up and down. 'Sure, she's a nice bit of work. But it ain't how rich folks are. It's what you'd take for her counts.'

Hakan shrugged. 'Silver.'

The merchant sucked his teeth. 'Not a lot of folk too free with their silver round here. Nope – none too free at all.'

When the merchant offered nothing more, Hakan grew impatient. 'Well, are *you* one of 'em or aren't you?' The last thing he felt like doing was haggling with this scrawny wretch. How could he be working trades when her body was hardly cold?

'Me! No, no. Besides, I wouldn't have no silver till I'm back from Torsvik.'

'Something else then.'

The merchant scraped at his chin. 'Suppose I've a horse I'd let go.'

Hakan snorted. 'Have to be some horse to make that a fair trade.'

'A boat takes some looking after, you know,' protested the merchant. 'If you want a horse, you can have one. Otherwise, you're stuck with your planks and nails there.'

Hakan considered his offer. Was this really what he wanted? The skiff could still carry him home. He could still give up this madness and return to Vendlagard, beg his father's forgiveness, weep with him. . . Bury her.

No. No! He couldn't. Wouldn't. The skiff was a bridge that had to be burned. 'Is it far?'

The little merchant turned and pointed eagerly up the slope. 'Halfway up the edge of the village. Be there quick as you like.'

Hakan nodded. 'I'll take a look.' And stepping onto the jetty, he threw his bundle over his shoulder with a clank.

'Nothing but a bit of worthless tin there, I suppose?' said the merchant, eyebrow cocked.

'Nothing worth your bother.' The warning edge in Hakan's voice wasn't missed.

'If you say so, friend.' The merchant didn't seem the type to start trouble, least of all with a man a head taller than him. Instead he led Hakan up the slope, shouting to the boy slouched nearby to watch over the goods on the jetty. Hakan hobbled after him, joints grating like rusted iron, his ankle sorer than ever he remembered.

'Something up with your leg?'

'Bit of sea-stiffness is all.'

The merchant grunted and led on.

Other folks went about their business – mending fishing nets, loading up meagre handcarts, stirring fire-pots filled with pitch. No one paid them much attention till a man on a pony rode over, heading them off. The rider's face was half-hidden under a hood, but his long chin jutted out under a nose sharp enough to crack an oyster.

'Good day, scrote! Got anything good for me?' growled the rider.

'Not today, Arald.' The merchant gave a servile duck of his head. 'Might be I'll have something for you from Torsvik next week.'

'You'd better.' The man turned to Hakan. There was the glint of a rheumy eye from under his hood. 'Who's this then?'

222

'An outlander. Me and him's working a trade.'

'Can't he speak for himself?' snapped the man called Arald. 'Well? What's your name?'

'It's not important,' said Hakan.

'Listen – I'll decide what's important and what ain't! Who the Hel are you?'

'No one.'

'What the fuck kind of answer is that? Where you from?'

'Nowhere.'

'No one from fucking nowhere.' The man snorted and spat out a gobbet of black phlegm beside his horse. 'What are you – some kind of ghost?' he sniggered.

'Just a man making a trade.'

'Is it? What we trading then?'

'That's between me and him. No business of yours.'

'Everything round here is my fucking business,' he snarled, leaning down at the stranger. Hakan caught the reek of his rancid breath on the breeze.

'It's nothing, Arald,' broke in the merchant. 'Just small beans.'

'Shut it, Arik! Now what you got in that bundle?'

'Nothing worth having.'

'Everybody's got something worth having, fella. Even if it's only the skin off his back.'

Hakan's hand went to the knife at his belt. 'You're welcome to come take a closer look. Can't promise you'll like the trade, though,' he said, loosening the knife in its sheath.

Arald ran a contemplative tongue along his rotten teeth, looking the stranger up and down. Suddenly, he smacked his lips and turned to Arik. 'You be sure to find me when

223

you're back from Torsvik. I want first call on the best of it. Understand?'

Arik nodded quickly. Arald spat at their feet. 'And you, stranger – I hope you know your shit from your clay. Arik's a sneaky little scarecrow.' He sniggered again, tugged on his reins and rode off.

'My kinsman.' Arik pulled a sour face. 'An arsehole, as you doubtless gathered.' He sighed. 'Come on, stranger. Ain't much further.'

They trudged along the edge of the village till Arik trotted ahead towards a modest-looking dwelling with a byre out back.

A towering woman with a greasy blonde plait appeared. Arik's wife, Hakan guessed, wondering how a man so small kept a woman like that where he wanted her. But the merchant soon dispatched her to prepare some hot food and she went docilely enough.

A boy's head crept around the doorpost, peering shyly at the stranger through a filthy fringe.

'Get on in and help your mother,' snapped Arik. The head vanished. 'My lad, Haki. The littl'un. T'other's down there.' He nodded back towards the jetty. 'Now, wait till you see my beauty.'

Arik's 'beauty' was a dusty-coated mare that had a pig and a couple of goats for company. Hakan wondered whether he wouldn't do better riding one of them instead.

'You actually feed this thing?'

'Every day,' crowed Arik. ''Course, I've seen handsomer animals, but she's got grit. She ain't fast, but she'll get you there.'

Hakan grunted, far from convinced. She was a sorry sight, but he just wanted to be away. Away from the sea. Away from this place. Away from other people. 'Toss in a bridle, a couple of rye-loaves, five marks of cheese and a skin of ale, and you have a deal.'

Arik pulled at his chin and made a show of weighing up the offer, but they both knew he could have thrown in his son for free, and still been on the better side of the trade. 'Aye – I reckon I could stretch to that.'

'And a few hours' sleep by your fire.'

'Whatever you wish.'

Hakan ran his palm down the horse's nose. 'She have a name?'

'We named her after the goddess Idun. On account of her love for apples.' Arik winked.

'Idun,' Hakan repeated, the horse's breath warm against his fingers.

The food Arik's wife had prepared was little more than gruel mashed up with chunks of salted herring, but it was scalding hot. Hakan devoured it without a word, trying to remember the last hot meal he'd eaten. It was before. . . Before his father, before Inga, before Konur even. Everything good was *before*. The small merchant sat by, whittling a piece of wood in silence, letting him eat uninterrupted.

When Hakan had finished, he murmured his thanks and, still clutching his bundle, fell back on a sheepskin and let exhaustion engulf him at last.

He had longed for dreamless sleep. But his eyes were hardly shut than he dreamed he was gulping from a skin of ale, more and more until the liquid was gushing from his mouth down his body. The ale rose around him, submerging him, drowning him. And suddenly it wasn't ale but the freezing sea, and he was kicking and kicking for the air. He touched sand, broke the surface to see the strand at the Skaw. Above him, the stars were shining, and a wolf was there on the dunes, calling to the cold night. Inga was there in a linen shift. He looked and the shift grew darker, as if the moon had cast a shadow, till he saw it was no shadow, but blood; blood running down her breasts and bare arms, over her fingers onto the handle of an axe. She ran at him, screaming, and he saw now he held a child, and Inga was raising the axe, and he was shouting for his father, but he knew his father wouldn't save him because he had foresworn his oath. And the child was wailing, and Inga screamed and screamed, and the axe fell, biting deep into his arm.

Hakan sprang up, breathing hard, his cheeks wet with tears. The scars in his arm ached. His head throbbed. He saw two solemn eyes staring straight at him. Arik's little son. Startled, the boy rushed outside, yelling that the man was awake.

Hakan looked about, feeling groggy. The fire burned on; a different pot hung over it, but otherwise the room was the same. Footsteps squelched in the mud. Arik appeared in the doorway. 'Had a good rest?'

'I think so,' Hakan whispered, his head still pounding.

'Must've needed it. Been out half the afternoon.'

'I'm grateful. You didn't have to do this.'

'A man never knows when he might need a favour back,' said Arik, cheerfully. 'Anyways, my lad has secured your boat. And everything's ready for you. Horse's all set. So now – where're you headed?'

Where, indeed?

It was a bitter question.

226

Hakan stood up. Pain crackled down his legs. Suddenly, he had to get out of there, had to clear his head. 'I need some air,' he mumbled, snatching up his bundle and shoving past Arik.

'Well, we ain't going nowhere,' the merchant called after him.

But Hakan wasn't listening. He blundered on, away from the village towards a bluff overlooking the harbour and, beyond, the sea.

Reaching its lip, he threw down his bundle and dropped to his haunches, looking west, out over the waves. Towards his home.

Except it isn't my home any more.

Loneliness weighed like lead in his heart. Suddenly he wanted to see his land again. Had to. He looked about, and there, a little back from the bluff's edge, stood an old beech tree.

He threw himself at it, hauling himself up through its branches as if pursued by the slaves of Hel. When he reached as high as he could go, he turned to the west and scanned the horizon. There, faint in the distance, he could just make out a sliver of land.

Jutland. The land of his fathers.

Would he never go back? Never?

His gaze lingered on the horizon a long time until he noticed a mist slipping down from the north, swallowing up everything. The seam of land in the distance disappeared into the greyness until he could see it no more.

That's how you must remain to me. . . For ever. I shall never return. Let my life to this day be cloaked in darkness, sealed by this vow. I swear I will never tell of it.

'Never,' he said aloud.

His father had named him Hakan – his 'Chosen Son'. But the Chosen Son was dead. A stranger now walked in his shoes. That would be the name by which he was known.

Erlan: *Stranger.*

Hakan's life must end. The life of Erlan would be his new beginning.

On the ground, picking up his bundle, he realized he still had no answer to Arik's question. Where *was* he headed?

Trudging back, he tried to figure what to do. Until yesterday, he knew his path. But love had led him only to death. He'd foresworn his land and his birthright. He was no farmer. No craftsman of any skill. He had neither the cunning nor the greed of a merchant. What else had he to offer? What had he ever done?

He had a killed a man. More than one.

Was that all he was? A killer.

He could kill again.

Hadn't his father impressed on him again and again what a bloody world they lived in? In a world like that, there would always be need for a killer. But if he put himself in the service of some lord. . . Such a man should be a lord worth serving. A lord greater even than his father. Maybe the greatest lord in all the land. No – in all the wide world!

Who is that man?

He turned the question over in his mind. It was something. Some scrap of purpose. Some frayed thread to cling to.

Service to a great lord.

He tried to imagine himself there – in another man's hall,

taking another man's salt. Another life. A life alone. *A life without her.*

Suddenly he was bent double, emptying the contents of his stomach into the grass. Bile tasted bitter in his throat. Bitter as his own fate.

He swore and spat into the dirt. What was another lord to him now? What did any of it really matter? What were blood-oaths or honour or loyalty? Maybe he should just wander the earth. A man cursed. An outcast. A stranger with a sword.

His hand fell absently on the sword hilt buried under his cloak. With a sudden jerk, he pulled it clear of the bundle and unsheathed it. Even in the dull afternoon light, the blade gleamed like a sunray. *Wrathling* – a sword to grace the very gods. For long years it had lain idle in its sheath, hanging unblooded on the wall of his father's chamber.

He cut the salted air. Once. Twice. The blade sang with each stroke. Here was a different call: the call of steel. The call of red deeds, and valour.

If his own fate had fallen into death and darkness, surely the fate of this shining sword was not yet done.

He grimaced, and slipped it back in its sheath.

It was but a thread. His only thread. And yet, in the darkness of his pain, it seemed to shine like gold.

Like the first ray of a mighty dawn.

'I'm looking for a man,' Erlan began, back in Arik's yard. 'A lord. . . in need of a warrior.'

'You are a warrior, then.' Arik cocked his head. 'I knew it. Said so to my son when you pulled in.'

'Then tell me – is there any king in this land? This *is* the land of the Gotars?'

'Aye, we're Gotars of the west, for many leagues wherever you go. But we've no king. We have chieftains, seated in different places.'

'Who is yours?'

'There's our clan headman, Ingvar Bardasson. You met his son, Arald. But Ingvar's a scabby-arsed bully, worse than his son. You're better spending a lifetime shovelling shit than serving him. Anyways, his hall isn't a great one – more a farmstead. Same as most of the Western Gotars. We have our leaders and councils and that, but you want a king, or some fella who needs a warrior like yourself.' He gave a crafty smile. 'But it ain't just a question of need.'

'What do you mean?'

'First off, you're an extra mouth to feed. Fine, if another warrior's wanted. But who wants another mouth with winter coming on? Those that go raiding are likely done for the year. And none of our folk plan on any fighting. Least, not till next spring, if they go at all.'

'I could be useful in other ways till then.'

'The crops are gathered and most sown for next year by now. It ain't much work keeping animals through winter. It don't help you're no Gotar, neither. People are wary.' He added, 'Don't suppose it'd help no more if you told the truth.'

'There must be something,' exclaimed Erlan, nearly choking on his frustration.

'I wish I could say different. But you'll struggle to find anywhere'll welcome a big man like you, who'll eat a sight more than some southern slave-girl, say,' said Arik. 'Hel, if you were one of them, I know a few places'd take you!'

'So you can suggest nowhere?'

Arik tugged at his beard. 'Hmmm – well, it's not much to go on, but now you press me, there is somewhere. I couldn't tell you much about it for certain.'

'Go on.'

'Best I know, it's a kingdom. A kingdom that lies far north and east. You'd have to cross to the land of the Sveärs. They're a fine bunch of villains if you ask me, but I've heard they have a mighty king.'

'You know his name?'

'Not I.' Arik shrugged. 'But the Svears are strong. Rich, too. Huh! Now I think on it, if they're rich, they'll have plenty of enemies.' He nodded. 'A place like that might use a fellow like you.'

'How far is it?'

'Couldn't say. It's a couple of weeks' ride to the edge of Gotarland, travelling north, maybe more. Hard going too, especially once the snows come. All forests and lakes, far as I know. As for the Sveär kingdom beyond. . .' He shrugged.

'A kingdom to the north,' mused Erlan. The gods knew it was little enough to go on. But little was all he had. He nodded. 'Very well. That's where I'll go. Is your horse ready?'

'Ready as she'll ever be.'

He fetched Idun, who looked about as dubious about taking a rider as Erlan was about getting atop of her. The promised provisions were slung over her rump. Erlan fastened his bundle over them and threw his shield on his back.

'You're sure she can take me?'

'Certainly,' returned Arik, with a grin that made him look more gaunt and greasy than ever.

Taking the reins, Erlan swung himself onto her back. Idun stumbled sideways. It wasn't much, but enough to make him catch his foot against the bundle. There was a clang of metal and Idun shied away. Erlan snatched at her mane, keeping his seat, but his bundle jerked loose and went crashing to the ground.

The cloak fell open, and Wrathling lay exposed in the mud.

Erlan swore, regaining control, but Arik was already picking up his sword. The little merchant gazed at the magnificent twin-gilt rings of Wrathling's hilt, bright eyes round with greed. 'Why, she's a beauty,' he whispered.

Erlan held out his hand. 'My things,' he insisted. But Arik seemed unable to tear his eyes away from the beautiful sword. Erlan snapped his fingers. 'Now!'

'Of course, of course,' replied the merchant hurriedly, wrapping up the cloak and passing up the bundle. 'Hoho, friend! Now if you wanted to trade *that*, you'd get a sight more for it than a horse.'

'I'd sooner trade my arm.'

'Aye,' muttered Arik to himself, 'it may come to that.'

'What did you say?' snapped Erlan.

'Oh, I was joking – just joking of course! Well, may the gods give you luck on the road, friend.'

'And you on the wave.' With that, the stranger touched his heel to Idun's flank and set his face to the north.

CHAPTER SIXTEEN

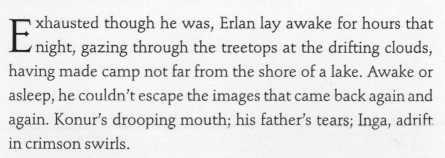

Exhausted though he was, Erlan lay awake for hours that night, gazing through the treetops at the drifting clouds, having made camp not far from the shore of a lake. Awake or asleep, he couldn't escape the images that came back again and again. Konur's drooping mouth; his father's tears; Inga, adrift in crimson swirls.

Questions chased images; images chased questions – each expanding and expanding, filling his heart and mind until it seemed his soul was a rudderless ship, adrift on an ocean of pain. He kept hoping he would come to the end of his grief, somehow slip his fingers round the edge of it – somehow contain it. But then another wave would rise up beneath him, and he would glimpse another endless horizon, rushing away from him.

He could only lie, looking upwards, the lonely ocean of grief lapping all around him, vast and deep and cold. At last, through the sheer exhaustion of his turning mind, sleep did come, dreamless and heavy.

And it was some hours later that he was awoken by Idun's warm, oaty breath on his face.

'Go away,' he hissed irritably, turning over under his cloak. Undaunted, Idun only butted him harder. He groaned, reaching out to shove her away.

But instead, all of a sudden, he sat up.

He sucked in deeply through his nostrils to see if his mind was playing tricks. . . There it was again, faint but unmistakable. No animal of the forest smelled like that. A sickly, sour reek that could only come from the stinking body of a man. A man he'd smelled before.

In a heartbeat he was on his feet, seizing his weapons and Idun's bridle. The dawn light was seeping under the branches. A little down the slope, he could see the lakeshore fanning out. He swung onto Idun's back.

'There's the whoreson!' cried a voice Erlan recognized all too easily. *Arald*. 'Quick, after him.' He glimpsed two figures stalking through the wood, each leading a horse. Jamming in his heels, Idun sprang away.

He hadn't expected much from her. Didn't get much either. But she went for the shoreline all the same.

'He's coming out – look sharp, lads!' shouted Arald, as Erlan cleared the trees. The lake opened out like a giant's silver platter. A few wreaths of mist lingered over its surface. He heard a clatter of hooves, and looked right to see two other riders kicking their horses over the flat grey stones.

He hauled the reins left, driving his heels, with only an instant to mark that one of the riders looked familiar.

Arik.

The weasel! So much for Gotar hospitality. Ahead of him, there was no one to bar his way, but his heart sank anyway. A large shoulder of rock sloped out of the trees, stretching fifty yards into the lake. The shoreline was blocked. Idun was struggling on the loose stones. There was no hope of going round in the water, no time to break back into the trees.

An arrow fizzed overhead, clattering against the rocks.

'Don't shoot him yet, you dopey potlicker!' yelled Arald. 'He's not going nowhere.' There was a loud half-witted cackle.

Erlan looked back. The four riders were closing in. He had little choice: he had to face them. He sawed on the bridle. Idun whinnied in protest as he jumped down, grabbing his shield and unsheathing his sword.

The feel of its hilt gave some comfort. Wrathling moved like a thing alive, as if it would guide his every stroke. He prayed to the Spear-God it would be so.

The men dismounted at a distance and came forward in a line. He swallowed, throat dry as dust.

Little Arik's grimace made him look more like a skull than ever. He had a throwing-axe in one hand and a cudgel in the other. On his left walked a much bigger man, helm pushed down tight, with a long-spear and a mailshirt covering his body. *He at least looks like he can fight.*

To Arik's right was a lad with wide-set eyes and a filthy tunic, wearing an open-mouthed grin and carrying a bow with a nocked arrow. On the end was Arald, long tongue licking wolfishly at blackened teeth, brandishing a double-headed axe.

Four men. Though Erlan judged only two were any use in a fight.

'Fancy finding you here, stranger,' sniggered Arald. The boils on his face were angry red. 'Far from home, ain't you?

Bet you're sorry you left off sucking your mama's teat now, uh?'

'Why didn't you kill me when I slept?' Erlan was addressing Arik, but eyeing each of them in turn. The lad with the bow was giggling like a simpleton.

'Well,' drawled Arik. 'Gotta be some standards of hosting, ha'n't there? Besides, I reckoned you a runaway outlaw, and a beggar one at that.' Arik cocked his head craftily. 'Till I saw that sword. Now there's a pretty thing.'

'You like it that much, come here, and I'll shove it up your arse.'

The simpleton laughed madly at that.

Arald chortled. 'We couldn't let an outlander come through here without some kind of contribution to my father's chests.' He twisted his neck till it cracked. 'Just wouldn't be right. Where's the respect? Now we gotta take it for ourselves, see?'

'If you didn't stink like pigshit, your work'd already be done.'

Arald's grin melted away. 'You're a dead man, stranger. You can make this easy, or you can make it hard. Give us the fucking sword, and we'll only slit your throat.'

Suddenly the simpleton whimpered, shuffling about like he was about to soil himself. 'You said, brother. You said.' He spoke with a lisp, like his tongue was too big for his mouth.

'Said what?'

The halfwit grinned and bucked his hips back and forward obscenely.

Arald snorted. 'Oh, aye. See, my idiot brother here doesn't have much luck with the sluts back at Freyhamen. And you with your pretty face, 'n all, he reckons you might oblige him.' Arald gave a lewd sneer. But Erlan didn't see it. He was watching the arrow pointing at his chest, how it wavered with every idiot chuckle.

'Didn't I tell you, stranger?' crowed Arald. 'Every man has something another man wants. What do you say? My brother might have cowpat for brains but he's hung like a mule!' They all broke out in gales of laughter.

But Erlan was remembering Garik's words. A shield is useless if you're outnumbered. Use it for one thing:

To narrow the odds.

He flung it at the halfwit.

The shield spun like a discus, straight for his head. But the halfwit saw the danger and, in shock, loosed his string.

The arrow whipped past Erlan's shoulder, the same instant the shield-edge caved in the idiot's face. The lad slumped to his knees and fell forward, quivering.

His arrow was heading straight for Idun, but startled by the sudden movement, she was already recoiling. The tip raked her neck, then skittered off into the rocks with a clatter.

The mare reared up with a shriek, barrelling past Erlan like a thunderclap, slamming full tilt into Arik and the big man in the byrnie. Arik went flying. His head hit a rock with a thud and he lay still.

Erlan didn't see what became of the big warrior because Arald had recovered his wits and came on with a scream like Hel's own spawn.

There was plenty of hate in his snarls, but his blows were ugly as his face. Erlan parried each blow, feeling a savage thrill as Wrathling danced in his hand. But he knew he had moments to win this fight. In the tail of his eye, the big man had picked himself off the ground and was coming to Arald's aid.

Erlan fell back a pace and drew his knife. Left-handed would have to serve. He threw it hard as he could. Arald saw the flying steel, flinched away. The movement saved his life, but only for the butt to smash into his eye. Arald squealed, doubling over, clutching his face.

Wrathling scythed upwards.

Erlan felt the blade slice bone and sinew. Arald screamed louder this time and dropped his axe, staggered back, shield gone, groping at the mess where his arm had been. His forearm hung by a few scraps of flesh. He fell writhing in the shallows.

But Erlan had no time to celebrate. The big man was there, squaring up. 'You won't find me so easy.' His voice rang through his helm. Through the eyepieces shone a cold glare. The man gripped his spear so tight, seemed his biceps would burst his byrnie. *Aye, and the biggest bastard biceps I ever saw.*

'They call me Barth the Boulder! Ain't no man living nor dead who's taken a slice off me. I will crush you.'

'Barth the Boulder?' Erlan gave a mad laugh. 'Is that for the rock in your head? I name you Shit-for-Brains if you do the bidding of that stinking fuck.' The sound of Arald's screaming still filled the air.

The Boulder came at him with a roar, spear-point darting like an adder. Erlan's arm worked fierce to keep his guard, springing forward when he could to cut at the Boulder's neck. But the big bastard was quick on his feet. Quicker than he ought to be.

Erlan's mind was working as hard as his blade. He had to get past that point, had to slow those feet so he could land a killing blow. But the Boulder didn't look like tiring.

Then he saw a way. He gave ground, edging into the shallows. Icy water filled his boots. The spearman came with him, and soon they were up to their knees. Wrathling cracked against the spear-shaft in a shower of spray. But his ruse was working. Now when he attacked, the Boulder struggled to stay clear.

He saw fear curdle the big man's face. The lunges became erratic, the Boulder's skill draining as he tired. But the Spear-God wasn't done yet. The rocks under Erlan shifted. He floundered, his guard faltered. The point shot past, its cold iron slicing his side.

The cut stung like a whip. He yelped in pain. The Boulder allowed himself a laugh. But the cut wasn't deep, and the gloating grimace under the Boulder's helm only maddened him.

Fury tore through him like a tempest. This wasn't how it would end. He wasn't going to die in some strange land at the hand of stinking thieves. Suddenly it wasn't the wound that incensed him. It was the pain inside, it was the darkness, it was the cold sea, it was the rage against the Nine Worlds and the gods that ruled them. . . it was Inga.

The Boulder must have seen something fearful because his grin vanished. Now it was his turn to retire, drawing them back into the shallows. Erlan rained down blows, muscles burning.

The water was ankle deep when the Boulder tripped. A fallen birch shimmered underwater. Barth went sprawling. Erlan leaped forward to finish him, but the Boulder swung his spear one last time, smashing the shaft against Erlan's wound. He screamed, falling, his point jamming in the rocks, twisting away, as he crashed on his enemy. The Boulder's face was inches from his. Instinctively, he seized his throat and began squeezing.

The warrior thrashed about, jettisoning his spear; Erlan crushed his hands tighter, rage strengthening his grip. Barth's head writhed, fighting for breath, his helm falling away. And suddenly, there was his face.

Erlan froze in shock. The cold, blue eyes, the hair black as jet, the heavy brow – they were *his father's*. They were – and yet. . . *couldn't be*.

Suddenly a meaty hand shoved back his head, thumb hooking his jaw. Pain jerked Erlan back into the fight. He squeezed tighter, bit down hard, tasted blood. That face, so familiar, raged, eyes wide with fear, bubbles of air streaming in silent screams under the shallow water.

But bitter fury filled him; his whole body burned with it. 'Die, you bastard, die!'

The Boulder's mouth gaped not two inches beneath the surface, but it was enough. Finally his hand weakened and fell away. The muffled screaming stopped. The terror went out of those ice-blue eyes. His father's lifeless face stared back at him.

Erlan flung himself away, gasping, arms and legs weak as a kitten. Relief enveloped him like the waters of the lake.

I must be losing my mind.

His chest heaved, and suddenly he began to sob with great lung-wrenching moans welling from the pit of his soul. He lay there, in the freezing water, weeping and weeping and weeping at how alone he really was.

You're to be a man, my son. Not a monster. His mother's words echoed, stark as winter. How in black Hel was he to survive this world without becoming a monster? How!

But his mother could never answer that. . . not now.

He'd always despised self-pity – yet here he was, a slave to it. For a long time, he lay staring at his shaking hands.

Murderer's hands.

At last, his sobs faded. He wiped away his tears and lifted his head. Arald was no longer screaming. Erlan sat up, listening to his own breathing, watching its mist float away on the still air.

Somewhere in the trees a crow cawed, jolting him from his daze. He scrambled up and turned to the body beside him, a heavy dread weighing on him.

But when he looked, the Boulder's face had changed. The dark hair and light eyes were the same, but the jaw was wider, the mouth oddly small. Erlan felt uneasy. The features were no longer his father's. A passing similarity maybe, but that was a stranger's face.

Slowly his anger ebbed away. He rubbed his eyes. The image was so clear. The look in those cold, blue eyes so wounded.

Yet I killed him anyway.

He shut away the thought, suddenly shivering with the cold, and turning his back, he went to retrieve his sword.

Arald lay motionless at the lake's edge, the stones all around him slick with blood. His arm was bent double, the flesh twisted, his face ash-grey, his long tongue drooping out of his mouth.

He was dead.

Erlan found his knife nearby, washed it and returned it to its sheath.

Arald's halfwit brother was a crumpled heap of limbs, his face smashed to a bloody maw. Erlan went over to Arik and found the merchant still breathing, but laid out cold.

241

'Come on, runt – wake up.' He gave Arik's leg a sharp kick. The merchant began to come around, blinking groggily up at the sky. Seeing Erlan over him, his eyes grew wide with fear.

'Seems Idun's none too fond of her old master.' Erlan put his boot on Arik's chest and drew his knife.

'Please, I beg you – don't kill me!' Erlan caught the acrid smell of fear leak into Arik's breeches.

He grunted. 'You think you deserve more of a chance than you gave me?'

'But it wasn't me,' he whined. 'I swear – Arald forced me to it.'

'Sure didn't look that way.'

'No, it's true. When you left, he asked all about you. I wouldn't tell him nothing – I swear. But he beat it out of me anyways.'

'I saw it in your face, liar. The moment you laid eyes on my sword, you wanted it.' Erlan ground his boot harder.

'No, no! Please – you're hurting me.' Arik tugged frantically at his tunic, trying to pull it up. 'Look, I've the marks to prove it. I swear!' Curious, Erlan relaxed his foot a little, and Arik eagerly rolled over and showed him his back. A few bruises ran purple and black under his skin. 'See – see? They made me do it.'

Erlan thought a moment, then shoved him over again. 'A man never knows when he might need a favour back – isn't that what you told me?' Erlan smiled coldly. 'I reckon you're in need of a favour about now, aren't you?'

'Please. I'll do anything. Take the horses. Take my purse. Just don't hurt me!'

Erlan made no reply. Only watched the little man squirming under his boot. 'Are you – are you going to kill me?'

Erlan shook his head. 'Those boys of yours need their father. Even if he is a rat.' He saw relief flood Arik's hollow cheeks. 'Maybe you need a lesson in hospitality all the same.' Erlan dropped his knee into Arik's chest, and jerked his head to one side. 'A reminder – to treat the next poor bastard who stays under your roof a sight better than you did me.'

'What? No! What are you going to do? No – stranger! Please! NO!'

Arik's screech split the still air as Erlan put the knife to his ear and, with a quick twist, cut half of it off. Blood leaked onto the stones. Flinging away the chunk of gristle, he hauled Arik, whimpering, to his feet.

'Well, friend. Freyhamen's that way.' And he sent him on his road with a shove. The merchant scuttled off along the shoreline, clutching his ear and muttering curses.

The dead men's horses had scattered and were nowhere to be seen. Erlan cursed. He didn't want to linger there. Freyhamen wasn't far away – it wouldn't be long before someone else was along, and they weren't like to take his part in this little altercation.

A movement in the trees caught his eye. Idun appeared from the shadows, her ears flat with suspicion. He clicked his tongue and held out his hand.

Warily, she approached. He could see a bib of dried blood down her chest where the arrow had cut her. Her muscles quivered as he bent to check it.

'Could be worse.' He was suddenly aware of his own wound. He pulled up his tunic and peered down at it. 'Aye, could be a lot worse. I'll get us cleaned up. We've a long road ahead.'

Above him, the crows began to circle.

CHAPTER SEVENTEEN

Their journey led into thick forest, which shrouded the day in perpetual gloom. The trees at least gave cover from the rain, which came more often, and from the deepening cold. They skirted many lakes, on which shone shimmering reflections of silver birches, sentinels around their edge. Moss smothered everything, muffling the woodland to a brooding silence.

Of people, there were few enough, in lonely farmsteads or shabby little hamlets. Places where folk had cleared some forest and begun cultivating new land, but come harvest, it seemed to Erlan, they would reap a beggarly sort of crop from ground so thin.

At best, these inland folk offered him suspicion. The more so since his hair was dark along with his features, and darker yet was the air he carried with him, where they were blond-haired and of paler complexion. At worst, they closed their doors and shut their hearths to him and bid him move on. In his Jute homeland, custom held that folk must give a stranger shelter, vittles, some little kindness. For in welcoming a stranger from the road, some were said to have hosted even the Wanderer himself, or other lesser gods. And such visitations were said to bring great blessing on any household so fortunate in its fate, if a god was well fed and aled, and left in all ways satisfied.

But Gotar folk seemed not to share this custom. Even those that gave him shelter would give him little more than scraps to fill his shrinking belly, and those for a night at most. And he would wake to find the door propped open and Idun tethered to the frame, the sooner for him to move on.

Anyone he met, man or woman, thrall or freeman, he questioned about the kingdom to the north. Some knew of it. Others had never heard of any king. But he discovered little more than that he must continue north and east.

The homesteads became fewer, then thinned to none at all. Wilder forest closed in around them. Pathways shrank to tracks and then vanished altogether. And all the while Idun plodded north and east, north and east. The cold bit harder with each passing day. Erlan's cloak offered meagre protection against the first frosts. Each night he did his best to find shelter for them in the lee of fallen trunks or in the crook of huge boulders breaking out of the earth, sleeping beside fires that burned out in the night, and each morning fighting off the first nips of frostbite from his fingers and toes.

The last frosts became the first snows. Light and wet at first, or sharp sleet lashed by a blinding wind, chilling him through bone and sinew; and then falling softer, heavier, smothering the forests and lakes in a white pall as silent and final as death.

Erlan was no skilled woodsman. He could hunt, of course – but with a yew-bow and finely fletched arrows, each honed to perfection by his father's smiths. But in this endless wilderness of green and white, with nothing more than knife and axe to catch his meat, he ate frugally if he ate at all. Squirrels and rabbits were the best he hoped for and the best he got. And soon the pangs of hunger were familiar to him as the pangs of his heart and the throbbing in his wounded side and the old ache in his crippled heel. His lips cracked with the cold. His knuckles split like over-ripe berries. His backside chafed so raw he had to lead Idun for hours on end, slowing their pace to a miserable trudge.

And all the while, his ghosts rode with him. Konur. Tolla. Garik. His father – the great Vendling lord. His unborn child. . . but most of all, his beloved sister, Inga. All of them whispering, taunting, pleading, chastening. Each rebuking him in turn with their special grievances, as though in death, their only aim was to weigh him down with guilt and grief. He was lonely and yet he was not alone. He longed for an end to the bitter reproaches that voiced on and on in his head, or took on monstrous form, torturing him again and again in the tumult of his dreams. Even the sad distant cries of the wolves at night were warmer comfort than the cacophony of sorrow inside his head.

North and east, north and east, and all the while the snows fell thicker. Idun fared little better than him, with less and less to forage, shrinking to a filthy hide of sharp ribs and jutting haunches. At times, he feared he would wake to find her dead. But every day she found something more in her weary limbs. Plodding on – north and east, north and east.

More than once she baulked at scaling the shoulder of some jagged cliff face or crossing some boiling stream thundering down from the hills over splintered rocks. Then he would set to dragging her forcibly onwards, step by stubborn step, until the obstacle was overcome or they came to terrain she found more to her liking. Sometimes no amount of goading could make her hazard the path ahead, and they would have to turn back and find another way.

One day, under a steel sky when the snow was falling a little lighter, they found themselves skirting a lake. Erlan's gaze was dragging dejectedly along the snowy rubble passing under his feet as Idun picked her way along the lakeshore when suddenly she stopped. Wearily he looked up.

Ahead of them, a sheer wall of rock, perhaps a hundred feet high, rose up out of the water, barring their progress around the shore.

He cursed, his voice now little more than a croak.

To the left, among the trees, the ground rose steeply to form a kind of bowl of land on that side of the lake, swinging round to meet the cliff-top. His heart fell as he realized he would never get Idun up ground so treacherous, not with the ice and snow and the loose stones beneath.

He looked behind. The thought of turning back again, of finding some other way onward, seemed too much to bear this time. Instead he scanned ahead for some other answer. In the near distance, the lakeshore curved around to the right. He could see through the swirls of snow that not far beyond the cliff the ground fell away again. His gaze moved out onto the white expanse of the lake.

The smaller lakes were frozen now. Only the very largest had yet to be sealed completely with their winter covering. So far he hadn't chanced his luck on the ice, but it seemed like days, maybe weeks, since the first snows had come. And only the day before, the temperature had dropped more bitterly than ever before.

He decided to test the shallows. If the ice there held, he would rather try his luck than be thwarted in his progress yet again. He hopped down from Idun's back, wincing as his ankle jarred against the ground. But the pain merited little heed. Discomfort was a familiar companion now.

Cautiously, he led Idun onto the ice, their footsteps crunching the pristine blanket of snow. He listened hard for any signs of the ice cracking, but there was nothing. He moved out a little further from the shore, trailing Idun behind him. No sign of any weakness. He halted, and then jumped a couple of inches. The ice held.

'What do you reckon, girl?' he said, chuckling at his own nervousness. 'You ready to get your feet wet?'

The horse looked back at him with docile eyes, her only reply a shake of the withers. This time, he jumped higher. His feet thumped in the snow.

Nothing.

He allowed himself a sigh and gazed around. The soft patter of the falling snow was barely audible. He heard wings flutter in the treetops across the lake and then settle. For one blissful moment, his mind was still, and he took in the quiet beauty of winter now that it had settled over the land. Just for a moment.

Then he looked down at his hands. They were gnarled and cracked, dried blood clogging the deep sores across his knuckles. It was only he that was ugly in this place. Only he that didn't belong here. He was a blight that marred this small corner of the world, that robbed it of its perfection. But he would be gone soon enough, and in a few more hours all trace of him would have disappeared for ever, and the lake and the forest could go back to their silent contemplation. They could begin to forget, until the shadow of his passing might have been nothing more than a dream in the mind of whatever woodland spirit haunted this place.

He turned and led Idun further out, circling round the great looming cliff face, gazing up at the rippling cascades of ice as they poured with exquisite slowness down the jagged rocks encased beneath.

They passed the apex of the promontory and Erlan saw beyond that the cliff receded, cutting away and shrinking until the ground sank back down to the level of the lake. Another hundred yards and they would be back on solid ground. They were going to make it.

They padded on through the powder.

It began so quietly that at first he mistook it for some distant echo floating down over the trees. A faint groan, and behind it the crumpled sound of snow shifting. The groan grew louder, higher, almost to a whine, and then there was a sudden, sickening crack. Panic flooded his veins.

They were still fifty yards out. He didn't know whether to run or stand still. In the end, his fear chose for him. He froze, listening with dizzying dread to the sound of cracks racing in every direction. Idun sensed the danger too, tossed her head, tried to push past him, but he gripped her reins tighter to stop her bolting. *As if that would make any difference now.*

Something instinctual made him reach for his sword in the bundle slung over her rump. He'd hardly got his fingers to it when there was a lurch beneath him, a loud ripping sound and then he was tilted headlong up and over her back. His one thought was to snatch his bundle, to cling to it tight, and then he was plunging into a whirling, sucking world of ice and water.

The shock of the cold slammed his chest like a war-hammer, jolting his heart. He flailed blindly, unable to breathe, not knowing up from down, but sensing the mass of thrashing horseflesh beside him. He tried to get clear, fearful of the flailing hooves or that he would founder under her.

The cold was crushing, a vice at his temples, the icy water sucking at his boots, turning his woollen clothes to lead. A chunk of broken ice banged against his head. He cried out, clawing to get a grip on something, anything, with his free hand, kicking madly to keep himself from going under. And then, out of the maelstrom of movement came a leaden blow – his head burst into a thousand pieces and the world went black. . .

When he opened his eyes, his first thought was that his hands were empty. His second that his lungs were filling with liquid. Everything was obscure; he was underwater. He felt his knees butt against something massive and solid. Praying it was the lake bottom, he pushed against it with all the strength left in his legs, tearing at the water above him. In only a few moments, he broke the surface, hacking and spluttering and spewing up icy water.

He steadied himself against the jagged edge of the ice. There was a splashing sound behind him. He turned and saw Idun, smashing, stamping, staggering her way through the ice, mad as a berserker, breaking it up any way she could, intent only on getting out. Somehow she had made it all the way in to the shallows. Behind her trailed a passage of bobbing chunks of ice.

Erlan was shaking violently – from cold or shock, it hardly mattered – and his head was pounding from whichever body part Idun had struck him with. He set out after her, dragging himself weakly through the freezing water, his only thought to get to shore.

A minute or so later his toes scraped the bottom and he managed to haul himself, slipping and tilting, the last yards out of the water. At last he flung himself down on the shore, exhausted. But within a heartbeat he was over on his belly, heaving out half the lake onto the stones.

When there was nothing more to come, he lay there, breathless, shivering like a palsied man, staring up into the grey sky while the falling snow flecked his cheeks.

Slowly he lifted his hands and looked at them. They were shaking uncontrollably. And they were empty.

He swore.

His sword was still out there. Everything was. Everything except the long-knife he kept at his waist. He sat up and looked back out over the lake. Its clean white surface was now disfigured by the ugly black gash out to the ragged hole where they had fallen through. The sheepskin he used as his bedding was floating pathetically among the bits of broken ice, but there was no trace of anything else.

His breath was coming in strange short shallow pants. He needed to get warm and dry, fast. But he needed his weapons more.

Never be more than two paces from your weapons on the road, his father had taught him. But he never said what to do when they were at the bottom of a fucking lake.

He couldn't go on without them. He had to retrieve them

if he could. So, forcing himself into action before he had time for second thoughts, he stripped to his breeches, pulled off his stockings and boots, and crept gingerly to the water's edge.

Idun stood nearby under a tree, looking about as miserable as any horse ever had. 'What? Aren't you coming in again?' muttered Erlan past chattering teeth. But she only levelled an accusing gaze at him, as if to say, in her humble opinion, that he was the stupidest son of a whore she'd ever had the mischance to meet. 'Don't look at me like that. It was time you had a bath anyhow.' But then he remembered that Gotars never did have much of a sense of humour.

It took him three trips out and back before he couldn't stand the cold any more. He looked down at his haul: the sheepskin and the shield had been easy enough. The axe he found on the second trip, though it took him two attempts of foraging around in the murk ten feet down before he had laid his hands on it. The third trip had taken him to the very brink of what he could bear. But Wrathling had been his reward. Four times he had dived to the bottom. Four times he had stayed under, scrabbling around in the pebbles and the silt, his lungs strained to bursting. Four times he had resurfaced empty handed. But on the fifth, his fingers had closed around something flat and hard. He'd recognized Wrathling's leathern sheath, tugged it free and resurfaced with a yell of triumph that sent a flock of nearby crows flapping into the sky.

The rest – his other knives, his cooking pot, his aleskin – he had to leave for the lake. He looked down at his naked torso. His skin was blue.

He needed a fire, right now. But moving quickly was not something he was capable of any more. Even so, luck had not completely abandoned him. There was an old dead tree, half-fallen, leaning out of the forest over the stony shore. He took his axe, hobbled over and went at it. By the time he had gathered enough wood to make a fire under the shelter of the trees, the quivering in his muscles was completely beyond his control. The cold seemed to have seeped right through him now, saturating him, stiffening his veins, hardening his lungs, turning his heart to stone. Even his eyelids seemed weary. All he wanted to do was lie down and sleep and sleep and sleep.

But he knew if he did, he would die.

The fire was laid now. All he needed to do was light it. But when he reached into the pouch on his belt, he found that his firesteel wasn't there. He thrust his hand in deeper, nails scraping at the sodden leather, but the familiar ring of steel was gone. Desperate now, he scrabbled among his other things, praying that it had only fallen out after he came ashore. But it was nowhere to be found.

He groaned in despair.

Without firesteel, how could he start a fire? Rage at his impotence welled up in him. He screamed into the pitiless sky, snatched up his axe in fury and hacked and hacked at the nearest tree until his arm was burning with fatigue. He flung it down. As it hit the ground, there was a crack and a stone shattered into pieces.

Erlan stopped screaming and looked dumbly down at the broken shards. Of course, he thought.

He snatched up two pieces, threw himself down beside his fire and set to knapping one shiver against the other, willing the senseless stone to birth a spark. His whole life seemed to be concentrated in those two jagged pieces. They were to be his judges. They would decide whether he should live or die.

He was weeping like a child, gibbering prayers to he knew not which gods. To anyone who could hear him. To any*thing*.

Again and again, he chipped away, desperate for the little orange shower of sparks to rain down on the wisps of moss and twigs he had gathered for tinder.

Then he stopped, tears and snot stringing from his nose.

Maybe this was his end. He could feel this cold death taking hold of him from within. Why not just let it take him? Why not give up, just as Inga had given up? What was there to live for anyway?

He let his hands fall limp into his lap, and his head fell forward. A kind of darkness seemed to rush forward in his mind, as if it had only been waiting for his surrender all that time. He would sleep, and then he would die.

So be it.

He heard a faint *click, clack* on the stones behind him. He hadn't the will even to lift his eyelids to see what it was. Something warm blew behind his ear, then butted against his neck.

He opened his eyes. He could see the blur of Idun's dark lips. They pushed against his face. He groaned.

If he died, she would certainly die. *More blood on these hands.*

He shook his head. *No. She at least doesn't deserve this.* For her sake, he would try again.

He lifted his hands and began doggedly striking stone against stone. On the sixth strike, the sparks flew. His mind was so dazed, he went on hitting the stones even as the tinder caught fire and started smoking. Suddenly, he saw it – yelped in triumph – and blew gently until the flame caught in earnest.

The wood cracked and popped; the flame surged, ready to devour more.

Erlan rolled onto his back and pulled the damp cloak and sheepskin over him, his eyes rolling back in his head.

They had fire.

They would live.

When he awoke, there was nothing of the fire left but dying embers. It was dark, but whether the night was nearer the mark of midnight or the coming dawn, he couldn't tell. His head was thundering mercilessly, the left side worst of all. He lifted a feeble hand to touch it and immediately regretted his curiosity. Pain shivered through his skull. That side of his face was all swollen.

His coverings were still damp, but they seemed wetter on the inside now. He was shivering still, but realized that he must have sweated in his sleep. Sweated enough to fill a bucket.

He cursed, sensing a fever's cruel fingers slipping around his body, settling its grip on him. If he could only hold on till morning, they could at least leave this lonely place.

They had to keep going. To stay there was death for both of them.

He staggered to his feet, took up his axe and stumbled back to the fallen tree, weaving like a drunk. It had stopped snowing at least. But the weakness in his arms scared him as he worked to cut enough fuel to reach daybreak.

Back at the fire, the heat was not yet all gone from the embers. He managed to coax a flame out of them and lay on more firewood. Then he stretched out again, exhausted. And while the heat of the fire warmed his face, the heat of the fever burned within.

The morning came like some grey-veiled dream. Somehow he roused himself from the ground, limped around gathering his things. He was burning up on the inside, though the sweat beading on his face was chill as ice. There was nothing to eat so he bundled up his things, heaved himself astride Idun's back and touched his heels to her flank.

That was the last conscious action he took for many days. Afterwards, he couldn't tell whether what he saw was real or else mere conjurings of his fevered brain.

North and east, north and east – words whispered in his ear, over and over, like some hideous lament, unshakeable as a curse. And the endless rocking as Idun picked her way over the terrain, directing her course whichever way seemed best to her. She was the master now, he nothing but her burden. Or more truly, she the mother and he the helpless child, borne away to horizons he knew not where.

To say he was lost had no meaning. For to be lost would mean there was some place he meant to be, some road he meant to take. But if there was such a place, it was far, far from his thoughts, if what his mind beheld could be called thoughts.

Later, he would recall things that could not have been: corpses hanging from branches, murmuring songs to the Slain-God, their tongues black, eye sockets long-empty, faces half-eaten away. Wolves kept pace beside them, sometimes whole packs at a time, as if accompanying them in a kind of funeral march in honour of the beast and its burden as they plodded onwards to hunger, exhaustion and death.

Surely, death awaited them at the end of this road. Or perhaps its threshold had already been crossed and this world was his to wander until the end of time and the coming of the Ragnarok.

Sometimes other riders would appear, warriors with snow-blond hair, faces stained bloody, mouths racked with screams and war cries, yet no sound came from their throats but silence. Silence laden with messages from some other world beyond this endless forest, which would never be heard. Silence like the quiet of his mother's barrow-grave, set on that lonely hill. And sometimes, she sat behind him, drew him close, ran her fingers through his hair. 'My son,' she whispered sweetly in his ear. 'My son. My monstrous son.'

Day and night flew like winged creatures across the sky, dragging the shadows after them. All colour had fled the world. All was black and white. Even his blood, caked around the wounds of his weathered hands, was black.

Once, he saw a bright light above him, when all around was cloaked in murk. The light shimmered, as if struggling to reach him, and he suddenly knew he was underwater. Perhaps he had never left the lake after all. And faces appeared above him, peering down at him. His father shaking his head in sorrow and shame; Konur laughing down at him, mouth a cold and vengeful sneer. And Inga. . . always Inga came last and longest. Weeping at first, smiling sadly at him as he called to her from below. But she couldn't hear him. And as he looked up, it was almost as though her sadness was some pretence she could not keep up for long. So that soon there was laughter dancing on her lips, and she was mocking him for an oath-breaker, for a coward and a fool.

Why did she laugh at him?

He recalled a haze of lakes and forests and streams, snowfalls and the winter sun's blinding shards piercing the forest veil, the rustle of the wind and the patter of scattered snow. But he never knew where he was or where he was going.

And last, and most vivid of all, was a clearing. He thought he lay upon a soft blanket and beside him he sensed something warm and very large. He awoke to see a pair of bright eyes staring at him from the shadows.

He sat up.

The eyes moved, and in the dimness he saw it was a deer – a beautiful red doe with almond eyes. When the doe spoke to him, he knew he must be dreaming.

'Are you a fool, my love?' she said.

But he didn't understand. And the doe circled around him, just beyond the clearing. She passed behind a pine and when she appeared again, the doe had gone and Inga walked in her place.

He cried out her name, but she only smiled and said, 'A fool shuns a friend on the road.'

But he didn't understand. He reached out to her and cried, 'Come back!'

She passed behind another tree, and there was the doe once more.

'Inga!'

But the doe only replied, 'Are you a fool, my love?' He rose to go to her, tried to run, but his ankle weighed like lead.

'Wait!'

The doe only laughed Inga's laugh and leaped away towards a bright light glowing through the trees. He pursued her, dragging his ankle like a curse, but it was all for nothing. He could only watch the doe's silhouette grow smaller and smaller until the light had swallowed it completely.

He sat upright.

Something was different.

His mind felt. . . clear. He put his hand to his brow. It was cool and dry.

He stared wide-eyed about him. He was in a clearing. It was a few moments before he recognized the shapes of the trees, faint but discernible in the half-light. *The dream.* He looked up and saw beyond the treetops the sky, already paling with the dawn.

Suddenly a pang of hunger hit him so hard he thought his stomach would turn inside out. He wondered when he had last eaten. Wondered if he had eaten anything at all since his fever had taken hold. He turned and saw Idun lying beside him. There was something starkly striking, even beautiful, about her that caught him in the throat. He leaned over and touched her neck. She flicked her head round at him, and then got stiffly to her feet. He hauled himself up after her.

He smiled.

It was good to smile. Good to think a straight and simple thought.

'Hello,' he said.

She looked back at him, blank as ever. He took her face in his hands and laid his forehead against hers. She didn't

259

seem to mind. He let his breath blow in and out in time with hers.

It was good to breathe.

He would have stayed like that for longer, but a sudden sharp light came lancing through the trees. Distracted, he turned to look at it. It took a moment or two before he realized it was only the rising sun. But then he remembered the dream – the fleeing silhouette swallowed up by the light.

Curious, he went towards it. As he did, he saw the trees ended hardly fifty yards further on. Picking his way through the snow, he breached the treeline, staggered out into the morning light and found himself standing on a rocky ledge overlooking the biggest lake he had ever seen.

The easterly sun was slanting off its frozen surface. From his elevated perch he could just make out the far side, but to the north and the south, the shoreline stretched beyond the horizon.

Down and to his left, perhaps half a league along the shore, a tiny village huddled, smoke roiling cosily up into the empty sky.

Are you a fool, my love? she had said.

It was time to find out.

CHAPTER EIGHTEEN

The first human he had seen in days was an old greybeard fisherman who was sat on a boulder, plucking away at a net that looked almost as frayed as he did.

'Saw you a ways off,' croaked the greybeard, as Idun clopped wearily up to him. 'Hel's teeth, but you're a skinny son of a bitch close up, ain't you? Why, you'd make a scarecrow feel sorry for yer.'

'I need food. . . And shelter,' said Erlan, each word strangely awkward on his tongue.

'I'll say you do!' cried the old man. 'And plenty of it.' He hawked up a gob of ancient phlegm and shot it like a bolt out the side of his mouth. 'If it's shelter you're needing, ask at the house with the painted gable.'

Erlan soon found the house. In front of it, a small shrewish-looking woman sat on a log, scraping busily at a fox-skin. Erlan greeted her and asked if she had any room for a traveller.

She glanced up and snorted, but didn't break her work. 'What hole did you crawl out of then?'

'The south,' he replied vaguely. 'I've been sick.'

She grunted and bobbed her head. 'Well, my husband's out on the lake just now.'

'Think he'd give me a place by your fire?'

'No doubt he'll give you a night.' She stopped what she was doing and eyed him properly. The cold had marked ruddy stripes down her thin cheeks. 'Maybe two if that's what you need. Depends what you're about.'

'I need rest. Then I'm heading north. Looking for service.' He touched his hilt.

'Haven't no need for service like that,' she said, twitching her head. 'Nope – can't help with that.' She went back to her scraping. 'We're quiet folk – trappers, skinners, fisherfolk. Th'a's all you'll find here.'

'You heard of a kingdom to the north? The land of the Svears?'

'Have I heard of Sveäland?' She glared at him, incredulous. 'Take me for a halfwit, do you?' She jabbed her knife up the lake. 'Your road's that way.'

'So you've been there?' he said, suddenly all eager. 'What do you know of it?'

The woman gave a loud laugh. 'Me – in the land of the Svears! You must be joking! Ain't got much in the way of brains in that skinny head of yours. What would I want with going to Sveäland? Half of them are murderers, the other half thieves. No, no. You won't catch me up that way.'

Erlan wasn't sure what to make of this. 'Well, is it far?'

'Far? My lovely, the other side of the village is *far*. Sveäland might as well be the other side of the moon, for all I care of it.'

'You must have some idea.'

She shrugged. 'We've had travellers through here talk of it. And that's the way they come. That's all I know.'

But then, seeing the disappointment in his face, she relented. 'Oh, cheer up, handsome! If you're so interested, my husband might tell you more, though you can't always get much sense out of that block head of his.' She chuckled, flashing a couple of lonely teeth. 'Best catch him before he gets to his ale-cup.'

Erlan didn't answer; he was looking out over the lake. The blanket of snow shone brilliantly in the morning light. He could see a few figures dotted about, huddled over holes in the ice. He guessed they must be fishing.

The woman cocked a look at him. 'Well, you're welcome!'

'Oh – thank you,' he mumbled.

'Should say so. Now you can put your animal round the back of them halls. Then you can get a feed inside. There's bread. And broth in the pot. The girl will sort you out.'

To call them halls was generous. They looked more like over-sized cowsheds with ill-fitted planks just about holding up each roof. But Erlan thanked her and led Idun away.

'Give her some hay, too. Looks like she needs it!'

He found the stall easily enough and tied Idun between a pair of stocky little ponies, found her some hay, and stood by till she'd eaten her fill.

After enduring the long, cold nights in the forest, entering the house, with its hearth blazing away, was sweet beyond telling. He let the warm air wash around him, swaddling him like a babe.

Inside, he found a thrall-girl scurrying about her chores who soon obliged him with the bread and broth promised him. He devoured it all in moments, each mouthful another wave of relief. Afterwards, she let him drink his fill from a bowl of warm goat's milk and then, at last, he lay flat out on a bench by the fire, closed his eyes and went to sleep.

It was well into the afternoon when he awoke. This time, no dreams had come to disturb his sleep. He got up, feeling not exactly refreshed, but at least human again, and taking an apple from the barrel, he went to check on Idun.

She stood looking indolent as ever, and returned his pats with her usual languid expression.

'Don't say I never spoil you,' he said, slipping the apple into her mouth. She crunched away, swishing her tail, the closest to grateful he'd ever seen her. The gods knew, she had little enough to thank him for.

He was about to wander back to the lakeshore when something caught his eye. A great fire was burning beyond the next dwelling.

It seemed strange to light a fire so big in the middle of the day. But he was drawn to its warmth like a thirsty man to water. Circling the house, he came closer, enjoying the heat prickling his face. For a long while, he gazed vacantly into the glowing embers.

When he looked up, he started. A pair of eyes was staring at him through the flames.

At first, all he saw were the eyes. But through the shimmer, he put the eyes in a face, the face on a head, the head on a body, hanging by the arms between two posts.

It was a boy.

He was stripped to the waist, his torso filthy as his face. Indeed everything about him was wretched. Everything except for his eyes, which brimmed with intensity. Erlan circled the fire to get a better look at him.

The boy lifted his head, trying to take the weight off the ropes that bound him. His wrists were lashed just high enough that he could ease the strain only on the very tips of his toes. Whoever put him there wanted him to suffer. And from the state of him, Erlan guessed that he had.

His hair was greasy blond, hanging in flicks over eyes blue as meltwater. His mouth was broad – too broad for his face – with thick lips tinged purple with cold. He was too young to be bearded, but he was certainly no child. He wore nothing but a pair of threadbare breeches belted with a bit of hemp. His bare feet were blotched red from the slush.

'Fancy trading places, friend?' The boy's voice was hardly a shiver.

'Can't say it looks tempting.'

'I was so hot, so I took off my—' Suddenly his toes slipped, and the bonds yanked cruelly at his arm sockets. He winced, hanging limp a few moments, before finding his toes again. His ribs were heaving just to breathe. 'Numb feet,' he croaked, by way of explanation. Then he twitched his head. 'Down there.'

Erlan looked about him. There was a filthy-looking tunic discarded next to a pair of ill-cut shoes. 'These?' He made to pick up the clothes.

The boy stretched even higher on his toes. 'No! There,' he gasped. 'The wood, the wood!'

Erlan looked again, and saw what he wanted. Nearby there was a pile of chopped wood, ready for the fire. One flatter piece had fallen apart from the rest.

'Can't speak. . . long. . . like this,' the boy managed.

Erlan finally understood and fetched the block, kicking it under the boy's feet. Once he got himself on it, his bonds went slack, and he sucked in an enormous breath.

'Obliged to you, friend. Much obliged.' He gave his shoulders a roll and winced.

'How long you been here?'

'They strung me up this morning.' The boy was looking a good deal happier now. 'Take me down at dawn tomorrow.'

'Overnight? You'll freeze.'

'Well, I haven't so far,' he winked. 'It's not my first time. They know how to make it hot enough I don't freeze, but they hang me far enough away that I spend the night wishing I would.'

'Then they let you go?'

'Not exactly. I get a beating. Old toad-face, Alvis, does it. Swear the old bastard enjoys it. There's no bigger fool in this stupid village, even if he is the headman. I tell you, I've seen quicker wits out the back end of a pig.'

Erlan snorted. 'Why did they put you here?'

'I stole a chicken, if you must know,' he said, without a trace of shame. 'Tasty little flapper she was too.'

'So you often spend the day like this?'

'You could say that.'

'Can't be much of a thief.'

The boy looked sore. 'Hey, I'm good enough. These days, I get blamed anytime, anyhow, whether I did it or not. Besides, folks round here gotta have something to smile at,' he added, bitterly. 'People ain't never happier than when someone else is taking a good beating. 'Course, if I took anything bigger, they'd stick my head in a noose and say they were well rid of me.'

266

'Why d'you keep at it then?'

'A lad's gotta eat. Look at me – I'm skin and bones.' He wasn't wrong. His body was streaked with mud and bruised around his ribs, every one of which Erlan could count where he stood. 'My father's a niggardly old fart. Does him good to see me go hungry, he says.'

'Is he poor?'

'No poorer than anyone else round here. He just doesn't like me.' He shrugged, as if nothing could be more natural. 'Oh, he's not my *real* father. . .'

'Where's he then?'

'Died five winters back. Some sickness. . . He was all right I suppose, but my mother soon bedded up with this useless sot. More fool her. He's a lazy bully and has her chasing around dawn to dusk. No, I get no help from her. She baked him a couple of younglings and a finer pair of brats you never saw. Fat little brutes too, just like their father.'

'Didn't your father have any kin?'

'I suppose. But far as any of them reckon, my mother and her fella take care of me. That's an end to it.'

Erlan nodded, but said nothing.

The boy licked his lips. 'Now I got a few questions of my own.'

'Well?' Erlan shrugged.

'What the Hel's an outlander doing here? It's a long bloody way from the sea.'

'How do you know I'm an outlander?'

'By the hanged! Ain't it clear as water? If I didn't know better, I'd say you were a slave.'

'A slave?'

'Aye, a bloody thrall – they're the only dark-hairs we have round here.'

'I'm no slave. I promise you.'

'If you say so.' Though he looked doubtful. 'Still, thrall or no, look at the state of you!'

'What do you mean?'

'You look like a fucking corpse!'

'I've been sick,' offered Erlan. Truth was his bones still felt hollow as reeds.

'Sick? More like bloody dead!' And the boy threw back his head and laughed till his body shook.

'Not yet,' observed Erlan, drily.

'That, I cannot deny,' the boy replied, recovering himself. 'So what brings you through here?'

'I'm headed for a kingdom in the north, beyond the land of the Gotars.'

'Sveäland.'

'You know it?'

'Some. A king called Sviggar rules there.'

'Sviggar? You're the first I've met who knows that.' He narrowed his eyes, curious. 'What else can you tell me?'

'Sviggar's a great king, they say. Lives in a hall bigger than bloody Valhalla, waited on by a thousand servants, surrounded by fabulous wealth. Every night they drink from silver cups, and the king leads a host so strong he fears nothing but the fangs of Fenrir.' He winked. 'Least, so they say.'

'What's the place called?'

'Some call it Vendel. That's what I heard. Or Sviggar's Seat. Maybe other names. . .'

Vendel? The name of his ancestor, Vendal the Grey, stirred in Erlan's mind. Old Vendal lived twelve fathers back. But then Erlan remembered his oath: he had foresworn his blood. Foresworn his line of fathers. The thought brought a pang of regret. Meanwhile, the boy was warming to his talk.

'They say Sviggar's halls are filled with maids so comely you wouldn't even dream of 'em, and there's nowhere in the wide world with feasting so grand nor songs so noble. A whole troop of skald-singers sings of Sviggar's deeds, and round his hall smiths work night and day hammering out wondrous things of gold and silver and steel.' The boy's eyes sparkled.

'You seem to know a good deal about this place.'

'You think you're the first traveller through here?' the boy crowed. 'Come off it!'

'Well it's not exactly thick with 'em, is it?'

'Huh! Perhaps not many, I grant you, but we have our share. A couple of merchants – so-called. . . though they were more like beggars if you ask me. Bonier-arsed than you even! Then there was a man who'd fled Sviggar's kingdom for killing his cousin – he wasn't right, that one. Then the skaldman – a teller of sagas and such. . . now *he* was a fine fellow.'

'You seem quite struck by him.'

'I *did* like him. Even the bird-brained folk round here listened once he got to singing. . . Anyway, I suppose you could call me curious.'

'You surprise me.'

The boy chuckled. 'That skaldman, why he was a one! He got sick, and we let him stay a while. There was one woman – a widow, and no great beauty I must say. . . fell out of her mind in love with him.' He laughed gleefully. 'He was a rogue! She

269

nursed him, let him stay in her house, did whatever he wanted. And I mean, what-*ever*. . . Why, he treated her like a slave! "Go here – do that!" And didn't she jump to it?' He shook his head in admiration. 'He never had it so good. Anyway, once he was on the mend, I'd sit by him for hours and he'd tell me about the places he'd been and things he'd seen. Aye – and the women he'd bedded. Ho-*hoa*!' The boy's face was aglow. 'Taught me some of his songs, too.'

'*You* can sing?'

''Course I can!' said the boy, indignant. 'Though no one round here wants to listen. Dumb as cattle this lot, I tell you. Still, it'll be different when I'm older. . .' For the first time, Erlan caught a trace of dejection in the boy's dirty features.

'I'll listen.'

The boy's eyes snapped up in surprise. 'What, now?'

'Sure – why not?'

'Oh, right.' The boy nodded eagerly. 'Let me see.' His eyes scanned the clouds, memory working. At length he hacked, spat, and began.

Skadi's man, the sea-spray god
blows and moans by bubbling foam;
surf-birds fly where once his bride
by strand on ice-shoes roamed.

Thiazi's girl, gone to the hills
their high peaks her heart long called;
heavy-heart, she sits, her huntsman eyes
drop tears like spring dew-fall.

Sick with loss, the sea-god shrouds
war-farers in winter squall;
for snow-heart Skadi loves him not
so dear as her mountain hall.

The boy's voice was strong and clear. Erlan's mind flew back to the gulls that swooped above the sands of his boyhood. He remembered the cries they uttered, how Inga would make him laugh with her perfect imitations. . . Abruptly, he curbed his wandering memory, lest it took him too far. But the boy stopped just as sharply. 'That's part of one. Here's another. The skaldman was always singing it.'

Bring your voice to the songster's fire,
His ear is open, the folk are fed,
Give power, proud word-father,
To flush the cheeks of maiden love,
Or rouse oak-shields to fells run red.

Sight of things that never were,
From poet-prince, the runesmith god,
Which folk may see in the wood-blaze warmth,
Snow-battles, sky-faring, dwarfish hoards,
A living dream – Bragi's gift to low blood.

The boy finished. Erlan said nothing, letting the last words linger.

'That's your lot,' chuckled the boy. 'Any more and you'll have to pay me.'

Erlan smiled. 'Your kin are fools indeed.'

Are you a fool, my love?

The words sounded so clear in his head he almost spun around to see who had spoken.

'Oh, no doubt about that.' The boy cocked his head. 'Anyway, what's your name, stranger?'

'Erlan. And yours?'

'Kai Askarsson. Though my stepfather wants me to say Torolfsson now. Bah! The fat fart can suck a goat. So where you from, Erlan?'

A shadow crossed Erlan's face. There he was once more, at the door he'd sworn never again to open. He could almost feel her presence there, on the other side. Waiting. Breathing. *Hurting...*

He gave a sniff and stretched back his shoulders. 'Well, I'm sorry for your treatment, Kai. Once you're through, I wish you well. Thanks for what you've told me. Farewell.'

'Wait – don't go! Why won't you answer me?'

Erlan gave Kai a lingering look. 'Better take this away.' And before the wretched boy could answer, Erlan had kicked the block aside.

Kai gasped, his weight suddenly wrenching his shoulders. 'Wait!' he cried.

But Erlan had already turned away.

'Please!' cried Kai, struggling desperately on his toes. 'Take me with you.'

Erlan spun round, incredulous. 'Take you,' he snorted. 'You must be crazy.' He kept walking.

'How you going to fare in Sviggar's... land, eh?' called Kai after him, struggling to speak. 'All alone?'

But Erlan only shook his head and walked on. He knew more about loneliness than this boy ever could.

'You know. . . what they say!' Kai sounded desperate now. 'A fool. . . shuns. . . a friend on. . . the road.'

He could hardly get the last words out, but Erlan had stopped dead. Turned back. 'What did you say?'

Kai was gasping, wresting at the ropes. 'A fool. . . shuns a friend!' was all he managed to groan.

Are you a fool, my love?

Were the Norns laughing at him again? Was this pitiful wretch, this scrawny thief, to be his *friend*? He looked at him hanging there.

This cannot be.

And yet, as he stared at the boy's wasted body, at his filthy rags, something made his heart burn within him.

He walked back over to him. Kai was peering through his greasy flicks of hair, eyes pleading, his ribcage straining with each breath. Erlan kicked the block back under him. Kai hopped on it and Erlan saw the relief flood his body.

'You want to come with me?'

'Yes!'

'Just like that.'

'Hel, yes!' Kai spat sourly. 'I'm done with this place. And these folk. My mother won't miss me and Torolf'd be glad to see the back of me. Anyway, the old whoreson can hang for all I care.' An expectant look shone on his grimy features. 'Take me with you. I'll be no trouble, I swear.'

'That I find hard to believe.'

Erlan stepped back. Kai was truly a pathetic sight – all but his defiant eyes. Something in them fascinated Erlan. Yet the boy was also garrulous beyond anything Erlan reckoned he could stand.

And then he considered the alternative – the stillness of the forest filled with the voices of his dead and lost. Something about the boy made him forget the Hel of his loneliness for a while.

Kai looked like his very life hung in the balance as he waited for Erlan's next word.

A fool shuns a friend on the road. . . Aye, but would this curious boy prove a friend? Or dead weight? Or something worse. . .

He made up his mind.

He shook his head. Kai winced like he'd been struck in the face. He was about to argue, but Erlan cut him off. 'I'll probably live to regret this, but. . . all right then. You can tag along.'

Kai yelped with delight. 'You won't regret this, Erlan. I swear you won't!'

'Aye – well you make sure I don't. All right, I'll wait till nightfall then I'll come for you. Longer even – till everyone's asleep.'

'Bah! Most of 'em are drunkards anyway – they wouldn't wake if the fires of Loki were tickling their toes.'

'Will you be all right till then?'

'Hah! I've seen off colder nights than this one. Don't fret about me. I'll be ready.'

'Good.' He nodded at the sorry-looking tunic in the slush. 'You have more clothes than these?'

'Aye, at home. But I'll fetch 'em in a moment, you'll see. They won't stir any more 'n if I were a mouse.'

'Fine. Bring a cooking pot and an aleskin too, if you can.'

'Ha! Easy,' grinned Kai.

Erlan looked up. 'If the skies stay clear, it shouldn't be too hard to follow the shoreline by night.'

'We can't go by the lake! Soon as Alvis discovers you've run off with his whipping boy that's the first way they'll go.'

'Is there another route into Sveäland?'

'Sure – through the deeper forest. There's a path by the higher ground further north. People don't go up there unless they really have to.'

'Why not?'

'Frightened what they'd find.' He winked. 'Or what'd find them.'

'What do you mean?'

'Spirits of the forests and the like. Or the dead. That's the talk. But I'm not afraid. Most folk are just scared 'cause up that way folks hang outlaws. Blood gifts, you know.'

'You mean sacrifices?'

Kai nodded. 'Could be wolves or bears up there too. But then, you've got that bloody big sword there.' He nodded at Wrathling.

Erlan grunted. What more terrors could the forest hold than he'd already faced? 'We'll have to risk it. Watch for my return.'

'Ain't got much else to do, have I?'

Erlan kicked away the block.

CHAPTER NINETEEN

The fisherman proved a deal less friendly than his wife. Nevertheless, he agreed to host Erlan for the night. But once at table, he was far more interested in getting to his first draught of ale than entertaining his guest. After that, he settled down like a babe at its mother's teat.

The window of talk, once drink loosened his host's tongue, was brief. Erlan got little from him about Sveäland that he didn't know already, and before long the man's eyelids were drooping, slow and heavy, and Erlan saw that any more words were wasted. The fisherman's chin went back and he fell sound asleep.

His wife managed to drag him, half-stupefied, to his bedding, and soon the household was quiet, save for the man's snores and his wife's slumbering sighs.

Erlan bedded down across from them and lay awake watching the fire-shadows skip among the rafters. At length, he decided it had been a while since he'd heard any movement, inside or out. His weapons were already wrapped up tight, and so he decided the time had come for their departure. He was about to get up when he heard a noise.

A rustle of covers, then heavy footsteps across the room, accompanied by senseless grumblings. He listened as the fisherman fumbled his way to the door, watched his shadow pull aside the door-drape, heard the full stream of his piss spattering into the snow and the satisfied sigh when he was done.

Erlan deepened his breathing, pretending sleep, as his host crept past him back to his bed. *It won't take long for the ale-soaked old bastard to nod off*, thought Erlan. Then he would be away.

But it seemed another urge had been aroused in the fisherman. There were half-hushed mutterings in the dark, smothered whispers passing between the man and his wife, and then a giggle. Erlan lay there in shadow, listening to the shuffle of covers, bodies rustling over one another, more giggles, and eventually familiar grunts and moans as they found their stride.

Erlan had to give the fisherman his due – the old boy had legs, as Garik would have put it. He closed his eyes and tried to imagine what it would have been like if he and Inga had had their way. If the Norns had let them live out their love in peace, to grow old like these two. And before long, the woman's moans and sighs awakened the memory of a younger voice, a younger body, smooth as amber in his hands. The teasing tongue, the whispered words of tenderness, the brush of her hair against his chest.

His sister. Aye – there was the horror of it.

The only woman in all the world he desired. The only woman in all the world he *could not* desire. Must not.

Beauty and love are slaughtered like swine.

Inga would never grow old. Her breasts would never wrinkle and sag. Her long dark curls would never pale with age. Death had stolen her, and yet somehow it had saved her too. For now she would never change. She would remain the same. For ever.

He looked up at the smoke-hole above the hearth. Flecks of snow were floating down out of the night into the house, only to vanish in the rising heat. Erlan imagined Kai hanging between his posts, his body turning blue. Waiting. On a night like this, the poor little bastard might freeze to death after all.

He looked over at the couple. He could see the silhouette of the fisherwife astride her husband now, cajoling him on to the finish.

He cursed silently, willing the old trout to get on with it.

At least the pair shared one virtue between them: once it was over, they dozed off faster than he could have snapped his fingers. He hesitated just a little longer until the chorus of snores assured him that the fisherman and his wife, sated at last, were both sound asleep.

Wasting no more time, Erlan rose, gathered his things, and slipped out into the night. Outside, the sky was dark, the snow still falling. And behind the silhouetted dwellings glowed the fire where Kai was strung up.

Erlan stole through the shadows, and within moments, he was creeping up behind the boy, knife in hand, stealthy as a murderer. Kai's silhouette was completely still.

'You didn't die on me, did you?'

The boy uttered a pitifully weak moan.

'Hey!' he hissed. 'You still with me?'

'Odin's eye, you took your time,' Kai murmured.

'Aye, and you don't want to know why. Now hold still.'
He put his knife to the rope; cut one bond, then the other. The
boy fell forward into the snow, his greasy hair hanging over
his face.

'Kai?'

The boy said nothing.

'Kai!' he hissed again, throwing his cloak over the boy's
shoulders. 'Say something. Are you all right?'

The boy looked up, pushing back his hair. In the gloom, his
cheeks had a purplish tinge. 'I bloody will be soon.' He climbed
stiffly to his feet and stumbled over to his tunic and shoes.

'Good. Then fetch your clothes and the other things, and
meet me over there.' Erlan pointed to the line of trees bordering
the edge of the village. 'Hurry.'

'I'll be there.' Kai's teeth flashed in his dirty face, and then
he was away into the shadows.

Erlan went to untether Idun. There was something reassuring
about seeing her long face again, about having her beside him.
He led her into the murk under the trees. There, he waited.

It was a while before he heard anything. But then he caught a
soft, deliberate sound. At once, he recognized a horse's footfall.
Kai appeared leading a sturdy-looking pony.

'Where the Hel d'you get that from?'

'Collecting on some trades I've been working up for five
years or so.'

'Whose is it?'

'Torolf's. The old bastard came in pretty handy in the end.
Thought he probably had no use for this either.' In one hand,
Kai had a sword. 'Not as good as yours, but better than a set of
knuckles.'

'Did you find a cloak?'

'Better than that – I got us a couple of furs. Finest lynx. See.' He put down his sword, and slid something off the pony. 'Your horse'll appreciate that.' He slung a grey-brown fur over Idun's back.

'Your old man's going to be in a fine fury tomorrow.'

'He's not my old man,' rebuked Kai, sharply. 'Anyway, I've earned these, putting up with his horseshit, and the dungheap knows it.' He shrugged. 'Then we have this.' He produced a knife from his belt. 'I figured we needed something to cut the bread and cheese I took.' He unslung a bulging linen sack from his shoulder and gave it a reassuring pat. 'Your aleskin and your pot are in there too.'

'Did you leave them anything?'

'It'll do 'em good. Especially those fat-faced brats. They could do with feeling the pinch of an empty belly for a change.'

Erlan shook his head. 'If these folk ever catch you, the next rider through here will find you roasting *over* the bloody fire.'

'Oh, I almost forgot,' said Kai, fishing around in a pouch at his belt. 'I've one more thing. Ah, here we are.' He held out his hand. Even in the dark, Erlan could make out the little metal hoop in his palm.

'Firesteel.'

CHAPTER TWENTY

T he next few days, he discovered two things about Kai. The boy could talk to drive a man from his wits, and he could cook as well as Tolla.

'If you don't get much to eat, you learn to make damn sure it tastes good,' Kai had said, by way of explanation. Which was just as well, because once the bread and cheese were gone, there was little on offer beyond what winter berries they could find and the odd squirrel if they were lucky. Once they snared a beaver, and by the time Kai was done with it, it would have graced the table of any Yuletide feast.

Besides the gnawing hunger, the cold weighed hard on them all, and Erlan was grateful for the stolen furs. And – he had to admit – for the company. It turned out a fire shared was a far less miserable affair than the lonely piles of ash he'd left on his way through the forest. And with two, it was easier to gather wood and to keep it fuelled through the night. He even gained some respite from his troubled thoughts, and often fell asleep to the sound of one of Kai's songs in his ear.

One evening, a few days after leaving Kai's village, they reached a small woodland pond, frozen hard. A chill wind was dancing through the trees. Erlan drew his fur tighter. 'There any dwellings up this way?'

Kai shook his head. 'Shouldn't think we'll see another soul till we're into Sveäland now.'

From the pond, they tracked uphill, past boulders breaking from the earth, while overhead the canopy knit tighter. Night was coming on.

'We should stop while there's some light,' said Erlan. 'Much darker and a man won't find his prick to piss with.'

'Comes from having a small one, I guess.'

Erlan scowled at Kai. The boy never missed a chance to make a joke. 'Once we find somewhere dry. . . an overhang or some—'

He halted abruptly.

'What is it?'

'*Hush!*' hissed Erlan, and pointed ahead. 'Torches. Through those pines.'

Kai followed his arm, peering into the gloom. 'I see 'em. They're close.'

Erlan was already sliding off Idun's back. 'Leave the horses. Let's take a look.'

Kai hit the ground with a crunch.

'Quietly,' growled Erlan. They tethered the horses, and were soon stealing towards the bobbing flames.

To Erlan the snow seemed deafeningly loud underfoot, but ahead of them were noises even louder. Muttering voices, cracking wood, and muffled moaning.

Through the trees, he could see torches moving, each flickering above a man's silhouette. He counted nine, perhaps fifty paces off, all intent on their business. Certainly, they wouldn't be watching for a pair of runaways skulking in the dark. He signalled Kai to a nearby tree. The boy nodded, reaching for his sword, but Erlan shook his head.

'Not yet,' he mouthed. He didn't want him tripping over the thing and making a racket. Instead, they crouched in the darkness and watched.

The trees opened into a glade. At its centre burned a meagre little fire. He heard mutterings, and then something was flung up into a tree. When it fell, he saw it was a rope. There was a wail, two men hauled on its end and the wail suddenly stopped.

A shadow jerked into the air. The two men grunted, their victim bucking like a fish on a hook, heels scraping at the bark.

It took only moments. Then the shadow hung there, twitching.

'A hanging,' whispered Kai.

'I can see it's a fucking hanging! Keep quiet.' His eyes tracked around the clearing. He saw another shadow hanging from a tree.

Then another. And another.

Erlan wondered how many would be left there to rot.

Turned out, they were six: five men, one woman. The woman was the last. She fought the hardest. It took three to get the rope on her, three to choke her. She kicked and shrieked like some devil was in her, and when her bowels emptied, the stench only earned her more curses.

Their grisly work complete, one of them – perhaps a holy man or *godi* – muttered some prayer, doubtless to the Lord of the Hanged. Then they departed.

Erlan motioned to Kai to stay still. It was a while before the forest had muffled the last of their footsteps, leaving only the wind and the creaking ropes.

The fire was dying. Erlan was about to signal Kai that it was time to go when a shadow slid from the circle of trees.

Erlan froze. Kai's face was a question. Erlan put a finger to his lips.

The shadow was queer indeed. In outline, like some beast – perhaps a small bear – but in movement, like a man, plucking sticks from the ground and throwing them onto the embers until the flames returned to life. As the light grew, so did the figure's shape. Erlan saw small antlers, and when it turned, the face of a dog. Yet those were human hands.

What the Hel kind of creature is this?

The fire now well lit, the creature crouched down, pulling a drum from under its fur. Peering into the flames, it began beating the drum, chanting low and guttural sounds that Erlan had never heard before.

Kai nudged him and shrugged. Erlan rose in response, and together they edged forward, hands hovering over hilts.

The snow must have given them away at once. But the figure only sat there, as if in some trance, apparently heedless to their approach. The smell from the dead woman poisoned the air.

At Erlan's signal, they jumped into the pool of light.

Immediately the creature came to life, snatching up a firebrand and leaping to its feet. Now visible was a bearskin covering, from head to toe, and a dog mask hiding the face. In its hand was a gnarled stick.

'What are you?' murmured Erlan.

'He's a *seidman*,' answered Kai.

The figure said nothing. But then brittle laughter pattered through the mask, and the weird figure began beating the drum round his neck. There was no rhythm to the beat. It was jerky, irregular, and he capered about, brandishing his burning stick.

Erlan tried to fix his gaze on the mask, but the flame kept dancing before his eyes, its brightness making them weary.

'What are you doing here?' he said, trying to see past the flame.

'Sitting out,' the other replied, beating his drum. 'Under the hanged. The dead speak. I listen.' The voice sounded pinched and high.

'You *are* a *seidman* then,' blurted Kai.

'How can a man speak with the dead?' asked Erlan, shifting his feet to see better the *seidman*'s mask. But the *seidman* hid stubbornly behind the flame.

'The way into darkness is through the light.' He suddenly swept the torch between them and the flame roared. 'I do what you are doing. I focus on the flame. See how it dances? How it's alive? The fire is the wave carrying you into other worlds. The fire burns and bears away your spirit into the arms of Yggdrasil. Deeper and deeper to the very roots of the World Tree.' He gave a guttural laugh. Erlan's eyes were growing tired, the fitful tapping of the drum confusing him. 'See deeper into the flames – as I do. The dead dwell beyond the light. They call from the darkness. They want to speak. They long for a living ear. Through the fire, their words come. And so the trance comes on me. Slowly. Surely. Until—' *BANG!* The *seidman* gave a violent rap on his drum. 'The threshold is crossed, Yggdrasil is ready, and the Nine Worlds are mine, to fare whither I will.'

285

The bang had startled Erlan. He shook himself as if waking from a dream. For a moment, he couldn't remember where he was.

Then he heard Kai speaking.

'There was a story once,' the boy was saying, though his voice seemed unnaturally laboured. 'About a man cursed, dwelling in these forests. They said he danced with dark spirits. That he summoned the *draugar* from the lands of mist. Folk said when a baby died, it was because he had put the black eye on that house.'

The *seidman* sounded his brittle laugh, drawing closer to Kai. 'You think the story true?'

'I had a baby sister. She died. Here, in my arms.' His eyes hardened. 'Was that you – you furry freak?'

'Now, now, youngling – you should watch your tongue.'

'I'm old enough to draw a sword and give you a taste of it.'

The *seidman* only laughed harder.

'Why are you laughing?' Kai's voice was drowsy, his sword still sheathed, almost forgotten.

'I laugh because you're much bolder than you are able. In a moment, you *will* draw your sword, but you'll be unable to lift it any better than your beloved baby sister. Is that all you are, friend? A big baby?'

'You dog!' cried Kai, seizing his hilt at last. But it was all he could do to unsheathe it. The point hit the ground like lead. Puffing and straining, Kai heaved it up, then took a swing. The blade arced lazily over his shoulder and hit the snow with a thud. The *seidman* skipped aside, laughing. 'A brave effort, lad! And again!' Kai tried a second time, boiling with frustration, but with the same result.

Erlan watched the two of them as through a dream. He wanted to move, but somehow his will felt as leaden as Kai's sword. Eventually, he managed to force his hand onto Wrathling's hilt.

'No, no, friend,' said the *seidman*, seeing his move. 'Before that, first heed my warning.'

'What warning?' His tongue felt thick and slow.

'Beware my friends.'

'What friends?'

'Why – the spirits of the dead! They are all around us!'

'Your talk won't fool me, *seidman*.'

'No fooling,' cried the other, dodging another cumbersome blow from Kai. 'The dead are here. And far stronger than you, I promise.'

'Lies.' Erlan's fingers tightened. 'Just lies.'

'You don't believe me!' The *seidman* laughed wildly. 'Then I'll prove it. When you go to draw your sword, you'll find it stuck fast. The dead will stay your hand.'

Goaded by his taunts, Erlan tried to draw his blade. But however hard he tugged, the thing wouldn't shift.

'*Heeheehee!*' giggled the *seidman*, prancing about with glee. 'See – the dead are my friends! They always protect me!'

'What witchcraft is this, fiend?'

'Now, now – no need for such names.' Kai lunged again, while Erlan wrestled on, but to no avail. The *seidman* hopped aside, unharmed.

'A baby like you shouldn't be fighting at all,' he crowed.

'I'll show you baby!'

'You're a game little fellow, I'll give you that. All the same, I could knock you out with barely a touch.'

'I'm tougher than you think, old dog!'

'That so?' The *seidman* fell back a step. 'I warn you – soon as I touch you, you'll drop senseless.'

Kai bellowed his defiance, mustering the last of his strength for a killing blow. His sword wheeled, sluggish as ever, but before he could swing it any further, the *seidman* darted forward and struck him on his back. It was the lightest of touches, but Kai toppled like a felled tree into the snow, out cold.

'Wretch!' cried Erlan. 'I'll snap your neck with my bare hands.'

'My dull-witted friend – I don't want to fight you. And I won't. All I need do is tap this drum and your feet will be stuck fast as your sword. *Heeheeee!* My friends will bind you tighter than Fenrir's leash!'

Erlan squared up, ready to grapple the strange little man, who stood completely still, the nose of his dog mask sniffing the air. But the moment Erlan moved, the *seidman* struck his drum. When he went for another step, his feet stuck fast. He pulled and wrenched in a frenzy of frustration, but he couldn't budge an inch.

'Didn't I warn you?' jeered the dog-face, hopping around, poking him with his stick. 'Some warrior you are! Outwitted and outfought by an old man! I told you,' he squawked gleefully. 'The spirits of the hanged always help me.'

'This is damned sorcery!' shouted Erlan, furious at his helplessness.

''Tis the play of children! No more.'

'I swear we'll make you sorry.'

'Will you?' The voice darkened. 'And how will you do that? I have power over you of which you know nothing at all.'

Erlan lunged for him, but immediately fell over, feet stuck fast.

'A man should know when he's beaten.' The *seidman* gave him another jab in the ribs, this time hard enough to hurt.

'Ow!' exclaimed Erlan.

'See, your friend.' The *seidman* poked his staff at the prostrate figure of Kai, still lying unconscious. 'You *do* see him, don't you?'

''Course I fucking see him.'

'What if I could send him to the blackest caverns of Helheim, simply with the tap of a drum?'

'You're a liar,' said Erlan, scornfully.

'Maybe. . . And maybe I'm telling the truth. Even so, when I hit this drum, you won't see your friend any more.'

Without delay, the *seidman* struck his drum, and Erlan nearly fell over a second time. Kai had vanished.

'Where's he gone?' he yelled. 'What have you done with him?'

'I told you. The boy is languishing in the halls of the dead. I don't imagine he much likes it there.'

'Bring him back, wretch.'

'I can,' snapped the *seidman*. 'But I won't. Not till I have your word you won't try to harm me again.' He chuckled. 'Believe it or not, I've no interest in killing you or your fierce young friend.'

'Swear you'll bring him back first.'

'You have my word. . . now give me yours.'

'Very well. You have it. Bring him back, and we'll leave you in peace. I swear it.'

The dog mask twitched side to side. Erlan could see the bright eyes within, weighing him up. 'All right – I believe you.

289

It's a simple thing. Another tap of the drum and you'll see him again.'

He did it. And there was Kai, just as he had been. Erlan tried to go to him, but he was still stuck. 'Aha!' laughed the *seidman*. 'Time for the spirits to be on their way.' He snapped his fingers and hissed, 'Release!'

Erlan fell to his knees, his feet finally free. His mind felt lighter too. Suddenly clear. He hurried to Kai.

'Don't fret yourself. He's only asleep.'

And so he was. Erlan roused him. The boy awoke with a confused look. 'What just happened?'

'I. . . I have no idea.'

'A small encounter with the other worlds,' declared the *seidman*. 'Unless I miss my guess, you were seeking some excitement – weren't you, youngling? For you,' he added, handing Erlan the torch. With a quick movement, he removed his mask.

He was old. Old as the forest, it seemed, though his features were sharp as a hawk's. The skin of his cheeks was taut and cracked like old leather and his eyes were ringed with hard living.

Kai eyed him suspiciously.

'My name is Grimnar.' He fixed Kai with a warm smile. 'I'm sorry about your sister. Truly. . . It was not I who was responsible for her death. Now you must be hungry, youngling. I have food and shelter not far from here. I'm not well-practised at hosting, but you're welcome for the night. Do you accept?'

The companions exchanged glances. Kai gave the slightest shake of his head.

'A watchful fellow, aren't you? But you've nothing to fear.'

290

'We accept then,' said Erlan. Kai scowled.

'Excellent,' croaked Grimnar. 'Then follow me.'

It was long past midnight when they sat in darkness in Grimnar's hovel, listening to the *click-click* of flint striking steel. Outside, the horses waited in the shelter of a vast slab of granite spewed out of the earth, under which Grimnar had built his dwelling.

Sparks burst like tiny stars onto a char-cloth, and the tinder caught. In moments, fire illumined the hut. The first wreath of smoke curled up through the turf-roof.

Erlan looked about. The earthen floor was empty, apart from a few pots and a pile of furs in the corner. But what drew his eye were the masks on the wall, each a different animal. Wolf, deer, eagle, raven. Besides these, two crooked switches of ash. The place smelled of earth and sweat and smoke.

'Not always a dog?' Erlan gestured at the masks.

'Depends where I wish to go.' Grimnar gave him a crafty look and threw off his bearskin onto the pile of furs.

'Meaning?'

'There are more ways a man may fare through this world than by walking on his legs.'

'Shape-shifting?' murmured Kai.

Grimnar gave a ringing laugh. 'You have much to learn, both of you! Now, let's see what we have.'

He ducked out for a few moments, only to reappear shortly with a wood pigeon in each hand, plucked from the dead menagerie he had hanging from the branches of a withered old oak tree outside.

'These should keep you happy.'

Grimnar went to the corner to prepare them. Kai leaned over and whispered, 'Guess a pigeon's better than one of them rotten old stoats.'

'So what do they call you?'

'I am Erlan. This here is Kai Askarsson.'

'Just Erlan?' A ghost of a smile. 'Don't you have a father?'

'Every man has a father. Not every man chooses to bear his name.'

Grimnar stopped his cutting and shot Erlan a curious look. 'Where are you from?'

When Erlan didn't answer, Kai spoke up. 'Not far from here, from—'

'Oh, I know where *you're* from.' The corner of the old *seidman*'s mouth gave a complacent flicker. 'Tyrstorp, on the shore of the Lake of Two Forests.'

'How . . . ?' Kai shook his head. 'But how can you know?'

'More witchcraft?' suggested Erlan.

Grimnar snorted. 'It's simple enough. Your blond hair and speech mark you for a Gotar. You have the wide mouth of many folk who dwell around the shores of that lake – kinsfolk, no doubt. You still carry the stench of fish on you – though here we are in the middle of a forest – so your home must be a fishing community not far from here. The sword you wield so expertly has an unusually shallow point – a style crafted only by a pair of brother smiths who dwell on the lake. The older makes his hilts of ash. The younger, of oak. The younger dwells at Tyrstorp. . . Your hilt is of oak.'

'His name is Ketil,' said Kai, eyes wide with admiration. 'Do I really stink that bad?'

Erlan laughed and gave Kai a friendly kick. 'No worse than the rest of us.' He nodded at Grimnar. 'For a man who lives alone in the forest, you're uncommon well-informed.'

Grimnar shrugged. 'One has only to listen. And to look.'

'And me?'

Grimnar looked long at the stranger. 'You. . . You do not want to be read. So I will not.'

'Huh!' shrugged Erlan. 'Indeed, nor will I tell. To do so would break a vow.'

'An intriguing guest then, as I thought.' The *seidman* smiled to himself. He had finished preparing the birds and came to the fire where a pot of water was already boiling. He tossed in the meat and began to drop in different herbs.

'Well, stranger, speak of what you can. Where are you headed?'

'We ride to the court of King Sviggar.'

'Sviggar,' he repeated. 'And what do you know of this king?' Erlan thought there was a trace of mockery in his voice.

'Not much, I grant you. In truth, Kai knows a sight more than I.'

Kai nodded, but said nothing, his eyes intent on what was going in the pot.

'So tell me.'

Erlan sniffed. 'He's a great king. The greatest in all of the northern lands, the way this one tells it. He commands unrivalled power in men and gold.'

'Indeed, he has been a great king,' Grimnar agreed. '*Is* a great king.' He chuckled. 'But will he be a great king in time to come? Who can tell?'

'It sounds like his luck is good enough. And if his hall is

half as grand as its renown, he must need men who can wield a sword.'

Suddenly, Kai snatched Grimnar's wrist. 'What's that, old man?'

'This?' Grimnar held up the sprig of herbs he'd been about to toss into the stew. 'Why, it's good. Better when fresh, but still good enough if you dry it out. I call it Frey's Fern.'

'I've never seen it. I'll bet it's poisonous.'

'Ha! You are a good watchdog, aren't you? Still don't trust me?'

'For all I know you plan to murder us, slit our bellies, and read our entrails, or some such devilry.'

'What an imagination you have!' the *seidman* laughed. 'No – this is quite safe. And rare. It only grows after a warm spring in the sunny parts of the forest where the soil is dry. Try some.' He held out the sprig.

'Not likely.' Kai folded his arms.

Grimnar shook his head. 'Very well, I shall eat it.'

So he did, popping the sprig in his mouth and chewing with the few teeth he had left. 'Delicious.' He held out another. After a time, Kai conceded, took it, and very doubtfully put it in his mouth. He chewed a few times, eyes fixed on Grimnar, then swallowed.

'Well?'

'Not bad. . .' nodded the boy. 'Not bad at all.'

Grimnar suddenly burst out laughing and slapped him on the back. 'Come, young wanderer, what do you think of me? We're all friends! Even if some of us must keep their secrets.' He tipped his head at Erlan.

His laughter faded and for a while the only sound was the

bubbling of the pot.

'What do *you* know of this king then?' asked Erlan.

'What do *I* know? That is the question. . .' He took a long spoon and stirred the pot. 'What I know I haven't learned from the mouths of men,' he began. 'The forest is alive with talk. Wood spirits, lake spirits. . . They carry long memories of the past, of things that even those with the far-sight have never known. And the chatter of the birds and beasts of the forest seldom ceases.'

'What do they speak of?'

'They call to one another of what they've seen – of tidings from afar – beyond the forest into the realm of this great king, and further still.'

'What do they tell of Sveäland?'

Grimnar sighed. 'For many moons, I've heard rumours of an enemy that troubles the old king. They say it cannot be seen nor heard. Folk disappear. Murders abound. His kingdom is awash with bodies slaughtered. And none knows why. Fear feeds on the hearts of his people. But what can he do?' There was a mischievous twinkle in the old man's eye. 'A man cannot fight an enemy no one has seen.'

'It's not a rival lord? Or raiding parties come by stealth?'

'Neither,' replied the old mystic. 'In truth, far worse. This much I've learned from the forest voices: it is an ancient enemy of mankind, which chooses to make itself known once more. They have many names. Earth-dwellers. . . the shadowfolk. . .'

'Where are they from?'

'From?' Grimnar grimaced. 'They dwell in the dark places now, but it was not always so. They worshipped savage gods who knew nothing of honour. Nothing of simple blessings like the good sun or a woman's kiss. Their gods were the great spirits of death and greed and deceit and all kinds of wickedness. But most men would not follow them. Only those who wanted this power for themselves, or those enthralled by it.' He stirred his spoon in the pot, as if stirring his own thoughts. 'Those who did changed. They began to become what they worshipped, feeding off the weak. Creating nothing, devouring everything. Wanting only to absorb whatever was weaker into themselves. Where they saw beauty, they wanted to despoil it. Courage and honesty they mocked. Mirth and kinship were the vilest of things to them. They were bound to one another only by chains of power: master to slave. They learned how to enthral the cruellest of nature, and became so disfigured in their corruption that they took to hiding from the light.'

'But then. . . are they men?' asked Erlan.

'Of a kind – aye. Yet not like any you've known. But they are remembered all the same – in old stories of old times.'

'I've heard no tale like that,' said Kai. 'Nor any songs of these. . . what did you call them? Earth-dwellers?'

'Oh, but you have,' smiled Grimnar. 'I'll stake my head you heard of them on your mother's knee. Though she would have called them the darklings.'

Erlan burst out laughing. 'Darklings! You are joking!'

'Why would I joke?'

'But those are just stories to scare little bairns who know no better,' joined Kai. 'Even they don't believe 'em long.'

'Aye – old yarns about dripping teeth and snatching claws,' agreed Erlan. 'Monsters that'll eat you up if you don't do what your nurse says. No one's ever seen one.'

Grimnar's impish eyes hardened. 'And you two have such wide knowledge of the world, I suppose?'

'Enough to know a tall tale.'

'Ha! You may as well be fresh from your mothers' bellies, the pair of you! So answer me this, my world-wise friends: where is the lightning born? What sorrows do the ancient rocks lament? What seed raised Yggdrasil to life? How old is the moon? How many are the stars? What dwells in the deepest caverns, or soars above the highest peak?' The mystic's questions fired like a volley of arrows. 'Who birthed the gods, or built the black halls of death? Tell me – I'm listening!'

But Erlan and his friend sat dumb as oxen.

'Come, friends – what is your answer?' demanded Grimnar, snappishly.

Erlan sniffed. 'Of course, we have none.'

'Of course. Then who are you to say what is, and what is not?' The *seidman* grinned sourly. 'No one has seen a darkling, you say. Perhaps not – in living memory. But a man would be wise to fear them, all the same. Men are no strangers to evil, to be sure. But a man's evil is his weakness – aye, even if it serves him well. The evil of the darklings. . . it is what they *are*, and nothing else.'

'What you say may be true, but it is a hard thing to believe.'

'I don't doubt it.'

Silence lingered between them.

'You tell a good tale, old man,' said Kai, at length. 'True or not, we've learned one thing: King Sviggar wouldn't turn away a willing sword or two.'

'Likely he'd welcome you. If he trusts you.'

'Why wouldn't he?' asked Erlan.

Grimnar smiled enigmatically. 'Trust is like gold in a fool's hand – hard to win, easy to lose. But don't trouble yourselves

297

with that for now. Here's food to warm your bellies.' He ladled the stew into a couple of battered bowls. With the steam still rising, they set about their meal – a salty pigeon stew with crusts of hard black bread to soak up the dregs. Better than Erlan had reckoned on eating that night.

'Delicious,' was Kai's verdict, delivered with a hearty belch when he'd finished.

Grimnar grinned. 'Now, my dear guests, I must leave you.'

'Where are you going?' asked Erlan.

'Why, back to our unfortunate friends! The spirits of the dead do not linger long in this world. If I am to learn anything from them, I must sit out under the hanged until dawn. At the breaking of day, they will depart.'

'We leave before dawn.'

The mystic spread his hands. 'So you will not see me again.'

'Well then – you have our thanks for the food and shelter,' Erlan nodded. 'Can you put us on our way to Sveäland?'

'Into Sveäland, it's simple enough. From this hill, the ground falls and rises twice more and then you come to two great cliffs, sheer and smooth to the left, jagged and rough to the right. Through the cut and beyond lies the land of the Sveärs. But from there, the journey on to Sviggar's Great Hall is yet many leagues and is by no means easy. Sviggar is the Sveär king, but in truth the forest still rules that land.' He smiled kindly at Kai. 'Even so, I've a feeling you're a resourceful pair. I'm sure you will find your way.'

He collected his bearskin and swung it over his shoulders. The headpiece dropped into place, and in an eye-blink, the odd figure they had stumbled upon in the glade was before them once more.

'Now, let's bid each other farewell.' Erlan took Grimnar's proffered hand, but no sooner had he than the *seidman* snatched him close, sharp fingers digging into his arm.

'Stranger – this is what I see.' His nimble eyes shone. 'A man running from his past will never be free of it.' He tapped Erlan's forehead with a bony finger. 'But for all you carry in here, remember this. Only when a man is truly lost is he ready for his destiny to find him.'

Destiny? thought Erlan. The word disgusted him. *What destiny of mine could be worth a drop of Inga's blood?*

Grimnar released the stranger and turned to Kai.

'And you, young friend.' Kai was looking more than a little wary of the *seidman*. 'Farewell, watchdog. Here, give me your hand.'

When Kai snatched it away, the *seidman* chuckled. 'You needn't be afraid.'

Doubtfully, Kai surrendered his grubby paw. Grimnar took it.

'The wind blows well for you. The thirsts of your heart will be quenched sooner than you think. But be careful what you seek – time hastens a man's doom as well as his dreams.'

Dropping Kai's hand, he went to the door and lifted the skins. A lick of cold air curled into the hovel. The bear's head turned one last time.

'Listen to the forest. Listen. And watch.'

The curtain fell, and the *seidman* was gone.

CHAPTER TWENTY-ONE

They found the rock cut just as Grimnar described. The horses trudged on to the other side at their usual plod.

'Sveäland,' said Kai.

It was the first word either had spoken all morning. The night had thinned into a fine day with the sun dancing through the pine trees on golden shafts.

As far as Erlan was concerned, Kai's uncharacteristic silence was a welcome change. The air felt crisp in his lungs, and they were making good progress.

It was midday when Kai spoke again. 'Strange way to spend your days, don't you reckon?'

Erlan glanced over. 'Grimnar?'

'He's a curious old bird. I mean, what does he actually do with everything he knows? Sitting out there alone.' He shuffled in his seat. 'I had the strangest dream last night, too.'

'Well?'

Kai shrugged. 'Not exactly easy to describe.'

'Dreams sometimes slip away as easily as they come.'

'Not this one.' Kai narrowed his eyes, remembering. 'I felt like the fire grew hotter as I slept, and then so hot I opened my eyes. But I wasn't in his hut any more. I was back where you found me. Tied up and stripped, just as I was. And I looked up and there you were – except you weren't beyond the fire, but right inside it. And you were burning. I couldn't hear your voice, but I could see your face. You were screaming. Screaming and screaming, and I couldn't do a thing about it. I tugged like a bull at the ropes, but couldn't get loose, my arms were stretched so wide. I wanted to help you, and I cursed and kicked the snow till my feet bled. Then it started raining, light at first, then harder till I was soaked through. And the rain was putting out the fire – you were still screaming but the flames dropped lower. Then I saw the rain on my skin, and it wasn't rain. It was blood – big fat droplets of blood, like the tears of the *valkyries* in the songs.' Erlan turned to look at the boy. Kai's face had a fey glow about it. His eyes were closed. 'The blood-rain was soaking me and putting out the fire. And I knew you'd be all right, and the blood was kind of washing me, till I was cleaner than if I'd been licked new by Audumla herself. You stepped out of the fire, which was all ashes now, and suddenly the ropes around my wrists broke, and I fell on my knees, just like when you cut me down.'

He paused.

'Go on.'

'That's it.' Kai looked up. 'What do you think it means?'

'How should I know? I'm no mystic.' Erlan snorted. 'Maybe it means you shouldn't eat pigeon stew.'

Kai chuckled. 'Maybe.' Then he seemed to think of something else, and he laughed even harder. 'I mean – darklings! Really?'

. . . .

301

At first, Erlan had been encouraged to reach Sveäland, and felt their journey must soon be over. But as day followed weary day, monotony and hunger began to take their toll, till he thought that they would never reach the end of the forest. His scrawny companion became even scrawnier, if that were possible. Erlan would look over at him and read his own hunger in the boy's face. His sunken cheeks, the wispish scrub of hair on his chin flecked with ice, his thin slumped shoulders, the dark rings of fatigue circling his now lustreless eyes. He wasn't exactly a fine specimen of a man. But Erlan feared to think what he must look like himself.

Weeks in the saddle had soiled his clothes beyond recognition, together with the feverish sweats that had soaked them again and again. His hair was matted, hard and stiff as straw, crawling with lice. His skin had broken out in sores all over his body. His joints ached constantly whether in the saddle or leading Idun by foot. And in his mind, the waking nightmares of his guilt and grief that had plagued him for so long began to be overwhelmed by fantasies of food. For hours, he would rock back and forward in his saddle, his eyes too weary to focus, dreaming of mountains of food: of swine-roasts or fresh-baked bread; of cheeses or steaming fish stews; of frothing ale-cups or hot spiced apple wine; of ladles overflowing with honey or dripping hunks of crisp burned beef. But there was precious little promise of anything like that on their horizon.

When a rabbit happened through their camp and Kai managed to brain it with his sword, the two of them danced about like children on a name-day. And again, when Kai spied a jackdaw's nest and skinned up a tree to find it full of speckled eggs.

302

Once, they surprised a boar leading a file of piglets across a clearing and gave chase, yelling and bawling loud enough to wake a dead man. But Idun was done in thirty paces, and Kai's pony had thrown him when the boar turned to defend her brood and charged them. Erlan found Kai flat on his back in the snow, venting foul-mouthed curses upon the lineage of every boar within twenty leagues. It would have been funny, but for the dull, gnawing ache that never left their bellies.

Another time they came across the carcass of a wolverine, its ribs laid open and being picked over by a pair of ravens. The stink was awful, although there was still good meat on the body, and Erlan had to think long and hard before he said they should leave the birds to their feast.

They pushed on through the gloom of their forest prison, listening to the winter winds gathering strength as they howled mournfully through the treetops, groping their way through sepulchral mists. They witnessed dawns pale as *draug*-spirits and sunsets red as blood, until they lost count of how many days had passed since their strange encounter with the *seidman*.

And then, one day, they came to the northern edge of the great forest. A wide white plain spread out before them and in the near distance, the first homely trail of smoke wavered up into the sky. Relief washed over Erlan, but disquiet soon took its place. Outlanders could never be certain of a warm reception, least of all a pair who looked at best like beggars, at worst like a couple of thieves. His wits had become dull on the road, blunted by the tumult of painful memories he had carried across that lonely land. The time had come to gather them. Sharpen them to a keen edge. He had a feeling he would need them.

They soon came to the first homestead where they begged a couple of barley-loaves. But even in their state, Erlan was ashamed to linger when he saw how little the family had for themselves.

It wasn't long before solitary dwellings and lonely little hamlets grew into bigger farmsteads surrounded by low-lying hedgerows that marked fields buried under the snow. The Sveärs were hardly open-hearted folk. But at least the pair had their bellies filled for the first time in a long while, and most folk were willing to direct them on their way towards Sviggar's Seat.

Kai's good humour returned. 'You wait till we ride up to the old bastard's big hall. They'll welcome us like a pair of bloody heroes!'

Was that what Erlan was? *A hero.* Not a beggar. Not a runaway. *Not a murderer?*

They came to a wide lake, which an old cart-driver had told them they could cross if the ice were thick enough.

'We've 'ad some good 'ard frosts by now,' he'd said, scratching at the dirty cloths swaddling his head against the cold. 'Reckon there's ice enough wot'll save you a day in the saddle, if yer going dead across.'

'Obliged to you,' nodded Erlan, his ear getting more attuned to the Sveärs' lilting way of speaking.

'If you go fallin' through, no use coming back to rattle me,' he'd called after them.

On this less than assuring advice, they had set out onto the lake with some hesitation. Erlan's heart was in his mouth all the while. His body still carried the memory of the awful cold that had seeped through to his marrow.

But winter had tightened its grip and the ice held.

They were halfway across when horsemen suddenly appeared from the trees on the far side.

'Riders!' cried Kai.

Erlan swore.

The horsemen turned at once to head them off, approaching at a canter, apparently with none of his qualms about whether the ice would break.

'Keep your wits about you,' said Erlan. 'And let me do the talking.'

He counted five men, all armed. Four carried long-spears on horses sleek and healthy. It was obvious that if they tried to run, they'd get a point in their backs before they'd even made the trees.

They sat motionless, hands on hilts, as the riders circled them, their animals snorting misty breath. The men wore mailshirts under heavy cloaks, and looked like they knew the business end of a spear.

One man stood out: the man without a spear. He had a predatory look, tugging his horse back and forth, never taking his eye off them. His rusty beard was longer than the rest, flecked white under a nose like a broken flint. He glowered with suspicion.

'Outlanders! What are you doing here?' he demanded, blunt as a cudgel.

'Who are you?' Erlan's eye darted from face to face.

'I'll ask the questions here, churl.'

'Why should we answer you?'

'How about because we're king's men, and you're a couple of whoreson beggars?' snarled the leader. 'Or because I could have you filled with more pricks than a Yuletide whore before you could scratch your balls?' The man leaned closer. 'How about 'cause I'm earl of the land you're fucking standing on!'

'Point of fact, we're standing on a lake,' said Kai.

'Jape like that again, boy, and I'll split that long mouth through the back of your skull.' The way he talked, Erlan could believe it.

This could turn ugly very quickly. It should've been good fortune to run into the king's men so soon. But somehow this wasn't feeling lucky. 'We've come from Western Gotarland.'

'You're no Gotar with hair that dark.' He cast a scathing look at Kai. 'The runt, maybe.' Kai's face showed he didn't much care for the handle. 'You're no trappers, nor traders. Hel, you look like someone just dug you up. What's your business in Sveäland?'

'We ride to offer service to your king.'

The spearmen rippled with laughter. The earl smiled. 'I'm sure he'll be fucking delighted.' To say the pair of them looked less than impressive was a towering understatement. They hardly looked fit to serve a swineherd, let alone a king.

'Will you take us to him?'

'The king'll want to see you, no doubt about that.' His men sniggered again. 'Who are you?'

'My name is Erlan.'

The earl shrugged. 'That it?'

'That's all I can tell you.'

Kai rolled his eyes.

'That's telling me nothing, stranger. Where are you from? Who are your people?'

'I cannot say. I've sworn to it.'

'That's a murderer's oath, stranger, and you know it.'

306

'I made it for my own reasons.'

'They'd better be damn good ones. So happens, we're looking for a murderer.'

'We came to Sveäland to serve, not to kill.' Erlan threw the corner of his cloak over his shoulder. 'But we will if we must.' The earl didn't fail to notice Wrathling's hilt at his belt. His expression suddenly changed. He brushed his hand over his mouth, thoughtfully.

'Who sent you here?'

'No one.'

'Was it the Wartooth?' he said, sharply.

'The Wartooth?' For a moment, Erlan was thrown. 'Why—'

'Or one of his sons?'

'I don't know what you mean.'

The earl nodded to himself. 'Aye – I begin to see it clear. Murder the son, then slither your way into the bosom of the king. A venomous bite for him, too. Is that the old boar's plan?'

'What son? Who is murdered?'

The earl chuckled, coldly. 'It's plain enough: you're an outlander by speech, and dark. A Dane, if I had to wager. Riding through lands where the king's son was killed, dressed like a beggar, but carrying a sword to rival any in the land. Doubtless a gift from the old boar himself. What Dane would come to Sveäland but by the bidding of Harald Wartooth?'

Erlan felt the spearmen bristle at mention of the name of the Danish king. 'We're here at no one's bidding but my own.'

'We'll take you to Sviggar right enough. And you'll answer his questions, oath or none.' The earl gave a signal and the spearpoints dropped. 'Throw down your weapons.'

307

Erlan wheeled Idun, glaring around at the lowered points. These men were of different mettle altogether than Arald and his gang of thieves. Kai was looking nervously for his lead, face white with fear. But his hand stayed steady on his hilt. 'We'll come with you if we must,' offered Erlan. 'But not as captives. We keep our weapons.'

'Not a chance.' The earl gave a brisk nod. 'Take them.'

His men moved forward. But Erlan was ahead of them.

He threw himself forward over Idun's shoulder, hitting the ice and snow hard. He rolled, came up at a crouch, Wrathling already in his hand. The earl's boot dangled only a foot away. He hauled it with all he had. The air was thick with shouting, the earl's bellow loudest of all as he toppled into the snow.

Erlan was on him at once, snatching his braids, yanking back his head, Wrathling's razored edge kissing his stubble.

'Erlan!' Kai's voice was raw with fear. He looked up. The blizzard of movement was suddenly over. All seven men were still. Three spears were sticking Kai in the ribs and back. The fourth spearman was poised, arm aloft, point aimed at Erlan's chest.

'Back!' snarled Erlan, dragging the earl backwards. 'Back or I cut him!' He guessed these men were vassals to the earl – sworn to do everything in their power to keep the gnarly old bastard alive. It wouldn't do their reputation much good to see him killed by a pair of scabby outlanders.

The earl growled his defiance. Erlan pressed the edge closer, feeling it bite. The earl stiffened. Kai was pale with terror, his sword halfway unsheathed. Erlan cursed inwardly. He couldn't just let them kill the boy.

'Release him – or your lord dies now.'

'You're in no position to bargain, outlander,' rasped the earl.

Erlan snorted. 'I'd say I've a fair opening position, wouldn't you?' He squeezed the blade tighter, and the earl gave a yelp. 'Now – we are going to keep our weapons. And you're going to drop your spears. Else I start painting the snow with your oath-lord's blood.'

The earl's head twisted. 'Fuck yourself, stranger. Kill the brat and skewer this whoreson next! When you throw his corpse before the king, tell him Bodvar Beriksson found his son's killer.'

One man grimaced with satisfaction. Erlan watched his knuckles tighten around his spear. Kai must have felt the point prick deeper because he screamed, long and loud.

'Wait!' cried Erlan. 'Wait. . .' The eager spearman stopped, poised like a dog awaiting his master's word. 'Don't kill him.'

'Your sword down, now!'

Bitterly, Erlan flung it in the snow. Earl Bodvar was up in a second. In the next, he put a fist into Erlan's jaw. Pain doubled him over, while the earl snatched Wrathling out of the snow.

'A fine blade,' he declared, admiring the hilt's workmanship. 'I'm sure King Sviggar will be grateful for it. I hope your boy is as grateful for his life.'

Erlan grunted, nursing his jaw. Next to his sword, the boy's gratitude was about as much use as a fire on a frozen lake.

A short while later, the companions were slung astride their horses, trussed like a couple of hens for market. Kai looked decidedly glum.

'At least we're headed in the right direction,' muttered Erlan.

'Your bloody oath,' spat Kai. 'Nearly had me stuck like a pig.'

'If your master pulls a trick like that on the king,' said Bodvar, overhearing, 'I promise you, boy – you both will be.'

· · · · · · ·

If their acquaintance with Bodvar had begun on a bad footing, the earl's prickly disposition did little to improve it. The most the earl would tell them was that Sviggar's Seat lay two hard days' ride to the northeast, three with the snow. 'Four with you two beggars on those things,' he said, with a scathing look at their mangy mounts.

He was right. It was hard work keeping pace with their escort, and Bodvar boiled with impatience at their slow progress. Each day when evening fell, the party sought refuge from the cold in farmsteads along the way. Under Sviggar's law, folk were obliged to provide the king's men with whatever little they had. The scraps that found their way into Erlan's belly after they'd had their fill were few enough. Even so, he was grateful for the roof overhead and the warmth of a proper hearth. Rest for his road-racked bones.

But his mind gave him little peace.

Perhaps Grimnar was right. *Destiny*, he thought. *The web of destiny.* He felt it now. For now it was not only his own past which had led him there, which stretched before him to shape the road he must walk. It seemed the threads of other men's lives were being woven into his – other pasts and other futures. Debts graven into the bark of the Tree of Worlds.

What must be...

The past, unchangeable. The future, inexorable. The debt of every deed, inescapable.

In the darkness, he saw the glint of Kai's bright eyes, still awake long into the night. Doubtless he too was anxious about the fate awaiting them at the hall of the Sveär king.

Soon, the waiting would be over.

On the fourth day, they rode the final leagues to Sviggar's Seat. A blazing sun lit up the land.

Along their road, trickles of passers-by swelled to a stream, the stream to a river. Traders with carts laden with pelts; bondsmen with mules labouring under grain-sacks; peasant women, so wrapped up they looked like bales of wool come to life, racks of dried fish propped on their shoulders. Everywhere children played, crunching their feet through icy puddles. Warriors and karls eased along on horseback, chatting and spitting and chuckling, indifferent to the low folk slopping through the slush beside them.

All stared, wide-eyed, as the earl and his riders passed, with the dark stranger and his scrawny companion in their midst.

Hammering rang out from the smithies lining the road. Erlan saw roaring forges, half-wrought blades aglow in coals, piles of leather cuttings, heaps of crude-cut brooches. Women huddled under stalls where wool-stacks awaited spinning on trestles straining under their weight.

The air brimmed with the homely smells of mead and barley-ale from brew-houses, sour milk from dairy-barns, bubbling broths from cookhouses, fresh sawdust from sawmills and carpenters' booths.

Erlan had never seen so much industry. Could hardly have imagined it.

'Look there!' cried Bodvar. 'The King Barrows of Uppsala. Sviggar's halls are beyond.'

Erlan looked. Beyond the bustling craftsmen, three huge earthen mounds rose up into the morning sky, each high as the grandest hall, each covered in snow, perfectly round, perfectly alike.

'They look like giant tits!' cried Kai. 'What are they?'

'The reason for all this,' said Bodvar.

'For what?' asked Erlan.

'All you see,' replied the earl, with a sweep of his hand. 'Long ago, the rulers of the Sveärs were mere chieftains. But later, the seed of Yng were named kings.' He nodded at the three mounds. 'Here three of the mightiest Yngling kings were lain. Since then, this place has been the seat of the Sveär king.' He leaned over and spat. 'Whoever holds it holds the right to rule.'

'Is Sviggar of this Yngling line?' asked Erlan.

Bodvar shook his head. 'The last Yngling king perished in the flames of his own hall.' He grunted. 'They say folk hated him like a boil on the bollocks by the end. He was mad. Sviggar's father – Ivar Wide-Realm – took the kingdom from him.'

Erlan was about to ask more, but his words died on his lips. Up ahead, through a grove of trees, he spied a vast structure looming like a mountain of oak.

'Would you look at that!' exclaimed Kai.

The hall towered the height of ten men. Each verge-beam alone must have been cut from an entire trunk, the wood now cracked by weather and age. Its gable was alive with carvings: beasts, warriors, weapons, horns, ships, shields, all tossed together in a squall of movement, as if the wood was but a breath away from bursting to life and spilling slaughter onto the yard in front. And above it all a monstrous eagle, wings painted black as midnight, spread for flight. But the figure had a wolf's head, with cruel fangs and pitiless eyes scanning the horizon – the lupine face of Fenrir, Odin's Bane.

Below, the great entrance gaped like the gullet of some giant of old.

'Close your mouth, stranger,' Bodvar chuckled. 'Welcome to Sviggar's Great Hall.'

CHAPTER TWENTY-TWO

Bodvar wasted no time finding them a cosy place to rest before their audience with the king.

Cosy, that is, if you happened to be a rat.

He shoved them into a dank cellar, dug under some storehouse. Or so it must have been once, but there was nothing there now, save for broken potsherds, a leaky-looking bucket and a brazier, stained black as Hel, which was making a bad job of keeping off the cold.

Bodvar had at least left them their cloaks. But their rope-bonds he'd replaced with shackles of iron. And now they sat, trussed tight, until it pleased the king to give them a hearing.

Erlan guessed they wouldn't have long to wait.

His jaw throbbed from Bodvar's punch. The thick scab from the Boulder's cut itched like a nest of ants. His hair was crawling with lice, picked up from some host's bedding. Even the burn scars on his hands from his fight with Konur were still tender.

That seemed a lifetime ago. Someone's else life. *The life of that other man – Hakan.*

But Hakan was dead. *He died with his sister. . .*

It seemed odd to feel that separation. Perhaps it was the only way to protect him from his pain – to contain it within another's life. *Another's death.*

Yet if Erlan's body could feel pain, he must still be alive. He had his doubts whether he would be, come the morrow.

'Makes you wonder whether we woke in some other world,' said Kai, interrupting his thoughts.

'Eh?'

'This place. That hall.'

Erlan grunted. 'I suppose. Sviggar must be a great king.'

'So he must,' nodded Kai. 'And you learn the lesson, master.'

'Lesson?'

'Aye – to drop all your arse-headed notions of secret oaths and what not. Speak true, and maybe the old fart will let us live.'

Erlan snorted. What would the truth serve him in this land of strangers? Bodvar had made up his mind. Why should the king do any different? Anyway, he would offer Kai no reassurance.

'I'd worry about my own head, if I was you.'

'What do you think I'm doing?'

'You were the one who wanted to come with me. That was your choice. If you don't like it, the joke's on you.'

'Aye – the thought had occurred to me,' replied the boy, miserably.

'And sooner or later, this old king will deliver the punchline.'

. . . .

315

Sooner, it turned out.

They came for them at dawn, hauling them out, damp and dirty, with wrists bound and sacks over their heads. Erlan's ankle felt stiff as a rusted hinge after the cold night.

Hemp smelled strong in his nostrils as he hobbled forward, blind to where they were being led.

'Bodvar never said he'd caught himself a cripple,' sneered his guard, with a shove that brought him to his knees. The other guard sniggered as he picked himself up. 'Keep up with the runt.' He felt a spear-butt jab his back and groaned, but staggered on best he could until he was yanked to an abrupt halt.

'Follow me.' It was Bodvar's voice. 'And you.' Kai gave a yelp. 'Keep your mouth shut unless the king asks you something directly.'

Erlan was pitched forward again, with no choice but to follow Bodvar's footsteps blindly.

The light through the hood grew dim. The air felt dead. They must be inside, perhaps in the Great Hall itself. He wondered what grandeur was to be seen without the hood. He smelled smoke, cooking aromas, and the dusty scent of ancient oak. He heard women's voices, hushed but hurried, then footsteps thumping on wood.

'Steps,' the guard said, too late. He tripped, cracking his knee, cursing under his breath.

'Move,' said Bodvar. 'The king is waiting.'

Swallowing the pain, Erlan let himself be dragged across some kind of platform. He heard men's voices murmuring ahead. And then abruptly they fell silent.

'Remove their hoods,' said Bodvar.

The guard snatched off the sacking. Erlan blinked stupidly, trying to focus.

The air was dense with heat. The first thing his eyes grasped were flames dancing in braziers in the corners of a large chamber. On the walls, he glimpsed fading tapestries, dusty war-banners and buckler-shields.

Dominating the chamber was a large table, around which stood a group of men garbed in fine cloaks and furs, despite the heat. They varied in age and colouring, but Erlan knew which was the Sveär king in a moment.

The first thing he noticed were his eyes, glistening in the low light, dewy with age. Yet something in them remained sharp. His cloak was of a sky-blue weave, trimmed with wolverine, and around his brow he wore a simple band of gold. Wrinkles cracked his face like weathered oak.

So this is what a king looks like. . . like any other man. *Except he holds my life in his hands.*

'These are the men?' asked the king. His voice, though frayed, carried the mark of authority.

'They are,' answered Bodvar.

'That one is no more than a boy.' Sviggar raised a thin finger at Kai.

'The other's servant, sire.'

'They don't look dangerous.'

'The boy isn't. But this one.' The earl shoved Erlan forward. 'He passes as a traveller, come to offer you service. But his sword gave him away.'

'So you said. Anything more?'

'We've crossed the Forest of Tyr many times. I've had men ride the length of Vestmanland, looking for any sign out of the

317

ordinary. In a month, none had anything to tell. Until we came upon these two.'

The king looked Erlan over with his colourless gaze. 'My earl thinks you're one of Harald Wartooth's men. Come to satisfy the blood debt he thinks he owes our line.' He turned and the councillors parted. Erlan saw his ring-sword there on the table. Sviggar ran a hand along it. 'Is the blood already spilled not enough for Harald? Must he take from me even my own seed?' With sudden violence, he slammed the table. 'Did you murder my son?'

The silence that followed was heavy as lead. 'Well?'

Eventually, Erlan spoke. 'I know nothing of your son. Nor of his death. Nor of this Wartooth king.'

'Are you so ignorant that you haven't heard of the king of the Danes? He's ruled these thirty years past.'

'I've heard his name,' conceded Erlan. 'Beyond that, little enough.'

'Who are you?'

'His name is Erlan,' offered Bodvar. 'But he refuses to say where he's from.'

'Is this true?' asked Sviggar.

'It is.'

'The insolence of a madman.' The voice belonged to a younger man, glowering across the table with eyes set a shade too close. 'Or else a fool.'

Are you a fool, my love?

'You have no friends here, stranger,' added the younger man.

Well, it wasn't quite true. Then again, his only friend's prospects looked about as rosy as a fat pig's in the month of Yule.

318

Not unlike his own. . .

'If Earl Bodvar has already spoken of me,' he replied, 'he will have told you of my vow – that I will never speak of my past. Neither for man nor gods.'

'This is supposed to make us trust you?' asked the king.

'Whether it does or not, I'm bound by the oath I swore.'

'Surely you realize how easily we could make you talk? Oath or not – I have men who could make you beg to tell whatever you're hiding before the sun reaches the mid-mark.'

'That is your choice.'

The king stepped closer. 'My son is dead!' A sinewy hand cracked across Erlan's face, jerking back his head. 'If you are responsible, you will admit it.'

The prospect of serving this man as lord was looking less and less appealing. But why else had he come?

Another man spoke up – one of the fair-hairs, not much older than Erlan. 'Sire, would you hear me?'

The king grunted his assent. 'As you will, Finn.'

'You know I loved your son like a brother. If this man – or any – were responsible, I would happily see Staffen avenged. But I was with him that day. I was first to him when. . . well, when he was killed. We saw no one. And we were leagues from the nearest village. All we found was the antler.' He paused, unsure whether to go on. 'Then there are these other killings. . .'

'Disappearances,' interrupted the man with the close-set eyes. 'Not killings.'

'As you say, Lord Sigurd. Disappearances,' Finn conceded. 'But, maybe there's another explanation.'

'Whoever heard of a deer charging a man?' This Lord Sigurd looked sceptical. 'There's no way my brother died like that.'

'I was thinking of something else,' replied Finn. 'Or someone. . . in the appearance of a deer.'

'Witchery, you mean?' Sigurd gave a derisive snort. Some of the others sniggered with him. 'That's clutching at straws.'

Finn shrugged. 'Maybe. But your lord father is a just king. Is it not true, sire – you seek only the one responsible?'

But Bodvar had lost patience. 'Man or beast – I've scoured the area, sire. I can offer you nothing but these two.'

King Sviggar scraped a wasted hand over his chin. 'We need not indulge these wild ideas.' He turned to Erlan. 'I only ask you again, stranger, and if you want to avert suspicion, you *will* make a defence. Who are you? Where are you from?'

I am from nowhere. That other man is dead. Erlan shot Kai a rueful look. The boy wore a mask of anguish. 'I cannot answer, my lord.'

'You warrant your own death if you refuse the will of a king.'

'A foolish king, perhaps.'

'Watch your tongue, vagrant!' snapped Bodvar.

'I know nothing of the Wartooth.' Erlan looked hesitantly at Kai. 'But. . . we've also heard rumours – of an enemy come against you.'

Behind the king, the councillors exchanged glances.

'What enemy?' asked Sviggar.

Erlan shook his head. 'I'll not waste words on what I don't know for certain. But I swear this: I came here to serve you. Whatever enemies you face, I will face for you. I will not speak of my past, but I pledge my future to you.'

It sounded grand enough, but Sviggar hardly looked convinced.

'This cripple makes mock of you, Father.' Sigurd took his father by the elbow. 'Beggar or murderer – look at him. His word is no better than a whore's to a prince.'

'Something you know all about.' Sviggar gave his son a withering look and turned away, scowling. 'Tell me. Has he any skill?'

'I'd wager he is high-trained,' answered Bodvar.

'And?'

'He has courage,' the earl admitted. 'If not for his loyalty to this boy, I might already be feasting with my fathers.'

'We've all heard how he bested you, Bodvar,' sneered Sigurd. 'That hardly makes him worthy of being a king's man.'

'I disagree,' said the king. Bodvar nodded his thanks, masking his irritation. 'Age slows the best of us – but not my faithful Earl of Vestmanland. And so you. . .' His watery eye turned to Erlan. 'Have I to choose whether you are the Wartooth's catspaw, or else some unlooked-for blessing?' His mouth curdled with irony. 'Well? Must we take you as a gift from the gods, dropped from the sky? Whichever it is, you come well disguised.'

'A rare disguise indeed,' laughed Finn. 'The pair of 'em stink worse than polecats.'

'Father, you can ill afford the chance of being wrong,' urged Sigurd. 'You always were too soft on the Wartooth. And yet, he mocks you as a usurper. As the Bastard King.' A ripple of discomfort passed over the other councillors. 'Staffen's death is sweet news to his ear.'

'Don't you say a word about my son,' whispered Sviggar, menacingly.

'Staffen was my brother too,' replied Sigurd, looking stung. 'The Wartooth and the rest of Autha's line won't forget the feud, even if you would.' He stabbed a finger at Erlan. 'You should kill him. If he didn't do it – make an example of him. Send a message that you will countenance no threat to your throne or your blood. And if he did do it, then he will die for the wrong he's done us all.'

'I tell you – no man did this,' insisted Finn.

Sigurd rounded on him, losing patience. 'You should know your place, vassal.'

Bodvar stepped between the younger men. 'Sire, I'm in the unusual position of agreeing with Lord Sigurd. This smells like the Wartooth's work—'

'Lord,' interrupted Erlan. 'I am blameless for your son's death. My past is nothing to you, I assure you. And yet the weaving of fate has brought me before you. Why, I don't know. Perhaps I *am* a blessing of the gods. If so, then you are surely too wise to destroy their gift.'

Sviggar snorted. 'Flattering words no better than horse's wind. What do you know of my wisdom?'

'He speaks these weasel words in plea of his life. If he's so precious to the gods, let's make an offering of him to them,' said Sigurd with a scornful laugh.

'The gods know my life is worth little enough,' answered Erlan. 'But I'm loath to give it up on account of another man's stupidity. Whatever killed your son – I swear on that blade, it wasn't I.'

'I swear the same,' cried Kai.

'Be silent, boy!' snapped Bodvar, striking him.

'There's been hatred between Autha's line and mine too long,' said the king, voice soft. 'And yet. . . And yet, Harald *would* do this.' He rubbed at his temple with a thumb

half-missing. 'But then there is this other thing. This. . .
shadow. . .'

He went to the table and seized Wrathling, throwing off its
sheath. The blade flashed, and all of a sudden, its point was at
Erlan's throat.

'My son has the right of it. I cannot take the chance.'

'Wait!' cried Erlan.

'Master!' shouted Kai, earning another blow from Bodvar.

'I will honour you by doing this myself, and with your own
blade. Hold him.'

Strong hands seized him; a boot kicked the back of his
knees. He buckled. Fingers like iron tongs forced his head down.

'Hold him still!'

Kai was whimpering.

*So the king is a fool after all. He and I both – and love and honour
and blood and oaths. The whole stinking world is a jape in the mind
of a fool! Hel take us all!*

Out of the tail of his eye, he saw the king stand ready,
heard the sweep of his cloak as he threw it back over his
shoulder.

Then he felt the cold kiss of steel on his neck as the king
measured his stroke. Suddenly the sword was snatched away.
Erlan waited for the end, a dizzying, dismembered nausea filling
his limbs.

'*Inga,*' he murmured, wanting to feel her name on his lips
one last time.

He waited. An eternity seemed to fill that moment – a
hundred thousand lifetimes between the rising and falling of
his blade.

But the stroke never came.

'What's this?'

Erlan twisted his head and saw Sviggar was staring at Wrathling's hilt, eyes aglow. 'Bring him here.'

The guard hesitated.

'Get him up, man!'

Sviggar thrust Wrathling's hilt into Erlan's face. 'What's this?' He pointed at a device cut into the larger of the two rings that formed the grip. 'That engraving – an eagle with a wolf's head – you see it?'

Erlan saw. 'Yes.'

'What does it signify?'

He hesitated, still trying to gather his wits. 'It's a symbol favoured by the smiths where I'm from.'

'But does it not mean something?'

Erlan knew exactly what it meant: the mark of the Vendlings, the line of his blood stretching back through his fathers, and theirs before them. Back into the mists of the past, back to Vendal the Grey, who had sailed down out of the north. 'It is the mark of my blood. I can say no more.'

Sviggar's face hardened. He went to his council seat and reached behind, produced another sword and unsheathed it. The firelight gleamed off a blade no lesser than Wrathling.

He thrust the point inches from Erlan's nose. 'Bjarne's Bane. The Sveär kings have borne this blade many generations. My father took it from the dead hand of Ingiald, the last of the Ynglings. Now, it is mine.'

Suddenly, he dropped the point and proffered the hilt to Erlan. 'Look. The same spot. The same mark. Not just similar. *Exactly* the same.'

Erlan looked. The mark was there, identical to the first.

'This is the mark of the Sveär people. And yet, you are no Sveär.'

'No, my lord.'

The old king laughed, a coarse, gravelly rumble in his chest. 'It is an auspice,' he cried. 'An omen!' He slapped Erlan's shoulder. 'I don't know why you've come, stranger. Perhaps you're from some brother line and we share something of this shadowy past of yours.' He nodded agreeably. 'Yes – I will spare you. You may serve me.'

Kai gushed a lengthy sigh. Erlan's wasn't far behind it.

'Besides, it's ill luck to make a man break his oath. And to bloody my hands on a gift from the gods will only bring a curse on my head. As if there aren't enough of those already – eh, Bodvar?' He looked around at the earl and the others for a response, but his councillors were struggling to share his mirth. 'Keep your oath, stranger, and add to it another.' He signalled to Bodvar's men. 'Release him.'

They did as commanded and Erlan dropped to his knees for the third time that morning. 'I'll gladly swear to you, my lord.'

'Sire,' began Bodvar, 'I would not advise—'

'I know, good Bodvar. But my mind is set. It is an *auspice*, I tell you!'

'As you please, sire.' Though the earl looked doubtful.

Prince Sigurd turned away, not bothering to hide his disgust.

'You – come forward.' The king beckoned Kai for the first time. 'Your name, boy?'

'Beg pardon, I'm no boy, my lord king, sire.' Kai shuffled closer. 'I've near sixteen winters behind me. I go by Kai, son of Askar. A Gotar by blood.'

'Well, forgive me, Kai son of Askar,' chuckled Sviggar. 'You're a man, indeed. And a Gotar, eh? Can you wield a sword?'

'Good as the next man.'

'A regular hero,' smiled Finn.

Kai cut him a scathing look. 'Well, it's true, my lord, I've not yet stood in a battle-line or shieldwall or such. But I know my strokes.'

'Ha! Doubtless you do. Well, there's plenty of time for that, lad. Can you do anything else?'

'He has a gift for singing, lord,' said Erlan.

'Gods spare us! Another blasted skald-singer, is it? These halls are infested with them – drinking my ale and bedding every maid in sight.' He peered down at Kai. 'Though you look a little young for that.'

'With respect, my lord – I'm not too young for anything.'

'In quite the rush, aren't you?'

'I'll face down whatever comes my way, my lord.'

'I wouldn't say that too loud. Some of our womenfolk are like to take you at your word. Now, stranger,' he said, turning back to Erlan. 'Keep your sword and your secrets. If you are honest and willing, you may eat at my table, fight for my honour, and die in my service.' He offered Wrathling's hilt.

Erlan took it. 'I am, lord.'

'Fine. Then here is my hand.'

Erlan dropped to one knee and bent over the king's withered old claw. 'Lord Sviggar, king of the Sveärs, I swear my allegiance to your person, your crown and your blood.'

'Excellent. Let all here know it.'

And with that, Erlan had himself a new lord.

CHAPTER
TWENTY-THREE

Lilla sucked smoke deep into her lungs and fell back against the tree. The bark was hard, but so familiar that it was comforting as a mother's arms.

She looked up, gazing through the branches of the ancient ash into the half-lit sky. The tree had stood for more than a dozen generations, her mother told her. When her eye roved along its long, sinuous cracks and among its crooked branches, she well believed it was so old.

Older even. Old as the land. Old as the world.

She closed her eyes, the smoke filling her blood, seeping through her sinews. Her limbs began to feel weightless. Soon she would fly.

She blew out through her nostrils, listening to the seeds snap in the pan, letting smoke tendrils float into the fading light. Among the treetops, night-dew was gathering into mist. Dusk, the borderland between night and day – a time for crossing over. A time to slip between worlds.

She reached beside her and took another pinch of dry

strands from her pouch. Urtha's Weed – the flower of fate. The key that unlocked the secret roads of Yggdrasil. She tossed it into the pan and watched the strands glow, then curl and cinder. Suddenly the little heap caught aflame and smoke started to billow in earnest. She bent her head and inhaled, this time feeling the rush to her fingertips and the edges of her body begin to dissolve.

She lay back on her furs. The cold couldn't touch her now. Weightlessness flooded her bones. She went on reciting the words, just as her mother had taught her. Although, in the end, her mother no longer needed Urtha's help to enter the world-between-worlds and ride Odin's steed. Her words and will alone were enough.

'One day you will do as I do,' she promised, never saying when. Now she never would. It was five years since they buried her. Five years since she abandoned Lilla, half-taught, half-ready.

Half-wise.

Queen Dalla was of the Dale Lands, whose folk, she claimed, were closer to the earth than all others. They knew the ways of the forest, the rivers and the hills; kept the lore of the birds and beasts; understood the earth and sky. 'Each must discover her fate through the mirror of time,' she would say. 'But not the Dale folk. We shatter the glass and ride upon the winds of fate like eagles on the wing.'

Lilla only half-understood. But Dalla insisted, 'The Dales are in your blood too.' Lilla was twelve when her mother began teaching her. But after three short years, she found herself alone. She remembered running back to the halls. Screaming. But no one could help. Her mother's lifeless body lay by the ash tree, her spirit flown for ever. *But where?* Maybe one day Lilla would find her in one of the Nine Worlds. . . Maybe, if she searched long enough.

But maybe she just refused to admit the truth: that her mother didn't want to come back. That she loved the other worlds more than her own. And sometimes, Lilla didn't blame her. Sometimes, it was hard to love this world. The places she'd seen were far more wonderful than this one. Here, she was bound by time and birth and custom. Here, she knew her purpose was to one day be the wife of a king, and afterwards the mother of kings. Here, love always abandoned her for death.

But there. . . there, she was free. There, she could soar as high as the stars. There, *everything was love.*

The world beyond the veil, her mother called it. 'Here is truth, my Lilla,' she had whispered, as they looked upon the ancient ash. 'The life you live is but a leaf on the tree. In that little life exists the whole of life – root, branch, soil and sky. All these have their part in how the leaf must grow. All is fate. Do you understand?' Lilla had nodded, half-understanding. 'I will show you how to ride the great Tree of Worlds.'

Lilla's spirit was flying now, her will climbing higher and higher, like Skinfaxi of the Shining Mane, chasing after the dying sun, drawing the cloak of night behind her. Her heart sang as the stars glittered above her, clouds scudding left and right, brilliant under the rising moon. She turned on the cold wind. Joy surged within her – an ecstasy of joy, the cramped prison of her body left far behind. She no longer soared in the sky; she *was* the sky – clear and bright and pure.

But then she perceived something far in the east. A tiny spot on the horizon, like a black tear. Seeing it, some part of her shivered. *But fear has no place in this world.* The teardrop grew, first into a stain, then a smear, then spreading to the ends of the sky. With it grew her dread. She fled the billowing blackness, yet it came on the quicker, towering over her in a wave climbing beyond the highest star, blotting every prick of light. Panic coursed like poison as she saw the darkness was a mist, thick and black as death, engulfing all. Suddenly she knew: this was some foul fog spewing from the bowels of Niflheim, the mist-land – the one world forbidden her. Hope died in her heart, and as the darkness swept over her, she opened her mouth and screamed.

She jerked up. A startled pigeon fluttered in the treetops. She was back in the Kingswood, but the horrors of what she'd seen in the mist still scuttled in her mind like scorpions. The fire was still burning beside her. She couldn't have been away long. Instinctively, she reached for the gourd lain out in readiness for her return. Her throat was dry as ash. She drained the bitter brew, which would bind her wandering spirit.

For now.

She dropped the gourd, her hand shaking, fixing her gaze on it till she could see only that – the flesh of her fingers, the glimmer of silver rings. She breathed a notch easier, the horrible visions loosening their grip, fading to a memory.

Suddenly, a horn sounded in the distance – three notes, short and clear. She recognized the call at once and laughed, despite herself. *Maybe there are some things worth lingering for in this world.* The horn was for her. Since she had been an infant, her father had had that horn blown to summon his children homeward. Most fathers would have given it up long ago. Not him. He knew her too well. 'If Lilla had her way, we'd live in the forest like a pack of wolves,' he often teased her.

Unsteadily, she got to her feet, brushing the dirt from her hands.

It was time to wear her mask once more.

The fires and shadows of the Uppland halls brought some comfort after the terrors of the mist, but by the time she was in her chamber brushing out her tangled hair, a different kind of dread began to take hold.

With Staffen dead, who was there to talk to now? He at least had been able to make her laugh, and laughter eased her loneliness. In truth, Staffen had been the one to make them all laugh.

With him gone, a dour mood had crept in. There were the trappings of mourning, to be sure, but this was something else. A part of each of them had died with him. As though Staffen had been the hub of the wheel. Without him, how long could the wheel turn before it flew apart?

Her father, under his brittle exterior, was a caring man. But he hadn't the patience to hold them together. If her mother was still alive, she might have. Instead, they had Saldas. . .

Once again, that strange discord of feelings. It had been three years – more even – since her father had taken Saldas to wife. Lilla was still wary of her. Jealous too, perhaps. Yet, there was something about her. . . Maybe only the same thing that dulled the wits of all the men around her. . .

But something in Lilla wanted to reach beyond the beautiful exterior. Reach inside where she was sure a fiery passion burned.

A passion seldom seen, a flame she was drawn to, which she wanted to reach out and touch. She wondered what it would be like to feel the heat of Saldas's love. But Saldas dealt only in cold formalities, offering no warmth in her affected words.

Lilla's head throbbed from the smoke. She felt more alone than ever.

'Lilla, child, are you ready?' It was her father's voice through the door of her chamber. 'It's time.'

'Just a moment, Father.'

She pulled the embroidered mantle over her long black shift. Her slender reflection shone back off the polished bronze mirror. Her father expected her to look fine whenever she appeared at the feast table, but that would never shift the drab feeling inside her. She adjusted the brooches at her shoulders. *Oh, that'll have to do.*

Sighing, she drew her braid over her shoulder and left the chamber.

A few moments later, she had joined her father's retinue, gathered before going in to the feast-hall.

Her father was speaking with the leather-faced Earl of Vestmanland. Her brother had his back to her, talking in hushed tones with his attendant. Several other men turned and murmured greetings. She returned each with a word.

'No, no, no! I won't – I won't!' The cries were embarrassingly loud. Everyone turned to see Svein, the boy Saldas had borne her father. He was all dark curls and cool, green eyes – startlingly bonny. But a little menace with a temper like a boiling kettle.

'You'll do as you're told, you little brute.' Saldas was crouched beside him, wrestling with his belt. 'There, now – leave it alone.' No sooner had she released him than he unhooked it and flung it on the floor, jutting his bottom lip in defiance.

'If you won't wear it round your waist, let's see how you like it on your backside!' His mother seized him by the neck, bent him over and would have given him a thrashing if Lilla had not caught her arm.

'You only make him more stubborn,' she said. 'Let me try. Please.'

Saldas scowled in exasperation, dropped the belt into her hand, and went to join her husband.

'She's so mean,' sniffed Svein. 'She hates me!'

'No, she doesn't. She just wants you to look smart for your papa,' said Lilla, wiping away the angry tears speckling his cheek. 'Won't you let me put this on?'

'It pinches! I hate it!'

She cupped his cheek. 'I'll fix it so it doesn't.'

He shook his head, crossing his arms.

'Listen – if you're good, I'll take you to the woods with me tomorrow. We might even find some lingonberries, if we're lucky.'

The boy's frown softened. 'Lingonberries?'

'I know just the place.'

With a little more persuasion, Svein relented, and Lilla fastened his belt, taking care not to pinch him.

'The brat needs a beating, not the coddling you give him.'

Lilla looked up and saw Sigurd standing over them. 'There'll be plenty of time for beating when he's grown. You must be tender with children, or their spirit grows mean.'

'Tenderness is weakness.' He turned away, uninterested.

Then you're the strongest man in this hall, brother.

There was a sudden banging. She straightened up. By the entrance to the main hall, the whitebeard Vithar was rapping his staff on the floor. Lilla smoothed out the folds of her dress.

It was time.

CHAPTER
TWENTY-FOUR

Erlan gazed at the sea of faces with his back against the wall. Chatter buzzed around the cavernous space, skeins of laughter swirling up into the smoke-stained beams.

Most were men, with the look of warriors or farmers. But there were a few women, perhaps wives of the men they stood beside.

All of them waiting.

Waiting for the lofty company of the king to fill the table running the length of the platform at the end of the hall. Behind the table stood the largest chair Erlan had ever seen, grand, empty and elaborately carved. To one side, he recognized the steps where he'd cracked his knee.

It felt odd – to have been within a glance of death one moment, and now, with the sun hardly set, he was about to take the king's salt with a hall full of strangers. But for the king's sharp eyes, he would be with his forefathers. Instead, he had what he wanted. A roof. A table. A lord.

Yet he still felt empty.

Had he been naive to think that finding a lord could even touch the dark abyss of pain in his heart?

He stood among these strangers. Yet he was the stranger.

He tried to remember the feasts of old at Vendlagard, when he'd sat with half a hundred friends and kin, faces ruddy with ale, eyes bright with laughter. What would a stranger have seen in those faces? A welcome table? An open hand? Or only the mark of death that overshadowed them all? Or behind each laughing face a killer, or the mother of a killer, or the child of a killer?

That's what he saw, in this magnificent hall, among these noble Sveärs. Killing faces all around him – hard and hostile.

All of them.

He looked down.

Well. . . all, save one.

'I don't know how many hedgehogs they had to kill to make this undershirt,' complained Kai, scratching himself madly.

'Stay still, can't you? Folk'll think you've got the pox.'

'Looking round here, there's a few lasses I wouldn't mind catching it from.' Kai leered at a passing thrall-girl, earning himself a giggle.

Incessant itching aside, Kai looked a new man. His freshly washed hair gleamed under the torchlight, and in the tan breeches and rusty tunic that Finn, Sviggar's bodyguard, found him that afternoon, he looked halfway presentable in spite of his gaunt cheeks. They'd tossed his old rags on the fire.

Finn had done no less for Erlan, and, although his breeches were loose and his tunic hot enough to melt the winter, he was grateful to be clean. He'd scrubbed his face till the water went black. Then, after trimming the more wayward parts of his beard, he'd had Kai comb out his hair to the last louse, before tying it back in a tail. He hadn't looked this well since his own Feast of Oaths.

The night that Inga—

'That skaldman wasn't lying, was he?' whispered Kai as another lissom servant went by, breaking the chain of thought that always seemed to be dragging him down and down. Kai dug an elbow in his ribs, eager for a response, instead catching his master's dark look. 'What's up with you?'

'No matter.'

'Suit yourself.' Kai shrugged. 'Oh, we're going to get along fine here. Aren't we just?' Seeming tickled at the prospect, he gave himself an especially vigorous scratch.

'What the Hel's the matter with you, boy?' said the man across the table, breaking off his conversation. 'You got that many fleas, why don't you go eat with the other dogs?'

'Sure,' returned Kai. 'You should come too. I saw a nice little pigsty outside. With a face like yours, you'd fit right in.'

The man's skin was pockmarked, with a couple of sores by his mouth weeping pus into his whiskers, and an eyebrow split by a badly healed scar. Not the kind of face with which a boy did well to trade insults.

'Shut it, shit-wit, or you'll find my fist down that big mouth of yours.'

'That's a relief!'

'Eh?'

'For a moment, I thought you might bleed pus on me!'

There was a scuffling of feet. Next moment, the man had reached across a meaty fist and hauled Kai out of his seat. Just as suddenly, everything froze.

337

'Let him be,' snarled Erlan, his dagger point at the man's throat. 'He's with me.'

'And who the fuck are you?' the man said, eyes brimming venom.

'A man holding a knife is all you need to know.'

'A man with no friends is what I do know.'

'We three manage well enough,' said Erlan, nodding at Kai and pressing the knife closer to make his point. The man's gorge rose and fell awkwardly. 'And I don't see *your* friends lifting a finger.'

Suddenly, a fart thundered loud as a horn-blast down the bench. 'How 'bout an arse-cheek?' drawled the man on Erlan's left, leisurely scratching his nose. 'That's about the wisest thing I've heard on the matter.'

Erlan glanced at him. The man had an enormous round belly, cheeks red as two cuts of beef, and a wry look in his eye. 'You know, you may well be right.' Erlan withdrew his point an inch. 'Well?'

The pock-faced man gave a grudging nod and let Kai sink down. 'By the hanged, Einar, you stink worse than Hel's breath.'

'You can blame my old woman's cooking.'

There was a loud rapping at the back of the hall.

'Our noble lord comes to plant his noble arse on his chair.' Einar gave Erlan a wink. The hall fell silent. Everyone rose as Sviggar and his retinue filed into the hall, one by one taking their places along the table.

At first, it was the king who caught Erlan's gaze. Even from there, he had the air of a man of well-worn authority. He was tall and walked surprisingly erect for a man of so many winters.

Erlan meant to get a look at the other high folk filing in, but his gaze never got past the figure behind the king.

He had never seen the like.

She was something impossible.

Stupefying. . .

Some mythic creature from the old tales, from another world even. No woman of flesh and blood could bewitch the eye like that. Her body moved like a lynx prowling through the forest. Beautiful. Dangerous. She wore a silk robe of shimmering black and midnight blue, which clung to her like a viper's skin. Her black hair fell, unbound and gleaming, over one shoulder.

He watched her take her seat, sweep up a cup of wine and put it to her lips. Then she settled back, tracing a languid finger along her collarbone, as if she could feel the weight of his eyes, and the eyes of every man, upon her body at just this place.

'You can sit down now.' Erlan looked down and saw Einar grinning up at him. Glancing round, he realized everyone was already seated. He sat down hurriedly.

'Something got your attention?'

'No, just. . . My mind was elsewhere.'

'Nestled between a fine pair of paps, perhaps!'

'Least you've got taste, master,' grinned Kai. 'I was beginning to wonder.'

'Just 'cause I wouldn't jump the village goat given half a chance, like you?'

Kai's smile died. Erlan felt suddenly foolish.

'Easy on the lad,' said Einar. 'There's no shame in it. The queen tends to have that effect on a man. Yep – you can't fault

Sviggar, the old bugger. He reckons a king deserves the best, and he damn well got it.' He snapped his fingers at a thrall carrying a pitcher. 'Here – let's meet properly.'

The thrall filled their cups and Einar raised a toast. 'To a long life!'

'A long life,' the others echoed, tapping beakers and sinking a few gulps.

'Though I did hear life might've proved regrettably short for you earlier today,' added Einar.

'I guess Sviggar decided we're more use to him alive than dead.'

'No thanks to you,' put in Kai.

'He would've been a fool to kill us.'

'Even kings can be fools,' said Einar. 'You were lucky. Fact is, folk like to know a man's story. I heard you weren't over-keen on sharing yours.'

'You hear a good deal.'

'A turd don't fall round here but that everyone hears about it.'

Erlan grunted.

'Well then – your names?'

'Erlan. This here is Kai.'

'I'm Einar.'

'The Fat-Bellied!' cried the pockmarked man.

'If you like,' grinned Einar. 'My wife ain't proud of the name, but what can you do? A fact is a fact.' He gestured at the other. 'That handsome devil is Aleif Red-Cheeks.'

Aleif shot Einar a hostile look but he ignored it.

'Then there's Jari Iron-Tongue,' gesturing down the bench. 'Ivald Agnisson; Eirik the Hammer – the hall-girls gave him that one. And Dofri, Gloinn, Flok. And on down the bench. Anyhow, you'll soon catch up.'

Those who'd caught their names gave a nod to the newcomers.

'I'm not one for names,' replied Erlan. 'But I never forget a face.'

'Some of these poor bastards are so ugly, you'll wish you could!'

Erlan chuckled.

'So, friend – what brings you to Sviggar's Seat?'

'You didn't hear that too?'

Einar shrugged. 'I'd rather hear it from you.'

'We came to offer service to the king.'

'What kind of service?'

'Well, we didn't come to wash his arse. We heard there was trouble in his kingdom. My sword for his salt. You know how it goes.'

'And him?'

'He has his uses.' He gave Kai a wink; the boy beamed.

'Charming pair. So this trouble you've come to save us from. What have you heard?' Einar leaned in, curious.

'We heard of murders. Disappearances.' He and Kai exchanged a glance. 'An enemy.'

'Oh, we have an enemy all right. Haven't you heard?'

'The Wartooth – aye. The Danish king has many enemies. But the way we heard, it's something else.'

Einar tugged at the curls of his beard. 'Talk gets around. So you think you can solve our little mystery?'

'Wouldn't say that. We needed a place. Sviggar needs protection.' He shrugged. 'His own son is already dead.'

'That was a deer,' said Einar, carefully. 'An accident.'

'Whatever. We're here now. If the king needs my sword, he's welcome to it.'

'And what do *you* know?' broke in Kai. 'Of murders? What are the stories?'

Einar leaned back, thoughtful. He beckoned a thrall, who went to pour some ale, but he stopped her. 'Second thoughts – if we're telling tales, it's mead we need.'

The servant called over another, who filled their cups with the golden liquid.

Einar took a long draught. 'Finest brew there is.' He wiped his lips.

'Well?' urged Kai.

'A story, aye. I heard one. Something my wife got from Vermland by way of her cousin. He told her some bondsfolk on his farm went visiting, not half a league from home, towards the forest. They reached their friends' house – pit-house it was. Tiny. But not a soul about, not a lick of smoke as they came up. Their boy was used to fooling with these other folk's son so on he ran into the house. He came out saying there's no one there, only it's dark and wet inside. His parents couldn't make sense of it, but as he walked about, they saw red footprints in the snow, and coming closer, they caught a foul smell on the air, and went on inside. What they found made 'em sick to their guts. The floor was thick with blood, near an inch deep. 'Course they raised an alarm and found neighbours to help search. But they never found a hair of 'em.'

'Wolves?' asked Erlan.

'Who knows? But that's the story.'

Kai's eyes were big as platters.

'Huh!' Aleif snorted across the table. 'If you want, I heard another like it.'

'Where from?' asked Einar.

'Up the Dale country.'

'Bah!' scoffed the Fat-Bellied. 'They spin nothing but long tales up that way.'

'Maybe, but this I heard direct from my brother. He's taking a wife from up there and he had business with her father. Anyways, on his way back last trip, he rode across a lake called the Birch Water – it was already frozen, mind.' Aleif leaned in, and Erlan caught a whiff of foul breath. 'So he comes across a fire on the shore, still burning. And beside it, a pile of furs and some other gear. He looks about, sees a hole in the ice and guesses some fella was fishing there. Well, he's hungry, ain't he? So he figures he'll wait and try his luck, figuring this fella had only gone to drop his breeches. After a while, the man still hasn't returned so he goes looking. And in the shadows there, he finds something.'

Aleif was enjoying the attention. He paused, waiting for the newcomers to bite.

Kai obliged. 'Come on. What he find?'

'Bones. Human bones – piled up neat. He reckons there was some pattern to it. Like it had some meaning. Then up he looks and sees a skull hanging there on a branch. Was horrible, he says. Damn near pissed hisself, he says. The face was all torn away, but hair still stuck off the back. Poor bastard's braids were soaked red, but there wasn't a drop of blood to be found anywhere else. After that, my brother just comes away.'

'And was it the fisherman?' asked Kai.

'Who the bloody else could it've been?'

'I've another,' offered the man Einar called Jari Iron-Tongue.

'Aye – you would have,' said Einar, adding aside to Erlan, 'This one could out-talk Loki.'

'There ain't a man on this bench hasn't heard something,' returned Jari, indignant. He was young, with ale-stained whiskers that ruffled when he spoke. 'No blood nor bones with this one, though. Still, it was mighty strange. A trapper from Gestrikland was heading south with a cartload of furs to trade, his wife in tow and her with a babe in the belly. It was snowing heavy and he wanted shelter for her, so they stopped at a farmstead and begged a little kindness. Well, they settled in fine. But she was near her time and often up in the night. Sure enough, up she jumps in the dead of night, heads outside to make water. No one misses her at first. But on a sudden, the whole damn household is waked by screaming outside. They see she's missing and all of them rush out with torches to take a look. They find her footsteps easy, which lead off under some pines, but not a sign of *her*.' Jari slapped the table. 'None, I tell you! Nor any other marks, neither. Only the stain of her piss in the snow.'

Kai leaned back and released the breath he'd been holding in.

Erlan sniffed, unsure what to make of it. He was about to say something when there was another knocking from the platform. The company fell silent as Sviggar dragged himself out of his chair.

'The stranger, where is he? Our gift from the gods,' he croaked. 'Erlan, is it? Where are you, man? On your feet.'

Erlan stood.

'Hah! Come here, lad. We want a look at you.'

· · · · · · ·

The man that rose at first looked like any other. A shade darker than most Sveär men, maybe. Thin, though broad of shoulder. He stood up bold enough, but she saw at once he didn't like the eyes of all those folk on him. She soon understood why. The man was a cripple.

'The rest – eat up! Drink! Talk!' cried her father, which most were happy enough to do. But some watched to see how the encounter would go for this limping stranger.

Her father had become quite spirited when he described this man's arrival and the fabulous coincidence that had saved his life. When he told of the stranger's oath never to speak of his past, Saldas had mocked him.

'A foolish oath. Only a fool would trust such a man.'

But her father was adamant. The gods had sent this man for some purpose.

'You know nothing of him,' said Saldas.

'Then you shall see him for yourself.'

And now here was the man, standing before them, dropping his head in an awkward bow.

'I don't believe I'd have recognized you now you're not half-buried with furs and covered in dirt,' exclaimed her father. 'You look well enough cleaned up. Now we need to feed you up a bit too, eh?'

Lilla thought he looked a little better than well, despite the obvious marks hunger had left on his face and frame. The man was strikingly handsome. Oh, not like her brother had been: with sky-blue eyes, sharp cheekbones and all. No, there was something different with this one, something in his eyes. He was young, younger even than her twenty summers, she guessed. But his dark eyes seemed to carry in them wisdom beyond their years. The rest of his face was hollowed out, almost gaunt. A tight jaw, short-trimmed beard, thin in parts – hardly a beard at all – with a tousled mess of hair, a few strands of which fell across his eyes. He seemed content to leave them there, as if a strand of hair could hide him from this attention.

'Meet your queen,' her father said. 'She thinks you a fool already.'

'I'm grateful, lord.'

'Are you, by the gods? Why's that?'

'It'll take little to raise her opinion of me if she already takes me for a fool.'

'You flatter yourself that I shall keep any opinion of you at all,' murmured Saldas.

'A hard woman to please,' laughed her father. 'And I should know! Nevertheless, she is your new mistress.'

'I'm honoured to serve you, my lady.'

Lilla watched Saldas trace her finger down her jaw, pausing at her chin, her green eyes moving languorously over the stranger. With a tilt of her head, she offered him her hand. He took it, bending to kiss the ring on her finger. Lilla noticed how lightly his lips brushed the cold, yellow metal.

Saldas withdrew her hand, calling impatiently for more wine.

'My son, Sigurd, you've already met. Prince of the Sveärs and my heir.' Her brother received the stranger with his customary lack of grace. He stood, with that nervous jerk of his head that was his habit, and held out his hand. The stranger took it, bowing over it.

'You have my allegiance, my lord,' he said, mechanically.

'Save your oaths till you mean them, cripple.' When the

stranger didn't reply, Sigurd added, 'Well, are you going to stand there gawping like a fish?'

The stranger hesitated, unsure whether to stay or take his leave.

'I see you still have nothing to say for yourself,' went on her brother. 'My father let you live for reasons I won't pretend I agree with. . . At any rate, you must have luck.'

Lilla watched the other's face carefully. On it, she could read almost nothing. She wondered if there was any insult that her brother could utter that would ruffle this man's cold composure.

'Perhaps you'll find more favour with my daughter,' said her father, apparently enjoying this newcomer's discomfort. He waved Erlan on. The stranger shuffled along with that awkward gait, until he stood in front of her.

For a moment, those dark eyes looked right into her. His gaze was unflinching and yet, unlike other men's, seemingly without guile. He bowed.

'Since my father has forgotten to introduce me.' She held out her hand. 'My name is Aslif.' He took it and she felt his lips brush her fingers. The pounding in her head from the smoke of Urtha's Weed thumped a little faster. She wished it would pass. 'But you may call me Lilla. Everyone does.'

'My Lady Lilla,' he murmured. 'You have my allegiance also.'

'You are a man of secrets, my father says.'

'I made an oath. I intend to keep it.'

'Even if it costs you your head?'

'Every oath costs something.'

'I can see you are very stubborn,' she said, feeling suddenly uncomfortable under this man's cold gaze. 'Very stubborn or very foolish.'

'Why not both?' offered her brother with a snigger. 'Most beggars are.' She noticed a flicker of heat pass over his features. Perhaps there was a limit to this man's patience after all.

'Is that all you are?' she asked. 'A beggar?'

'Is this all you are?' he returned. 'A princess?' She felt her cheeks colour with indignation and heard her father's ringing laughter. His mirth was easily oiled by a cup or two of wine.

'Haha! The boy has wit! Very good. Well, that's enough of you, young Erlan. You have our leave. And eat hearty, boy! By the gods, you need it.'

As Erlan returned to his seat, Lilla wondered how this proud cripple would fare at her father's court. Whether he would even see out the winter. The life of a warrior didn't bear much prediction. Then again, nor did the life of a woman. She thought of the childhood playmates who had succumbed to sickness. And her dearest friend Fulla, buried with her half-born child last Yuletide. She wasn't the only one; there were many. Wisdom taught its lesson again and again. You must hold onto life lightly. The things you love will be taken away.

Why then was it such a hard lesson to learn?

When Erlan resumed his place, food had been served.

'I've been looking after your pig,' said Einar, nodding at Kai, who was scarfing down his food like a starved sow.

'The lad's earned it.' Nonetheless, Erlan had to lever Kai off his platter to slide between them. Before him sat a steaming plate of salt pork and kale, with barley cakes and garlic mushrooms. It was enough to make him weep.

'So?' prompted Einar, as Erlan fell on his food.

'So what?'

'You've met our lordly family. What do you think?'

Erlan stroked his beard between mouthfuls. Traces of the queen's perfume curled into his nostrils. He inhaled, savouring the last traces of that sweet, dark scent, recalling the curve of her upper lip.

He shrugged, and went back to his food. 'Saldas and Sigurd were cold. Lilla. . . I don't know. The high-born – they're all the same.'

'Odin's stars,' said Kai, spraying mushrooms everywhere, 'but the princess is a beauty! Got a chest like a pair of otters wrestling in a sack.'

Erlan shoved him. 'Just stick to filling your face.'

'Yep – the Lady Lilla is fine.' Einar drained his cup. 'There's more, you know. The queen's children. A little easier to win over.'

'You think?' Somehow Erlan had his doubts.

'A pebble for him, a doll for her and they'll be friends for life.'

Erlan scowled. 'So I have to win over kidlings now?'

'The son of a king grows up.'

'The son of a bastard king.'

Einar nearly choked on his mead. 'Keep your voice down! Remember whose salt you're eating, eh?'

'Sigurd called him that this morning when they spoke of the Wartooth. What does he mean?'

'Sigurd's the only one who could say it and keep his tongue.'

'Is it true?'

Einar sighed. 'Aye. . . Fact is, it's where all the bad blood between the Wartooth and Sviggar's line arises.' He leaned in.

'See, Sviggar's mother was never married to old Ivar. She was his concubine. 'Course, Sviggar's enemies say she was a whore.' He winked. 'Anyway, the only legitimate child that survived was Autha, the Wartooth's mother. The Deep-Minded, so called; and she was certainly clever. Oh, she's long dead. She was twenty-odd years older than Sviggar even. But she never gave up her claim to her father's realm.'

'If she was older, how did he come by the kingdom?'

'Ivar named Sviggar his heir, despite being bastard-born. He wanted to spite his daughter, see. Hel's teeth, there's a lot more to it! Ivar must've been a mean old rascal. He and his daughter finished up hating each other, and many would tell you, she had more cause to hate than him. The feud's run and run.'

'Between Sviggar's line and Autha's?'

'Yep. The Wartooth hasn't given up his mother's grievances.'

Erlan thought back to his ordeal that morning. Suddenly, the suspicions that he was the Wartooth's catspaw made more sense. 'Small wonder Sviggar suspects the Wartooth of his son's death.'

'Aye – and it *is* suspicious. *And* a heavy loss to lose his heir. Sigurd isn't the man his brother was.'

'No? He's ready to stand up to his father, and knows his own mind, at least.'

'Bah!' Einar pulled a face. 'Did you meet that man yet?' He jabbed his cup at the platform. 'See him? At the far end.'

'With the black hair?'

'That's him. If Sigurd has anyone's mind, it's his.'

The man was sat on the other side of the hall, obscured in shadow. His hair fell untidily, framing a thin face with dark curls. From that distance, it was hard to perceive more, except

350

that he sat very straight with sloping shoulders and spoke with no one. Almost as if he was invisible.

'His name is Vargalf. He is Sigurd's personal liegeman.'

'Meaning?'

'He's taken no oath to the king, so far as anyone knows. Only to Sigurd.'

Erlan considered him a while. 'How can a master have a servant's mind?'

'With remarkable ease!' laughed Einar. 'Oh, Sigurd's no fool, but nor is he as wise as he'd like to think. And Vargalf could put thoughts in a dead man's head.'

'You don't trust him.'

'Not many do! His heart is cold as the northern frost. But he has names – Merciless and Steel-Storm. Folk do well to keep right with him. Hey, you there!' cried Einar distractedly to a passing thrall. He bade her fill their cups.

'It's a strange old place you've come to. You may come to wish Sviggar had let the sword drop, and that be an end to it.' He laughed, not seeing the shadow pass over Erlan's face. 'Meanwhile, at least you can enjoy the finest brews in the land.'

Erlan forced a smile, raised his cup and swallowed down the beer. It tasted warm and earthy. Reassuring. He glanced over his rim towards the darkened corner.

Vargalf was gone.

Erlan stared at the empty space on the bench, and, for some reason, the more he stared, the more the warmth in his belly turned cold and bitter.

CHAPTER TWENTY-FIVE

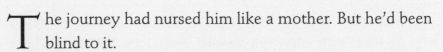

The journey had nursed him like a mother. But he'd been blind to it.

Only with the first days rolling into a week and then another, did he come to realize that even if he voyaged to the ends of the earth, he still had to face himself.

He settled into his duties quick enough. Finn, the king's bodyguard, saw to that. Affable, quick-witted, confiding, Finn had been a nomad in the far north. He'd stayed south after he won an archery contest and came to the king's notice.

'He made me an offer I couldn't refuse.' He winked. A fresh young thrall with a cloud of auburn hair who'd served as Sviggar's concubine. She and Finn were lately wed, and he was full of bounce at his luck.

Yet something about his easy nature, about his confidence – as if life owed him good fortune and would pay up without the slightest delay – made Erlan sick to his stomach.

Finn found them a place to sleep in one of the smaller halls, and assigned them people to report to, and tasks to complete.

Kai was put to work about the hall yards doing odd jobs. He complained it usually involved shovelling shit. 'Horse shit, sheep shit, pig shit, chicken shit, goat shit. Any kind of shit. I've become a regular expert. Ain't nothing I don't know about shit!'

Erlan rode long hours escorting earls or thanes or lesser men to one place, or returning with tribute from another. He stood guard or saw to the repair of someone's war-gear or bridle or some such trifle.

Most days, he joined in the weapons training. As the newest of Sviggar's karls, he taught the younglings. How to use a shield. How to cut and turn, thrust and parry. How to kill. He recalled his own first lessons. He'd seen hardly seven winters when his father put a short, blunt sword in his hand, saying, 'A sword and a heart, son – you need both to survive in this world.'

He watched the boys, faces taut with effort, struggling to hold back tears when they took a hit and felt the pain, and found himself wondering what was the use of either.

Something he couldn't control was creeping like a cancer into his thoughts. Through his bones. His duties were dull. But it wasn't the dullness he minded. It was the banality of it all. *The nausea.*

On the road, he'd been forced to think of what lay ahead. To stay alert. To stay alive. But now, here he was. And the black memories of what lay behind at Vendlagard that had followed him across these unknown lands returned to his mind like flies to a rotting corpse.

In his dreams, Inga's face grew indistinct, but she returned again and again – sometimes loving and sad, sometimes furious and vengeful. And his eyes would flick open with a catch of breath, cheeks wet, heart racing, a relentless pressure inside his head.

He was losing all sense of purpose. The goal of reaching this place – finding a lord – was done. Was this to be his life now? Running errands for the whipping boys of a king. Was he to find a healing love among the Uppland whores? What could they do for him, but mock his memory of Inga's caresses, of the intimacy that was gone for ever?

Intimacy that never should have been.

Everything he touched dripped with nausea – every hilt, every bridle, every cup. Every laugh was a taunt. He watched folk about their business, saw their smiles and scowls, listened to their talk. But all the while, he was suffocating in a darkness that seemed to smother everything.

How had he not seen it before? What were these pitiful things they all chased after but illusions, ethereal as mist? A piece of land, a healthy son, a beautiful daughter. Loveplay, drink, friendship. Songs of wonder, fine jewellery, a full belly. Even love came to nothing – no more than hate. Whether you were the lowliest pig-thrall or the mighty king himself – what did it matter? Nothing endured. Everyone was blind, going about their lives as if they meant something.

Was he the only one who could see? *Why?*

He was an outsider here, and always would be. He was an outsider everywhere. He had no home. Perhaps he was an outsider even to himself.

A stranger.

Many times, he longed to be blind again. Just to fit in. To come back, somehow. But perhaps now he never could. Instead, he was condemned to see, and the sight would drive him to madness.

Madness or death.

This life sickened him, and the sweet song of darkness began calling in his dreams.

Kai, however, was happy as a hungry tick on a fat swine. Truth was, he would have done any kind of work going around Sviggar's Great Hall, and been grateful for it. It'd take more than a few piles of shit to hold him down.

His mouth seldom got a rest. But even those who found him garrulous, and more than a shade annoying at first, were soon won over.

He was an upstart, but one who made folks laugh. For that, he was forgiven a good deal. He had the young stable girls shrieking with laughter, watching him race a pig around the yard. Or if one of the high folk needed something doing, Kai was on it at the instant, and running too, with a smile wide as the horizon.

He had a prodigious talent for gossip, confiding useless tit-bits in exchange for the fattest, juiciest secrets. He knew which maid swooned after which karl; which thane had slept with which merchant's wife; whose scales were honest and whose crooked. He knew which newborn was the bastard of some drunken tryst; which maid was promised to which old man, and what price her father settled for her, to the very mark. He even knew much that passed in the king's council. Councillors talked to whores, whores to stable-boys, and stable-boys to him. And so on.

Soon, there was no one who knew more of what went on about the Uppland halls than Kai Askarsson.

All this was very well. A picture of life, common enough when folk dwell together – men and women, thralls and freemen, good wives and scoundrels, kings and beggars. But he heard other tales, too. Tales of a darker shade.

Mud-spattered trappers came to the Uppland halls telling of hearths in the west where many tears fell. A foreshadowing of the Ragnarok, some said – the World Serpent was stirring, snatching souls for the final fight against Odin and his heroes.

Others said it was thieves with a taste for blood. Stories came, of crimson pools upon the ice, or snowdrifts sparkling scarlet with blood, or bones picked clean and white.

And the rivers of tears flowed down from the mountains, drawing closer to the hearth of the king.

Finally, it was her turn.

They all knew it was more fun to be the one hiding, which was why it took all morning before her older brothers let her have a go.

She knew just what to be. A raven.

They were the birds in all the stories – them or eagles. But eagles didn't sit in trees. Ravens did. And she loved climbing trees.

She left Ref and Raffen by the Shining Lake, skimming stones and counting to a hundred. She'd been scheming which tree was best ever since the game began. The big beech was usually the best, especially in summer. But it was Raffen's favourite too, and would be the first place he'd look. There was the hollow oak above the quarry. But Papa said it was dangerous and its branches might snap. Also, inside it was dark, and crawling with earwigs.

She'd settled on the old yew tree on the hill behind the lake. It was a bit spooky with its knotted old roots, but she knew a secret way inside its hulking trunk, and up onto the first big branch. Up there, no one could see her from the ground, but she could peep through the needle bushes and see her brothers coming.

She ran, breathless and giggling, snow flying about her heels.

Far behind, she heard one of her brothers shout, 'Coming, Namma – you'd better be ready!'

She squealed with excitement as she reached the yew tree. Grinning to herself, she crept inside, her short breaths clouding the cramped space. She'd soon picked her way up the footholds, and was inching along the branch. Her tunic had ridden up and the bark was scraping between her thighs. It hurt, but she gripped on tight all the same. She didn't want to fall.

At last, satisfied, she waited.

Before long she heard noises approaching. Scuffing, shuffling, crunching, cracking, and the murmur of voices. She leaned back against the tree-trunk, peering through the foliage.

Suddenly she saw them and had to clamp her mouth shut to stop herself from squealing again. They were coming quite slowly – criss-crossing each other, peering up into the trees. Ref, the younger one, kept calling her name. But she wasn't *that* stupid.

Raffen called Ref over to some rocks. She watched them check the cuttings and under the overhangs till they were sure she wasn't there.

Sillies – they must think I'm a badger. But I'm never a badger.

They changed direction. She heard Raffen shout, 'Over there.'

Her heart sank, sure he'd guessed where she was hiding. They were so close. She pressed tighter against the trunk, holding her breath, trying not to make a sound.

And then, unable to bear the suspense, she had another peek.

When she did, her blood froze.

There were her brothers, so close she could see their faces. But behind them, closing in through the trees, were the most terrifying creatures she had ever seen.

Stooped shadows, moving fleet as wolves over the snow, with barely a sound. Suddenly, there were lots of them, popping from behind each tree – as if they *were* the trees one moment, and these horrible creatures the next. They had arms and legs, like people, but their hands were all crooked; their skin, pale as the snow.

Her brothers hadn't seen the danger.

She wanted to warn them. Wanted to scream. She knew she should. . . But what if those things heard her? What if they saw?

Her throat was stone. And then, it was too late.

At the last moment, Ref turned and uttered a short, desperate wail before the creatures were on them. She watched, stricken – those hands, those horrible hands. Dozens of them, pulling at her brothers, clawing, crushing.

Her brothers kicked and struggled, their bodies disappearing under the writhing pale figures. And then, there was a horrible snap – like a branch breaking. Raffen stopped fighting.

As the creatures bore him away, Ref fought bravely. He had an arm free, was hitting out at them. But there were too many. He had one by the hair – long, greasy white hair – and pulled, twisting its head towards her, and she saw its face. A hideous sight – cheeks streaked black, eyes bright like white fire, and a ragged maw of a mouth and teeth that, even from that distance, looked sharp and cruel. Then another had a grip on his throat, and began squeezing.

He started shaking. She saw through the mob of white figures his arms quivering wildly. Until he went limp. There was another cracking sound. They threw him on their shoulders, his head jiggling like a broken doll.

And then – as silently as they'd come – they were gone.

Namma was rigid. Her fingers wouldn't move. She looked down and saw her nails had sunk deep into the bark. And between her legs, the branch was wet with her fear.

CHAPTER TWENTY-SIX

The day began in a grey smear. Ice-dust gusted across the snowbound fields. The cold had come. The deeper cold. Sparrows huddled in the crook of branches; horses stood shivering under byres, while the hall-folk hurried across the frozen yards back to the warmth of their fires.

'Winter's closing her fist,' folk muttered in passing, and those same deathly fingers seemed to have taken hold right through Erlan's bones. He had arrived back late the previous night, wearied from a long day's ride from the south as escort. If anyone ordered him back in the saddle that day, they could go to Hel.

On his way to report for his daily duties, he saw a crowd of men jawing in front of the Great Hall. He stopped another karl striding towards them. 'Is there special business today?'

'You didn't hear?'

'Hear what?'

'The king called an assembly of his sworn lords. Earls, thanes, the hird-lords – each with two karls. He speaks at noon.'

'What will he say?'

'If I knew that, he wouldn't need to say it.'

As the karl walked off, Erlan heard hooves snap at the hard ground behind him. He turned to see two riders appearing from the Sacred Grove.

He recognized Earl Bodvar, wearing a jet-black cloak and his customary scowl. Pulling up before the growing crowd, the earl nodded a greeting. 'Still alive, stranger?'

'So it seems, my lord.' He held Bodvar's bridle while the earl dismounted.

Bodvar snorted. 'Well, if Sviggar wants to take in stray dogs, that's his business.'

'How fares the Earl of Vestmanland?' said Erlan, with a servile curl of his lip.

'Badly. The king snaps his fingers and we must fall in like whipped pups. He cares nothing that a man's arse could freeze to his horse in this weather.'

'He seems to enjoy keeping you in the saddle.'

Bodvar gave a gruff chuckle. 'That he does,' he conceded. 'And always when there's business to be done at home. Damn miserable ride, too. And worse, one of my karls took sick on the road.'

'That's too bad.' Erlan noticed Bodvar was eyeing him up and down.

'Tell me – are you summoned to this thing?'

'No. Only the high men and their karls, I heard. Errand-runners aren't needed.'

'Huh!' Bodvar gave his beard a thoughtful tug. 'Then you can stand in for my sick karl. He had a fever like a furnace. I'd lay he'll not see out the week. Poor bastard,' he added.

'You want *me* to attend you?' Erlan couldn't conceal his surprise. *Has he forgotten I came within a whisker of slitting his throat?*

'Well?'

'I've duties to the king.'

'Bah! My need is greater than the king's. What say you?'

Erlan considered his offer. 'I suppose I say yes.'

'Excellent!' smiled the earl. 'You can begin by fixing some hot vittles and a drop of ale. I'm hungry as a hog.'

Erlan swallowed his pride for the thousandth time. 'As you wish, my lord.' As always, it tasted bitter.

It was well past the noon-mark.

Inside the Great Hall, the firepits burned high, but their heat didn't travel. Ephemeral clouds of breath wreathed the broad shoulders and tight-woven braids of the assembled men. The highest men in the land.

Fifty small-lords with attendant karls stood murmuring, fidgeting with brooches or buckles, now and then glancing at the king's council, who conferred in low voices on the platform.

All awaiting the king's arrival.

At last, Vithar, the white-bearded relic who'd stood council to Sviggar and his father before him, shuffled into the hall and slammed his staff on the floor.

'The old bastard likes to rattle his stick, don't he?' muttered someone. There were a few sniggers as their king entered.

The murmuring ceased. Sviggar came to the platform's edge, scanning the younger faces below him.

'You honour me to come at such short summoning. Every one of you,' he began, voice coarse as gravel. 'According to

Sveär law, it is not the season for an assembly, yet you have come. I am grateful.'

He paused, weighing up how to go on. 'It's common knowledge now, how my son was taken from me. No father would outlive his son. No king, his heir. Yet I'm not alone in mourning an untimely death.'

Erlan glanced over Bodvar's shoulder at the faces around him, but they were impassive as stone.

'Many shed tears for kinsfolk. People cry out for fathers and mothers. For daughters and sons.' He grimaced. 'I am old, but I'm not yet deaf. Their cries have reached my ear. These very tables bear witness to many a strange tale. You've heard these for yourselves, doubtless. Vanishings. Murder.' He spat the words like pip-stones. 'Blood.'

His eye swept over the upturned faces. 'And who is this enemy? Folk are taken from their halls and homesteads. They vanish on the road. Tell me. . . *Who has done this?*' he suddenly hissed.

If he expected an answer, no one uttered a word. In the silence, Grimnar and his dark talk came to Erlan's mind. The old *seidman* had an answer for this king. But now was not the time to convince these others of something Erlan could barely credit himself.

The king shook his head. 'You do not know. And how could I summon men to fight an enemy I couldn't yet perceive? My people bled, but this foe had left no trace. No one had seen them.' The lines about his mouth tightened. 'Until now.' He turned to the guard by the entrance to his council chamber. 'Bring her in.'

The guard vanished as a flurry of whispers rustled through the assembly, and reappeared clasping the armpit of a young girl. The little thing could hardly be six summers old. The guard shoved her towards the king, but she froze stiff soon as he let her go.

The sight of her silenced the voices immediately. Even for her age, she was small. She had tangled hazelnut hair and wore a rough-spun russet smock falling just below her knees. Her feet were bound in dirty cloths, and her bare calves were blotchy with cold.

'Come nearer, little one.' Sviggar's voice was surprisingly tender. Her tiny features were rigid with terror, but she managed to shuffle towards the king. When she reached him, he took her and turned her to the crowd.

She coloured scarlet, as if her fresh, innocent face couldn't endure the sight of so many grizzled, guilty ones.

'This girl has seen our enemy!' A murmur ghosted over the onlookers. 'And only two leagues from this hall.' He squeezed the girl's shoulders. 'Go on, child. Tell us again what you saw.'

But seeing it was her moment to speak, the girl was paralysed. Her eyes darted desperately for some hope of rescue, but when she saw there was none, she buried her face in her hands and bawled.

Sviggar stood by, looking awkward, unsure what to do. There were a few half-hearted suggestions from the crowd. But he quickly lost patience, and tried pulling her hands away from her face. Only she resisted him bravely, sobbing even louder.

With a last shake, he let her go. The girl dropped down and buried her head between her knees. Sviggar seemed at a loss when a figure appeared from the crowd and flew up the steps two at a time.

Erlan lurched in surprise.

How the Hel did he get in here?

'Isn't that your Gotar lad?' observed Bodvar, drily.

Erlan nodded. Though what the mad little bastard was doing in the company of the greatest men in the land, he had no idea. But without even a glance at the king, Kai went to the girl, crouched beside her, and began whispering in her ear. Gradually her sobbing abated and she looked up to see Kai smiling at her. She wiped her nose. He whispered some more, and at last, she nodded.

Sviggar observed all this with waning patience. 'Well?'

Kai murmured something and the king nodded. 'Very good,' he announced, 'the lad will speak for the girl.'

And so he did.

Piece by faltering piece, Kai drew out the girl's story, relaying each detail to the assembled men. The Shining Lake, the children's game, her hiding place, her brothers' approach. And then, the appearance of the killers.

'They came from behind the trees,' said Kai, crouching with his ear near the girl's mouth. 'She says they looked like ugly people. . . Kind of stooped. Long armed, but not exactly tall. They moved fast, without a sound in the snow at all.'

The girl lifted her hands, made them crooked. 'Their hands were bent. Like claws. And their skin was very white. But dirty. She could see their hands because of what they did to her brothers.' The girl burst into tears afresh. Only after more whispering from Kai did the assembly hear how the killers had snapped the boys' necks like kindling.

'She saw the face of one.' Kai listened some more. 'It made her afraid, she says. There were marks down its cheeks. And

365

it had white skin, all cracked like a snake's. She says its mouth was wide with teeth all black and sharp—'

'All right,' broke in Sviggar. While Kai had been relaying her description, talk had been swelling among the crowd. 'That's enough. Take her away.'

Kai hesitated, evidently wanting to stay and witness the rest of the meeting. 'Now,' commanded Sviggar.

'Go on,' urged Erlan, under his breath. Now wasn't the time to irritate the king. Finally, Kai acquiesced and led the girl out through the council chamber.

'The boys' bodies were found hanging in a tree half a league from there, on the other side of the lake.' Sviggar eyed the crowd. 'They had been flayed. Their eyes, noses and tongues cut away.'

He turned to his councillors. 'Lord Torkel, this happened on your land. Have you anything to add?'

A tall man with a long face and a wolfish nose stepped forward.

'The Earl of Tundaland,' Bodvar muttered. 'And lord of the royal arse-kissers.'

'Only that this time we found traces in the snow,' said Torkel. The assembly stirred at this.

'Can they be tracked?' called someone.

'I believe they can,' Torkel answered. 'There are visible tracks and signs of movement through the forest. I can't say it's much – and there'll be even less if we have another snowfall. But there is something. . .'

'Are these even men?' called out a karl near Erlan. 'What of the girl's description?'

'They sound like no men I ever saw,' Bodvar remarked to Erlan.

'No man can move across snow without sound,' declared another. 'How do we know these are the same killers as elsewhere, where there were no traces at all?'

'Is the girl to be believed?' asked a councillor.

'She's of sound mind,' said Sviggar. 'She described what she saw, best she could. Yet the like has never before been heard. Not even in the old tales.'

Vithar shuffled forward. 'With respect, my lord, that is not true.' He nodded his snowy head gravely. 'There were once stories – though never told these days – which this child's unhappy tale has dragged out of my memory. Even I have not thought of them since my boyhood.'

'Well?' demanded Sviggar. 'Speak of what you remember.'

'My father would tell of the Ragnarok That Was Not. It was during the age of gold, a time eight generations back or more, when Freya's golden tears flowed like a river to this land. . . not like these days of scarcity. But without warning, a terrible darkness fell for three whole years. The sun was blotted out, and men said the Ragnarok had come at last. Thick mists choked the land. The air was filled with a pestilential dust. Nothing would grow without the sun's light. Folk starved or slaughtered one another for the last scrap of food. The lords made gold offerings to the gods, pouring the last of their wealth into the earth in the hope that their fate could be turned – that the gods would restore the sun. Some said that the king even offered himself as a sacrifice.' He shook his head grimly.

'But there were many who gave up all hope that the world of men would survive. Instead they looked for another way out – away from the blackened skies and the terrible mists. They went down. . . down into the deep places of the earth to find some other way of living, taking with them their wealth and their women and children. However, after three failed summers and untold hardship and misery, the winds came and blew away the foul dust. The sun returned. That first summer, there was much gladness as the crops at last grew, and folk once more reaped a harvest. People went back to their living – poorer maybe, fewer, but glad to be alive. But of those other folks – those who went down into the depths – no one ever heard anything again.'

The old man had come to the end of his tale. For a time, no one spoke.

'But they died, surely,' said Sviggar, at length.

'I know not,' croaked Vithar. 'Nor does any man. Perhaps they did not die. All I say is that this tale has risen in my mind.'

'What the girl describes are like men. And yet not so.' The speaker was another councillor, a grey-haired earl named Heidrek. 'They move like *draug*-spirits, and have the appearance of fiends.' A few groans rose from the crowd – Heidrek was not popular. 'I may not have Vithar's long memory, but I'm old enough to remember stories which the land wants to forget. Of man-killers. Unseen, except in the darkest of dreams—'

'You sound like some old *vala*, Heidrek,' interrupted Sigurd. 'Talking of ghosts and fiends! Bah! I'll wager they bleed and die like men. And what's more, men of the Wartooth.'

The Wartooth's name kindled the blood of the assembly.

'Lord Sigurd,' called Bodvar over the hubbub. 'I'm curious. Tell us what it serves the Wartooth to skin two little boys?'

It was Heidrek's turn to laugh. 'Bodvar has the right of it. You call me an old woman, Lord Sigurd – well, I shall overlook the slander. There's many a hall-maid would rather wrestle with this old woman than the whole pack of you younger men.' An ironic cheer roiled through the crowd. 'Be that as it may. There are shadows that roam of which folk know next to nothing. . . only stories.' He broke off, cryptically.

'What are you getting at, Heidrek?' demanded Sviggar.

'He means darklings.'

It was the first time Erlan had opened his mouth. The hall fell silent as all looked to see who had spoken. Then someone sniggered, another laughed, and soon a resounding jeer echoed to the rafters.

But the ancient Vithar rapped his staff for silence. 'Many of you laugh,' he squawked, casting a withering eye over the assembly. 'But the worthy earl may have it right. Darklings, the stranger said. Aye, we've all heard the name. But what are these? Do you know?' He jabbed his staff at one of the men who'd laughed the loudest. 'Or you?' he demanded of Sigurd. Neither man spoke. 'You don't answer because you don't know. It is but a word. A name. A darkling might even be a kind of man! Who knows? You might use any word for a thing unknown – a thing dangerous and hateful. Is this not what we have here?'

The hoary old councillor drooped back against his staff, his anger spent. But no one laughed.

'There's another possibility,' came a voice from the floor. 'I hold nothing to our wise kinsman on such things, but can a man's spirit not take on many forms?'

'Who spoke?' snapped Sviggar.

'It is I, Arve, son of Asgeir.'

A spaced cleared around a stout man with a crooked nose looking up at Sviggar, eager as a hound. 'What do you mean?'

'Shape-shifters, lord.'

Another buzz of whispers.

'More cursed sorcery!' cried Sviggar. 'I spent my youth standing in the shieldwall against flesh and blood. There was honour in that.' He gave a bitter sneer. 'Must I grow old chasing shadows?'

'It may explain their appearance,' said Arve. 'Neither man nor beast, yet both at once.'

'No,' cut in Earl Torkel. 'Shifters take one form or another, never some twisted concoction of both.'

Arve shrugged. 'Perhaps you're right. But if these killers take form at all, and are no mere shadows, we can kill them.'

'And so we shall,' said Sviggar. 'Enough talk on this. The truth is we cannot say what they are. But we have their tracks. We shall hunt them. And destroy them.'

He beckoned the Tundaland earl. 'Torkel, the trail begins on your land. It falls to you to find them. Wherever it leads, let nothing turn you aside. Choose three men and go quickly, before another snowfall comes. Who will ride with you?'

'My brother, Torgrim.' Heads turned to a man standing near Erlan. He had Torkel's wolfish nose and angular brow on a younger face. The brother nodded assent.

'The second is Handarak of the Sami blood. None in these halls knows forest-lore so well.' Another man stepped forward: black-haired with a round face, narrow eyes, and cheekbones like polished oak.

'Good,' said Sviggar. 'And the last?'

'Sire, for the last, you make the choosing.'

'As you wish.'

For a long time, the old king scanned the world-worn faces of his vassal lords and their karls. Erlan fixed his eye straight ahead. He thought of Grimnar and his strange mutterings. The *seidman* knew. He could see into this darkness. Had powers to wrestle with it. Erlan recalled how powerless he had been – a captive to the mystic's slightest whim.

Strange. . .

Strange that around him he felt these men bulging with desperation for their king's favour. Yet he felt nothing. No desire to see these deaths avenged. No part to play.

Just then, Sviggar's eye alighted on him. When the king's gaze lingered, Erlan tried to imagine what he saw. A stranger? A warrior? A gift from the gods? If so, Erlan knew now the price the gods paid in others' blood to lavish their gifts on kings. Inga's blood stained the gift in this king's hands. But if Sviggar believed that he had been drawn there for some purpose, perhaps this was it. He felt his blood quicken.

But the king turned away.

'I choose Arve, son of Asgeir. You leave today.'

The king stalked out, his councillors scuttling after him. Erlan watched them go, as the assembly broke up.

Why should I care? he thought, trying to dislodge the splinter of disappointment in his throat.

Did he envy a muscle-bound buffoon like Arve the chance of glory? Or the chance of his lord's favour? Or even of the slaking of a thirst for vengeance? No, it was none of these.

It was something else.

CHAPTER
TWENTY-SEVEN

'Fucking Torkel,' snarled Bodvar, as they left the Great Hall. 'The man has about as much nerve as a constipated sheep.' The earl tramped off, muttering about some business that wanted attending, leaving Erlan alone.

Before long, the yard had emptied, the crowd of karls melting away to their duties, leaving the cold wind to lick at the frost on the ground.

Erlan stamped his bad foot. It felt the cold worse than the other. He ought to report to the spear-master. Even in this weather, the younglings would get schooled. Ahead of him lay many drab hours teaching the sons of lords how not to get themselves killed in the first moments of combat. Arrogant toadlings the lot of them, and tiresome beyond measure.

He'd turned with a sigh when a yelp carried around the corner, and out from under the hall buttresses ran a small boy.

The boy's face glowed with happy terror. He wasn't more than four winters old, with short dark curls and a high forehead.

His little fists pumped away, but despite great effort, he was hardly swift.

Though he'll soon be swifter than I am. A bitter thought.

It was Svein. The Spare Heir, as Kai had named him. The boy ran straight past, oblivious to him, only looking back with another wild laugh at his pursuer. But he was in no danger of being caught.

A still smaller figure rounded the corner: his little sister coming on, tiny leather-bound feet slapping the ground, her face determined. Behind her bounced the same silky hair that graced the head of her mother, the queen. Waddling for all her worth, she suddenly noticed the big warrior in her way.

The glance cost her.

She caught her toe in a rut and went skidding over, little hands grinding the dirt. She started bawling.

Erlan limped over and scooped her onto her feet. 'You're in a hurry, eh? Here, show me your hands.' She whimpered miserably, as he began rubbing some heat back into her fingers.

There was a good deal more wailing before the pain seemed to ebb and she took a good look at him. And suddenly he found himself staring into a pair of enormous brown eyes. The sight of them hit him like an invisible blow. Those eyes, so earnest, so full of curiosity, echoed another's, twisting the splinter in his heart.

The girl stopped crying suddenly. Maybe she read some change in his face, for she slid her arms around his neck, and laid her head on his shoulder. Hardly knowing what he was doing, he picked her up and held her, murmuring, 'It's all right, my love. It'll be all right.'

The boy had come back across the yard and was looking up at the pair of them, curious.

'What are you doing?' said a woman's voice behind him. He started round to see the king's older daughter picking her way across the yard. She wore a pale dress, and over it a fur cloak, black as pitch and gleaming even in the dull light.

'My Lady Lilla.'

'What happened? Put her down.'

'She fell.' He tried to put the girl down, but she clung on to him, burying her face in his cloak.

Lilla was eyeing him, taking his measure. 'She seems quite taken with you.'

'No doubt she'll soon learn better.'

'You're the one my brother calls the cripple, aren't you?'

'My name is Erlan,' he reminded her.

'I know,' she replied. 'The stubborn one.'

'You have a good memory.'

She snorted, tilting her chin. 'As it happens, I do.' Years of looking down on men like him was clearly a difficult habit to shift. 'So – how do you like it at my father's court?'

'I like it very well.'

She gave a sharp laugh. 'You're a poor liar, Erlan. Still, once you settle into your place here, you may like it better.'

'There's no shortage of people to remind me of it.'

'Perhaps you should be grateful,' she snapped, catching the sarcasm in his voice. 'Many lords would have turned someone like you away. You're fortunate my father has a kind heart.'

'Someone like me?'

'Well, you know. Someone with. . .' She trailed off, gesturing vaguely at his ankle.

He gave her a thin smile. 'We all have our weaknesses, my lady. Some are more visible than others.'

The princess looked uncomfortable, seeming unsure how to respond. 'Anyway, you can put her down now.'

'As you wish.' He set the little girl down on the ground. She ran to Lilla, grabbed two fistfuls of fur and looked shyly back up at him. 'What's her name?'

'Katla. And this little scoundrel is Svein,' she said, ruffling the boy's curls. 'They're the queen's, but they like being with me, so . . .' She shrugged. 'I let them tag along.'

'Where are you going?'

'Nowhere special. Into the woods. They have sharp little eyes. They help me find things.'

'Things?'

'You know – winter berries, roots, herbs. . . other plants.' She shook her honey-coloured mane of hair and pulled it over one shoulder. 'You'd be surprised at what you can find. You can survive a long while out in the woods, even in winter. If you know what to look for. . .'

What the Hel did this girl know about survival? 'And you do, I suppose,' he said, unable to conceal the disdain in his voice.

'Huh!' she snorted. 'Better than you, clearly. If you'd known half what I do, you wouldn't have arrived at these halls looking so like. . .'

'Like what?' he asked, feeling his temper rising.

'Well, quite so like a skeleton!'

'Fortunately, you'll never have to put your superior knowledge to the test.'

'Why do you say that?'

375

'You're the daughter of a king. . . I don't suppose you've ever wanted for anything.'

'How would someone like you possibly know what I want?'

He could see the anger flare in her eyes. They were deep blue, as deep and dark as the ocean. He'd always mistrusted the ocean. Too many mysteries lurked in its depths. 'I should go, my lady.'

'No doubt you should,' she replied, her composure regained. 'As should we.'

He was turning away when she stayed his arm. 'I suppose I should thank you,' she said stiffly. 'For her.' She laid her hand on Katla's head, her skin pale and delicate as a flower against the midnight black of the girl's hair.

'No trouble,' he said, looking down once more into Katla's big, wounding eyes. 'Farewell, little one. Till we meet again.'

Before she had a chance to reply, Lilla had turned and swept her away.

The following days, folk talked of nothing but Torkel and his men. Some said they were bound to return soon, empty handed; others that, with Handarak's forest-lore and Arve's wits, they were sure to send word within the week.

Meanwhile, the house-karls sharpened their blades and strutted like stallions, bragging how many of this furtive foe they would slaughter.

Erlan grew tired of it all. His thoughts drifted back to the men he'd stood with. *Before.* Men like Garik and Gunnar and Dag. Sure, they'd liked a tale and admired a man's courage, but the conceit of these Sveär karls was something else. Maybe it was inevitable. Most of his folk had been farmers in their way, but few of these had any land to call their own. Their food depended on the king's favour, and his favour on their renown. For what was a warrior without a name? Just another mouth to feed. And the great Uppland storehouses were not inexhaustible. . .

Yet beyond the boasting and the chatter, a silent doubt was discernible in everyone's eye: that Torkel, Torgrim, Handarak and Arve would never be seen again.

'The old goat,' as Kai liked to call the king, 'has been losing sleep, is what I've heard.' Kai heard a good deal. 'Pacing his bedchamber like a wolf – grinding his teeth to dust with all his worrying. And the queen just laughs at him.'

'How the Hel would you know that?'

Kai tapped the side of his nose. 'There's folk up there couldn't keep their mouth shut if their tongue was gonna run out of their head.'

'Well, just you be sure your mouth stays shut to anyone but me.'

On the sixth day, a heavy snowfall came in the night and for the whole of the next day. A blanket of fresh powder six inches deep covered the land. Everyone knew: if the trackers hadn't pinned their quarry by now, the snow would make their hunt all but impossible. Word of one kind or another was expected.

Another week passed and still nothing. And the talk began to turn from discussing nothing but their fortunes to avoiding mention of them altogether.

Two days later, a young lad rode in with a message. Said he was the last in a chain of five messengers carrying tidings from Torkel. The message was a week old, but told that they were still on the trail and heading to the northwest, into the high country towards the Dale of the Elves. Nothing more.

Naturally, this kindled the hopes of the court, that a summoning would follow, and they could ride to battle. Sviggar became quite renewed in spirit.

But after another day or two, the doubts returned, and fresh gloom spread like a pall over the Uppland halls.

Only they didn't have long to wait. For another message was on its way.

The guard stamped his feet in the snow.

The last night-watch was the coldest and darkest, by his reckoning, but he must be closing on the end. He yawned. Grey dawn-streaks had begun slipping through the mist that sagged on the fields and woods beyond the Great Hall.

He could see the outline of the road, the sharp triangles of the low folk's dwellings; walls dark, roofs white as fallen clouds. The wind had dropped. The air was so still he could hear the flap of a pigeon's wing from the woods beyond the King Barrows. Their bulging outlines were emerging like some new world, birthed out of a void of darkness and ice.

He shivered and imagined his wife bundled up in the bed-skins. The fire would be burning low. If only Skurrik would relieve him soon, he might get home before she awoke. Soon warm up then, wouldn't he just?

He decided to make another turn around the mounds. By then, Skurrik must've come. As for his duty, he'd long made up his mind that the only use of walking his circuit was to keep warm and awake. In three years, he'd never had to hold up anyone more menacing than a herdsman taking a piss.

His footsteps crunching in the hard-packed snow and the soft swish of his breeches were the only sounds. He walked along the road past the Sacred Grove, the ancient oaks emerging out of the gloom like the legs of giants. He passed the Tiding Mound, from where great announcements and decrees were proclaimed. It was half the size of the three royal burial mounds, but any man shouting from up there was sure to get a hearing.

He remembered the first time he'd come there as a boy, late one summer, and heard old Karak, a renowned warrior on the high council, recount to a herd of grubby-faced younglings and their work-worn fathers and mothers the feats of King Sviggar in his bloody battles across the East Sea. Karak's words had caught his imagination like a cub in a bear-trap that day.

And now here he was, in service to that same king. So much for glory. He was just bloody cold. It was so long since his last fight, he could hardly remember what it was like to kill a man or piss himself with fear in the shieldwall. Trudging around in the snow was hardly the stuff of the old songs.

He sniffed and spat into the snow, following the road in its loop away to the west. Then he cut north, off the road, heading for the edge of the Kingswood that nudged against the foot of the westernmost barrow. The outlines of the trees and the mounds were sharpening now as more light spilled into the sky. Following his earlier footsteps, he came to the far edge of the western mound.

All of a sudden, he stopped.

There in the snow, cutting across his path, barely visible in the half-light, were footprints leading straight up the side of the mound.

His gaze followed the prints to the top. Was there something up there? He peered into the lingering shadows. Aye, certainly, there was. Some shape with no connection to this or any of the mounds.

He looked harder. The silhouette was tall and very thin, becoming at its top bulbous and misshapen. His first thought was to get closer, but he hesitated – to walk on the King Barrows was an offence as grave as any against the king. What was the penalty? Was it death? Whatever, most folk were more worried about the curse they'd invite for disturbing a dead king's grave. No one he knew would be fool enough to do that.

But someone *had* been up there, and there was something up there now. He faltered, unsure what to do. But at last, he reasoned he was here to protect the king and his halls, and that included these bloody barrows.

He put his foot to the climb.

His breathing shortened with each upward step, but well before he reached the top he stopped dead. For now he *could* see.

It was a post, rough-cut from some blackened tree, but straight and tall. His gaze ran to its top, and there it stayed, seized with terror at the grisly thing that hung there. He saw a braid, glistening darkly in the rising light. Saw ragged chunks of flesh, torn and dripping. . .

A human head.

Beneath it, the post was slick with blood, not yet frozen. Suddenly, he caught the reek of flesh. His stomach lurched, settled, lurched again. And he doubled over, retching into the snow.

Too bloody long since I've seen a battle.

Cautiously, he climbed to the summit. He could make out some features on the head, contorted by the cold. The eyes were rolled back and a tongue-tip poked from a corner of the mouth, coal-black. The mouth gaped, lips stiff as bark. But then a flicker of recognition – the round face, the high cheekbones, the wide flat brow.

Handarak the huntsman.

The guard looked away, trying to goad his mind into some kind of sense. He must go and tell someone. But who, and what was to be done first?

He looked east, towards the onrushing dawn, over the other barrows and the Tiding Mound, which moments before had been swathed in shadow.

In the thin light, he saw three more posts.

Three more heads.

He started running for the halls.

CHAPTER
TWENTY-EIGHT

When Erlan and Kai arrived to see the wretched gargoyles, staring out like sentinels of doom, a crowd had already gathered.

Erlan could hardly have remembered their faces before. Now he would never forget them.

The low folk gaped, silence cloaking them like a mist. But after a while, there was a dry comment from one that he must fetch his son to show him what becomes of heroes.

'What's the old fella gonna do now?' asked one old woman.

'Same he's been doing – not a bean. Just hide hisself in that ruddy big hall, and rut away with his mare.' That brought a few laughs.

'He put away his sword long ago,' said another.

'One of 'em, anyway!' More laughter.

'A sword's no bloody good. What can he do against ghosts?' said a grimy smith.

'It's evil – straight and simple. Has to fight evil with evil, don't he?'

'That ain't easy with the power leached out of them mounds.'

'How do you mean?' asked Kai.

'It's a bad business, what's done 'ere. The King Barrows are sacred. But not no more. Their power's gone.'

'Aye – and the luck of the Sveär folk with it,' said another.

'Shouldn't wonder if bad fortune comes now. Children'll take fever. Crops'll fail. Mark me – it'll happen.' This cheery soul sounded like he wanted it to, just to prove him right.

'There's witchery here – fell spirits,' grumbled the old woman. 'The place reeks of it.'

Suddenly, Erlan heard his name called. He turned and saw Einar trotting up, cheeks ruddy in the pinching air.

'Fancy seeing something interesting?'

'More interesting than this?'

'I'm rounding up the king's councillors – those that are here. Sviggar's called an immediate council. Oh, he's in a rare fury!' Einar wiped away beads of sweat. 'Help me find them, and you can come see what happens.'

Erlan considered his offer.

'I'll bloody go if you don't,' blurted Kai.

Erlan snorted. 'Fine. I'll do it.'

Barely an hour after daybreak, Erlan took his post in the council chamber. The thralls had piled the braziers high for the hastily clad earls and thanes. Old Vithar was there, leaning on the gnarled staff that seemed stuck to him tight as his own head.

To one side, Sigurd paced. He was clean-shaven. Erlan hadn't before noticed that his jaw was slightly twisted. Perhaps some old break, giving his mouth a sloping appearance. He was chewing at his thin lips restlessly.

Erlan glanced at Einar, standing as close to erect as his belly would allow on the other side of the chamber. For once in his life, he looked serious.

Erlan looked around, studying the anxious faces, catching frantic whispers. And suddenly he felt a huge chasm open up between him and these Sveärs. It mattered nothing if they were high folk or low. He hadn't known Torkel and his men. Didn't care about the King Barrows. Oh, it was a grim sight. But inside, there was no anger, no indignation. At most, perhaps a mild scorn – that here were the greatest men in the land, reduced to whispering cravens.

He heard approaching footsteps; Sviggar entered, flanked by Finn Lodarsson. The king swept past his councillors, face like thunder.

'Are there tracks?' he demanded, flinging himself into his high seat among the furs. When no one answered, he bellowed, 'Odin's Eye! Am I surrounded by halfwits? Go and see! Before every soul in Uppsala tramples them to mud.'

Heidrek, the earl of Helsingland, shuffled off, muttering aimless apologies.

'This enemy plays on our blindness.' Sviggar's clear eyes glittered with anger. 'Where's the messenger?'

'Which messenger, lord?' ventured Vithar.

'The boy – damn him! Who brought word from them. I want to know exactly where they were last seen.'

'We know the trail took them to the Dale of the Elves,' offered Sigurd.

'Then there is our beginning.'

'What do you intend, lord?' asked Vithar.

'To raise an army! To rake the high country from peak to

dell, to hunt them down till the last one lies dead in his own blood.' Sviggar slammed a bony fist on the arm of his chair.

'Perhaps it is wise to take more counsel,' said Sigurd. 'You're upset.'

'Upset! This enemy makes mockery of me. They have violated the kingdom's sacred power. They have slaughtered some of my best men. You expect me to sit here and do nothing?'

'Not nothing. But I think caution is wise here. Had we the greatest host ever gathered, would it do us any good against an enemy that can't be found?'

'Everything that kills can be found. We will start with the Dale of the Elves.'

'That's many leagues away. Torkel and his men could've been lured there into a trap, nothing more. The truth is we've no idea whether this enemy dwells in the mountains, in the sky or in the earth under our feet.'

'We *will* find them.'

'And if we don't?'

Sviggar glared at his son, but said nothing.

'Men will die anyway – starving and freezing. Wandering around a wilderness on a fool's errand, looking for someone – or something – that refuses to be found.'

'So what is your counsel?' The old man's lips dripped with disdain.

'I advise before we blunder into the forests and doom an army, we understand what we're pursuing. Winter is no time for making war. Unless there is no other way.'

'With these deaths, this *is* the only way.'

'Why? To prevent the deaths of a few more thralls – or

bondsmen or children – you'd risk shedding the strength of the kingdom?'

'These were my best men.'

Sigurd's face curdled. 'Hardly your best. But now they're dead. Would you waste more good men then? Would you bleed the kingdom white?'

'You forget yourself, prince,' interjected Vithar.

'Do I?' Sigurd rounded on him with a look of scorn. 'What if this is all some ruse by the Wartooth to lure our strength away from these halls? Have you thought of that? We may return from stumbling around in the snow to find our women and children slaughtered, and the Wartooth with his ugly arse planted on that throne there.'

Sviggar leaned back, weighing his son's words. 'I will not do nothing,' he said at last, in a quiet voice. 'This insult cannot go unanswered. Their blood will not go unavenged.'

Just then, a rich perfume filled Erlan's nostrils, distracting him. Instinctively, he inhaled deeply, savouring its spicy tang. Before he'd turned, Queen Saldas swept into the chamber. She wore a long dress of dark blue that trailed behind her in a pool of velvet. Erlan watched her approach the circle of councillors, hips pouring from side to side, graceful as a serpent.

She had something in her hands.

'My lord husband,' she said, very calm.

'Who summoned you here?' Sviggar's tone was impatient. 'You know the council has pressing business.' The attention of every man in the room was fixed on the queen. Saldas was well used to that. 'Whatever you want, we cannot be disturbed.'

The queen tilted her slender neck, half-deferentially. 'Far be it from me to disturb such wise company. I shall return later. My king.' She lingered a moment, turning over whatever was in her hands. Some sort of garment.

When she turned away, Sviggar said, 'Wait. What is that you have there?'

'Oh, this?' She allowed herself a condoling look. 'It pertains to the news I bring. But I see I am disturbing you, my lord. Please forgive my intrusion.' She turned away again.

'What news?'

'Concerning your daughter.'

'Lilla?' The old king started forward. 'Speak, woman! Quickly.'

'As you wish,' replied Saldas, maintaining her low and unhurried tone. 'I imagined you would want to know at once. Lilla has disappeared. Her maidservant tells me she was in the Kingswood this morning. But after this morning's. . . events. . . it was a while before she noticed Lilla hadn't returned. She went looking for her, but all she found was this.' She let the garment fall to its full length. Erlan recognized the long fur cloak, sleek and shining. 'It was a gift from you, was it not?'

She tossed the thing into Sviggar's lap. The king caught it and crumpled it slowly to his face. 'I'm truly sorry,' she added. 'It's very distressing.' Though she hardly looked distressed.

'Was there any. . . blood?' asked Sigurd.

'None – though I didn't see for myself. I'm told the snow shows signs of a struggle. There—'

'Fiends!' cried Sviggar. 'Wretches – black devils! Curse the hands that touch one hair of that precious head!' He leaped from his chair, his eyes ablaze. 'I will hunt them down – tear out their hearts! Crush them to a stain in the earth, whatever they are!' He slewed, drunk with rage, and reached behind his throne, pulling out his sword, Bjarne's Bane.

He seemed half-mad, his blade half-drawn, but in a heartbeat, the queen was beside him, her delicate fingers enclosed around his gnarly fist, whispering in his ear.

The rage in his eyes subsided slowly. Gently, she pushed his hilt back into its sheath. Sviggar dropped back, limp, into his chair.

'Revenge must come first through wisdom,' said Saldas. 'There will be time enough for testing your mettle.'

There were more footsteps and Earl Heidrek entered. When he saw the king, he approached with faltering steps.

'Well?' croaked Sviggar.

'Many folk have been crowding around the barrows. They've made a. . . a terrible mess – but. . .'

'Are there tracks?'

'There are, my lord. Clear, this time. Footprints.'

'Can they be followed?'

'I think so.'

'Think?' growled the king.

'They can.'

'Then we ride at once. Summon the hird-lords. We raise the Uppland karls and vassals today. Send riders at once to the thanes of Sothmanland and Gestrikland to do the same.'

'This may be a trap,' said Sigurd.

'By the stars, your brother never would've been so timid! He'd already be astride his horse and after his sister. Yet you are still here!'

'I am not my brother.'

'We can all see that, plain as day,' his father scoffed.

'Staffen is dead. Lilla may be as well by now.'

'Then how can you delay even one moment?' cried Sviggar. 'Bah! Can you really be a son of mine?'

'It is not I who is the bastard.' Sigurd's thin mouth was unwavering. 'Father.'

The king looked fit to explode. 'How dare you—'

But Sigurd was quick to cut him off. 'No doubt Staffen would've blundered off swift enough. Sword in one hand, cock in the other. But he never would've stopped to wonder why there were tracks so clear now, and never before.'

'What do you mean?'

'Isn't it obvious? These creatures want to be followed. It's a trap.'

'Lord Sigurd may be right,' said Vithar.

'Of course, I'm right,' Sigurd snapped. 'Why else would they return with Torkel's head – and the others?' If they only wanted to kill them, their bodies would be buried under some drift. . . In the Dale country if those messengers are right. No, this was a declaration of war.'

'Well, then,' roared Sviggar, 'let it be war!'

'Aye, but war on their terms? Is that wise?'

'This enemy is more cunning than you allow,' said Saldas, her train sweeping behind her. 'They aren't to be cut down like some rabble of thralls. There is something of the other worlds in them. Until now, they make you seem weak.'

Sviggar bristled at his wife's slight. The other councillors shuffled uncomfortably. 'Oh, I know you are not,' she smiled. 'But, truly, they've made a fool of you. If you do not go about this in the right way, you risk appearing an even greater fool. Or a dead one.'

'What is your counsel?' asked Sviggar, his voice acid.

'You need allies.'

'Allies? What kind of allies?'

'Ones who have power over the unseen. Power in all the worlds.'

'You speak of the gods?'

'Naturally. You need their favour in this. Is Odin not Lord of the Ghosts? Is he not all-wise – the Spear-God who delivers victory? You must make him an offering.'

Sviggar snorted. 'An offering?'

'A full blood worship.'

'I knew it. The blood of your father's people runs thick in you, my dear. Thick and cold. But I am father of the Sveär people. *My* people. I ride to stop more killings, and you demand that I sanction nine more?'

The queen arched a finely plucked eyebrow. 'The All-Father's favour does not come without sacrifice.'

'You don't need to tell me that. Sacrifices, we can make. But I will not kill nine more of my folk. I will not allow it.'

Queen Saldas gave an elegant shrug and turned away. 'What you do not give to Odin freely, he will take in other ways. You will find out what it will cost you. My king.'

Sviggar considered her words, irritation spreading over his withered features.

'The queen is right,' agreed Sigurd. 'You must turn whatever power exists to your advantage. If the gods are so easily bought, then give them what they want.'

'And who decides, exactly, what it is they want?' demanded Sviggar. 'You? Her?' He shook his head. 'No – I am resolved to stop more deaths, not order them myself. But, my dear,' he continued in a biting tone, 'if you would fain make use of your skills, tell me whether my daughter still lives.'

The queen gave a tiny sniff of disdain. 'The bones will tell me.'

'Then ask them.'

Saldas thrust her fingers into a pouch at her belt, and pulled out a handful of squat bones, dirty white, and marked with tiny runes. She went to the table, pulled a small knife from her waist, and without the slightest hesitation, drew its edge across her thumb. A crimson line appeared at once. Squeezing, she sprinkled a few drops of blood over the waiting bones, then cast them on the table.

Sviggar leaned in, face eager.

Saldas gathered the bones together, and brushed a languid finger over them. 'It seems your daughter is bait,' she said. 'The bones say she still lives.'

The king nodded, seeming content. But then his expression soured, and he drew a weary hand over his face. 'Ah! These are scraps to go on.'

'The bones are seldom wrong.'

'Would that we all had your assurance, my queen.' He grimaced. 'I cannot do nothing,' he murmured. 'Even though we ride into a trap – we must ride.'

But the queen wasn't listening. She had scooped up the bones again, and scattered them on the table, letting her gaze wander over the misshapen lumps. 'Curious.'

'What?'

'The bones tell of a man alone.'

'A man alone? What is its meaning?'

'I cannot be sure.' She shrugged. 'Perhaps they show another way. If you must spring their trap, save your army. Do it with a man alone.'

'What good will one man do, if four of my best men fared so ill?' snapped Sviggar.

'I fancy I see it,' said Sigurd. 'A lone man could follow the trail to their stronghold – if they have one. If this enemy turns to spring a trap, we lose only one man, instead of seeing our army slaughtered.'

'But what would even that serve them?' said Saldas. 'They want to draw you on for some reason. If they allow a lone rider to follow them as far as their stronghold, he might send word. Send scouts ahead of your main force to stay close.'

'So Lilla must just wait and hope,' said Sviggar.

'If she yet lives, then what she must do is survive.'

'It seems a pitiful chance for her.'

'Better than none,' said Saldas, tersely. 'Lilla is gone. They have her. They may yet kill her, but if the bones tell it true, a lone rider may find the chance to bring her back to you.'

Sviggar sighed. 'At least they'll not expect this. Still, either we send a man to a very quick death, or it is our best chance.' He drew himself up. 'Very well. Who shall this man be?' He turned to Sigurd. 'She is *your* sister.'

'And I am your heir. Whoever this man is, he will almost certainly die. Do you want your legacy to die with me?'

The king looked unimpressed, but seemed caught.

'Sire, I will go,' said Finn, from beside Sviggar's oaken throne. 'I'm sworn to protect you and your kin. Let me go. I'm not afraid.'

Sviggar laughed warmly. 'My dear Finn – you are ever willing. You never disappoint me. But I must disappoint you.

You are far too valuable to me. I need you alive and by my side.'

'My lord.' Everyone turned to see who had spoken. 'The bones spoke of me.' Erlan stepped forward from his place in the shadows, his own words still ringing in his ear. He felt every eye upon him.

Sigurd reacted first. 'You! You're a cripple. And a beggar. What makes you think my lord father would entrust this to you?'

'Because if he doesn't, he will choose a good man. Perhaps the best man he has. And like as not, that man will die.'

'Then what conceit makes you matched to the task?' snapped Vithar.

'Because I'm nothing to him. What's another karl in his service? If I die, it's no loss to you, my lord,' he said, addressing the king. 'But if I succeed, then you'll have your daughter and you will have another proved sword in your household. You keep your best men and gain another.'

'What gain is it to you?' demanded Sviggar, eyeing him closely. 'If you're so sure that death awaits this man.'

It was a while before he answered. 'It's enough to have the chance to prove myself to you. However slight.'

'That's worth the risk you run?'

'It is.'

All the while, Erlan had sensed the emerald gaze of the queen upon him, moving over his every sinew. Suddenly she turned away and cast her bones again. Peering down, she looked momentarily troubled. 'Strange.'

'What is?' demanded Sigurd.

'The bones – they cannot read him.' She gave a light snort. 'At least the boy has ambition.'

'I'm no boy,' returned Erlan, meeting her gaze.

'But you are a cripple.'

Erlan turned to the king. 'Ask your Earl Bodvar whether I can fight, my lord.'

Sviggar gave a conceding shrug. 'It's true – he vouched for your skill.'

'You can't seriously be considering sending him?' cried Sigurd. 'You're squandering the only chance of saving Lilla.'

'Silence!' thundered Sviggar. 'If you will not go yourself, don't dare tell me whom I may or may not choose!'

He turned back to Erlan. 'As you wish. I shall trust in your sword, and the mark that joined your destiny to mine.' The king began to push himself out of his chair. Finn rushed to help him to his feet. 'I believe you came to my halls for a reason. It seems the Norns are now revealing to us what that is.'

'Perhaps.' The Norns dwelt in obscurity. The web they wove was dark with obscurity just the same.

'If not, you will die.'

'The Norns have woven what they will.'

'Very well,' declared the old king. 'You shall go ahead and follow the tracks, wherever they lead. I will lead the main force two days behind you. Together we will bring a red day upon this nameless foe.'

'A younger man should lead your host, father. The winter is unforgiving. Your old bones will not wear it.'

'They will wear it as good as any man under me!' growled Sviggar. 'But since you are so concerned for the safety of these halls, much more than the safety of your own sister, you will stay here, my son, and watch over them in my absence.'

'But, Father—'

'No argument! That is my last word on it. And you, Erlan – make your preparations. Take whatever you need. You must leave this very day. You understand what you must do?'

The stranger nodded to his lord.

It was very simple.

He had to die.

PART THREE

SHINING
WANDERER

CHAPTER TWENTY-NINE

The halls of Sviggar's Seat already lay many leagues behind. Erlan was away – back in the world of black and white, where the only sounds were the bridle's chink, the crunch of snow under-hoof and the sigh of the wind. Only now, the snow drifted deeper. The air bit sharper.

He'd never reckoned himself a tracker. On this trail, he didn't need to be. From the Kingswood, the tracks led always northwest, on towards the young mountains, brazen as the sun. He followed over farmland, round fjords, along half-buried hedgerows, across frozen lakes, through silent forests. Anywhere distant from the halls and hamlets of men.

Why this enemy never cared to conceal their path mattered little. If he was to be hunter or quarry, the Norns had made their choosing. He would follow these tracks to destiny or doom.

The landscape was made for solitude. Here, it made sense. Among the Uppland folk, his loneliness had been acute, cutting him at every turn. But in this place, with its grand skies and endless ocean of forest, solitude seemed a road to freedom.

Freedom or death.

And yet. . .

'Bragi's cock, it's cold!' Kai's exclamation was followed by an absurdly loud sneeze. Erlan looked down into his face. Even buried under a mountain of furs, he looked half-starved and half-frozen.

Solitude might well be a road to freedom. But he wasn't alone.

'If you weren't such a stubborn bastard, you could've been tucked up with one of your lithe little milkmaids.'

'Now there's a thought to warm the heart,' replied Kai. 'Still, I came along to get my blade wet, not watch my fingers fall off.' He blew into cupped hands. 'We've been a week on the trail and still not a shadow of 'em.'

'Turn back whenever you want.'

Kai didn't answer. Erlan pulled up. 'Well?'

'Baaah!' groaned Kai. 'Couldn't do that. You're such a bloody awful cook, you'd poison yourself 'fore you got within fifty leagues of the princess. And Sviggar'd have me on a spit!'

'Your scrawny arse would make a poor feast.' Erlan shook his head, wondering why he indulged the lad.

Back in Uppsala, he had left the king's council, headed straight for the stables, heart storming, while his head planned the journey's provisions. Before all else, he wanted horses. He'd picked out a sleek black mare and a strong bay stallion, and set about making them ready. He was so deep in his preparations he didn't hear the voice behind him.

'Master?. . . Master?. . . Erlan!' Finally he turned. Kai was standing there, still catching his breath.

'Go away,' said Erlan.

'But I just heard you're going after the princess.'

400

'By the hanged! Folk can't keep anything from your flapping ears, can they?' Irritably, he slung a blanket over the stallion's rump.

'Not if I can help it. Now, I've been thinking about what we'll need—'

'*We* don't need anything. I'm going alone.'

'Alone? But you can't. . . I don't understand.'

'What's so hard to grasp, boy?' he snarled. 'The king sends a man to pursue his enemy. He chose me. I go alone. If I succeed, the king has another proven warrior. If I fail, I die.'

'But surely you want me with you?'

Erlan shook his head. 'Actually. . . no.'

Kai stood blinking, eyes wide and wounded. Erlan turned and shook out his bridle.

'This is wrong.'

Erlan looked up. 'What?'

'Our fates – they're woven together. From the fire to this place, and onward. Our roads run together. Don't you see?'

'I see the road *I* must walk. Alone.' But seeing Kai's stricken face, he added, 'Look, I'm doing you a favour. You like it here. You're swimming in skald-singing and skirt. What more do you want?'

'What more?' Kai looked stunned. 'But all this is. . . it's nothing. It's a. . . a lark. I'm here 'cause you're here. Where you go, I follow. That's my path, and I see it clear as the sun.'

'You really think you're bound to me?'

Kai gave an eager nod. 'I'm sticking to you like the bloody pox.'

And so he had. They argued on a while, but Erlan soon realized Kai would never give in.

401

'The king won't take well to this change in his plans.'

'You're a smart fella. You'll talk him round.'

He had – eventually; persuading him Kai's presence would make contact with the scouts simpler, and that Erlan could fight better if Kai were there to handle the extra horse.

That same afternoon the Uppland folk watched the departing silhouettes of the two companions dissolve into the woods. Wrathling hung from Erlan's belt, and in his heart, demons whirled.

Despite the snow, they'd made seven or eight leagues a day. Fair going, by any reckoning, and now the last cultivated land lay far behind. Ahead lay a vast wilderness of woodland.

On the seventh day the ground reared up, folding the forest into ridged valleys and crooked dales. Cresting one ridge, the breath caught in Erlan's throat and he pulled up abruptly. The two sat, gazing out over the snowbound landscape, struck dumb by its cold beauty. There were no sounds around them. Nothing but a colossal stillness. As if silence were the god of this place. To break it was to smash something sacred.

For a long time, neither of them was willing to speak, until at last Kai whispered, 'Have you ever seen anything like this?'

Erlan shook his head.

'This must be near the place they call the Dale of the Elves.'

'It's well named if that's where we are. We must stay watchful. The others didn't get far beyond this.'

They watched the sunfall burn the horizon, gilding every tree with fire. And then the land sank back into a cold, vast gloom.

They dismounted and made camp – by now a well-worn routine. Kai darted around gathering wood while Erlan cleared space to lay a fire and prepared the kindling. Once the fire was lit, Kai began cooking, leaving Erlan to settle the horses and lay out a shelter and their sheepskins for the night.

Since leaving the Uppland halls, even Kai's excitement had slowly given way to disquiet. But he seemed especially subdued after they had squatted down to eat their supper. Erlan could see the boy was chewing something over.

'What is it?'

'Eh?'

'Something's bothering you.'

Kai only grunted.

'Come on – spit it out.'

'It's little enough. It hardly makes a difference now anyway.'

'What – curse you!'

'It's just I never asked you – don't know why – but I never thought to.'

'Asked me what?'

'Why you?'

'Me?'

'Yep – why did the old goat choose you? He had the pick of his men – loyal bastards to a fault and plenty of 'em know a sword's point from its pommel. . . yet he chose you. Did he say why?'

Erlan's gaze dropped into his bowl for a time before speaking. 'I asked him to go.'

'You asked *him*? For the privilege of coming to this miserable wasteland to freeze your bollocks off? Are you mad? What the Hel for?'

Erlan have a desultory grunt. 'They were talking of sending one man after the princess. Right or wrong – I wanted it to be me.'

The fire crackled beside them. A puzzled look settled on Kai's face, while he did some figuring. 'I see now,' he smiled at last. 'The glory. Yes – the glory! Ha! And why not – why let someone else win the old goat's favour when it could be you?'

Erlan shook his head.

'No?'

'No.' When he said no more, Kai threw up his hands in frustration. 'Then what?'

But Erlan only stared into the fire.

'It's Lilla, isn't it?' said Kai, his voice turning crafty. 'Of course – the princess! Am I right? Go on – you can tell me.'

'I don't want Lilla.'

'Why ever not? What's wrong with her?'

'Nothing's wrong with her. She's just. . . *Ach!* She's not why I'm here.'

'Then why the Hel are you? You wanted to come – yet you don't do it for glory. Nor for love. What then? Is it guilt?' He leaned over and gave Erlan a poke. 'The last princess you were looking out for didn't fare so well, is that it?' he chuckled.

His master didn't laugh. Instead his mouth hardened. 'I'm tired, Kai. We should get some sleep.'

'But you haven't answered yet,' the boy insisted. 'I don't understand. What else could you gain? The king's favour? The favour of a beautiful girl? A great name? But you don't seem to care what others think of you. It can't be for vengeance, since you're no Sveär.'

'Just drop it!'

But Kai couldn't, not now. 'If it's none of them, what else can you hope to gain except a swift and bloody death? There's nothing else down this—'

Erlan suddenly met his gaze, and the boy stopped.

'Wait. . . a. . . moment,' he whispered, gaping. 'It *is* death you seek.'

Erlan said nothing.

'Death,' murmured Kai. Suddenly he gave a violent snort, his face reddening. 'Why, you selfish, self-pitying son of a pox-ridden whore!' he cried, throwing his bowl at the fire.

'It's none of your con—'

'Of course it's my concern,' yelled Kai. 'You miserable prick! Haven't I followed you through enough? Don't I deserve to know some scrap of what goes on in that dismal block of wood you call a head? So you've got some dark story behind you. So damn what? I don't care! You are you, and I am me. That's it. The road lies ahead. I'd follow you to Helheim and back if that's where we have to go – but not because I want to *die*.' His long mouth was trembling with passion. 'Because I want to live! And live as high and wide and far as life will throw me. But you,' he snarled, 'you ungrateful bastard, you're living in the past, with your head stuck in some grave you've crawled out of. And all you want to do is crawl back there.'

Erlan suddenly thrust out a hand and seized Kai's throat. He yanked him so close and so hard he saw fear flood the boy's eyes. 'You can hardly call me ungrateful, little man. Haven't you got exactly what you wanted? Yet you stand there yelping like a bitch. The moment you saw me you wanted to drop your folk and tag along with me. More fool was I to let you. But I never promised you I would change. I never promised you a thing! If

405

you want to follow me into the bowels of death, it's your idiot eagerness got you here. By the hanged, if you weren't so like a bloody dog with a bone, refusing to let go of me. . .' He shook his head, infuriated. 'I'm not yours to keep, like some damned toy horse carrying you hither and thither to give you your next lark! I owe you nothing. I owe no one. Only myself, and the oath that I swore.'

'That's right,' sneered Kai. 'You serve yourself. You know how to do that well enough. And where's that got you?'

Erlan released his grip on the boy, and turned away with a scowl.

'You and your fucking oath.' Kai's voice was bitter as death. 'Whatever lies behind you, if it was that bad, you should be glad you're out of it, rather than living like the shadow of death is already over you. Be glad, you fool.' He reached out and gave Erlan a shove, but the stranger didn't respond. 'Death will find you soon enough without you seeking it.' But Erlan's stare was far away, into the fire and a thousand leagues beyond. 'Why do you seek it?' persisted Kai. 'Why?'

Erlan felt his anger ebb away as he watched the shimmering air rise into the night. 'It's not death. Or not only death. It's. . .' He shook his head, the fragile thread of his thoughts fraying. 'There is no answer to your question. A wise man once told me to open my mind to a friend. But I find I cannot.' He let out a long sigh. 'You are my friend, and I would explain why I chose this journey if I could. I don't rightly understand myself. Maybe it's all of your reasons and none of them. And if death hasn't the same meaning for me as for other men. . . I cannot tell you why. I swore I never would. You know I will not break my oath.'

The two sat listening to the flames snapping at the wood.

'I don't think we will return from this,' he went on. 'Maybe that is why I came. But now you know this, if you want to turn back, I'll not stop you. You're free to do whatever seems good to you.'

When Kai spoke, there was a rough edge to his voice. 'You call me your friend. I am.' He nodded. 'And if I haven't your wisdom, still I'm no fool. I see what I see in you. They call it the song of death. Aye, and it can be enchanting as any love, or any desire a man might know.' His eyes shone in the flame-flicker. 'You call me friend. Then I promise I will share with you whatever I have, as long as we walk the road together. And I have at least this much – I believe there is still much to live for. For me *and* for you. Maybe I've not known the world as you have, but I'll carry this belief until death rips it from my hand.' He held up his bunched fist. Suddenly he grinned. 'Hey – you're not the only one can make an oath.' The boy jumped to his feet, pulled up his sleeve and produced his dagger.

'What are you doing?'

'I make an oath to you – not as your servant, nor even as your friend. But as your brother.' He laid the point of the dagger against his naked forearm and, with a flick, made a cut in his flesh. The blood came quickly, running dark in the half-light.

Erlan saw him bite back the pain.

'I swear to you, by this blood, that I will stand with you as brother whichever road you walk, whatever your reasons. What gold or honour I win in this life, I'll share with you. I'll be your eyes, your ears, your hands – whatever you need me to be. And I'll not be separated from you by the will of any man.' His wide mouth beamed. 'Nor of any woman neither!'

Erlan gave a thin smile. 'I didn't ask for it,' he said quietly,
'. . .but I accept your oath. It was good fortune indeed to find
you, my. . . my brother. Here.' He pulled out his own knife, cut
off a corner of his cloak and threw it up to Kai. 'Cover that up.
We don't need to do our enemies' work for them, eh?'

'Stings like a bastard too,' hissed Kai, squeezing the cloth
against the wound.

'Aye – but no one ever tells you that.'

Kai sat down and wrapped himself in his furs. Now it was
Erlan's turn to rise. 'Put your head down. Get some sleep. I'm
going for a leak.'

'We need more wood.' Kai began to get up.

'I'll get it. You rest,' said Erlan, and stalked off out of the
pool of firelight while Kai settled back down. He just caught
the boy's murmur: 'Goodnight. . . brother.' Then a low chuckle.

Erlan smiled in the darkness.

He walked away from the fire towards their sunfall lookout
on the ridge-crest. The landscape spread below him in a wide
bowl. It was another clear night. So far, they had been lucky.
If the weather turned and the skies brought a fresh snowfall,
the trail would be covered and the princess as good as lost. But
there would be no snow tonight.

The moon had risen – a sliver of silver in the darkness – its
frail light enough to illumine the valley like a pale dreamland
beneath him. He lifted his face to the night sky. Thousands
of stars peered back at him. He looked down at his hand and
could just make out the blurred lines and calluses in his palm.

*Is this how a man turns blind? The light dims, the lines blur, and
soon he sees nothing but darkness.*

What *did* he want? Did he truly yearn for death? Or was it

only vindication? Must he now die to save one beauty to pay for the beauty he could not save? To turn back the falling drops of time? This was madness, he knew. *Or the road to madness.*

He looked up at the moon.

There were men who lost their reason for love of the moon. Perhaps he had lost his reason also. Or was death the only sane thing to seek in this world of blood and broken love?

How is it madness and sanity seem so close? Are they twins of the same father? The moon – the white queen of the night – who calls and calls to her lovers. She drinks down their love like a whirlpool, and yet they come no closer to her. She waits there, forever at a distance, inviting souls to her silken touch, weeping her moonbeam tears on lips that smile, cruel and taunting.

How like love she is, he thought bitterly.

They were riding into a trap – of that he was certain. But even the craftiest traps do not always catch their prey. Perhaps there was a chance. The words of the *vala* whispered in his heart. *You will bear much pain, but you will never break.* Yet the malice of the Norns seemed at odds with the *vala*'s telling.

There was no answer. There was only the road ahead.

He cast a last look across the valley, over which silence seemed to reign like the lord of all worlds, vast and eternal. And then he turned back – to find his wood and take his piss and return to the warmth of the fire.

CHAPTER THIRTY

They awoke to a brilliant blue morning and picked their way down the forested slope, following the trail across the valley floor and over the next ridge. There, the land climbed higher before flattening onto a white expanse punctuated by frozen lakes.

Around noon, clouds rolled in from the north. The shallow beams of the winter sun broke around their bulging shapes, colouring them black and gold. The sky, having dawned so clear, began to fill with a kind of foreboding. They pulled their cloaks tighter against the chill.

They were riding through a stand of pines; ahead a treeline was visible. That meant another lake. Kai was a few yards ahead, leading the third horse behind him. Erlan watched him emerge from under the snow-mantled branches. And then, abruptly, he stopped.

'What is it?' Erlan called.

'Come see for yourself.'

As he drew alongside, he looked down to where Kai was pointing.

410

There in the snow, the ragtag tracks they'd followed for so many leagues separated into three distinct trails. One led right, along the eastern edge of the lake; a second to the west, across the frozen lake; the third cut back south into the forest. Erlan jumped down.

Kai dismounted after him, while Erlan squatted over the fork in the tracks, examining them. He felt Kai beside him, and was startled when the boy suddenly kicked the snow and swore violently.

'I knew it was too bloody good to last! As if they'd lead us by the nose to their stronghold. *Baah!* They've been stringing us along like hogs to a roasting.'

Erlan gave a wry snort, and continued glowering at the three sets of footprints.

'This seems to be the larger pack of them.' Kai pointed at the middle path across the lake.

'Might be. . . But they seem to step in each other's footprints a good deal. Besides, we're to follow whichever leads to Lady Lilla. She may not be with the biggest pack.'

'Could any of these be hers?'

They looked again, squinting at every ruck and ripple in the snow.

Kai shook his head. 'It's bloody impossible.'

Erlan pointed to the trail leading back into the woods. 'Follow that one a little way – might be you'll see more. I'll check this one,' he said, striding out onto the lake.

'I doubt it's this lot,' called Kai. 'This way heads back to the lowlands. My guess is they dwell in the mountains.'

'Look anyway.'

A short while later, Kai appeared back at the lake edge.

'Anything?' he shouted. Erlan was a hundred paces out on the lake, peering at the marks in the snow.

'Nothing.'

They met at the split, and together followed the trail heading north along the eastern shoreline. After fifty paces or so, Kai snapped.

'This is hopeless! We just have to pick one.'

'Wait. Let's think. Why are they doing this?'

'How the Hel should I know? To piss us off?'

Erlan chuckled. 'Well, are they trying to throw us off or aren't they?'

'Why would they be so obvious this far, and only now stop us following?'

'To buy some time, maybe. Or else Sviggar's plan worked better than he knew: they wanted to lure his whole host, and somehow they found out we're just two, so they want to drop us.'

'Or split us up.'

Erlan stood, toeing the broken clumps of snow. Why had he never learned the skills of a tracker? The footprints seemed to taunt him – they knew the answer, but they were keeping their secret. Anger started boiling in him.

'Hel's spawn!' he spat. 'We're not turning back. Not now. We'd be a laughing stock.'

'So let's just pick one.'

Erlan rounded on Kai. 'Aye, but which fucking one? We pick the wrong way and we'll follow a fool's trail for days, if not weeks. We could be out here all damn winter!'

'Well, I know which I'd pick. That middle one. Straight on, the way we were going. Straight up into the hills.'

Erlan shook his head. 'Too obvious. If I had to pick I'd say the way back into the woods. My guess is they want to deceive us by cutting in a different direction. I'd wager this horse that path swings north if we keep on it.'

'Well, that's not your horse for a start,' observed Kai. 'No, you credit them with too much reason, master. That girl said they could hardly speak more than grunts. We're not trying to outsmart some old riddler here.'

'They outriddled Torkel's lot, easy enough. And everyone else. Look, I pick that path, so that's the path we take. I don't like it any better than you, but that's my decision.'

Kai shook his head and shrugged.

'Sulk all you like, that's the way we go.'

They were soon mounted and, with scant enthusiasm between them, set off along the left-hand track.

They were about to head back under trees when a bird swooped low and fast in front of them, causing Erlan to check his reins.

The bay stopped, and the company came to a halt. The bird, meanwhile, had settled on the branch of a small spruce that stood nearby, and began to call. Its voice was anything but sweet – something between a chirp and a caw.

Erlan had never seen a bird exactly like it. It reminded him of the wood jays he'd known in the land of his fathers. But this was an altogether drabber creature, its feathers shades of brown or grey, apart from the shoulder of its wings and the underside of its tail feathers, where there were a couple of splashes the colour of rust.

The bird strained its beak wide open, repeating its squeaky call. Erlan listened a while, then kicked on his horse. But no sooner had it moved off than the bird took off, flapping round and round his head.

'Funny little thing,' he said, but carried on. The bird alighted on another branch ahead and redoubled its call.

Erlan stopped again to watch it.

'What's the hold-up?' asked Kai.

'Just this bird. Noisy little brute.'

As he spoke, the bird took off and settled on another tree nearer the lakeshore, then began squawking away again. When Erlan turned to walk on, the bird flew back to him. He looked again and the bird flitted towards the lake and stopped in another tree.

'What's it doing?'

'It's a bird. They hop around. They make a racket,' shrugged Kai, still in a sulk.

'Maybe,' murmured Erlan, curious now. 'But this one's different. Watch.'

He pushed the bay on again into the wood, and sure enough, the bird flew ahead of him, then stopped in a tree at the level of their heads, and squeaked for all it was worth. When they stopped, it flew back towards the lake.

'You see what it's doing?' Erlan smiled.

'No.'

'He wants us to follow.'

'What? That's ridiculous.'

'Is it? Let's see.'

He pulled the reins around and prodded the bay back towards the lake. The bird went wild, flapping all over the place.

He followed and it flew off again in the same direction, first to a branch, then back with the riders, then ahead again, as if dragging along these men and beasts by force of its tiny will.

They were soon back at the fork.

'Let's see what it does now,' said Erlan.

The bird had flown eagerly ahead, around the eastern edge of the lake. It alighted and looked back, and seeing the riders had halted, quick as a whip, it was back, fluttering round their heads, badgering them onwards.

'It can't really be trying to show us the way,' said Kai.

'There's only one way to find out.'

They pushed their horses into a slow trot after it. The bird went wild with excitement, squawking and squeaking and flapping.

'The spirits of the forest, eh?' called Erlan, with a chuckle.

'What did you say?'

'The spirits of the forest. Might be they're helping us.'

For a moment, Kai came over all serious.

'What is it?'

'A thought, is all.'

'Well?'

'It's mad.'

'Yours usually are. Go on – tell me.'

'The bird. What you just said. . . makes me think of the old *seidman*.'

'Grimnar? What of him?'

'All his masks. You remember 'em?'

'Sure.'

'He said he was a shape-shifter. You reckon he told it true?'

Erlan shrugged. 'Suppose if anyone could, it'd have to be him.'

'You didn't notice a songbird's mask on his wall?' An uncertain smile was creeping over the boy's face.

'Wait – you think that bird might be him? You are mad!'

'What, as mad as you? Here we are in the middle of nowhere chasing a bloody bird.'

Erlan scratched at his neck, thoughtfully. 'All right, let's ask him.'

'What?'

'What was the last thing the old hermit said? "Listen to the forest," was it? "Listen and watch."' He gave a shrug. 'So then – let's ask the bird.'

They'd reached the end of the lake, and the clouds were spreading thick and dark overhead. The trail was there in the snow, and the bird had found a perch where the tracks disappeared into the trees again. The two riders came to a halt in front of him.

For a while, they sat silent.

'Go on then, master. Ask away.'

Erlan shot him a warning look, and then cleared his throat.

'Well, it doesn't need to be a bloody speech.'

'Just keep your mouth shut, you! Right then. . . erm. . . Spirit of the forest. . . or little bird. We know not which. . . Oh, what the Hel – this is stupid!'

'Go on,' urged Kai.

Erlan rolled his eyes. 'Little bird. Tell us. . . erm. . . if you can – are you Grimnar, the night-watcher?'

There they sat, waiting for any kind of signal from the bird.

The little creature continued to watch them, its bright eyes blinking. It no longer squawked, but now and then a short chirp escaped its beak as it hopped about.

'This is fucking ridiculous,' said Erlan suddenly. 'Let's get on.'

Kai roared with laughter. 'Oh, a fine tale this'll make if we make it back home!' he crowed, nearly choking. 'A tale to top 'em all!'

'Just try to keep up,' scowled Erlan, cantering off along the trail. 'We've wasted enough time as it is.'

'Of course, my master! Onward to glory!' cried Kai, kicking on his mount after him.

And as he followed Erlan under the trees, the first flakes of snow began to fall.

All that afternoon, the sky darkened and the snow fell thicker, until their hands and feet throbbed with the cold. And all the while the trail grew ever fainter.

When they saw the snow would continue, they made markers for the scouts following behind: broken branches or cuts in the bark showing the way they'd come.

'I hope they're better trackers than we are,' said Erlan.

'That wouldn't be hard,' observed Kai.

The woodland opened out into empty plains of windswept drifts, where only the hardiest bushes and stunted trees stood, leaning bleak and bare against the northern winds. A weird kind of a sunfall filtered across the horizon like a bloodstain, and then receded into darkness.

The bird was now leading them far more than the footsteps vanishing under the snow, until at last they reached the shelter of the trees again. They made camp with hardly a word, little doubting it would be a miserable night.

Later that night Erlan watched the eyes of his friend close in sleep. The bird was nestled in the crook of Kai's chest, lured there by a few morsels of bread. Erlan wondered where Lilla was that night. Maybe somewhere in this white world, wretched and cold. He gazed out from under their shelter at the flurries of snow settling on the ground. Soon all hope for her – like the tracks they had followed – would vanish for ever.

Far away, a wolf called.

He pulled his covers close, and let his eyes fall shut.

A few hours later, he started awake.

He looked over at Kai, eyes still blurred with sleep, and saw the boy was sitting bolt upright and looking like he was awaiting an answer.

'Did you say something?'

'I said, today is the day,' replied Kai. 'I know it.'

Erlan sniffed. 'Oh, aye – here's hoping. Anything's better than another night like that.'

'No – you don't understand. I saw Grimnar.'

At the *seidman's* name, Erlan sat up. 'You did? Where?'

'In a dream.'

'Oh,' sighed Erlan, settling back onto his sheepskin with a yawn. 'A dream, huh?'

'I saw him. He was grinning with that black mouth of his. Like he had a joke on us. . . or something. Least, that's how I remember it. And he said, "Today. The end of your road. Today."'

Erlan grunted, turning his gaze to the forest. The snow had ceased in the night. The air was still as a grave and a soft mist clung about the trees. Everything was bowed with fresh powder. 'It's the end of the road, all right. Unless we really believe this bird can help us find the way.' He nodded at the jay, perched on a nearby branch and looking a sight less cheerful than the day before. 'You see anything else in this dream?'

'The whole world was white. And he stood before a massive wall. It was huge – bigger than anything I ever saw. Seemed there was no way round it.'

'Did he point to it or anything?'

'No, it was just there.'

Erlan considered this a while. 'Reminds me of stories I once heard. You must know them – of the different worlds. The edge of Midgard, the world of men. Isn't there supposed to be a huge wall that separates our world from the land of the giants? Or else the land of the gods?'

'The giants, I think.'

'Then maybe we've come to the end of the world.'

'Bloody small world, if that's true.'

'No doubt. Anyhow, we have little choice.'

'Then let's get started,' said Kai, climbing to his feet with weary determination.

The horses were soon ready. Meanwhile, the bird flitted from tree to tree impatiently. At last, Erlan pulled himself onto the bay's back.

He looked at Kai with a shrug and then said to the bird, 'Lead on.'

At once, the jay set off through the forest, alighting, returning, chivvying along the riders. With the fresh snow, the going was much heavier, and often they had to jump down and lead the horses through the deeper drifts.

But their little guide kept them working all morning.

419

Soon they heard the sound of running water, and came to a river of jagged rocks slick with ice, swirling eddies and lingering mist. They followed the western bank of this into the afternoon, while the land to the west climbed higher and higher into the mist.

At a certain bend, the bird fluttered around them and made a show of flying off to the west, away from the river. By now, the companions had surrendered themselves wholeheartedly to following wherever their little friend led them, so they turned west obediently.

The path led upwards through an old, old forest of dead trees. The ground grew steeper, the snow deeper, the horses struggling on.

At last the trees thinned, and they emerged onto a slope that dropped away to the south. Ahead were two spruce trees, grown tall and thin, standing like silent sentinels, guarding their path. Beyond them, a tangle of frosted branches in a crystal scrubland of bushes and stunted trees, and still further ahead, something. . . Some vast shadow looming indistinct, yet immense. As they drew closer, the mist began to thin, and suddenly the travellers halted.

In front of them rose a massive wall of rock.

'I've seen this place,' whispered Kai.

'The dream?'

Kai nodded slowly.

'The end of the road.'

'Or the end of the world.'

'Could be the same thing for us,' said Erlan, gazing up.

It stood high as fifty men. His eye followed the line of its summit as far as it could, but the wall disappeared in each direction into fog. Its sheer face was dusted white, but much of the cliff was so steep that vast black rocks jagged out from the enshrouding whiteness, like the features of some giant of the earth. At its base, the snow had drifted deep.

The bird was perched patiently on a nearby bush covered in hoarfrost.

'Onwards. To the end.' Erlan led on through the snow, past the ice-bound shrubs. As they approached the cliff, he saw there was something else, at once weird, yet very beautiful.

The icefall shone brightly, glistening even in the dreary light, its smooth curves and jagged points cascading down over one another from the towering summit, down and down to the ground where they stood. They gazed, fascinated at the ice, which fell in a torrent of mad shapes.

Kai was first to notice the bird had settled.

'Look!' he said, pointing to a gap on one side where the falling ice had separated from the rock. There was space enough for a man to enter there. A void that seemed to beckon.

The jay sat on a splinter of rock beside the fissure, squawking hard enough to burst a lung.

'Take a look,' said Erlan.

Kai leaped down from his mare and struggled the last few strides through the snow to the hole. Cautiously he put his head inside, and then immediately recoiled.

'*Urgh!* It stinks like rotten meat.'

Erlan jumped down and joined him. They peered into the gloom, hands covering their mouths.

'It seems to go down,' said Erlan.

'We'll need torches. Unless you fancy groping your way to Lady Lilla.' Kai couldn't resist a smile.

But Erlan didn't smile. Instead he put a hand on Kai's shoulder. 'Listen to me. This is where our path together must end. At least, for a time.'

'What the Hel are you talking about?'

'I'm sorry, Kai. But I must go on alone.'

'You can't mean that!'

'I know you won't like it – but you can't come any further. If this leads to their stronghold, in some foul hole down there, someone has to stay alive to guide Sviggar and his men to it. Without us, he'll never find this place.'

Kai looked suddenly very young. 'But. . . but you'll need my help. . .'

'Your time will come, my brother. But you must stay here. What use is it to come this far, if we both of us disappear into an abyss down there and no one ever hears another thing? Maybe Lilla is dead. But I must try to find her. And if we don't come back, then Sviggar wants a red day – for his daughter and for his murdered people. Aye – and his murdered son.'

'But—' Kai began to protest, but seeing Erlan's mind was made up, he screwed up his face and swore. 'You are the master,' he said, in a brittle voice. 'What would you have me do?'

'Wait here. If I'm not back by sundown tomorrow, ride for Sviggar's host. They'll only be two, maybe three days back by then. You know the way – down to the river, then south and follow our tracks to the lake where the trail split. When you find them, bring them here. And meantime, pray to the Thunder God that it doesn't snow.'

'Snow or not – I'll find the way. What about you?'

'Me?' Erlan frowned. 'You can pray for me, too.'

A short while later, they had fashioned a torch: a pine branch, stripped, split into four, and stuffed with birch bark and a few strips from a blanket for kindling.

'Should last a while,' said Kai.

'A while – aye. Then what?'

For once, the boy had no answer.

Erlan took out his flint, his firesteel and a char-cloth from his pouch. He crouched down and the sparks flew in little arcs from the circle of metal until the cloth started to smoulder. He held it to the torch and soon the kindling began to smoke and crackle.

'Here,' he said, pressing the tools into Kai's hand as the flames caught.

Last of all, Erlan drew his sword. The ice-cracks echoed with the rasp of steel. Wrathling shone like a comet as he held it aloft.

He was ready.

'The gods go with you, brother.' Kai's face was pale.

'And with you.'

His dark eyes held the boy's for but a moment.

Then he plunged into the darkness.

CHAPTER THIRTY-ONE

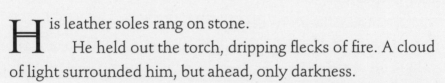

H is leather soles rang on stone.

He held out the torch, dripping flecks of fire. A cloud of light surrounded him, but ahead, only darkness.

He heard trickles of water and glanced back at the icefall, now a gloomy curtain against the dull afternoon.

Above him, the torch illumined the dank ceiling, which cut sharply down towards a black maw of shadow, no taller than a man. He crept inside, ducking away from the flame-heat. A foul smell seeped into his mouth and nostrils, foetid as a drunkard's breath.

The tunnel was short – hardly ten faltering steps before the torchlight expanded into a much larger cavern that loomed away into shadow. He stopped, astonished. The space could hold a feast-hall. His flame sent shadows dancing among strange shapes in the rock – cascades smooth as honey bubbling up from the floor, or dripping long and stringy as waxen candles from the ceiling.

Either side were smaller caves and hollows, framed by

pillars that gaped like Fenrir's fangs. Erlan shuffled forward and the shadows shuffled with him like living things, eyeing him silently as he went deeper.

He walked on, eyes darting at the eerie beauty around him. Ahead, light glimmered on something smooth. He saw the cavern shrank towards a pool. In its surface, rocky reflections shone sharp as knives. Seeing no way around, he put a cautious foot in the water and found it was only a few inches deep.

He felt soft grit underfoot. Treading warily, he had only gone a couple of steps when his weak ankle folded. Desperate, he threw out his sword to catch his balance. Wrathling's point jammed into the sediment. He slewed wildly, yelped, spilling sparks onto his face. Pain seared up his leg. But somehow he stayed on his feet. He grimaced at the precious flame. Still alight.

Sviggar may regret sending a man who can't even fucking walk.

Taking greater care, he shuffled to the other side, and looked up at the stark wall of rock. There was no way forward.

He was about to curse the bird for leading them to a dead end, curse himself for the folly of following a bird, when he noticed a shadow darker than the rest. He moved towards it. The torchlight slipped ahead, seeping into an enormous crack. Drawing closer, he saw it fell away into a darkness so dense it seemed it would smother his flame. And then, just below him, he saw something that made his skin prickle.

Steps.

Steps cut into the rock. Steps that went down and down into the abysmal shadow.

So their little friend had led them to something. *Or someone.* But just then, it was hard to feel grateful.

His hobbling gait echoed downwards, every other step a stab to his ankle. The torch burned dimmer now, gnawing its way towards his hand. He could see the hot resin at the foot of the flame only inches from his fist. There was no time to waste.

The path became ever stranger as he went down and down. Hundreds of steps, maybe thousands, wending a dismal path through many chambers, some small and cramped, others vast and fathomless; along passages smooth and dry; over rubble slick with slime. But always, he told himself, on a path that some*one* had made.

He came to another staircase. Sensing he was running out of time, he hurried down it, in spite of his limp, jumping the last two steps. But as he landed, the torch jolted, spilling scorching resin onto his hand.

He jerked in pain and before he could stop himself, he'd let go of the torch. He snatched wildly for it, but only knocked it further, and watched in horror as the stub skidded away into a patch of dank grit. The flame hissed. And he was plunged into utter darkness.

Blinking in panic, he tried to make out the rocks around him. Or *anything*. But open or shut, his eyes saw nothing. He was blind. Fear rose bilious in his throat, his heart thumping like a hammer. He wanted to get out – away – anywhere but this place – back to the light.

But breath by gasping breath, he fought down his horror until the fear that locked his limbs began to loosen.

He couldn't see, he reasoned, but he still had his other senses.

And Wrathling.

He shuffled forward, gripping the hilt tighter than ever. Already it seemed he'd been buried under the earth for hours. Or was it days? Or years?

He groped onwards, feeling his way, with only his breathing, the ring of his footsteps and the touch of steel for company. For hours he waded through the sea of shadow, blind to everything about him.

He had only the next step.

And then, out of the darkness came a noise.

It sounded like. . . a scamper of feet.

A rat? Something bigger? He stopped to listen and now thought he heard a shallow panting. *No rat sounds like that.* Then more. Not panting exactly, but breathing, and from more than one direction. Behind him. To the side. Both sides.

Then he smelled it – acrid and stale. But unmistakable.

Human sweat.

He braced himself, listening for the slightest signal of an attack, fear snaking round his heart, his feet edging doggedly onward.

Suddenly, up ahead, he perceived something in the abyss. A light? It was. . . *something*. A sort of blue smudge. *Hardly a smudge.* A dim prick of light, like the ghost of some fallen star.

Fixing his gaze, he headed towards it. It seemed to grow. He closed his eyes, then opened them. Yes, there *was* something there.

Suddenly something glinted to his right. It was very close, and in the suffocating shadow, it shone brilliant as a blazing sun. He recognized it at once.

An eye.

Without warning, the darkness erupted into a babble of

shrieks – shrill and wild – and beyond these, he heard an awful scraping. They were coming for him now. He readied Wrathling for the onslaught.

A rush of air as something shot past him. He slashed blindly, but his sword rang on stone. A low snicker. He spun, wild with fear, lifting his sword.

There was another rush of air, and another. Then hissed whispers, low and quick, were dancing round him like demon wasps. Still he crept on towards the blue light, sweeping Wrathling in front of him, its shadow just visible.

Suddenly there was a terrible scream and a body slammed into him. He stood firm and then, glimpsing another shadow, slashed down Wrathling. The blade tore flesh and something wet spattered his face. Then the blackness was filled with scampering feet, pitter-patter, coming for him.

Erlan put both hands to his sword and lay about him. He felt the steel bite, ripped it free to a shriek like a tormented gull. His leg kicked against something on the ground, and still he pushed for the light.

But the shadows were all about him now. Hands grappling at his legs, pulling at his cloak, snaking around his body. He tried to cut his way free from the tangle of limbs, but they were too many, too close, miring him in flesh. He wrested free his dagger, stabbing and slashing. Voices hissed and wailed when the edge found flesh. Foul breath blew in his face. Then stronger hands had his shoulders, then his arms, pinning them back. Clammy fingers crept around his throat and began to squeeze. He slewed drunkenly under the weight of pressing bodies, but then his ankle buckled and he collapsed under the writhing shadows.

The fingers were squeezing and squeezing till each breath burned like fire. He felt consciousness slipping away; waited, helpless, for the last sound he would ever hear in this world – the snapping of his neck.

But the sound didn't come.

Instead he was drowning. Drowning in the shadows. Drowning in the darkness. And he knew he would never find his way back to the light.

Kai wriggled about under his fur. His backside was numb with the cold.

The pale firelight was growing more vivid as the cloak of night settled. He listened to the steady breathing of the horses and the crackling song of the fire. The faint smell of spruce dusted the air.

He was tired, yet restless. Bored, yet worried. He tried to distract himself by singing a song he knew, but his heart wasn't in it. The words trailed away after only a few lines.

How long should I wait?

That was the question that was bothering him.

Erlan had said a night and a day, but what if there was still no sign of him by nightfall tomorrow? He couldn't just leave. Couldn't watch his friend disappear into that hole, never to come out, and do nothing. . .

I couldn't do that.

He'd never felt so useless. He flicked the twig he'd been slowly shredding into the fire. What did it matter if he stayed alive to lead the king here if Erlan was already dead? He might have helped him – might have been the difference between life and death. Instead he was out here with the frost biting at his arse.

The gods'll do for you, Erlan, and your damned stubbornness!

'What do you reckon, you old bastard?' It was the name he'd taken to calling the little grey bird. 'You were happy enough to lead him into that hole, but you ain't much for leading him out again.'

The jay hadn't flown away yet and Kai had given up trying to fathom why. Still, it was the closest thing to company he had right now and he wasn't about to chase it off. Instead, it had flitted around while he set up camp, before settling on a low-hanging branch a few feet from him, feathers puffed, neck tucked against the cold. Seemed a long while since it had made a noise.

He tore a morsel of bread off his loaf and was about to toss it to the bird when he stopped. A note, forlorn and unwavering, rose into the winter sky. The sound was unmistakable. *A wolf's howl.*

Kai cocked his ear and waited. Sure enough, a few moments later, there it was again. He felt the blood turn cold under his skin. It was one thing to hear a wolf-cry when you were tucked up in bed under a roof of turf and timber. Another to be out in this wilderness. Alone. The wolf howled again. He listened carefully and found he could breathe easier when he judged it must be far away. Anyway, the spruce trees would conceal the fire, and the scent of the horses surely couldn't travel that far. No, there was nothing to fear.

Still, best to keep an ear open.

He threw the bread over to the bird and watched it swoop, pluck the crumb from the snow, and return to its perch.

'Aye – you're welcome, you old bastard.'

Despite his worries, he smiled. And soon the weariness of their journey was smothering his thoughts like a wet cloak. So he lay back and yawned, dragging his sheepskin up to his chin.

He gazed into the fire till the flames started to blur. But just as his lids were closing, he caught a dart of movement.

He glanced over. The bird was agitated, fluttering from branch to branch. All at once it began squawking madly.

Kai was about to curse the old bastard for disturbing his sleep, but just then he saw, perched on a higher branch across the clearing, a pair of eyes gleaming like beads of jet. They were set in the head of a large bird, silhouetted against the darkness.

A raven.

He watched it drop its head, its hackle feathers rising like claws. Its beak rolled side to side, all the while those black-bead eyes following the jay from tree to tree.

Kai caught another movement in the tail of his eye. He turned and there was a second raven, big as the first, stretching its wings. Like the first, its hard eyes followed the jay, its beak snapping menacingly.

Kai was about to sit up when, as if at a signal, the ravens flew at the jay. But the smaller bird had seen the danger and launched itself upwards. The ravens went after it, black wings beating the air.

The jay dodged and darted, trying to shake the ravens through the tangle of branches, but they were always there, scattering powder everywhere. With growing rage, Kai watched the dark wings turning and diving above him.

And then, high overhead, a shadow smashed into the little grey smudge and the jay fell. It was dropping straight onto the fire, only suddenly its wings caught and it pulled out onto a branch. But one of the ravens was already landing with it, dashing snow to the ground. The raven's head jabbed, again and again. Then the other raven had joined the first, pecking and stabbing at the jay without mercy.

Moments later, something fell. Hardly more than another lump of snow, thudding to join the rest that had fallen to the ground.

Kai went to the hole in the powder and reached inside. His hand came away with a small soft body. The bird looked pathetic in his palm, its drab plumage now gaudy with spots of blood.

His hand closed around it, feeling the last of its body heat seep into his fingers, and he looked up.

Four dark eyes, brimming malice, glared down from their perch. They only watched him a moment, then their wings flapped and they were gone into the night.

His eyes dropped to his hand.

It was only a dead bird lying there. Hardly a tragedy. But for no reason he could have explained, he felt a cold rage fill his heart.

That was when the wolf howled again.

Closer now. Much closer.

CHAPTER THIRTY-TWO

The stranger opened his eyes.

His cheek was pressed against something cold and hard. His neck throbbed. The same coldness touched the back of his hands. He turned them and felt rock. Pushed and his face was free.

He was lying on the floor of a cavern.

There was light, though but a little. The first thing he saw was a brazier of black iron. In its grate danced a blue flame, its light rippling over the walls with an icy glow. But the fire seemed to give out little heat.

A putrid damp filled his nostrils.

He looked about. The cavern was not big. It extended perhaps a dozen paces in each direction, curving into darkness at one end, while at the other there was a shadowy doorway cut out of the rock. He sat up and saw another shape – a stack of slated stones. At its top, the stack spread into one wide piece that formed a kind of tabletop, except that it stood as high as a man's head.

What is this place?

Something moved in the tail of his eye, something in the shadows beyond the doorway.

One of the creatures?

He rose unsteadily to his feet, and took a first cautious step towards the doorway.

'Don't concern yourself about him,' a voice sounded behind him. He turned in an instant, but could see no one. 'He's there to see we are not disturbed.' The voice came in strange deep pulses through the stagnant air, filling the chamber like the echo of a far-off horn, though each word had a sibilant edge.

The gloom stirred, and the shadows fell away to reveal a figure that caught the breath in his throat.

His blood turned to ice. Instinctively, he shrank from the figure advancing towards him step by measured step. But what he saw would be carved for ever into his nightmares like some runic curse.

The figure had the shape and aspect of a man, yet his head towered ten foot from the ground, crowned with pale hair that shone blue in the flamelight. But the figure didn't look old as a man looks old. *Ancient.* . . Beyond old – like the sky is old, or the ocean. His features were of perfect symmetry: a long straight nose, a smooth brow, a sharp hairless jaw with eyes that burned like coals. Yet it was the mouth that gripped him. The lips were white as snow – almost beautiful, if not for the sneer they wore, of such malevolent scorn that his heart trembled.

The huge figure drawing closer, Erlan saw his skin was all cracked, and so pale it looked chill to the touch. His hands were massive yet elegant, with knuckles the size of shield studs. He wore a long dark cloak, obscuring the immensity of his limbs, yet he moved with a kind of grace that belied his colossal appearance.

Erlan backed away.

'You needn't run,' the giant began. 'Where would you run to in any case? Back to your world?' He uttered a deep throbbing laugh. 'You could search for a hundred years and you would never find your way out.'

Erlan checked his steps, but said nothing.

'That world is lost to you.' The huge head turned to the cold fire in the grate, his long cloak dragging heavily across the cavern floor. '*This* is your world now. The world of your end. . . Or a new beginning.'

The eyes turned and bore into Erlan's like hot iron.

'What is this place?' whispered Erlan, his voice at last overcoming his fear.

'This is Niflagard. The realm of the Nefelung. I am their king.'

'I've never. . . heard those names.'

'What of that? Men are ignorant, and the Nefelung have been known by other names. Some have called them the earth-dwellers, some the *mørklunger*, others only darklings.' The giant smiled.

'What are these. . . Nefelung?'

'It is well that you should know. Many, as it goes, are just like you. They eat, they drink, they rut, they *spawn*, just as does the race of men. Others. . .' He looked away. 'Well, I shall come to that.'

'How have men come to live in this. . . this deathly darkness?'

'All men may learn to live in darkness if they have a good

435

enough reason. And when they know no better. . .' His eyes narrowed cruelly. 'Then, this *is* life.'

'No reason would be enough to dwell in this hole.'

'You think not? How about the end of the world? Faced with certain destruction, men will seize any scrap of a chance to keep their pathetic lives from extinction. Especially when guided by another.'

'You?'

Slowly, he stroked his chin with a long white finger. 'Yes. A man will do many things if he believes he is guided by his god. But how pitifully weak is the mind of man, how pitifully easy to seed his thoughts with ideas that are not his own. Fear, a lie, a way out – with these I have built my kingdom.'

'A way out of what?'

'You call it the Ragnarok. You watch and watch for it. But when the final destruction comes it will not be as you imagine, nor as those first ones I drew here thought of it. Yet once a few were convinced, they persuaded many others to follow. After all, men are like cattle – they prefer others to do their thinking for them.'

Erlan thought of Vithar's tale in the assembly. Of those trying to escape the death of the sun.

But the sun had not died.

'If you are no god, are you of the *jötnar*?' Every child knew of the giants who dwelt in a land far, far to the north – every one of them bane to the gods of Asgard.

'Ha! Your people are fond of growing tales out of the shadow of the truth. Your *jötnar* are not as you believe. But those tales took seed in the old times – when the great ones still dwelt among you. Now they are scarce in number and seldom known.'

'The great ones? Who are they?'

'They were the offspring of my kind and the most desirable of the daughters of men.' He stroked his chin in that disturbing way, as though remembering. 'When we took them.'

'I don't understand. If you are no giant, what are you?'

'I am one of the Watchers.' He sighed, a sound like the heaving of the ocean. 'We are older even than the world of men.' A troubled look passed over him. 'Once we dwelt in a realm. . . Well – far from here. We were the mightiest. The brightest. Yet the lord there was nothing but a small-minded tyrant. A glutton for his own glory, yet denying the glory of those who secured his power. There was a war. But he couldn't be torn from his throne. So the first of our kind came here, to the world of men.'

'You were defeated.'

'Do the defeated wield power as we do?' he boomed, eyes flaring with anger. But he mastered himself quickly. 'There were others who left, not from war, but from desire. I was such a one.'

'Desire? For what?'

Before he answered, a strange luminescence rippled over him, from the crown of his head down over his face and body. Within it, Erlan glimpsed a beauty so startling he never could have dreamed it: golden hair, eyes bright as suns, silken skin and blinding white robes. But it was gone so fast he thought he must have imagined it.

'We only wanted the daughters of the men of this world. We left to take them for ourselves. And afterwards, that other realm was sealed to us. The tyrant would rather we thirst and beg like dogs but never receive – our only crime to desire something he meant to be desirable.' His voice dripped bitterness. 'He punished us. Once we climbed on the air like eagles. Now we crawl in the earth like worms. And he gave us a sign to remember him by.'

He made the faintest of gestures behind. Erlan saw the Watcher's cloak sweep across the floor with a hiss, but could make nothing of it.

'Who is this tyrant then?'

'He is nothing in this world now. I will speak no more of him.'

Erlan didn't press him. 'Well, if you're king of the Nefelung, do you have a name?'

'I have many. In your tongue, I am Asasterk. In other lands, Azazel. Some have called me the Destroyer. In these caverns and the northern forests, I am known as the Witch King.'

'The Witch King,' Erlan repeated. The gods knew he had reasons enough for hating witchery. Now he had another. 'The Nefelung are your thralls then.'

The Witch King snorted. 'Not all of them. Some are my sirelings. I told you, our offspring were the mighty ones of old. Here, they are overlords, ruling over my thralls. After the great darkness above, the people found their way into these caves, lured by my call. They had their leaders, naturally, and with them wives and children and every last ounce of gold they could carry. But after I first appeared to them, they soon worshipped me as a god. For down here, they were lost.' He laughed his loathsome throbbing laugh. 'So very lost!'

Erlan listened on, enthralled by his strange words, and heard how he had taken for himself all their choicest women and many more besides. They bore him sons who grew into mighty men, with sharp minds and hard limbs. To them, he gave his dark knowledge – of sorcery, of bewitching men's minds, of power over nature to change their form. And these overlords had a choice. They could stay in the darkness, masters over the Nefelung thralls; or they could go up, to live among the race of men. There, to foster every kind of wickedness – chaos and deceit; murder and treachery; bloodshed and greed.

'This they do well,' the Witch King said. 'Through them, I've been leading the men of the north to blood and destruction since long ago. Soon it will be visited on all the world.' His lips curled in a pale smile.

Blood and destruction, thought Erlan, scathingly. *That* is *the world of men.* 'Are there people like this now? These overlords – even in Sviggar's realm?'

'Certainly.'

Erlan tried to imagine who at Sviggar's court might be more than what they seemed, and found he thought of a good many people. Too many. 'And their seed too?'

A look of irritation passed over the Witch King's cracked face. 'Their seed. . . No. They have sired many offspring, but they are. . . tainted. They do not grow as do the children of men.' The Witch King seemed reluctant as he described how the overlords' progeny were deformed of limb and face, and so wantonly cruel that they were difficult to control. These were named the Vandrung. 'They feed on only one thing. Human flesh.' Erlan listened in disgust as the Witch King told how the Nefelung thralls were bred to keep these Vandrung sated.

'They grow in number, but it is no matter. When they are too many I send them up to find what flesh they will elsewhere.

Sometimes they return, but often they turn on each other or disperse. I let them go. . . Unless they can be of use.'

'The Nefelung are but slaves and fodder then.'

'They are worth nothing more. We put them to working in the mines or forging weapons or fashioning the gold they love so much. And many of their newborn are taken, of course. But here they are free from the bonds that choke your world. Free to glut themselves as they wish – with fighting or the pleasures of the flesh. I do not stop them. A man is happiest when he is most like a beast. He needs only the lash from time to time to remind him to fear.'

'But I still don't understand. Why stay so long hidden from the world above – and then suddenly make yourselves known? The killings – why now?'

'Why now?' the Witch King snarled. 'Why not? Real fear comes from meaninglessness. If there is no reason, then you are afraid. If I wanted Sviggar's Seat – or the seat of any king – I would take it. But it pleases me to sow seeds of warfare and jealousy and murder and betrayal in the hearts of men and women. Best of all are the blood sacrifices to your gods.' His voice rang off the walls of the chamber. 'Your gods don't listen. . . We *are* the gods and we do just as we will! When you slit the throats of your women and children to gain some blessing, we laugh. Their blood changes *nothing*.'

Erlan had no response. The Witch King's words were too much. In this netherworld, he was sure of nothing any more. He groped for something. Something solid. Something real. . . Lilla.

'Sviggar's daughter? What do you want with her?'

The Witch King gave an indifferent shrug. 'She'll be mine for a time. When I saw the Vandrung had her, I wanted her.

The time has come to sire a new brood of sons and daughters. They will be the masters in the new age of destruction that is coming. For a time, she will birth my seed and when I am done with her, I shall give her to the Nefelung. They will use her as they wish.'

A wolfish smile spread across the Witch King's face, goading Erlan. But he shut his revulsion away.

'You've struggled all this way. Would you like to see her?'

Erlan nodded.

The Witch King called out over Erlan's head in a strange tongue. There was movement in the darkness, the pad of footsteps receding.

'You come to save her,' the Witch King sneered.

Erlan said nothing.

'A pathetic hope. Perhaps you knew this. But we shall soon see whether you're as foolish as the lord who sent you.'

'Fool or not, Sviggar is a lord of war. Your Vandrung have brought his sword to this place.'

'Lord of war? Baah! The Watchers gave men war! Taught them its ways. If this little lord wants to follow the crumbs I've thrown him, he will be swallowed by the darkness.'

'If he falls in battle, you give him what he seeks. A glorious death. A seat at the All-Father's bench.'

'The All-Father's bench!' The Witch King boomed with laughter. 'Hah! You still don't understand, do you? There are no gods! No, his carcass will rot and his soul will remain in the shadows with us. And his heroes with him.'

The sound of footsteps approached.

Three figures appeared at the chamber entrance. Erlan hardly glanced at the two guards, with their lesioned skin, lank

441

white hair and dead-looking eyes, each gripping an arm of the girl between them.

She was barely recognizable: her dark blonde hair tangled into a great knot; her eyes, pools of shadow fixed on the cold floor; her cheeks hollow and grey. Her mouth was curled into a weird half-grin and her dress torn to rags. With each limp, her naked and bloody toes, just visible under her tattered hem, buckled with pain.

At last, she looked up and saw Erlan. Shock, pain, despair all chased across her features, fusing into a hard look of defiance. Or perhaps it was anger. She kept her eyes on him.

'You must not think too ill of me, child,' began the Witch King. 'My servants are brutes. If your journey was discomforting, soon, I promise, I will make you feel most. . . *comfortable*.' Erlan saw again the strange luminescence ripple down his body.

Lilla said nothing. Her only sound, ragged breathing. The Witch King paced around her, his long cloak sliding across the floor with a sibilant hiss. But she wouldn't look at him.

'We shall see how that delectable maiden belly takes my seed.' A repulsive leer smeared his pallid lips. 'You are fortunate, my dear. Many women have learned there is no pleasure more exquisite than a Watcher feasting upon her body. To give up your flesh to a mere man – what an intolerable waste! Women of such beauty are worthy only of *our* desire. You will soon need my flesh more than the air you breathe.'

Lilla looked at the Witch King for the first time. 'I don't care what you do,' she whispered. 'You'll always be as foul to me as the stinking air in this demon hole.'

The Watcher's laugh throbbed around the chamber and he stretched out a long white finger. She tried to move her head out of his reach, but the guards held her tight. The tip of his finger traced her jaw. 'Good!' he hissed, red eyes flashing. 'It is better you are unwilling. That is how it should be – one beauty consuming another.' The sinister pulse of light passed over him again, and he took away his hand.

'I shall not keep you waiting long, my dear.' He gave a command and the thralls turned and began dragging Lilla to the doorway, but with the last of her strength, she screamed, writhing against their grip. And suddenly she was screaming Erlan's name again and again until the cavern echoed.

Erlan turned to throw himself at the guards, but he'd hardly moved when fingers like iron seized his neck and threw him at the wall. His head cracked against rock, the wind thumped from his chest, and he slumped to the floor.

Lilla's screams shrank into the darkness.

Erlan looked up through a fog of pain. The Watcher didn't move, only glared with scornful eyes at Erlan's crumpled body.

'Get up.'

Painfully, Erlan pulled himself upright. 'Why tell me all this?' he gasped. 'Why not just kill me?'

The pale lips curled. 'If death were all I intended for you, I wouldn't waste words.' He smoothed his chin. 'I offer you a choice. My call has drawn you here, inexorable as a tide.' He made a mocking flourish in the air with his hand. 'You are a hero of the realm.'

'I'm no hero,' muttered Erlan.

'Oh, they don't see it yet. But they will – your destiny draws you on. No man will be able to deny it.' He fixed Erlan with his burning eyes. 'Why do you think we are called the Watchers? I saw you far off. And I have voices and eyes among the spirits. I

443

heard of you from your friend in the west who thinks he sees. How easy it was to persuade him to lead you here! Though now, alas, he's gone to see his beloved dead face to face.'

'Grimnar is dead?'

The Witch King answered with an enigmatic smile.

Erlan shook his head, struggling to make sense of the Witch King's words. 'What destiny do you speak of?'

'Perhaps nothing. A shadow that might never be. It depends on you. You must choose. Naturally, you may choose death. But there is another path for you.' The Witch King went to the huge slate table. Its surface lay just above Erlan's eye level.

'See how free you are? You are not bound. Your own sword lies here.' He reached out and plucked something from the slate surface. 'You may have it back in a moment if you choose well.' Wrathling flashed blue in the firelight, its steel blade seeming small in the Witch King's hand. Even so, he tried a couple of cuts at the foetid air. 'A fine weapon. Though quite useless here.' He tossed it back on the table with a clatter.

'So you are free to choose. Die now for Sviggar. Or serve me as your lord.'

Was this what this strange king was bringing him to?

The Witch King snorted impatiently. 'Come! You waste my time.'

'I swore an oath to serve him. Swore on the sword of my fathers.'

'Bah! You creatures are so pathetic, with your notions of honour. Or your hunger to win a great name. It makes you all so *predictable*. . . You think power comes from oaths of loyalty and wealth and laws and a strong arm? No. Real power comes from chaos. Real strength throws off the shackles of honour or

444

the petty rules that pander to a man's conscience. We are strong because we are bound by nothing. No law, no duty.'

The Witch King's eyes glowed like embers.

'Your heads are filled with stories of your gods and goddesses. Thor – a petulant fool! Odin – the so-called Father of All who wants all his best children slaughtered! The All-Wise who knows nothing!'

He leaned forward, his voice dropping to a whisper. 'Honour makes you a slave, chained by an illusion. Freedom is to satisfy whatever your head or heart or body desires. Freedom is to have *now*. Freedom is to answer to no one and nothing. Not to honour, not to kings, not to gods, not even to the tyrant.' His face seemed to cloud with a terrible darkness. 'Freedom is to *be* a god among men. That is what I offer you.'

Erlan couldn't tear his eyes away from the pale lips. With each word, a mist was creeping into his mind, smothering his reason. But as the stream of words continued, he began to hear sense in the Witch King's meaning.

'*I know you*. You cannot hide behind an oath, Chosen Son. Swear fealty to me, and I will make you lord over every other man. Free to answer to no one but yourself.'

The words flowed like a sweet melody he had always known and yet had never heard.

'*I know you*. Join me and you can sate all that lies within you. A woman's flesh? Poor fool, you've eaten one dish and now it's gone, you insist on starving! Feast on a mountain of flesh and be free from the curse of love. You'll soon forget the scraps that once satisfied you.'

Erlan shook his head, trying to loosen the cords tightening around his mind. But the Witch King spoke on.

'*I know you.* Anger fills your heart. It festers like an unbound wound. Then let the whole world feel your wrath. I will slake your anger. And the world will pay for the wounds you bear.'

Erlan fumbled for an answer under the deluge of words. 'There is anger within me.' He nodded. 'Anger from which I would be free.'

'*I know you,*' the Witch King said a fourth time. 'You want to control your own destiny. I shall cut the weave of the Norns' needles – you alone shall be master of your fate. The world will tremble and bend to your will – the world that laughs while you suffer will be made to bleed.'

'Men will hate me,' Erlan murmured as if from some reverie.

'Let them hate,' soothed the Witch King, 'so long as they fear. Look only to me. I will give you everything. I will be your lord.'

'Yes,' whispered Erlan. 'Yes.'

The Witch King's voice hardened. 'Now. . . kneel.'

Erlan hesitated. The Witch King laid a heavy hand on his shoulder.

'Kneel,' he repeated, pressing down. The stranger sank. 'And bind yourself to me for ever.'

He inched lower and lower until his knee touched the floor, the exact moment a scream stabbed the dead air, sharp as a needle. It rose from far away in that strange world of shadows, flaring like a spark thrown from the furnace of his mind. Its light died in an instant, but it was enough. He had seen.

Seen the anger burning in his heart, seen the thirst for vengeance that prowled there, eager to devour something. *Anything.* . . Yet why should the whole world feel its bite? A lie had struck this wound. A hand of death had robbed him of love. Was love a curse? Was the world only counting the days until its descent into fire – when the Ragnarok would consume everything? Or was that all just another lie? He was certain of only one thing: he, Erlan, was the enemy of lies. And this king in the darkness, this Azazel – he was the lord of lies. He was his enemy.

Vengeance could drink of his blood.

He sank still lower until his fingers found the rock and he felt his feet grip. Behind the veil of his ragged hair, he inhaled deep.

Then he leaped.

CHAPTER THIRTY-THREE

K ai spun around, the howl nearer now.

A lone voice arching into the night.

But that's impossible. A wolf couldn't have covered that distance in so little time.

He dropped the dead jay, his hand moving to his knife. The long weary cry fell silent.

He listened.

Then he heard a soft patter of snow in the darkness a way off down the slope.

Or had he imagined it?

He listened again. Something *was* moving through the bushes. He heard the tinkle of falling crystals, the scuffle of fur in the snow.

His knife suddenly felt pathetically small. He cursed himself for a lazy fool. His sword was against the tree by the horses where he'd left it. Only twenty strides away, but just then it seemed an abyss. Without a second thought, he lurched towards it, the scamper of paws now all too audible in the shadows.

448

The horses whinnied, tossing their heads, while he heaved through the snow. Then, out of the night, a growl, sickeningly guttural, sounded beyond them. The bay reared up, hauling at its tether; the bridle snapped and he took off into the night. The others weren't far behind.

Kai swore. Without horses in a wilderness like this, they wouldn't last long. Though right now, admittedly, he had a more pressing problem.

The growl skirted around him, rattling in the wolf's gullet. He had to get to his sword, or an axe, or any bloody thing that had an edge. The weapons were only five paces off now. He was going to make it.

But suddenly, there it was.

The cruellest sight he ever saw. Yellow eyes, malignant with hunger and hate, staring at him out of the darkness. He froze as the wolf padded into the light of the fire. His weapons were not two strides away, behind the tree. But it was too late now.

All too late.

The wolf advanced, a rasp like gravel in its throat, lips curled to reveal vicious white fangs. Kai backed away, trying to squeeze courage from his knife haft; but there was precious little to be found.

Pace by baleful pace, the beast became visible – a hulking body of black fur, shoulders jolting menacingly up and down. Those yellow eyes, intent as the gaze of Hel herself.

Kai shuffled his feet, bracing himself for the moment that was coming. His mind flicked back to those hall-yard scraps he never could seem to avoid when he was a kid. Every time he'd take a beating from the bullies who were bigger and stronger. Every time he made damn sure he got back on his feet afterwards. But this was a fight from which there would be no getting up if he didn't win it.

He gulped, his back a slick of sweat, watching those pitiless eyes, hardly able to move for fear. A bead of sweat broke from his hair and he felt it trickle slowly down his spine. The exact moment it reached the small of his back, the wolf leaped.

A blood-chilling bark filled the air. Kai saw the jaws flying at him, then the wolf's paws hit him in the chest, the force knocking him flat in a cloud of snow.

He cried out – but there was no one to hear. No one to come to his aid. The wolf's great paws pinned his shoulders and he was too scrawny, his arms too weak to roll from under it. Pain was burning the side of his head, his ears filling with slobbers and snarls as the wolf thrust his snout, hungry to sink its teeth into his throat.

But the gods had a sense of humour. In the tumble his jerkin had ridden up around his neck. Instead of flesh, the wolf had a mouth full of sheepskin and hair. Fangs raked his head; he felt blood pouring into his ear. And then at last, his wits jolted into action. Gripping his wretched blade tight, he slammed it, hard as he could, into the wolf's body.

He felt the knife go in, but he knew that wasn't enough. Suddenly he was filled with rage, determined to wrestle his life out of the jaws of this slobbering mutt. His fist smashed into the wolf's ribs, again and again, till his wrist ran slick with blood.

The wolf yowled, its snarls rising almost to a scream. For an instant, the wolf opened its muzzle, only to lunge for his face. Instinctively, Kai raised his arm, blood and foul-tasting spittle splattering his lips. The wolf was convulsing, but even as its life

450

gushed away, its jaws locked down on his arm. Kai wailed as its fangs crunched bone.

But just when he thought he'd seen the last of his hand, the grip slackened, and the hulking body began to shudder; the snarls became shrill, fading almost to a whimper. And then, with a final wheeze of rancid breath, the beast gave over and sank dead as stone onto his chest.

He lay, listening to the silence, until, realizing he could hardly breathe, a fierce panic seized him. He heaved and wriggled and squirmed until he'd prised himself out from under the weight of stinking clotted hair.

He staggered to his feet, then immediately doubled over, retching his relief into the snow. When the nausea had passed, he wiped his mouth, catching his breath.

The wolf lay still. A heap of fur and blood and twisted sinew. A dark stain seeped from its wound into the snow. He took a step closer. Then he saw something strange. Something about its limbs. He moved to see better in the firelight. The flames lit up one side of the wolf. Its fur seemed to have thinned almost to nothing in patches and its hindquarters were contorted into something that looked. . . Well, if he didn't know better, he would say looked like the legs of a man.

Curious, he came closer – still wary it might not be completely dead. But the creature was still. He put his foot to its flank and gave it a shove. The body rolled over.

Kai nearly vomited a second time. There, where the wolf's front paw had been, was a human hand.

He didn't need a second glance. He went to the fire, seized a burning branch and put it to the body. The flames began to lick and catch at the fur. He took another, and another, and soon the clearing was filled with the crackle of hungry flames and the smell of burned hair and flesh.

Kai retrieved his cloak and swung it across his shoulders. Then he settled down to watch the thing burn. It was long before he turned away and looked up at the trees and the ice, and the shadows of the night.

He hugged his injured arm close and shuddered.

All around him, he felt the brooding whisper of evil.

Erlan smashed against the Witch King's chest.

It was hard as iron, but the Nefelung lord wasn't ready. He reeled back and Erlan slipped from his grasp.

Next instant, he ran at the wall, burying the pain in his ankle. Three strides up the wall and he leaped again, his momentum slinging himself up onto the giant table.

He skidded across it, mail screeching against stone. And there was Wrathling. He threw a hand, snatched the hilt, missed, his heart lurching. The ring-sword spun, he grasped again, and then he had it. He yelled in triumph going over the edge and clattering to the ground below.

'So,' hissed the Witch King, unhurried, 'you choose death.'

Erlan crouched, ready, watching his foe tear off his cloak and fling it away. The demon drew himself up and reached behind his head. With a rasp that filled the chamber, he unsheathed a huge double-handed blade, far longer than any man could wield. But in that moment, Erlan saw the strangest sight of all he'd seen in that pit of darkness.

Behind the Nefelung lord was a long slithering tail. It was thick as a man's fist, black and gleaming, with a point of coarse hair. Erlan stared in horror and would have stared longer, but for the looming figure of the Witch King.

His eyes flared with hate, his sinews tightened, and the massive blade arced out of the shadows. Erlan lifted Wrathling to meet it. The blades rang loud as a battle-knell. Erlan dodged, his arm shaking with the blow, but his mind still sharp.

Black curses were pouring from the Witch King's cruel lips. Erlan retreated, looking for space, but the demon came on. Erlan dipped left, ankle jarring, cutting at his opponent's flank. But Wrathling was batted away as though no more than a twig.

Azazel sneered. 'Pitiful! I *gave* men weapons. Taught them how to craft steel. You think you can touch me? Come – again!'

Erlan went the other way, stretching under Azazel's blade to slash at his knees. The huge blade clubbed Wrathling aside. But Erlan was ready. He spun, scything at the Witch King's waist. His left felt horribly open, but he thrust in, muscles stretched to burning, and felt a thrill as Wrathling bit flesh.

The Witch King screamed in rage. Erlan felt the whistle of the blade, but threw himself past the demon, to the sound of ringing steel smashing unblooded onto the ground.

Azazel put his hand to his side and Erlan saw a stain spreading through his robes.

'You bleed,' he said through heaving breaths, feeling his mouth twist into a grimace.

'I may bleed. But you will die.'

The pale lord set again, feet slapping the rock, arms even faster. Erlan parried the first two, tried to dodge the third, but felt the bite of steel. Pain shrieked from his arm all over his left side. Then another lunge caught his leg. He staggered backwards, barely parrying the killing blow aimed at his neck.

And then he felt a huge kick. Falling, he gave a desperate slash and his edge caught the demon's calf.

Next moment, he smashed against the wall. Wrathling flew from his hand with a clatter. Erlan pushed himself off the ground, dizzy, his movements slow as sludge. He flopped forward on hands and knees and began crawling to the hilt gleaming dully ahead of him.

But he was tired now, so tired. . . he could see the massive white feet astride his sword.

'Kneel, slave.' Erlan stopped and sat back, exhausted, on his heels, head limp as a dead ear of corn. His left arm was burning. 'You had your chance to submit. Now I'll take your head.'

Erlan couldn't move. He knelt, beaten, awaiting death. *Was this the death he had been seeking, through all those long leagues in the snow?* The Witch King swung away for the killing stroke. The blade swept round, singing through the foetid air with the demon's massive frame behind it.

No!

Erlan flung himself backwards, flattening against his calves. The point sped past, close as a lover's breath, and on.

The force of his momentum spun the demon away. The hideous tail whipped round after his sword. Erlan stretched out a hand, caught the thing's coarse end, and with his other snatched for Wrathling's hilt.

The tail was thick and Erlan hauled so hard his heart might burst. The Watcher jerked backwards, spinning the other way out of control.

Erlan sprang into the Witch King's embrace. He felt no pain. Had no doubts. He thrust Wrathling with all his strength upwards, into the demon's body, burying it to the hilt into the broad chest. Erlan felt a slick of blood gush over his hand.

Azazel's pale face was high above him, his red coal eyes flaring with death. His arm curled over Erlan's back, almost tenderly, and then his long fingers released the sword. It fell with a crash of steel.

The Witch King sank back, pulling Erlan down like a lover to his bed. At first he sagged with him, the massive arms too heavy, but then his knees hit the rock, he pushed hard and he was free.

Azazel lay on his side, a foot of Wrathling protruding wetly out of his back. He said nothing. Only his eyelids moved, blinking weakly.

Erlan put his boot to the chest and heaved his sword free. The ancient Watcher fell onto his back, dark blood bubbling from the gaping wound.

Erlan limped around to his head. The eyes glimmered like dying embers. His life was leaving now, would soon be gone for ever. Suddenly, strangely, the cracked skin began to fuse, becoming smooth as glass, and a spectral beauty settled on the Witch King's face that seemed outside of time. A word passed over those pale lips – one Erlan didn't recognize. A name, perhaps? He didn't know. And then the eyes went black for ever.

Erlan lifted his sword high and brought it down. Blood splattered in wet gobbets over his face and the massive head rolled away.

Without thinking, he licked away the blood. It was cool on his face, but past his lips, it burned like a living flame. He tried to spit as searing heat raced along his tongue, down his gullet, boring its way into him. He collapsed, choking, tearing at his throat, hacking desperately to vomit up the demon's blood.

But it was in him now.

He crushed his eyes against the pain as the heat blazed like a straw fire through every sinew. Then it passed out through his hands and his feet, and was gone.

Slowly he opened his eyes and looked at his hands. They were trembling. And yet, they felt strong. Hardened somehow, as if metal flowed where only blood had flowed before. He stood, and though he felt his wounds, he didn't feel weak.

He looked around.

The light from the brazier seemed warmer. Many of the shadows were somehow not so dim. He looked down at the remains of the Watcher, the head rolled away, upturned like a broken statue. Even the pale skin seemed warmer. Almost golden.

What have I killed?

Suddenly curious, he stooped and laid hold of the Watcher's huge shoulder and hip. He heaved and strained until at last the body rolled onto its side and over, flopping face down.

Erlan gazed long at the Watcher's weird appendage. The tail was nearly seven feet long and scaled like a serpent. As he looked, a terrible dread seemed to come over him. He felt his courage wilt, as though the thing itself could suck the mettle from the bravest heart. He hated it. Yet he knew he must take it.

He raised Wrathling a second time, and down it came, biting through bone and gristle.

He picked it up.

The tail was hard and something about the light rippling off its surface made his flesh crawl. But it also felt powerful. He noticed the pain in his left arm had lessened.

He flicked the thing out in front of him. And, almost without thinking, he raised his fist and whipped the tail down with a resounding crack.

He grimaced at his trophy, feeling some dark power welling within. He had slain this demon king. And now he would escape this black Hel in the bowels of the earth. He would reach the light.

And Lilla was coming with him.

CHAPTER THIRTY-FOUR

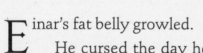

Einar's fat belly growled.

He cursed the day he'd bought that damned cask of rotten wheat-beer off Vanta the brewer. Cursed his damned insatiable thirst. Cursed his damned wife for telling him he'd make himself sick. And double-cursed that, as damned usual, she'd been right.

His guts gave an ominous gurgle. Einar squeezed his spear-shaft and clenched his arse-cheeks tight as he could. It was one thing to soil your breeches; another to soil them in front of a queen.

He could feel greasy sweat beading on his face and wished he could loosen his belt another notch. In fact, he wished he were still in bed. That's where he damn well deserved to be. But as a council guard, he had to stand stiff as a board, unobserved but ever-ready to attend to Lord Sigurd's merest fart. Anything but the slightest movement would draw attention to himself, and the prince would bawl him out. He wasn't about to give that axe-faced son of a bitch the satisfaction.

He'd been listening to Sigurd's moaning all morning: that his father was an old fool; that he, Sigurd, was the match of the best of Sviggar's hird-lords; that it was shaming for a son and heir to be left behind when every other Sveär lord rode with their king; that his father meant to provoke him, or make a fool of him; that thanks to his father's incompetence, they were probably all dead already and some dark horde was swarming towards the Uppland halls this very instant.

Queen Saldas meanwhile had been prowling around the chamber like a she-wolf, tickling a teasing finger under the chin of a small grey kitten – though the gods only knew where she'd found the thing. From time to time, she smiled and whispered something inaudible into the creature's ear.

Watching her was certainly a duty he was happy to endure, and right now he didn't have to look very far. She'd come to a halt immediately in front of him and was peering at him – as if he were some carving worth an idle moment's scrutiny. Meanwhile, his stomach was leaping about like a sack of toads. It was most disconcerting. He wished she would look away before some disaster happened from which neither he nor his breeches ever recovered.

Instead, she drew a little closer, her emerald gaze steady.

'Do you know, my little terror of mice?' she said, loud enough to stop Sigurd's complaining. 'I believe that if I were one day to be a great king, I should be more careful what I said within hearing of your young and tender ears.'

Sigurd looked over, while Saldas began tickling the kitten's ears. The little brute closed its eyes and waggled its head in ecstasy. Einar tried to remain expressionless. Not easy for a man so beset from both ends, as it were.

'What are you talking about?' asked Sigurd.

The queen released Einar from her gaze and turned back to Sigurd. But she went on speaking to the damned cat. 'All this railing, my princess of pouncers – it is hardly becoming, is it? An heir to a kingdom should remember he cannot hope to rule without the good opinion of the men under him – do you not think?'

'Well?' scowled the prince, sunken eyes glowering even darker than usual.

'Oh, little puss, see how angry he gets at a little counsel. It is funny to see him strutting around like a stallion, no? Yet, for all he actually does, the mares need be no more frightened of him than a gelded colt. Is it not amusing?' She gave the kitten another tickle under its chin and it swished its tail in delight. Then she held the little beast's nose to her ear. 'What's that? You think he should talk a little less, and act a little more?'

'Leave off that cursed animal, won't you?'

'It seems a pity to,' replied Saldas, resuming her rich, low voice. 'It strikes me she has the right of it.'

'What the Hel am I supposed to do? My father would have me remain here like a chained puppy, expected to do nothing but wait on his word.'

'You are here to rule in his place. You have power to act in any way you see fit.'

'What can I do but sit and wait?'

'There are different ways of waiting,' said Saldas, a trace of mystery in her voice.

'Meaning?'

'You're angry because you feel impotent. You have no way of influencing the outcome of your father's... adventure. Is that it?'

Sigurd dropped his eyes sullenly. 'In part, I suppose.'

Saldas snorted, a curve of derision in her delicate mouth. 'You men reason in such straight, unimaginative lines. You think if you were with him you might draw your big sword, stick it in a few other men – or creatures or whatever they are – and you'd win a great victory for your father and folk. You'd be a great hero. Men would raise their cups to you. "All hail, Lord Sigurd – the mighty man of the hour!"' She shook her head, her mouth twitching with mockery. 'How terrifyingly dull.'

'Well I can do no better from these halls.'

'Can you not? There are far more powerful ways to influence the sway of things, but they require a will unlike the blunt bludgeoning of you men. Do you not know that a god may be beguiled the same as any man?' She moved a little closer towards him. From his post, Einar watched her lithe hips stir beneath her shimmering gown. It was, he conceded, as beguiling a sight as a man could hope for to soothe his present woes.

Nor was the sight lost on Sigurd. Though he turned askance, a little discomforted, Einar noticed his eyes move up and down the queen's figure. 'A god?' was all he said.

'*The* god. The High One. The Slain-God. The Father of Victory. The Father of All.'

'Odin.'

'Indeed. Listen, my good son. I do not speak lightly. Oh, I know men utter plaintive prayers to him in the shadow of their battle-dread. Perhaps he listens. But I doubt he does otherwise than just as he chooses. But we . . .' She smiled, seeming pleased at her own craft. '*We* may be far more persuasive.'

'How?' demanded Sigurd, bluntly.

She was about to answer, but then checked herself and gave a light, low chuckle into the kitten's fur. Then she was back at her old trick of listening to the damned cat. Einar reflected that if this woman were his wife, the leather of his belt would get a good airing, and no mistake. 'What's that, my little glutton of milk? You are shy? Your little schemes are for his ears alone. Oh, very well. It shall be as you wish.' She smiled at Sigurd. 'Shall it not, my lord?'

He considered her, his jaw twitching. Then, he gave a sharp snort and turned to the guards. 'Leave us.' Einar didn't need telling twice. He had urgent business of his own to attend to. But turning to go, he heard Sigurd say, 'You too.' He glanced back to see the solitary figure of Vargalf, Sigurd's oathman, delay a moment before uncoiling himself from a bench in the corner and following him out of the council chamber.

A short while later, in a quiet spot round the back of the nearest dungheap, Einar was enjoying a moment of profound relief. He'd awoken that morning feeling like the bottom had fallen out of his world. Now he'd let what felt like a world fall out of his bottom, he was feeling a Hel of a lot better.

He was just pulling up his breeches when he heard a giggle behind him. He turned to see a pug-nosed brat making a poor job of suppressing his sniggers. Einar snatched up a stone and threw it at him. The boy dodged it easily.

'Go on, you little tyke!'

The boy stood there, brazen as you like, hands on his hips. 'Vargalf's looking for you.'

'Is he now?' Einar wondered what that pale-faced bastard wanted now. 'Where is he?'

'Back of the Great Hall,' said the boy, and scampered off.

'Toe-rag,' muttered Einar.

He found Vargalf easy enough. As usual the two of them didn't bandy words. Vargalf gave him the names of three women to find and bring to the Smith's Hall – one of the smaller halls among the jumble of buildings spread out east of the Great Hall.

'What do you want 'em for?'

'Just get them,' was the curt reply. Before Einar could object, Vargalf had turned and stalked off.

'If that son of a bitch took his head out of Sigurd's arse for half a minute, I'd gladly knock it off for him,' muttered Einar. He was the king of the late comeback. But he couldn't be too glum. He was feeling a new man, after all. 'Right then, lassies. Where are you at?'

It didn't take him long to find the first of them: Klarika, the wife of Finn the archer. She was easy to spot in the crowd with her bouncing auburn hair and a pair of fine shoulders. He found her haggling over a pile of homespun among the wool-halls. The girl she was dealing with looked mighty glad for the interruption. Beautiful as Klarika was, she had a mouth like a shitpit and was stubborn as a mule, neither of which made her an enviable woman to barter with.

'What – right now?' she groaned, when he said she was wanted. 'I'm right in the fucking middle of something.'

'Afraid so, sweet-cheeks.'

'Least tell me what it's about.'

'Would if I knew myself. Just have to come get you. That's all I know.'

'Fuck,' she said, and dumped the homespun on the trestle. She wagged an elegant finger in the girl's face. 'I'll be back. And don't you go giving this to anyone else till I do. You hear me?' The girl nodded slavishly.

It was a pleasant stroll around the halls, Klarika chattering away, while they found the other women. Finn's wife had a garrulous tongue and knew a hoard of filthy stories from her days as a concubine under Sviggar's roof. But she admitted she preferred married life with Finn. 'There's no doubt the man knows what he's doing.' She thought about it, adding, 'Least, now I showed him what's fucking what, he does!' She laughed a great beaming laugh, and Einar couldn't help wishing he'd learned to shoot an arrow straighter if the likes of her were the rewards.

They collected one of the kitchen wenches – a pretty little thing with an elven face and short cropped hair. Lastly, a raven-haired wanton who – as everyone knew – spent her days in the dairy and her nights in the bed of any visiting nobleman who happened to stray near the Uppland halls. She had a string of little bastards to show for it.

They were merry company, gossiping away, and as they arrived at the Smith's Hall a little later, Einar was reflecting that some days a council guard's duty had its pay-offs. But between them, they couldn't fathom the reason they'd all been summoned.

The Smith's Hall was a dismal hovel compared with Sviggar's Great Hall, but its blazing hearth was welcome relief from the cold outside. He hustled them in, telling them to keep their voices down, better yet be quiet – though he had little hope of that. But when they saw who was waiting on the dais at the end of the hall, they soon hushed up.

Lady Saldas was dressed in a finery of blacks and forest greens, looking, by Einar's reckoning, as striking as any queen in the north ever had, and this time with not a hair of that damned fool kitten in sight. Beside her was Lord Sigurd, with his customary glower, though Einar thought he saw a trace of nervousness – or was it excitement? – in his eyes. Positioned around the hall were armed guards. In a moment, Einar's practised eye told him seven in all, including that savage son of a bitch, Aleif Red-Cheeks. And glancing behind, he saw by the doorway Vargalf, whose face, as usual, was unreadable.

Nevertheless, Einar's eye was drawn inexorably to the young women assembled at the foot of the dais. It only took a scan of their faces to see this was no ordinary collection. True, Einar had been enjoying the company of the three bonny girls he'd brought with him, but he'd thought nothing of it in particular. But this group of. . . he counted them. . . with his three, there were nine. . . Well, seeing them together, it was as though someone had handpicked the nine brightest beauties in all Uppsala.

Excepting the queen herself, of course.

'Thank you, gentle sisters, for coming here at such short notice,' Queen Saldas began. 'I realize you are all busy. But I also know you are aware these are times of great peril and uncertainty. There is not one of us here who is not bearing a heavy burden of care for at least one of her menfolk, and some of you more. Like me, you must feel so very powerless to help them in their task. We women are weaker in limb, naturally. And for that reason perhaps, we have to be stronger in heart.' She indulged them with a smile.

Einar scanned the women's faces. A few of them, he knew, would already have an irreverent joke or two on their lips in response to the queen's words. But for the moment, they all looked up at her, attentive enough.

'But,' continued the queen, 'a woman's role may be further reaching and more profound than any man could understand. Yet we should not judge them too harshly for that.' She turned and smiled at Sigurd, but his face was stone. One or two of the women tittered. 'It is because we have the greater power that often from us is required the greater sacrifice. Gentle sisters, you have an important role in these perilous times. You have the power to seal your menfolk's victory. A victory for all our people. You are honoured indeed.'

Just then, Einar found himself distracted by shadows moving on the wall. He glanced behind and saw Vargalf discreetly closing the doors. He watched him ease the second door shut, then gently drop the bar in place. His head turned and Einar noticed his mouth curl into a smile. Something about it gave him a bad feeling in his stomach. A very, *very* bad feeling.

This time, it had nothing to do with Vanta's rotten ale.

CHAPTER THIRTY-FIVE

E rlan peered into the shadows.

Before, he could see nothing but pitch darkness. Now everything seemed to have a dull luminescence. A line of braziers with pallid flames trailed into the gloom.

His heart was galloping, the blood in his veins surging like a storm-swell. He didn't understand what was happening. Yet his senses were sharper than ever.

He stopped and listened. Behind, silence. Ahead, a jumble of far-off murmurings, the pulse of drums, the ring of iron. Lilla must be that way.

He limped towards the noises. The light was growing. At least he could see more and more. The rock walls rose about him. Looking higher, he saw nooks and hollows; a few at first, then more and more until the cavern was riddled like a honeycomb.

He came to a crack between two shoulders of rock, followed the path round a bend and halted in surprise. Steps descended into another chasm, this one filled with light and noise. A fresh stench filled his nostrils. He recoiled, disgusted.

Suddenly a figure appeared with lank white hair and a hunched body. *A Nefelung thrall?* Whatever it was looked up, eyes straining, hesitated a moment, then turned to run.

Erlan leaped after it. The Nefelung had no time to escape. Erlan was on him at once, kicking away his legs. The Nefelung fell headlong down the steps, crashed against a rock, then turned, cowering away from him.

For the first time, he saw its face clearly. Like a man's with all the colour leached out of it. Eyes darting, with ugly sores, blackened teeth, a nose crossed with scars. But there was no time to inspect any closer.

He put his point to the Nefelung's chest.

'Where is she?' The response only a craven babbling.

'The woman?' But the creature shrank back, a jabbering heap. Erlan shook the tail in his face.

'The woman!' he cried.

When the Nefelung saw the tail, he screamed, his face twisting in sudden terror, desperate to get away.

Struck by the tail's effect, Erlan hesitated, long enough for the Nefelung to throw himself over the edge into the darkness. There was a scraping noise as he slid into the abyss.

Erlan beheld the tail, wondering what power he had in his hands.

But there was no time to waste. He limped on, able to see quite well now, the pain of his wounds somehow dulled. At the bottom, he turned a bend and emerged from a cut.

A vast cavern opened about him.

The path continued straight. Either side of it, the ground fell away into deep pits. He saw steps down into some, and further on other paths and stairways leading into higher caverns and cracks.

The noise grew all the time – a din of murmurs and shrieks and scrapings – drums – metal hammering. He stumbled along the pathway, a new dread seeping into his heart.

And looking down into the pits, he saw things of such horror as he never would forget.

In one, a writhing sea of bodies, and from them moans and gasps rose up in an unbroken sibilant breath. He heard women's wails and saw many muscular backs at work, something twisted and brutish in their shape.

In another, drums echoed off the walls around a horde of Nefelung leaping about in a mad frenzy, pale arms whirring overhead.

He shuffled on, gagging at the stench rising from the next pit. There, he saw figures stirring a boiling stew of blood and body parts in huge vats, and seated around them other figures clutching bowls, slopping the grisly contents into their mouths. But these ones were somehow different. Bigger, with rounded shoulders and crooked hands. He remembered the Watcher's words – of the Vandrung, the deformed sirelings of the overlords. He shook his head, bewildered at this demon's nest of horrors.

He moved to the next pit. There, the smell was worse, of open viscera and human filth. There too, the cries of infants – newborn sons and daughters of this strange race, lying wretched and helpless. One by one they were put before a Nefelung with a knife, whose long hair was soaked red. He slashed the tiny throats and pushed them, still wriggling, to another who slit them loin to chin and began disembowelling them. Erlan tore his eyes away, his stomach heaving with disgust.

Forcing himself on, he saw more pits on the other side: one in which bodies were strung up, stretched out and skinned.

In another, rows of the Nefelung lay prostrate before a great stone likeness of a serpent; in yet another sounded the ring of metal, with molten iron glowing in smiths' faces, and stacks of all kinds of weapons and outlandish objects, embellished with spikes and hooks. But none of them looked up and saw him. All seemed too intent on their grisly business.

This is all some mad nightmare. It must be. He felt his mind slipping under, drowning in revulsion.

Suddenly a scream pierced the deathly air. Far closer this time, and from above.

Lilla.

Just ahead, a staircase led up to the right, disappearing into a dark hole. He took it and began climbing. At the top the steps narrowed into a passageway. He stopped to listen, eyes probing the gloom. Ahead, he heard a whimper, just for a second, then a low snicker.

He steadied his sword and edged around a curve in the passage until at last he saw two figures standing guard at the entrance to another chamber. They were peering inside, each clutching a long-spear.

He took a deep breath and ran at them.

He was onto the nearest guard at once. The spear-point lowered to meet him, but it was too late. Wrathling scythed into the guard's side so deep Erlan felt its edge scrape his spine. The guard gave an agonized shriek. Erlan ripped his blade clear and turned to face the other.

The Nefelung braced himself. Erlan flicked out the tail. The effect was that same craven look. The guard flung down his spear and turned to flee, but Erlan was quicker. He whipped the tail. With a crack, it coiled round the pale neck. He jerked his hand, pulling the creature onto its back. In an eye-blink, Wrathling was wet with fresh blood and the Nefelung sighing his last breath.

Erlan stepped over the body and went inside.

A brazier, flaming yellow, stood on one side. Along the wall were apertures in the rock through which came the sounds of the hideous scenes below, and in the middle was an enormous bed.

On it lay a naked woman. Her limbs were bound to the corners, her skin slick with oil. In another place, another time, he might have reckoned the contours of her body beautiful. But here, there was something horrible about the way she was splayed out. She lay quite still.

'Lilla!'

The princess stirred, moaned, tried to lift her head. 'You!' Her voice was a broken whisper.

He moved around the corners of the bed, cutting her free.

'Don't look at me,' she said, writhing in shame. 'Look away!'

'Believe it or not, Princess, I didn't come here to gawp at you!' he snarled, severing the last bond.

Once her hands were released, she covered herself.

'Put this on.' He unfastened his cloak and threw it over her.

She sat up, hugging the cloak to her chest. 'Is he dead?'

'Yes.' Her eyes looked half-dead with fear and fatigue.

'Are you sure?'

'I cut off his head. Good enough for you?'

Her face curdled. 'What's that?' She nodded at the dark coil he had tossed on the bed.

'He had a tail. I took it from him.'

'Why would you do that?' she asked, shrinking away from it.

471

'Listen to me – we need to get away from here – now!'

But she didn't hear him. Her shoulders started shaking and her mouth curled into laughter. Cackling laughter that grew and grew, until her whole body shook and her eyes became wild. And then she was sobbing, gasping for air, tears staining her face.

Erlan took her in his arms, squeezing her, feeling her shudder against him. Suddenly she pushed him away.

'Why are *you* here?'

'Your father sent me.'

'You? Of all his men, he sent you? I don't understand. You're a . . . a . . .'

'A fucking cripple, I know! You're hardly in a position to be picky, Princess.'

She stared at him, wide-eyed, and then seemed to regain some control. 'I'm sorry. I should thank you. . . For coming for me.'

'Coming is one thing. Getting out is another. Can you walk?'

'I think so. But how can we get away? There are so many of them!'

'We're going to try.' Though just then the surface seemed about as far off as the moon, and no easier to reach. 'At least I'll get you away from this place. But to find our way back to the surface—'

'I know the way!'

'You do? How?'

'Even in darkness, a quick mind can see.'

'What? You think you could find the way back through that warren of caverns? You must be out of your mind!'

'That's the whole point. It was to stop myself going out of

my mind that I forced myself to memorize it.' She tapped her head, eyes ablaze. 'When they brought me here, I carved every step, every turn, every echo right here. It was my only hope.'

It was a thin shred to go on, but what choice did they have?

She must have seen the doubt in his face. 'Trust me. I've retraced those steps a hundred times in my head already.'

'All right. Do you have any things?'

'My dress,' she gestured at a heap of rags in the corner. 'What's left of it.'

'It'll do for now. Up there, we've plenty of things for you.'

'We? You mean my father is up there with his men?'

'Not your father. My servant, Kai.'

'What! That little clown of yours?'

'That's right,' he scowled, running out of patience. 'The clown and the cripple got this far, so I suggest you shift your noble backside if we want to get any further.'

At last she did as he bid her, climbed off the bed and snatched up the remains of her dress. 'Do you mind?' she said, over a naked shoulder.

'Just get on with it.' He turned away, glowering, and gathered up his sword and the tail from the bed. When he looked back, she had the dress over her head.

'Ready?'

She nodded. 'What about light? We'll go much faster with a torch.'

'Don't worry about that. I can see in the shadows.'

'You can?' It was her turn to be surprised. 'How?'

'I don't know.' He thought about telling her what happened. But how could he explain what he didn't understand himself? 'I just can. You'll have to trust me.'

For the first time, she smiled at him. A forlorn smile, true, but it showed there was still some fight left in her. 'Your eyes and my mind, huh?' she said.

'Let's go.'

Outside, Lilla immediately stalled, horrified at the two bodies.

'Leave them!' he shouted.

But, half-dazed, she bent down and picked a spear out of the lake of blood that had leaked across the floor.

'Come on!' Erlan urged and led her to the staircase and the cavern of gruesome pits. 'That way,' Lilla murmured. 'Past the demon's other chamber.'

They hurried along the pathway. 'They're monsters,' he heard her moan.

'Don't look!' They were passing the pit where the Nefelung were carving up their newborn. He kept his eyes fixed ahead. They were about to reach the cut that would lead them away from that hall of horrors when footsteps echoed down the stairway towards them.

Suddenly another figure appeared. In his hand was the severed head of the Watcher. Erlan stopped in surprise. The figure was like none he'd yet seen in this kingdom of nightmares.

He was taller than the slavish Nefelung, with the appearance almost of an ordinary man by features and proportion. But his extreme paleness and the sinewy strength in his limbs were unnatural, and in his eyes shone a cruelty born of pure darkness.

An overlord. A son of Azazel.

His eyes gleamed with bloodlust. He lifted a long streak of blackened steel. Erlan felt Lilla's hand on his shoulder, her breath in his ear, whispering words he didn't understand.

The overlord raised the Watcher's head and shook it, then spoke in a voice hard as granite. Whatever he said, his meaning was clear – he wanted revenge.

Erlan brandished the tail, half-expecting, half-hoping the overlord to cower from it. But he stood his ground, spittle flecking his pale lips as foul words poured forth.

'Take this,' he said, proffering the tail to Lilla.

'I'll not touch it.'

'Take it!' he snarled.

Bridling her disgust, she did as bid.

He stepped forward. The overlord came to meet him, uttering a last vengeful cry; then dropping the massive head, he took his black blade in both hands.

'You talk like your father. I took his head. Yours will fare no better.' Erlan laughed – a cracked, crazy laugh – feeling something dark welling inside him. The overlord bellowed in reply and hurled himself forward, hacking at Erlan's open flank.

He shoved his sword to meet the blow, but with no shield and little space, his position was weak.

'Back! Back!' he shouted.

He heard Lilla retreat, still speaking her prayers or spells or curses or whatever the Hel she was saying. He cut upwards, knocked away the overlord's blade, his opponent's mouth curling into a sneer, hissing something in his demon tongue, shaking his head in contempt.

But Erlan didn't wait to listen. He lunged – once, twice. The overlord fell back, slashing down on his arms, but Erlan blocked and lunged again. Still no blow landed. And suddenly he'd over-reached and saw too late the cut from his left. He felt steel hit his side, waited for the blaze of pain.

But it never came.

Both froze, stunned that Erlan was still standing. Lilla's stream of words was louder than ever. Erlan recovered first and struck at the other's arm. This time the blade bit. The overlord screamed in rage.

The cut was deep but he was far from finished. He flew at Erlan with fresh fury. A gap flashed ahead and Erlan lurched through it, switching places.

There was no way to win this fight on the narrow pathway, but now he had his back to the steps. He inched back – step by step, readying himself – planning to leap wide for a killing stroke. The overlord pressed harder. Erlan gave another two yards.

Suddenly his weak ankle jarred against something heavy. It rolled. He tripped. Saw he was going over, cried out. His back smashed against the ground, and he glimpsed the Watcher's deathly face past his feet. The overlord's eyes blazed in triumph as he leaped forward to skewer his foe.

But Erlan was still moving, gaining speed, slipping down the lip of rock and over the edge.

In horror, Erlan felt himself plunging headlong towards one of the pits. The drumming below was deafening. The last thing he saw as he went over was the overlord's victorious sneer.

He snatched at the dizzying air – for a heartbeat, nothing – then he smashed into something hard. There were shrieks all around, the stench of sweat and rancid flesh. The drumming ceased suddenly. Under him, someone was groaning. And then weird pale faces were crowding over him.

Their eyes were dead, their jaws working; sweat dripped

from their scarred faces. He hauled himself to his feet, Wrathling still welded to his hand.

The Nefelung he'd landed on was moaning, his body broken. Erlan looked up. The overlord was leaning over, shouting down into the pit. One by one, the Nefelung around him began to look up, began to heed what he was saying.

His face was a mask of urgency, but then a long blood-slicked spear erupted from his chest – just for a second – and was gone. It was so brief, Erlan thought maybe he'd imagined it. But the overlord's sneer melted, his sword fell and then he tumbled forward into the pit.

Erlan threw himself aside as the body thumped onto the miserable Nefelung, the sword following hard after it. The others went wild, leaping about like the ground was burning. He got up quickly and looked about. The overlord lay on one side, limbs wrenched like a broken doll, his chest a gaping hole.

'Erlan! Erlan! Are you down there?' Lilla's voice. *Of course, Lilla!*

He bellowed her name. Then there she was, peering into the pit. The Nefelung were closing in on him, jaws gurning. They looked like they'd tear him limb from limb.

'Lilla! The tail – throw down the tail!'

He saw her look behind her, and then a shadow was flying like a flailing serpent through the air. It splattered to the ground beside the broken bodies.

Erlan snatched it up, brandishing it in front of him. The nearest Nefelung recoiled with a whimper. He pushed forward, driving them away in confusion, but with no idea which way to go.

'Can you see a way out?' he yelled.

'I can't see!'

'Look again!'

'I'm trying!' She leaned forward, straining her eyes into the shadows. Suddenly she pointed. 'There, on the far side. There are steps back up.'

He turned to where she was pointing. The hideous faces surged around him. He cracked the tail and the Nefelung nearest to him trembled, pushing back.

The shrieks and yells faded into wails and whimpers, each Nefelung cowering from him as he moved through the throng. At last, he saw steps out of the pit.

He hurried to them and, ignoring the pain in his ankle, took them two at a time. Below, the Nefelung were herding around the foot of the steps as if, at a distance from the dreaded tail, they dared come after him.

At the top, he saw a pathway disappearing into darkness one way. The other, it skirted the pit-wall back to Lilla, waiting with the bloodied spear in her hands.

He hurried along it, hundreds of pairs of eyes on him from below. At last he reached her. He wanted to hug her from pure relief, but she'd already turned away.

'Hey!' he said, taking her elbow. 'You saved my life.'

'Not yet I haven't.' She pointed down at the crowd of Nefelung, who were halfway up the staircase and seemed to be growing bolder every moment. He glanced down and saw one of the larger Nefelung had picked up the overlord's sword, was turning it in his hand. 'Come on!' Her cheeks were ash-grey. 'Now!' she screamed.

'My eyes, your mind, right?' he said, looping the tail over his sheath.

She nodded.

'You'd better be as smart as you think you are, Princess.'

'We're about to find out.' She put her hand in his and they set off up the stairs.

CHAPTER THIRTY-SIX

K ai had waited longer than a night and a day.

Course, he'd known he would if Erlan hadn't emerged by then. But it was well on in the third day, and still no sign.

If Sviggar's scouts were worth their salt they shouldn't be far away. Though he doubted even the best huntsmen could've followed their tracks after that snowfall. Unless they'd found their markers, which he supposed was some hope.

Anyway, if Erlan was gone, what did he care if Sviggar got his revenge?

So he went on waiting. And with a bloody raw arm into the bargain, and ever the chance some other wild beasty would come and have another go at him. But after the wolf – or man, or whatever the Hel it was – and after he'd rounded up the horses. . . well, the truth of it was he was bored out of his skull.

He'd sat staring at the icefall for three days now, under grey skies and drifting mists, thinking there couldn't be a more miserable place in all the world. He'd waited, buried under furs, moving only to chuck more wood on the fire, and dreaming up snatches of songs about the shapes in the ice. And above all, he watched that dark hole, hoping for something. . . *anything* to happen.

While he waited, he got to thinking. Supposing there *was* a whole pack of murderous creatures down that hole – was Erlan likely to chop 'em all to bits on his own? He might get out – maybe with the princess if she was lucky – but there'd still be plenty of 'em left to cause a heap more trouble.

If someone blocked their way out, they'd be corked down there like flies in a bottle. That'd be the end of their trouble-making, eh? They'd have to stay down there for ever. Although he guessed the king still wanted his 'red day' or whatever he called it. He could hardly have that if he couldn't get at them. Even so, it seemed a happy solution.

So long as Erlan got out.

And looking at the icefall, he wondered – supposing it was the best thing that *should* be done, *could* it be done?

The entrance was maybe fifteen feet high, top to bottom. And you could only squeeze two men at a time through the gap at most. So it was hardly a big hole to fill.

Either side of the icefall stood two cliffs of black sandstone. In the last three days, his eyes had scaled them a hundred times. Each went straight up, more or less, but there were jags and cracks and ledges all the way to the top.

On the morning of the third day he'd noticed a crack on the right-hand cliff that was long and deep and – far as he could see – uninterrupted. The cliff looked steady enough, but he'd picked out a slab the size of a small hall that seemed hardly attached to the rest. It was a wonder it hadn't fallen already, by his reckoning.

481

The slab was mostly all of a piece; except right at the bottom, where the crack emerged, the last few feet splintered into smaller fragments. These appeared to act as a sort of foundation, holding the slab in place.

What if someone knocked that away? It was only a collection of little rocks, after all. If you knocked any of 'em away. . . Why, wouldn't the whole cliff come down?

He smiled at the thought. He'd like to see that!

Wouldn't be much of a hole after that, he chuckled. There wouldn't be much icefall left either.

He shrugged. It might work. And looking at the cliff, he set about figuring a way up to the bottom of the slab. By late afternoon, he reckoned he had a route. And so on to his next problem. It was one thing to drop an enormous rock onto the gap. Another thing entirely to get the Hel out of the way.

He'd just begun thinking this one through, when there was a noise from the crack.

His eyes darted to the darkness. He listened. This time he was certain, and then he was throwing off his furs, pulling his sword from its sheath, and heaving through the powder fast as he could. He reached the crack and leaned inside.

'Hello!' he yelled. 'Erlan!'

He pricked an ear. No answer. He listened again. Another noise.

'Erlan? Is that you?'

This time, there was a reply, muffled and smothered by echoes.

'Erlan!' he cried again. 'I'm coming!' He made to go in, then realized he had no light. 'Hel take me for a fool!' Three days to make a torch and he'd never even thought of it. He went inside, tried to grope forward, but it was no good. The back of the cavern was black as pitch.

The fire – of course!

He waded through the snow a second time, pulled a half-burned branch from the fire, then turned back. He was still a dozen yards from the icefall when he heard footsteps and two ragged figures tumbled out of the gap.

'Erlan!'

'Kai!' cried his master, gasping at the cold air. His face was black with dirt and blood; his hair matted red; the arm of his mailshirt cut, with a blood-soaked flap hanging loose; and his eyes wild. But it was certainly him.

Beside him, the princess was shielding her eyes from the blinding glare looking like some spectral handmaiden of Hel, face streaked with grime.

Kai dropped the burning stick and ran to his friend. 'You're alive!'

'Aye – for now – but we've no time to lose.' Suddenly a terrible shriek rose up out of the depths of the cavern.

'They're coming!' cried Lilla. 'They were hard behind us in the caves.'

'Where's the king?' said Erlan. 'His men – are they here?'

'No. Just me. How many are following?'

'Many,' said Erlan, grimly. As if to seal his words, another howl rose up from the darkness, and then another, nearer now. 'Quick! Fetch the shields – we'll need them.'

Only now did Kai notice the long-spear in Lilla's hand, blood crusting half its length. 'If we must die, at least it'll be breathing the clean air of this world,' she said.

'But master – we don't need to face them! There's another

483

way. I can seal them inside. All of them.' Seemed like as good a time as any to make a bold claim.

'What are you talking about?'

'This entrance – I can close it.'

'How?'

Kai threw down his sword and clapped his hands in delight – then regretted it. His left arm was still mighty tender. 'Just watch, master!' And seeing the doubt on Lilla's face, he cried, 'Fear not, my lady – I can stop them!'

Not waiting for an answer, Kai set himself at the cliff. He looked up and gave a low whistle, his hand going to the back of his belt where his hand-axe was safely tucked. 'Ain't much in this world a bit of hammering can't fix,' he muttered, then put his hands to the wall.

The rock was ice cold to the touch.

'What the Hel are you doing?' asked Erlan, caught between curiosity and impatience. 'We need you here with us – with a sword in your hand!'

'You'll see.'

His fingers were strong and well used to the cold, but as soon as he gripped the rock, he felt a twinge deep in his forearm. *All right then – this was going to be unpleasant.* He gritted his teeth and took his weight anyway and found he could keep his grip. In his head, he rehearsed the sequence of holds he'd mapped out from the comfort of his furs. And up he went.

He soon discovered some holds were better than he'd figured; others a good deal worse. But, the pain in his arm notwithstanding, he reckoned he could get there. After all, hadn't he climbed a thousand trees as a kid? He'd never come close to falling, though his mother always said one day he would.

Not me, I'm as agile as a squirr—

Suddenly his foothold gave and he found himself dangling twenty-five feet up with his fingers wedged liked pegs in a crack. He winced as his knuckles tore.

'Hey!' yelled Erlan. 'Be careful up there!'

Kai released a long breath. 'Aye – the thought had occurred to me.' *Maybe squirrels do fall after all, just no one's around to see it.*

He looked up. Maybe ten feet to go. He drew up his legs and found another toehold. *Ten feet. And then?* There was a yell from below. 'They're here! Kai – hurry – for all our sakes, hurry!'

He glanced down as another shriek burst from the darkness, and with it figures appearing into the open. Two of them – then a third.

Dirty little tykes, he thought, watching Erlan lift his sword and the princess brace her spear. 'Guess we're all in now.'

He was out of time. Already the shouts and yells of combat carried to his perch. He shinned up the last ten feet like a cat up a tree, at last within reach of the shattered rocks he reckoned held up the big slab.

Satisfied with his grip, he reached behind and pulled out his little axe.

He heard Lilla scream below and glanced down. There were a couple of darker shapes motionless in the snow, then more creatures emerging from the icefall.

'Kai! Kai!' cried Lilla, sounding desperate. 'Do it now!'

He looked up and grunted. Aye, this *was* the weakest part of his plan. Getting out of the way of a falling rock the size of a house. Still, he reckoned the main weight of it was off to the left. Once it started to go, he could scoot right and be out of the way. He scanned that way and noted two or three good handholds and a decent ledge for his feet.

I'll be fine. It's all about timing. Knowing when the thing's about to go.

He started hammering at the rocks with the butt of his axe. Below him, Erlan was bellowing like a bull. Chips of stone skittered off down the cliff. His arm was burning. He had to use his left arm, of course, so he could escape to the right, and he wasn't sure that wolf hadn't cracked his bloody bone. Still, he went at it busily, chunks of rock flaking and falling away, and then a lump the size of his fist cracked and broke off.

He grinned at his progress, but it still wasn't fast enough for them below. Suddenly a bigger piece of rock swivelled, leaving the end jutting out. He leaned away to give himself more room, and with a backhanded blow sent it sailing into the air.

Now he was getting somewhere.

But before he took another hit, there was a cracking noise as the rocks above began to give. And then the noise grew louder, rippling up the long deep crevice above him as the ice fractured.

He looked up and suddenly it seemed like the whole cliff had started to shift.

'Shit.'

He flung away his axe and lunged for the handhold to his right. But suddenly everything looked the same. His ears filled with the roar of shearing rock, loud as thunder, bursting on him from above. He snatched for a handhold – any one would do. Then he had it and he looked up and the sky was collapsing on his head.

There was no time.

Jump! Did he shout the word or only think it?

The cliff face rumbled under his hands. He felt the ledge under his toes, sucked in a breath and then leaped as far and high as his legs would send him.

The whole world was crashing down in a cascade of ice and thunder. And him with it. He felt a beautiful moment of weightlessness – falling, falling into the white abyss below.

So this is what it is to fly!

And then there was a shock of cold – and after that, nothing.

Erlan pulled Wrathling from the last of the Nefelung. There were bodies all around. Pathetic things now. Each one the stain of a life that used to be. But was death so much worse for them than the life he'd seen them lead?

He was breathing hard. Too tired to feel any pain. He looked across at Lilla. She was on her knees, head hanging, blood splattered across the rags of her dress. But alive.

Whatever Kai had done had worked.

Snow dust was still falling in glittering sparkles all around. But there were no more Nefelung to fight. And they were alive.

The roar had filled the sky. But when the worst of the shattered ice and rock had settled, it revealed a great heap of stone and scree and smashed icicles sloping from the foot of the icefall to the cliff nearly twenty feet above them. Higher still, there was a large smooth hole where the huge slab had fallen away.

The gateway to Niflagard was gone.

And so was Kai.

There's the justice of the gods for you – I sought death, yet I'm alive. Kai sought life and he's dead. For all his wounds, nothing hurt so much as his heart just then. Somehow the lad had weaselled his way in there.

He grimaced, wiping his sword on his filthy breeches, and turned back to the princess. Her face was a mask of exhaustion. 'I saw him,' she said, voice hardly a whisper.

'Who?'

'Kai.'

Erlan shook his head in confusion. 'What? Where?'

'Over there.' She pointed to a deep drift of snow a little way right of the heap of fallen rocks. 'He fell clear.'

But Erlan was already lumbering through the snow, wading into the drift, heart in mouth. And there, in the deeper snow, was the perfect outline of a body. He dragged himself over to it and peered down.

There was Kai, face down, unmoving.

Erlan reached in, grabbed his belt and hauled him out of the hole. He turned him over. The boy's hair and scraggy stubble were plastered with snow. His mouth was contorted with pain, but his eyes were peaceful as a slumbering babe.

'Kai!' Erlan shook him. 'Kai!'

Nothing. He shook him again, harder this time. 'Kai!'

The boy groaned and rolled his head.

'Hahaah!' cried Erlan. 'Kai – you mad little bugger! You're alive!'

'Am I?' the lad moaned, blinking. 'Keep saying that till I believe it.'

'You're alive – you lucky son of a bitch!'

'My face. It smarts like Hel. . .'

Erlan could hardly contain his delight. 'If it's your face you're worried about, I'm afraid you're as ugly as ever.'

'Since when did you grow a sense of humour?' said Kai, gingerly brushing the ice off his chin.

'About when you grew a pair of bloody wings! By the hanged – you must have fallen forty feet!'

'Did it work?'

Erlan grabbed his scruff and hauled him to a sitting position. 'See for yourself.'

For a while Kai sat there, admiring his work, a grin slowly working across his mouth. 'That. Is. Fine. . . Yep – just *fine*!'

Lilla had waded over to them. She looked gaunt as a ghost, her eyes wide with shock. 'Is he all right?'

'His body's in one piece,' answered Erlan, 'but his mind's clearly cracked.'

Kai sat in the snow, blinking artlessly, but alive, his hair a crazy splay of white spikes, his tunic caked with powder.

'That's a rare kind of courage you have,' said Lilla, seeming truly bewildered by what Kai had just done. 'Some might say a rare kind of madness.' She gave his shoulder a squeeze. 'I'll be sure to tell my father what you did.' She turned to the jagged debris. Her voice hardened. 'That place is full of evil.'

She glared at where the entrance used to be, then closed her eyes tight and stretched out her arms.

The others watched.

Suddenly words came pouring out of her mouth, words flooding in an undulating stream of sound, words far beyond their understanding.

They listened, absorbed, until she gave a sudden shriek, clenched her fists and thrust them at the debris. She stood like that a while, perfectly still, until, very slowly, she let her arms drop.

At last, her face relaxed and she opened her eyes.

'What the Hel are you doing?' asked Kai, bemused.

'It's a telling my mother taught me. For sealing things.'

'So they're stuck down there now?'

'I'd say a few thousand marks of rock would keep them in there just fine,' said Erlan, irritably. 'I don't see the need for all this jabber in some witch's tongue.'

'It's not jabber,' she protested. 'It's a language my mother taught me that she learned from the spirit world. It has power beyond the understanding of men. Beyond what I understand myself.'

'Then what fucking use is it?' snarled Erlan.

'The telling is to seal in the things unseen,' she snapped back. 'You saw the evil down there.'

'Come on, master,' said Kai. 'You know, she means—'

'You did the same down there, didn't you?' Erlan's eyes flashed fiercely. 'Spewing up your witch's prattle all over me.'

'And it saved your life!' she exclaimed. 'You should be grateful.'

'I'll be grateful if you keep your damned sorcery away from me. Spells and curses – I've had a bellyful of 'em.'

'My tellings speak only to heal or protect. I never speak to anyone's harm. My mother—'

'Your mother is dead. Dead!' cried Erlan. 'You understand? I don't care what she taught you.'

'How dare you speak to me like that?' Lilla's blood-streaked features hardened into anger. 'Anyway, you know nothing of the realm of the dead.'

'So people keep telling me. But I know this much. I know the dead don't come back.' He turned away and added in a whisper. *'The dead will never come back.'*

She shook her head in frustration. 'Just take me to my father. I'm sure he will reward you richly. Isn't that why you're here?'

'Think whatever you will,' murmured Erlan, looking away down the hill.

'Well,' broke in Kai, clapping his hands. 'Those ugly little brutes are shut up in there good and proper, one way or t'other! And aren't we all bloody heroes, eh?' He looked eagerly between the princess and Erlan. 'You too, my lady! So then – what now, master?'

Erlan turned. Lifted his sword and swept it wearily over the bodies strewn about them. 'We burn them. And then. . . we take her home.'

CHAPTER THIRTY-SEVEN

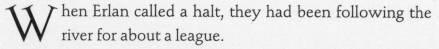

When Erlan called a halt, they had been following the river for about a league.

Kai had scouted ahead and found a campsite close by the river under some tall pines. It had only been two or three hours on horseback, but Lilla felt nearly delirious with fatigue. Kai had produced food enough to strengthen her till nightfall. But the memory of that place wouldn't be as easy to shift as an empty stomach.

Erlan had hardly said a word since they'd ridden away from the horrible stench of burning bodies. She'd noticed him cradling his arm most tenderly. If he felt anything like her, he'd be happy to curl up in the snow and die, there and then. Though after all they'd been through, that was probably a bit of a waste.

Her feet were the worst. She'd bound them with a few strips of cloth, cut from a cloak they'd brought for her, but that was hardly enough to stop the slow creep of pain up her calves from the cuts and bruises and swelling. Being astride a horse was some relief. But now it was time to dismount.

She looked down, reluctant to surrender her distance from the ground. Dreading the pain. Too stubborn to ask for help.

Stupid. Why do I have to do everything myself?

She just did.

'Something not to your liking with this spot, Princess?' asked Erlan, tying off his horse next to Kai's. The boy was already off searching for firewood.

'No, I. . .' She looked around. 'It will serve.'

When she didn't move, he sighed. 'A princess requires a hand down, that it?' He came closer and proffered up his arms. 'Come on then.'

'I can manage on my own,' she said stiffly.

'Suit yourself.' He turned away.

She swung her leg over the horse's withers, biting her lip in anticipation. She dropped to the ground. Pain roared up her legs. She whimpered, staggering against the horse.

Erlan could hardly fail to notice. 'Come on – take my arm.'

'I'm fine,' she insisted, swallowing the tremor in her voice. She lifted the blanket off her horse, meaning to dump it with the rest of their gear, but on the first step, her knees folded into the snow.

'And you say I'm stubborn,' he growled, scooping her up and swinging her into his arms. When she didn't answer, he just snorted, carried her over to the pile of furs and put her down. 'You sit here.'

She was too tired to argue. Too tired to find some proud retort. She sat huddled up, while Kai chased around gathering more wood and Erlan lit the fire. Before long its familiar heat was warming her face and the soles of her battered feet. It felt good beyond description.

'Don't you move a muscle, my lady,' crowed Kai. 'I'll soon whistle you up a dish worthy of your father himself.' He insisted his master should do no more than her, so Erlan soon limped over and dropped down beside her.

He had in his hands a knife, an undershirt and his sheepskin coat.

'What are you doing?' she asked.

'You need these more than I do.'

'Won't you be cold without that?' She gestured at the coat.

'Out here, I'm cold with it – cold without it. So what's the difference? Give me your feet.'

Hesitatingly, she moved them towards him. He took them gently and, one by one, undid the bindings and peeled away the cloth. She winced at the cold air. The firelight revealed soles rubbed raw, swollen with blisters, mottled with bruises.

'By the hanged.' The stranger gave a low whistle. 'It's a wonder you can even walk.'

'Like you.' She'd said it before she'd even thought it, and immediately regretted her sharp tongue. *Why can't I keep my stupid mouth shut sometimes?*

She saw he was offended. But this time he only raised his eyebrows and murmured, 'If you can bear just a little more of the cold . . .' He didn't wait for an answer, but took a handful of snow and began cleaning the wounds. She bit her lip, groaning at the fresh torment. But he was soon done, drying each foot carefully, cutting the undershirt into bandages and wrapping them up.

Then he began carving up his coat to fashion a pair of sheepskin coverings. 'These'll last you until. . . well, as long as they last.' By the time he'd finished binding them tight with twine, the pain had eased a good deal and her feet felt snug.

'Thank you.' She meant it.

'Nothing more than my duty. For the daughter of my king,' he added, voice laced with sarcasm. He sheathed his knife and sat back, gazing into the fire, cradling his arm.

'Let me see that.' She nodded at his arm.

'You?'

'Of course, me,' she said impatiently, trying to get hold of it.

'It's fine,' he protested. 'I've had worse.'

'Any worse and your arm would fall off, idiot. Show me.'

So he showed her, pulling off his tunic and draping a fur across his shoulders. The wound was a long, deep cut from the back of his bicep to the crook of his elbow. Much of the blood was congealed, but for a dark line glistening down the middle.

'It's deep,' was her verdict. She peered closer. 'Although . . .'

'What is it?'

She looked up at him. '*When* did you receive this?'

'You know when. Just before I found you. Why?'

'The healing is already well advanced. *Strange. . .*' she muttered. It didn't make sense. Then again, there was still plenty of need for her skill. 'Anyway, it should be cleaned and bound.' She began dabbing at the wound with a damp scrap of linen, feeling his eyes on her as she smoothed away the dried blood.

'Your lips are moving,' he murmured.

'Oh.' She hadn't even realized she was doing it.

'More sorcery?' He cocked an eyebrow.

'Just a habit, I guess.'

'You do know you're dabbling in something you don't understand?'

'I understand it a Hel of a lot better than you,' she replied, indignant. 'So if you don't mind. . .'

495

'You promised.' She noticed a smile flicker across his mouth.

'Did I? I don't remember that. Besides, men don't know what's good for them.' She felt the trace of a smile on her own lips.

'And you do, I suppose?'

She looked up, fixing him with her gaze. 'Yes. I do.'

He gave a low chuckle. 'Hel – I'm glad someone does.'

'Hold still.' She bound the wound with the strip of linen, ignoring his yelp when she pulled it tight.

'Now,' she said. 'Take down your breeches.'

'What? I know you're used to servants doing your bidding, but—'

'Your leg – I must look at that too.'

He gave an ironic snort. 'I *think* this oversteps my duty, Princess. I'm pretty sure your father would agree.'

'Don't be so coy. You must let me bind it. Unless you want to be limping for the next year?'

'I already have a limp, as you've so graciously pointed out.'

She cursed inwardly. 'Of course, I didn't mean . . .' What was it about this man that made her so clumsy with words? 'Just let me bind it – for all our sakes. We need you strong. You flatter yourself that I care a barley crust for what you have under there.'

'Steady on, my lady,' piped up Kai. 'You'll hurt his feelings.'

'You just keep to your damn cooking,' growled Erlan.

'Sure, sure,' chuckled the boy.

'You're being ridiculous,' Lilla snapped. 'The wound needs dressing.'

He let out a long sigh. 'Very well.' He got awkwardly to his feet, unhitched his belt, unlaced his breeches and dropped them.

496

The firelight spilled over his thighs. But she averted her eyes from the absurdity between his legs. She had always thought men unclothed not much better than comic. Erlan was no different. On the other hand, the play of light over his skin was pleasing enough. At least, she imagined a lot of girls might think so. But for her... that kind of thing only led to wounds that never healed. Right now, she was interested in dressing one that might.

She traced a finger the length of the cut on his thigh. He sucked sharply on his teeth. 'Cold hands.' He smiled down at her. 'Cold night, come to that.'

'He's just making excuses, my lady,' sniggered Kai.

'This wound is strange too,' she said, ignoring their childish talk. 'It was also deep, but it's showing signs of healing already.'

'It hurts bad enough.'

'I'm sure,' she said, cutting short her curiosity. 'You're lucky, though. I've seen many wounds, but none so sure to heal.'

'I guess I'll have to take your word for it.'

'I guess you will.' She disliked the way he picked at everything she said like some scab. Suddenly she wanted to be done with this. She set about tending to the cut, and in a short while she was binding it with a woollen shawl from the bundle they'd brought for her.

'That should see you most of the way to my father's halls,' she said, as he pulled up his breeches.

'Much obliged.' He chuckled. 'I don't suppose many could claim to have been serviced by the daughter of the king.'

'Listen – you don't know anything about me,' she snapped. 'So I'd appreciate it if you kept your stupid japes to yourself.' She didn't like his familiar tone. Liked even less the assumptions he made about her.

'As you wish.' He shrugged, and they both settled back on the furs in silence.

She supposed there would be some talk. Some answers to her questions. Like why, out of all his men, her father had chosen this unlikely pair to rescue her. How had they found her? How had the stranger slain that horrible fiend?

But she was too weary to ask now. The answers would keep. Instead, she gazed into the fire, drinking in its heat.

Fire is life...

She had often thought that on her terrible journey through the snow.

'Something the matter, my lady?' asked Kai, interrupting her thoughts.

She realized she was frowning. 'Just the fire... Would've been good to have heat like this when they carried me to that horrible place.'

No one said anything for a few moments.

Erlan was first to break the silence. 'What happened, Princess? I mean from the beginning...'

She stared even harder into the embers crackling and spitting in the fire's depths. And then she told her story. Of an early morning that began like so many, of the sense she was not alone. Sounds in the snow, shadows skulking in the trees. Of the figures surrounding her, those strange, strong hands reaching for her, slipping round her throat. Of her waking to incessant motion, the pain shooting up her back. Of the hard poles they bound her to, the tight bonds sawing at her flesh.

'They moved at a speed beyond anything you could imagine. They were relentless, hardly needing any rest.' She had watched the branches and clouds and stars passing overhead, her body racked with aches and gnawing hunger. She told of the degradation of being force-fed forest carrion, the shame of relieving herself before her captors, the teetering brink of madness. The pendulum swing between delirium and determination – the songs she sang in her mind to keep it from shattering.

'All the while, the cold burrowed into me. And when we came to the icefall and plunged into darkness. . . That's when I made my last resolve. To remember the way down. The rest. . . the rest is best forgotten. I was dead.' She nodded at Erlan. 'Until I saw your face.'

A tear welled unbidden and fell in a silver stream down her cheek. She brushed it away hurriedly. The last thing she wanted was anyone's pity, least of all the stranger's.

'My wounds are nothing to what you've suffered,' he said. For some reason, the trace of tenderness in his voice annoyed her.

'Well, my lady, here's something better 'n carrion, I hope.' Kai passed her a steaming bowl, and held out another to his master.

Erlan was about to take it when the boy pulled it out of reach. 'Uh-uh!' he chuckled.

'What?'

'It comes at a price.'

'Well?'

'I want to know *what happened* down there,' whispered Kai. 'And above anything else, what the Hel that weird rope thing you're keeping so precious is all about.'

Erlan sighed. 'I suppose that's fair. Give it up then.' Kai passed over the bowl and his master sank his fingers into the stew and scooped some into his mouth greedily. After a few more mouthfuls he began to talk. *And talk.* Lilla watched the boy hanging off every word like a dog begging scraps, his bright eyes wide. Many times he interrupted, straining every last detail from Erlan's memory until the boy was satisfied he had it right.

'Has anyone ever heard the like?' cried Kai when Erlan had come to the end of his tale. 'Hohoooah! And here you both are! Why, my skaldman friend would've given his thumbs to hear this. Oh, he'd make a fine song of it – wouldn't he just!'

'Song of it?' Erlan grunted. 'I'd rather forget all about it.'

'Tsk! You would, master,' the boy scolded. 'That's 'cause you're a miserable son of a bitch at the best of times.'

Lilla couldn't stop herself laughing at that.

Erlan just shook his head at them both.

'Still,' said Kai, leaning in all sly, 'if we're making a song of it, there ought to be a verse or two for me.'

'You've more to tell?' she asked.

'Might be I do,' he replied, with a wink. She found it impossible not to return his smile. 'You haven't noticed, have you?' he said to Erlan.

'What?'

'The *bird*.'

Erlan looked about him. 'Of course – I'd forgotten. Where is it?'

'Dead,' declared Kai, with a jut of his chin. 'Two ravens came and did for him. I never saw the like.'

'What do you mean?'

'It was like they were sent for it. Deliberate, you know.' And then Kai told how the ravens had hunted down their winged friend.

Lilla still didn't understand. 'What was this bird to you?'

Her companions exchanged glances, apparently unsure how to answer. Eventually Erlan spoke. 'It led us to you.'

'A bird? How?'

He scratched at his tousled hair, searching for an explanation. 'We came across it in the forest. It was a jay of sorts. . . It seemed to know which way to go. No, it *did* know – because it led us to the icefall.' He shot Kai a look. 'We came to think it wasn't what it seemed.'

'How do you mean?'

'Shape-shifting,' he said.

Naturally, she knew of it. Her mother had sworn her never to do it, but she knew there were some who could. 'Before we came to Sveäland,' he continued, 'we met a *seidman* deep in the Forest of Tyr. He told us he was a shape-shifter and knew the forests. His name was Grimnar.' Erlan looked at Kai again. 'The Witch King *told* me he was dead.'

'You think the bird was this Grimnar?' asked Lilla.

'I couldn't credit it myself,' said Kai. 'But like he said, it did lead us to you. And something else happened while you were down there.' They listened as Kai told more. With peculiar relish, he recounted his fight with the wolf and the twisted deformity of its limbs once it was dead. The human hand. He pulled back his sleeve and revealed his swollen arm where the wolf bit him.

When he'd finished, Erlan gave a long whistle. 'I'd say you've earned your verses, boy. More than that, even. How does Kai Wolf-Hand sound?'

'Better than it feels,' grinned the boy. But she could see how it pleased the boy to impress his master.

501

'You did well,' she agreed. 'This Witch King has many servants who do his bidding.'

'Had,' corrected Erlan.

'So you hope,' she replied sharply. 'But if they're alive, even though he is dead. . . what evil might they yet do?'

Her question hung unanswered in the air. In the fire the wood snapped and popped.

'Where did you come across this bird?' asked Lilla at last.

'Where the trail split into three. We had no way of knowing which would lead to you.'

Lilla suddenly felt a dreadful chill inside her, a memory lurching out of the shadows of her mind. Why had she not remembered earlier, when she had related her journey? She felt the blood leach from her cheeks.

'My lady? *My lady!*' Kai's touch jolted her out of her nightmare. 'Are you all right?'

'I . . . don't know why. . . I had forgotten till now. But it's coming back to me.' She looked up at them. 'There were others.'

'Others?' echoed Erlan.

'Yes. But different from the ones who took me from the Kingswood. Different from the creatures in the caves. They were larger. Fiercer. Fell creatures that could only have been spawned in the darkest caverns of Hel.'

'The Watcher spoke of others called the Vandrung. The sirelings of the overlords. A mongrel race.'

'I know nothing of that.' Lilla screwed up her eyes, put her head in her hands. 'My memory is not clear. It is more like trying to recall a dream. But there were some. . . some who stood much taller than you.' She nodded at the stranger. 'The smaller ones were cowed by them.'

'You saw none like them below?'

'I couldn't say. The darkness obscured so much.' Lilla shook her head. 'But now I remember that when the company split, in spite of my fear, I felt relief. The smaller ones are full of malice. But those others – *they were not human*. Their very breath was evil.'

'How many did they number?' asked Erlan.

She shook her head again. 'I can't say for certain.'

'Try!' he urged, his voice rising. 'You must remember more.'

'I was in agony. Trying to keep my sanity.' Her voice quavered.

'How many?' he barked.

'I don't know. Dozens, at least. Perhaps more.'

'More than a hundred?'

'I don't know,' she cried. She didn't want to think of those horrible creatures any more.

'Were there more than a hundred?' he said again, seizing her arm.

'No. . . I don't think so. I don't know. Leave me be!' And she tore her arm free.

Wings fluttered in the treetops. All three of them started at the sound and looked about them. Suddenly, the darkness seemed full of menace.

'So much for sealing that place with your sorcery and spells,' grimaced Erlan.

'What should we do, master?' For the first time that night, the boy looked fearful.

'Ride faster.'

'I'm serious,' returned Kai.

'So am I!' Erlan snarled. He got to his feet, went to the pile of gear and pulled out the Watcher's tail. He flung his grisly trophy out to its full length. 'Whatever evil these things possess, here's the proof that it can be beaten. With sword and sinew.'

Lilla shuddered. The tail glistened black as tar in the flickering flames. 'Why do you have to keep that thing?' she said quickly.

'What would you have me do with it?'

'Burn it! A thing like that can bring nothing but ill from a place so dark.'

'And yet it has power,' he whispered, looking on it with wonder. 'I saw it. So did you.'

'The thing is ill-fated!'

'No! It's the proof that the Watcher and his foul kingdom can be destroyed.'

'Why keep a memento of what you have destroyed? You're no better than a child!'

'I keep it not to remember what I destroyed. . . but what I won.'

'And what was that?' she said, her tone acid.

'Life!' he cried, looking up into the night. 'A reason to live.'

His cry sailed off into the darkness. After a few moments, she murmured, 'Are there not many?'

'For some, maybe. But not for me.' His eyes met hers, and in them she saw for the first time a deep, deep wound. 'Not for me. . .'

It was a while before she spoke again. 'I would bring nothing from that place. It is all accursed.'

She could see him wrestling the question in his mind as he gazed upon his trophy. 'Very well – I won't keep it.' She let out a sigh of relief. 'But I will at least keep something from it.' He didn't wait for her protests, but took out his knife, sat down on the fur and began skinning the smooth surface off the tail's thick core.

There was no convincing him, she could see that much. But that only disturbed her all the more. Instead she and Kai watched him in silence.

The skin seemed strangely dry, peeling away in tough, supple strips. Erlan lay each one beside him until, in the gloom, they looked like so many dead serpents.

'What are you making?' asked Kai, at last.

'A belt to remember this by.'

'This?' she said.

'The life I won back. The fire can take the rest.' So saying, he flung the monstrous tail into the flames.

It bucked and snapped like dry wood, tongues of fire flaring around it. And before long the blaze had devoured it all, leaving nothing but embers and ash.

CHAPTER THIRTY-EIGHT

They smelled them before they saw them.

The scent of pine and spruce mingled with sweat and horseflesh. Then they heard the crackle of dawn fires and muttering voices.

'Sviggar's scouts!' cried Kai.

And suddenly a shout went up. There was a clatter of armed men getting to their feet, a babble of startled voices. The three of them rode on into the camp, nodding at the dirty faces gawping up at them. For the first time in a long while, Erlan felt secure. Kai was grinning like his head might split.

'By the fires,' said a hoarse voice. 'We never thought we'd hear from you again!' Earl Bodvar was pushing his way through his men. For a change, the flint-faced old bastard was smiling.

'You nearly didn't,' returned Erlan.

Bodvar slapped Kai's leg. 'And you, young rascal – we can't shake you, can we?' He turned to the princess. 'Lady Lilla – your father will be overjoyed to know you're safe.'

'Where is he?' Her beautiful face was creased with anxiety.

'With the main force. We're just ten. The king and two hirds are perhaps half a day's ride behind us.'

'How many?' asked Erlan.

'Nearly three hundred men in all.'

'You took your sweet time. You're nearly four days behind us.'

Bodvar gave a surly grunt. 'We lost the trail after the snowfall. Eventually we found your markings and by then the king's force was catching us up.'

'Can we go to him?' said Lilla. 'He must know I am safe.'

'Of course, my lady. My men can be ready at a moment.' He turned to the other scouts. 'Well, you heard her. We leave immediately.'

The huddle of men split obediently and set about breaking camp.

Bodvar gave Lilla a craggy smile. 'I promise you'll be with your father before nightfall.'

And he was right.

Three leagues further on, they made contact with the king's vanguard. Sviggar's hirds buzzed with excitement to see the princess and the stranger among Bodvar's men. But Lilla hastened on through them all, impatient to greet her father.

It was Earl Heidrek who told them that her father was a little way back among his men. The earl's wiry face was even paler than usual. 'He's not well, my lady.'

'What do you mean?'

'The king is no longer a young man.'

'Oh – why do you always have to talk in circles!' she snapped. 'Tell me quickly – what's wrong?'

'Forgive me, my lady. The weather has worn hard on him. He suffers from a breathing sickness.'

'Take me to him at once,' she said, hurrying on. Erlan followed with Bodvar, Kai bringing up the rear.

They found him soon after, propped up on his horse's back by Finn the archer and another attendant. But he seemed hardly able to keep his seat. His head hung low, his body slumped like a half-filled sack of grain.

Lilla cried out, slid from her horse and hobbled to him as fast as her injured feet would allow, pushing aside Finn's horse. 'Father! My father, I'm here! I'm alive.'

Erlan was shocked to see the old king. His breath rattled in his throat like the sea sucking shingle. Sweat beaded along the wrinkles of his hanging brow.

'Lilla,' he croaked. 'My child – you're returned to me.' His cheeks flickered a smile.

Lilla reached up and caressed his thigh. Her cheeks were wet with tears. Sviggar blinked down at her, almost in a stupor, then bent over to stroke her hair. Suddenly he slumped forward and would have fallen on her but for Finn's quick reaction holding him on his horse.

'The old goat's in a fine fucking state,' whispered Kai sidelong. Erlan shot him a warning look. Now really wasn't the time.

'This is madness,' Lilla cried. 'He shouldn't even be on a horse.' She tried to ease him out of his saddle, and glanced angrily round at Erlan. 'Help me, can't you!'

Within moments, furs had been thrown on the ground and the ailing king lain upon them. By now, the whole force had come to a halt and was dismounting. Lilla sent Kai off to fetch water and the lad scurried off to retrieve a skin from his horse.

'I'm all right, I'm all right,' croaked Sviggar, trying to prop himself up, while his daughter fretted over him. 'A winter fever, nothing more. Here, help me.' Lilla got him comfortable and pulled the fur tighter round him.

'You must lie down and rest, Father.'

'Of course,' he wheezed, 'but how could I rest till I knew you were safe?' Suddenly the fever shivered right through him. Kai arrived with the water. Lilla snatched it from him and put it to her father's lips. The old man drank a while before pushing it away. She moistened a corner of her cloak and started mopping his brow.

'You mustn't fuss, child. I'm not dying.' He coughed a deep rasp in his chest. *He bloody sounds like he is*, thought Erlan. At last, Sviggar recovered himself. 'Where's the stranger? Is he with you?'

Erlan stepped out of the circle of men.

Sviggar looked up and smiled. 'So my bet was a wise one.'

'Or lucky.'

'Ha! Either way, you've rendered me a service greater than any man alive or dead. I'll not forget it.' He coughed again, hard. 'Tell me. I must know. What is this enemy? You have seen them?'

'Aye.'

'And? Are they men? Or beasts?'

Erlan glanced at Lilla, then back to her father. 'Perhaps men who've become beasts. Though they had a king who was certainly no man.'

'Had?'

'I killed him.'

Sviggar grimaced. 'Bravely done. You'll be honoured for it – you have my word. What manner of king was he?'

So Erlan told him, and all the company lent a full ear as he described his descent into that demon's warren. He told of the Witch King and the Nefelung thralls, of the overlords and the mysterious Vandrung. They listened to his account of the hall of horrors, of their escape through the darkness back to the light. And lastly, how, thanks to Kai's madcap plan, they had sealed them in the depths for ever.

'For ever?' Bodvar sounded doubtful.

Erlan exchanged glances with Lilla. She gave a curt nod. He shrugged. 'Say until the Ragnarok. That's long enough for me.' It would take a giant to clear through all that rock and rubble.

'From what you describe of the place, much of the entrance is sealed by this icefall. Is that right?' When Erlan nodded, Bodvar gave a sharp snort. 'And what happens when the spring thaws come? What seal protects the kingdom then?'

The truth hit him like a slap in the face. How could he have missed it? Perhaps it was the shock of his ordeal, or relief at their escape, but something had blinded him from seeing what was so damned obvious. Blinded all of them. 'Fuck.'

'Quite,' agreed Bodvar.

'Perhaps summer doesn't reach this part of the land,' piped up Kai, ever the optimist. 'You wait, my lords. It's the very end of the world! The ice – why, it's thicker than the walls of the greatest hall – ten times higher than the tallest tree. I'd bet my arm that icefall would stand a hundred years if it stands a day!'

'The lad's arm will be poor recompense if these Nefelung are able to break free again,' said Bodvar.

'I fear, my lad, your confidence may prove ill-placed,' said Sviggar hoarsely. 'How many of them were left?'

'Many,' conceded Erlan.

'Then the business is not finished.' Sviggar grimaced. 'The kingdom won't be safe until they are slaughtered in this stronghold of theirs.' A sudden fit of coughing racked his body. Erlan saw blood fleck his withered lips. 'A red day,' he croaked. 'Is this not what I've promised my people to avenge their blood? A red day for my son.'

'Father, is it not revenge enough that their king is dead?' exclaimed Lilla. 'You're sick. You can't fight. You know you can't.'

A grim expression settled on his face. 'If I can but hold my sword—'

'Father, you must not break the seal on that place! Though you kill every last one of them, there are things unseen down there – things not of this world – which must not be released. If they are, I fear for all of us.' She turned and appealed to Erlan, eyes imploring him. 'Tell him, Erlan! The seal must not be broken!'

But the king spoke before he could. 'How you talk like your mother, sweet Lilla! You must forgive an old man his obstinacy. I deal in things of flesh and blood. These ill spirits and such you speak of – it is beyond a king to protect against these. But the kingdom must be secured.'

'Lord, like you I know little enough of any spirit worlds,' said Erlan. 'But your daughter is right. There is untold evil down in those caverns. Perhaps what you have now is the best you can hope for. Perhaps, as Lady Lilla says, it is best to let it lie.'

'Do you expect all these men to have ridden through this bollock-freezing wasteland just to crawl back to Uppsala with their blades still dry?' said Bodvar, the lines in his face hardening. 'Now? When the road to their enemy is finally clear?'

'Oh, how the talk of you men sickens me!' cried Lilla. '*I* have a blade wet with Nefelung blood. Am I more of a man than you because of it?' Her gaunt features flushed with passion. 'Well? Am I?'

The grizzled earl only returned her question with a wan smile.

'Many of these men will die if you break in there!'

'And when the spring comes?' was Bodvar's gruff reply.

She shook her head, seeing these men were not to be persuaded. 'You should not disturb what you don't understand.'

'My child, I understand your misgivings,' said Sviggar softly. 'But the thing must be done. And done now.' He seemed about to say more, but was suddenly overwhelmed by another fit of coughing, the worst yet.

Finn, his bodyguard, laid a hand on his shoulder, finally voicing what everyone was thinking. 'Sire, on one thing at least, your daughter has the right of it. You're too sick for this fight.' The archer glowered at Bodvar to say something decisive.

'Let Earl Heidrek and I be your hands,' offered Bodvar, albeit with a circumspect look at the other earl. 'Let us win you your revenge.'

The king's breath rasped noisily while they awaited his answer. At last, he whispered. 'Very well – I will heed my daughter's counsel. You will do my killing for me.'

'We shall not fail you, sire,' said Bodvar.

Erlan had followed this, seen the way it was going. So

when Bodvar turned to him, he'd already been turning over the question that the earl now asked.

'If the entrance is sealed, do you think we can still find a way in?'

Erlan nodded. 'Aye – I believe there's a way.' Though the prospect of going back down into the darkness was bitter as poison.

'Is it far from here?' asked Heidrek.

'A day's hard ride, no more. Maybe less with our tracks. I'll show you myself.'

'No,' said Sviggar firmly. 'You've done enough already.'

'Lord, I'll go again if I must. Don't think my wounds would stop me.'

'Wounds or no, my word is final. Your servant will stay with us too.'

Finn suddenly laughed. 'Stranger, you're a glutton for the king's favour! Let these murderous bastards have their day.' He jerked his head at the two earls. 'I'd say you've had your fair portion, wouldn't you?'

Aye – enough to burst my belly.

Erlan looked from Bodvar to the sagging figure of the king, and to Lilla beside him. 'Then I'll do as you wish, my lord.' Relief washed over him. He suddenly realized he was nursing his wounded arm. A rest would be good. 'But there is much I must tell you, Lord Bodvar.'

The earl chuckled. 'There's much I would know.'

The rest of the day Erlan spent in conference with Bodvar and Heidrek. He disgorged every detail he could recall of Niflagard and had them repeat it all till they knew it as well as him.

'Above all, you need light. Without it, you're blind. With it, you can defeat them.'

Bodvar asked how they could break the seal into the place. 'I have an idea, but if it fails. . .' Erlan shrugged. 'Maybe they're fated to stay buried down there.'

'We'll not let the bastards off so easy,' returned Bodvar. 'Tell us.'

'When you come to the place, you'll find a huge fall of ice and rock.' He threw a glance at Kai, who sat warming himself a little way off, but within earshot. 'That one's doing. Half the cliff blocks the entrance now. But on the left, the ice seals a large part of the cavern behind it. My idea is this. Build a furnace against that part of the icefall. Pack it tight. Pile it high. The fire's heat will melt the ice and the way will be open into the hole.'

The two earls considered this.

'Are you certain it can be done?' asked Heidrek.

'Certain – no. But there's a chance it could work.'

'At least it stands to reason,' said Bodvar. 'Ice yields to fire.' Erlan's skin prickled with the memory of Lilla's strange spell and he felt a pang of guilt, imagining her reproach.

The next day, long before dawn, the two earls rode out at the head of a column of karls and thanes and high-born lords. Two full hirds, nearly three hundred men. They left behind only a dozen who would ride escort to their king and his daughter, back to the Uppland halls.

Kai and Erlan rode with them.

'Onwards!' cried the old king, astride his horse, watching his warriors move out. 'Onwards to a red day and victory!'

514

Lilla tugged her horse around and rode off. Curious, Erlan did likewise and caught up with her.

'You still have misgivings?'

She looked at him and he saw the foreboding in her dark blue eyes. 'Sometimes defeat looks like victory,' she said, kicking on.

'Then we should pray the gods this isn't one of them,' he called after her.

But then he recalled the Watcher's web of words and a doubt sprang into his mind.

Were there any gods to hear their prayers?

CHAPTER THIRTY-NINE

Sviggar's health improved not a whit as they journeyed homeward.

Each day they rode slower as his need for rest grew, and Lilla insisted they move on only when he felt strong enough to sit atop his horse.

By late afternoon on the third day, whatever gladness there might have been in returning home had long leached away.

'This feels like a bloody funeral march,' murmured Kai, as they rode along. A fair wind was gusting through the trees. 'Not exactly the triumphant procession I imagined.'

'Knowing your imagination, I'm not surprised.'

'I should've been with Bodvar's lot. I'm not all cut up like you. It's past time I got *my* sword wet.'

'Catch,' said Erlan, chucking a flask of water. Kai caught it with his left hand and yelped in pain. 'Wolf-Hand,' winked his master, point proven.

'Baaah! My sword arm's good.'

'Save it for a fair fight. Down that hole you're not like to get one. Anyway there's plenty of—'

'Time – yes, I know. So everyone keeps bloody telling me!' Kai glanced back at the king, flanked by his faithful Finn. 'I'll be wheezing away like the old goat before I get a decent fight.' He pulled a face. 'Still, there's a thought! I could take the king of all Sveäland just now. Easy! Hey – would that make me king?'

Erlan gave up trying to follow his friend's meandering mind.

'First law I'd make – every new king gets three wives. In fact, I'd have all the fairest women fight it out for the privilege.' He grinned to himself. 'I can think of some of them Uppland minxes who wouldn't mind.'

'Isn't it usually the other way round?'

'Men fighting for women? Oh, I know that. But these darlings couldn't stop 'emselves! With old King Kai on the throne, show me the beauty who wouldn't want to share his bed.' His face fairly glowed at the prospect.

Erlan answered his question with a nod in the direction of the princess riding behind. 'How about our frosty maid back there?'

'Hmm. . . Tell you what – a king should be gracious. She could be a prize of office. A reward for my most loyal servant, the famous earl of bloody Niflagard,' he said, grandly. 'And other stink-holes he'd care to conquer. The noble lord Erlan – son of no one, heir to nowhere in particular. There you are – what a generous king I'd be!'

'Reckon I'd be warmer sharing my bed with a block of ice.'

The two of them laughed long and loud.

'What's so amusing?' a soft voice sounded behind them.

They turned as Lilla nudged her horse between theirs.

'This one's foolishness isn't for your ears, princess.'

'Sometimes there's great wisdom hidden in great folly.'

'Then Kai must be the wisest man in the kingdom.'

Lilla laughed and Erlan discovered that it was a beautiful sound – free and fresh and full of life. *She should do it more often,* he thought.

'Hey, it's not *that* funny,' protested Kai, as Lilla struggled to recover herself. 'Now if you'll excuse me, my lady. I must be *alone*.' He gave a mocking little bow, pulled off to one side and dismounted, already unbuckling his belt.

'A friend is a valuable thing,' said Lilla, as they watched him disappear off into the trees in a hurry.

'So it is. You should try it yourself.'

Her mouth only twitched in reply.

'How's your father?'

'Stronger today. In his limbs, at least. His breathing is still weak. Sometimes he coughs blood. But the draught I gave him is helping.'

Erlan sucked on his teeth. 'Well – a long life to him.'

She looked at him, scanning his face for sincerity, apparently unsure.

'I mean it. My life is bound to his now.' He glanced back at the slumped figure of the king. He had to admit that, just now, the withered old man looked a pitiful sort of protector.

Lilla gazed up at the wind gusting in the trees. 'I fear what will become of this land when he dies.'

'I suppose your brother will become king and rule as your father does.'

'He may rule, but not like my father. A son is not his father.

When kings die, bonds of fealty are tested. And kingdoms quickly fall.'

'Are there any to challenge the Sveärs?'

She scoffed as if she couldn't believe his naivety. 'Many! There are always many. But the most jealous are blood kin.'

'You mean the Wartooth's line?'

'You know about that?' She sounded surprised.

'I heard a little talk. That and your father nearly took my head for being King Harald's catspaw.'

'You're lucky he didn't.'

'As are you.'

She ran a tongue across her dry lips. 'I suppose so,' she said, eyeing him carefully. 'The jealousy of kings is long-lived and never simple. In the times of our fathers, there wasn't the peace we have now. My grandfather was a great king. His power spread beyond Sveäland to Denmark and the lands of Eastern and Western Gotars.'

'Ivar Wide-Realm?'

'Indeed. So named because far and wide, kings paid him tribute. He lived long. Long enough to outlive his first wife, who'd given him a daughter called Autha.'

'The Deep-Minded.'

'So you know all this?'

'Some – but little more.'

'He married Autha to King Rorik of Denmark and they had a son called Harald. Later Ivar took another. . . My grandmother.'

'But they were never married.'

Lilla looked up. A nerve pricked. She shook her head.

'So both wine and mud run in those royal veins of yours,' he teased.

'You think I care about that,' she snapped. 'Except that it gives other fools reason to slander my father's name.' Her eyes fixed his. 'They call him the Bastard King, but there was never born a bastard so noble. And as for my grandmother – she was a matchless woman. She had more dignity in her little finger than the blood of a dozen kings or queens.'

'So why didn't he marry her?'

'For no better reason than he was a stubborn fool.'

'But she gave him a son. Your father.'

'Yes. For that he was grateful.'

'So where did the bad blood between them arise?'

Her brow furrowed as she told how Autha had demanded that her father name her heir to his realm as his only legitimate child. Ivar was riled and instead named Sviggar heir, and schemed to murder her husband and take Denmark for himself.

'He murdered his own daughter's husband?'

Lilla nodded.

'Small wonder she hated him.'

'There were wars. First in Denmark and then across the East Sea in Estland and beyond. Harald, Autha's son, won great fame for himself there, as did my own father. But this strife came to an end when Ivar died suddenly. He drowned off his boat one night, but no one knows how.'

Afterwards the young Sviggar had returned to Sveäland to secure his throne, while Autha sent Harald home to Denmark to take up his inheritance. Lilla sighed as she came to the end of her story. 'There he now rules – over Danes and Eastern Gotars. And my father kept Sveäland and draws tribute from the Western Gotars.'

This was all new to Erlan. He had heard of the Wartooth, of course, but never how he had come by the Danish crown.

'And now there's peace between your lines.'

'For now – yes. . .'

'You think it will hold?'

'I don't know.'

'Would Harald still try to take your father's kingdom?'

'Harald isn't strong enough to do that. As for my father, he's long lost his appetite for finishing Autha's line.'

'So a balance is struck.'

'While my father lives. And if my brother Staffen had lived. . . He understood the limits of the kingdom's power. Oh, he was conceited, but he wasn't stupid, nor blinded by grand ideas.'

'And Sigurd?'

'He's not the same. He always speaks of the "true kingdom" – the Wide-Realm of our grandfather, in which Danes and Gotars and Sveärs were all under one king. That's how he believes the kingdom should be and he's forever goading my father into restoring it.'

'And what do you think?'

She laughed. Again he was struck by its sweet sound. 'What a strange question!'

'Why?'

'One thing you learn as a girl raised in the halls of kings – it's not a woman's place to speak openly her opinions on realms and war.'

'Only whisper them into their menfolk's ears at night, perhaps?' He smiled. 'Is that not a woman's skill? To make a man believe her thoughts are his own?'

'Are you so distrustful of us?'

'Some of you.'

'Well, you needn't fear on my account,' she smiled. 'Kingdoms are ideas in the heads of men seeking glory. I care not for ideas, but for people. For my folk and family and those I love. If I want glory, I need look no further than the woods I walk in or the first glimpse of a sunrise.'

'Men die for glory. Would you die for those you love?'

She thought for a moment, and then said, 'Yes. . . Yes, I would.'

'Hel of a gale up!' They turned to see Finn smiling at them from atop his grey mare. It was true – the whistle of the wind overhead seemed to be getting louder all the time. 'How's the arm?' he asked Erlan.

'Stiff. Sore.'

'Well, what wound isn't? But you're a big lad now, eh?' He leaned over and thumped Erlan on the back. 'If it's not keeping you from amusing our fair princess here, I won't be worried on your account.'

'I'm about as far from fair as ever I've been,' said Lilla, demurely.

'And yet a lot closer than most women are ever like to get.'

She gave a flick of a smile in reply.

'What about him?' Erlan nodded at the king. 'Are you worried on his account?'

'I'm always worried on his account,' joked Finn. 'But you're right. I doubt he can go much further this evening. We're losing light fast.'

'Seems we cover less ground each day,' said Erlan.

'Well, the days are getting shorter.'

'It'll soon be the winter solstice,' observed Lilla.

'Yep,' replied Finn. 'By rights, we should be wrapped up cosy in our halls, toasting our way through the long nights and feasting on a fat Yuletide hog. Hel's teeth – I can't remember a night out here I haven't dreamed of getting home. One thing that wife of mine can do is keep a man warm in bed!'

'We'll reach there soon,' said Lilla.

'Not soon enough for me,' he grinned.

'You surprise me,' said Erlan. 'Didn't you want to join Bodvar and his men?'

'I suppose there was a time I might have wanted to,' admitted Finn, cheerfully. 'But a man can't do everything. And I realized long ago, if you miss one fight, there's usually another round the corner. Besides which, once you've figured where your duty lies and you stick to it, life becomes a lot simpler. Mine – for good or ill – is beside that fella.' He tipped his head at Sviggar.

He seemed to have all the answers. Erlan found himself envying Finn his untroubled mind.

Behind them, there was a thud of hoofbeats approaching. Kai rode up at a canter, shot straight past the king and pulled up beside them, eyes wide.

'What the Hel's up with you?' asked Erlan.

'There's something out there,' Kai gasped breathlessly.

'Out where?' demanded Finn.

'Back there,' he puffed, pointing off into the gloom to their rear. 'I heard something moving around. I swear!'

'There's nothing out in this bloody wilderness.'

'I know I heard something!'

'Probably a snow fox.'

'It wasn't,' insisted Kai. 'It was much bigger than that.'

'Ha!' snorted Finn. 'Well – there's no need to be jumpy. We're a dozen armed men. No beast would take us on. Anyhow, whatever it was, you and your bare arse probably frightened it off already.'

But Kai looked anything but reassured. Finn laughed and shoved him. 'Your face!' He shook his head with mirth. 'I was like that when I was a lad. This time of year, my mother warned us not to get caught outside on a winter's night like this. Used to turn my liver white with her tales of the Wild Hunt. You heard of it?'

'Maybe,' said Erlan. 'You mean Odin's Hunt?'

Finn nodded, smiling. 'Aye – some call it that. She'd tell us bairns if we ever heard the sound of thunderous hooves and terrible cries and whoops in the treetops, we were to throw ourselves flat on the ground and keep our eyes tight shut. 'Cause anyone who happened to look up, curious at what was all the racket, was like to have his soul snatched away, scooped up by High God Odin himself, riding like fury at the head of the hunt, with his bloodthirsty maids and heroes in his wake, all baying like mad bloody hounds. And that poor bastard would drop stone dead and be found next day stiff as a post.' He gave Kai a wink. 'Not a merry prospect, you'll agree. We once played a trick on my baby brother and scared the poor little bugger so bad, he soiled himself. Oh, we got a beating off my mother I never forgot. Gods, she was a tough one though!' He laughed to himself.

Erlan had heard tales like it, sat at Tolla's knee beside the hearths of Vendlagard. He felt a stab of longing for home. For its worn old smells and familiar voices. *Never going back*, he reminded himself.

524

Never is a long time. . .

Kai wasn't looking any happier. But before he could reply, the wind licked up as wild a gust as they'd heard, blasting at the pines, tossing the treetops till there wasn't a flake of snow left on them.

A gale was on them and Erlan saw Finn was about to speak when, all of a sudden, the whistle and howl dropped to nothing. Total stillness. . .

The stillness of the grave.

The companions swapped uneasy glances. And then, out of the silence rose a whine, faint at first, then louder and louder, till it was high and piercing sharp through the dead air.

'What the Hel is that?' murmured Kai.

In answer, somewhere off in the thickening gloom, something started barking. . . then another bark replied, much fainter.

'You hear that?' asked Kai, wide-eyed.

'We're not bloody deaf,' said Erlan.

'One of them is near,' said Finn, unslinging his bow. 'That other's further off.'

'Is that a wolf or a dog?' asked Lilla.

'Out here, likely a wolf,' said Finn. 'But that other sound. . .' He grimaced, and the whining droned on, high overhead.

'We should get to higher ground,' said Erlan. 'And quickly. We need fire.' The last of the light would be gone soon and they hadn't a torch alight between them. A little way ahead to the right was the outline of a rise in the ground.

'There!' pointed Finn. Higher, the slope gathered into a broad knoll, at the top of which Erlan could make out a thinning in the trees and a jagged outcrop of large rocks. 'Head for those rocks.'

'My father,' exclaimed Lilla, twisting round. 'I must go to him.'

But Finn was already wheeling. 'I'm with him, my lady – don't fear. Go with Erlan. We'll be close behind.'

Shouts passed round the company, and one by one they broke off and followed Erlan up the slope. The crunch of snow and crack of fallen branches under-hoof sounded loud in the still air.

'Go ahead,' he called to Kai. 'Start a fire, quick as you can.' Kai nodded, kicking on. 'A big one!' he yelled. 'You go with him, Princess.'

'What about you?' she cried.

'I'll be right behind you. Now go!'

Lilla did as he bid, while he turned to look back. He could just make out the other riders, and the gaggle of men and mounts around the king. There were a dozen men, plus him and Kai, to guard the king and his daughter. He tried counting them off, shadow by shadow, but the trees obscured much, and the gloom was bleeding every outline into darkness.

The barking had stopped. Maybe the wolves or wild dogs or whatever had moved on. But it was better to be cautious. A rider passed him, then another. He recognized the brothers Beran and Jovard.

He had turned to follow them when a terrifying scream rent the night. He felt his horse shudder under him.

Is that a man's voice? It sounded again and again. Horrible shrieks punctuated by imploring whimpers that communicated only one thing – unspeakable, agonizing pain.

'Shit,' he whispered, putting his heels to his animal's flanks, heading uphill. Ahead the shadows of the rocks loomed out of the forest, and then he was passing through a gap between two of them onto the summit of the knoll.

He saw Kai on foot, hastily throwing down an armful of branches on a surprisingly sizeable pile of wood. *The lad works fast.* No doubt of that. Nearby Lilla was holding the horses. He jumped down.

'Let's have that fire started, Kai.' He was trying to keep his voice steady, but he wouldn't be happy till they had a blaze going.

'What's that noise? What's happening?' Even in the gloom, Kai's face was pale with fear.

'Quick as you can, lad.' Kai obliged, dropping to his knees and getting to work with his flint and firesteel. The sparks shone bright as new stars in the gathering darkness.

Other riders were coming through the gap now, and at last Finn and the king appeared. The men already afoot went to the king and helped him down. 'See to it every man is here,' ordered Sviggar, voice rough as rust.

The screaming had stopped. So too the whining. It seemed like the whole forest was holding its breath.

'Sellvar is missing,' said Finn. 'I count thirteen beside the king and the princess. You?'

Erlan scanned the men. 'Aye – the same. Did you see him?'

'Not I.'

'He was in the rear,' offered Jovard, the younger of the brothers. 'I heard him following behind us.'

Well, he wasn't there now. Wherever he was, Erlan didn't imagine he'd make a pretty sight.

One of the other men cursed. Lilla asked what was going on.

'We don't know yet. But we should secure this place.'

Erlan looked around the circle of the outcrop. As Kai's fire took bite, the shadows turned to pitch, but the flames also revealed the ground they'd chosen. They were inside a kind of enclosure, formed by two massive curved boulders bulging out of the ground like granite garlands around the crown of the hill.

'Is this the only way up here?' He pointed at the gap they'd just ridden through.

'There's another gap on the north side,' answered Kai, who'd been scavenging around for wood.

Erlan limped a few paces north and could make out the second gap, perhaps twenty feet across. The southern gap was no more than a dozen. Inside this outer perimeter the ground rose higher, peaking in a steep-sided granite platform with three gullies running to its summit.

'Whatever comes up this hill, we hold them at this outer ring. If we're overrun here, we fall back to the summit. Finn – you take that larger gap to the north.'

Finn barked a sarcastic laugh. 'My thanks for that, friend.'

'Take six with you.'

He named Gakki, Jovard, Falger, Manulf, Dani. . . and Kai.

The men began separating. 'If there's any fighting to be done, I'm doing it with my brother,' insisted Jovard.

'Fine,' said Erlan. 'Beran, you go with them. Dani – you're with me.' Danel the Sami herdsman, a bead-eyed terrier of a man who could take a crow on the wing with knife or arrow, nodded. 'We'll take the southern gap with Vakur, and the rest.' A burly brute draped in cowhide swung his axe up to his shoulder. The others divided accordingly and went off to their places.

The king was seated awkwardly on the stone jutting from the earth. 'Lord, you stay close to the fire. Lady Lilla with him.'

'You know,' said Finn, scratching his chin. 'He made me swear an oath I wouldn't leave his side.'

'Best way you can protect him is to see nothing comes through that gap.' Erlan pointed north into the menacing darkness.

'No, no,' protested Sviggar, 'I'll not sit here idle.' Though he looked haggard. 'You need me to fight.'

'We don't know what's needed yet, my lord. Might be we sit watch through the night and no more. For now, you should rest here by the fire.' With a grunt, the king acquiesced, settling back on his stone.

'And the horses?' asked Lilla.

Erlan considered their animals. *Aye – what the Hel could be done with them?* That much horseflesh could cause serious disruption if there was a fight coming. And likely, they'd be far more trouble to the defenders than to anything attacking out of the dark. There were a couple of saplings straining out of the earth near the granite summit.

'Tether them to those.' Lilla looked where he was pointing and nodded, understanding. She went to the horses, then stopped. Looked back. He could see in her eyes they had the same thought. 'Erlan – if it *is* the Vandrung. . . They aren't like the others.'

'I know.' He held her eyes a moment longer and turned away. 'Just see to your father.'

'Be careful,' he heard her call.

Be careful? That was the one choice this night would *not* leave him.

'See anything?' he asked when he reached his place at the southern gap. Dani's crouched silhouette was peering into the darkness, his bow across his knee.

'Nope.' The Sami spat sourly into the snow. 'Whole lot of black is all.'

'Keep watching.' Erlan unslung his shield from his back and drew out Wrathling. He looked at the blade's dull sheen. *Demon's bane.* A fair new name for the sword, he reckoned. *If I ever get to use it.* His shield weighed heavy on his wound, but he gritted against the pain. There'd be time enough for healing if they ever got away from this place.

He crouched beside Dani. Beyond he could see nothing but the tall shadows of the trees and the pale snow clinging to their branches. Around him, the others readied their weapons for the watch.

'Going to be a long night,' muttered Vakur. The big man was fairly bristling with steel – a huge axe in his hand, a sword on his back with a spear leaning against the rock.

'Who can bloody sleep in this cold anyway?' replied Dani.

Suddenly, a shout went up from the north. 'I see them! I see them!'

Kai's voice.

Erlan looked ahead. 'Be ready,' he whispered, squeezing his hilt tighter.

And then the darkness came alive.

CHAPTER FORTY

One moment the night was a sea of blackness, the next the shadows had sucked together into dozens of wild figures. There was a yell, high and grating, answered by another, and another, until the forest was a din of inhuman cries.

Beside Erlan, Dani strung an arrow and stabbed a handful of others into the snow. 'Where the Hel are your bows, lads?' A fair question.

Dani loosed the first shaft.

'Too soon!' Erlan hissed as the thing skittered off, harmless.

'Big bastards, eh?' growled Vakur, hefting his shield.

'Quick too,' said another named Foldurr.

So these were the Vandrung. The bastard offspring of the demon's seed. Erlan could see them now, filthy hair jangling, brutish blackened blades, outsized limbs twisted and bulging, clothed in little more than sacking.

A different foe from the pallid Nefelung.

Dani snatched a second arrow and loosed it. This one told, slamming a Vandrung flat, clawing at his throat. To the north,

Erlan heard the whoops and war cries of Sviggar's other men.

The screams grew louder as the first wave approached. 'Keep firing!' Another fell and over the tumbling body leaped the foremost Vandrung with a savage shriek. Erlan braced his bad leg, gripping his shield.

'See you in Valhalla for a cask of Odin's ale,' laughed Vakur, and then the Vandrung hit.

There was a shriek and a streak of metal. Erlan raised his shield, the blow shuddering through wood and bone. He knocked it away, lunged for the screaming face, felt Wrathling scythe flesh. The Vandrung fell choking, but there was another at once.

Vakur was bellowing like an ox, axe whirling at the onrushing bodies. Erlan smelled foul flesh, flipped his shield, driving the rim into a snarling face. Another jumped into the gap; he kicked hard, slamming his boot into a Vandrung's chest.

Sveär voices were baying all around. He heard the twang of Dani's bow, his yell of triumph as another Vandrung fell. The din was appalling with snarls and screams, the clang of metal and thud of wood. Erlan struck a shadow with pitiless eyes, spattering blood, glimpsed a flash and threw himself against the granite, feeling the wind of the blade and a shower of ice. His shield arm screamed with pain. He turned, smashed away the sword, shoved with his shield, throwing the Vandrung into another.

Dani was there – face a mask of savagery – his long-knife slashing into a Vandrung's neck. But before he'd turned, another was on him. Erlan yelled a warning, but the blow caught him. Dani screamed, black steel slicing his legs. He fell to his knees. The Vandrung lifted his sword to finish him, but Vakur's axe was crashing down. The arm fell in the snow, pissing blood.

There were more, surging into the gap. Dani was clawing at the snow, trying to pull clear. Erlan threw his shield behind him, seized Dani, dragged him over two dead Vandrung into the enclosure. The Sami was babbling murderous curses.

'There's more coming – look out!' he yelled. Erlan had already seen them, snatched up a spear and lurched forward. Ahead was a rush of bodies, wild faces and limbs – he slashed his sword, arm jarring against Vandrung iron, then lunged with the spear.

The point found flesh. He screamed, twisting the blade deeper, but the shaft was wrenched away and a body hit him, knocking him down. His vision swam, his ears rang. Soft through the ringing came snarls from the creature on top of him. He butted hard, smashing the Vandrung's nose. It reared up. Erlan saw its short crude blade. Saw the hate in its eyes – and suddenly he was tired.

Bone weary.

He felt thunder in the ground and thought it strange.

The blade was falling. He lifted his wounded arm – he had nothing else to offer. There was a deafening crash, a shower of snow, a shadow flying over him and the Vandrung was gone. The thunder was all about him.

He lay, dazed, wondering why he wasn't dead.

Then he realized the thunder was the beat of hooves.

Gakki was dead, his head split in two.

Manulf was dying, guts half-spilled in the snow.

Jovard's face was a mask of pain, one side slathered in blood. And outside the cut were the bodies of a dozen or more of *them*.

The Vandrung. . . They were ugly sons of bitches. That hadn't stopped Finn from killing a heap of them.

'You sure know how to use that thing,' said Kai, nodding at Finn's bow.

'Not my first time,' returned Finn, with a rueful grin. 'Could be the last, though.'

Kai was breathing heavily. He didn't know why the Vandrung hadn't pressed home their attack. But he was mighty glad. 'Where did they go?'

Finn wearily pushed a braid behind his ear. He was sweating, despite the cold. 'Not far is my guess. Doubtless, they'll be back.'

'We'll never last the night,' said Beran quietly. He was hunkered, nursing his axe, staring into the darkness.

Finn gave him an encouraging tap on the shoulder. 'You won't mind if I give it a try though, eh?'

'Horn half-full, brother,' said Jovard, his blood-slicked grimace ghastly in the dim light. 'You always were a gloomy bastard!'

Kai was regretting his wish for a proper fight. He'd always imagined it different, with him all fired up and brave. Instead he'd shaken with utter terror, start to finish.

At least he hadn't run. That was a great feat. Still, it wasn't like there was anywhere to run to.

It had been a mad, arse-loosening tempest of shouts and shrieks and shoving and sticking and slashing and the gods knew what else. By the time the first Vandrung had reached the gap, seven lay dead to Finn's arrows. But the rest had arrived quick enough, and there ensued hand-to-hand combat the likes of which had never yet disturbed his worst nightmares.

Manulf was groaning.

'Poor son of a bitch,' muttered Beran. 'Someone should finish him.'

'You gonna do it?' said his brother, irritably.

Beran only hugged his axe closer.

It made little difference. Manulf wouldn't groan much longer. Kai had never liked the man, but this was a fate beyond any he would've wished him. He wasn't exactly sure how he wasn't in the same state. His sword was bloody and his left arm ached like a bastard so he must have taken some blows. But he could have sworn to precisely nothing of what just occurred. Only that when the ugly brutes pulled back, he was still there. Still breathing.

'What do we do now?' he asked Finn.

'We wait.'

He was afraid that'd be the answer. He didn't fancy sitting all night in the freezing cold, while nauseating fear chewed its way through his innards. He'd rather the thing reached its conclusion. Except there was only one conclusion likely to be reached, and he had to admit. . . it wasn't that appealing.

He watched Finn count up his arrows and curse.

'What is it?'

Finn gave a bitter snort. 'Couple more attacks like that and I'll be chucking snowballs.'

'Does no one else have any?'

'Only Danel, over with your master.' He winked. 'Funny thing, luck. Never enough archers around when you need 'em.'

'Shall I go ask him?' At least it would give him something to do. Better than this awful waiting.

'My guess is his need is as great as ours. 'Less he's dead.' He turned to gaze out the gap and swore again. 'Must be fifteen shafts out there.' He shot Kai a bitter grin. 'Not a lot of fucking use to us any more.'

Kai followed his gaze. He could just make out the shape of a Vandrung body a few paces down the slope beyond the cut, an arrow jutting out of his chest.

'How many have you left?'

'A round dozen.'

Kai grunted. A dozen wouldn't go far if they came again. Out in the shadows everything was quiet. No whining, no wind. Nothing. And looking at that nearest arrow, a mad idea entered his head. He swallowed hard. 'I'll go.'

'What?'

'I'll go out there and fetch you that one. Here, take this.' He shoved his shield at Finn, stuck his sword in the snow, and before Finn could say a word he was hopping over strewn bodies through the cut. He heard Finn's fevered whispering, but shut it out. Strangely, it felt better to be doing something.

He snuck to the edge of the cut and stopped, sniffing the air like a fox. He smelled pines. And blood.

He scanned the trees for danger. They must be out there. But they weren't moving a muscle. The nearest body was a few feet away. Teasingly close.

He skulked over. Hel, the fire must have lit up his silhouette clear as the sun, but he could do nothing about that. Then he was there beside the body.

He dropped to his knees and seized the arrow, half-buried in the Vandrung's chest. The muscle was hard as oak. But the wound still oozed blood. He tugged. It resisted. He tugged harder and suddenly the barbs gave and the shaft released with a sucking noise.

He nearly whooped with delight. One arrow was a small victory, but it was something. He looked back, ready to scurry to safety, but then his eye caught another shape a few yards down the slope. Another shaft in another motionless hulk.

One more couldn't hurt. . .

He hesitated, listening for the slightest sound, and hearing nothing, snuck over. In a few moments, he had his second prize. He grinned. With Finn's sharp shooting, each arrow was another kill. He listened again. Nothing.

Right, my friend. This is when you earn your bread.

A short while later, he pulled the sixth arrow from a Vandrung's throat. It was grisly work. His hands were sticky with blood. But he had quite the collection now. He'd cursed when he found two arrows beyond repair, but luck had flicked him a scrap – he'd pulled another couple from the same tree.

He glanced back. He was maybe fifty paces out. A bit of a run, now he thought about it. But the last body was only another twenty feet further on, slumped in a shallow gully.

Last one. And he would have it.

When he reached the gully, he found the snow had drifted and his legs sank in deep. He laid his arrows aside and set about freeing the last one. It was lodged tight in the side of the creature's rib cage. He tugged and twisted, wiggled and wrenched, but the thing stuck fast.

Still, he wasn't giving up that easy. The reek of the body was overpowering, but he managed to get on top of it to give himself more purchase. He was about to give another tug when he heard a noise that stopped his heart.

A low bellow some way off in the trees, so rasping it sounded like a wood-saw.

He first thought of an ox, albeit one that sounded mighty unhappy and – surely – very lost. Whatever it was, he needed to get out. He yanked again and still it wouldn't budge.

There was another bellow. This time with a cracking of wood and heavy blowing. He peered down the slope and saw a hulking shadow lumbering through the trees.

'Kai!' It was Finn.

The bellow again, angrier this time. 'Kai! Get back here!'

'Just a second!' he shouted, wrestling even harder with the shaft, cursing its damned obstinacy.

'Leave it!'

This time it was a roar, and for a moment, the shadow detached from the surrounding trees.

What. The. Hel.

A bear. The biggest bloody bear he'd ever dreamed of. And coming his way.

Suddenly, there were other shadows advancing out of the darkness towards him. 'Time to go,' he grimaced, with one last desperate tug. All at once, the arrow came away, the force toppling him off the body and into the drift.

'Seven!' he cried, and could hear the snarls and yells of the Vandrung over the bear's bellowing, as he scrabbled about in the powder, clutching his prize. Then, above them all, sounded the howls of wolves.

'You must be joking,' he moaned. But he knew that sound better than any other.

'Kai!' Finn screamed, as he struggled to extricate his legs. 'Get back here! They're coming!'

'Gods blind me – you don't say!' At last he touched solid ground, was out of the gully in a blink, snatched his heap of arrows and ran.

He didn't look back – mustn't look back. But he could hear them, closing in, thumping footsteps, and they were a sight faster than his. Only thirty paces to go and he could hear a Vandrung's panting breath.

Twenty paces and there were the moon faces of Finn and his companions ahead. The arrows rattled in his hand. Fifteen and the raucous breath behind filled his ears. Ten and he could stand it no longer. He glanced back and saw the looming shadow nearly on him, cruel mouth gaping, black blade scything down. He closed his eyes, knowing his last moment had come.

Something whipped past his cheek, the air snapped, there was a grunt and the footsteps behind him ceased.

Half the horses were gone.

But then half the men were dead.

Lilla had listened to the opening onslaught, the clash of steel and iron, the din of Sveär shouts mingled with the bestial wails of the Vandrung. She'd never felt so helpless before something she didn't understand. If these were the creatures that separated from the scavenging party that carried her to the holes of Niflagard, they had grown in number. Or else her delirium had been worse than she knew.

There were dozens. Her gaze had flicked frantically, north to south, as she tried to relay to her father what was happening. At first, she was sure the north must cave as the Vandrung rabble threw themselves into the wider gap. But it was the south that had faltered. She saw one man fall, then another, and then the horrible creatures pouring into the breach.

Her instinct had been to run and throw her spear into the fight, but her eye had chanced upon the herd of nervous horses pulling at their reins. Without a second thought, she'd untethered the beasts tied to one sapling and with cries and slaps cajoled them down into the southern gap.

The animals had reared in panic, barrelling into the Vandrung at a gallop, sweeping them aside like autumn leaves. It was enough to tip the balance, and next thing she knew the Vandrung were falling back, leaving their dead and soon-to-be-dead companions to the wrath of her father's men.

She had noticed Erlan picking himself up from the carnage and was surprised at the relief that washed through her. But relief couldn't live long that night.

Had it been hours? Or only a few snatched moments? She couldn't have said. Time was bleeding along with the bodies. The night was black as ever. But all at once, the forest was a storm of furious sound and they were back, the shouts of the men at the northern gap more desperate than ever.

'What can you see?' cried her father, looking to the north, fists bunched on his knees.

'More of them, Father. The men are hard pressed.'

In truth, all she could see was a mayhem of limbs and shadows. On one side, Finn shot arrow after arrow in a pitiless rhythm. The others – those still alive – were laying into the Vandrung with desperate blows, though even then, she watched a warrior skewered to the ground. Another dispatched the Vandrung at once, but they could ill afford to lose any man.

Her lips moved in a feverish stream, but even she doubted any magic could work to save them.

Then there was a warning shout, the ragged line of warriors threw themselves aside and into the enclosure ran a bear.

Its hulking frame dwarfed the reeling men around it; its bellow, exposing fangs big as daggers, struck awe in her heart. The bear spun at once, lashing out at a warrior's shield, sending him flying on his back. In a heartbeat, the animal was on him. Lilla saw the huge skull shake and jerk away, taking the man's throat with it. The bear kicked him aside, limp as a doll.

Her father was on his feet. 'I must go.'

'Father, no – it's too dangerous.' She tried to push him back down onto the stone, but he had new strength in him she couldn't resist. 'You must live!'

'Some deaths offer the only way to live,' he said, touching her face, and drew out Bjarne's Bane – the sword of his father and of the line of Sveär kings before them. 'I must go.' And as he stood, sword raised, face hard as stone, she glimpsed the young warrior king he must have been. The sight silenced her.

Perhaps this is his fate. Who was she to turn him aside from destiny?

He raised his shield and hastened down the slope fast as age and fever would allow. She glanced south. Erlan and his men were sore pressed, cleaving about them like woodsmen. But their little band was few and growing fewer. She wondered what to do, and then grimaced, snatching up her spear.

If she was going to die here, it would be with her own blood. She stumbled after her father.

Ahead King Sviggar's battle cry sounded fierce over all that noise. The bear turned, perceiving a new threat. So too

Finn, hearing his lord's voice, but there was no time for him to protest. Lilla saw him loose a last arrow and draw his sword.

The bear squared up to her father, its muzzle dripping blood, eyes menacing as winter. The king drew himself to his full height and screamed in its face.

It was pure madness. *But then what's left us but madness now?*

The bear's hackles bristled. It opened its mouth and roared. Yet her father was undaunted, slashed Bjarne's Bane at the massive head. The animal batted it away and dashed forward to butt him. His shield took the brunt, the force tossing him in the air, landing him on his backside in the snow.

'Father!' she cried, fearing for his throat, but Finn was there, driving his point into the beast's shoulder. The bear reared, lashing out at Finn, sending him tumbling against the rock. Another warrior leaped forward: Beran – face a mask of dread as he beheld the beast. He slashed wildly, caught the animal a glancing blow; there was a fearful ripping sound – the long claws swiping through his head.

Beran fell back, clutching his face, dying. But he had saved his king, if only for an instant: Sviggar was on his feet. Lilla was still behind the bear, her spear weighing heavy as lead. Her father raised his shield, sword ready. Finn was yelling, struggling to untangle himself and get back into the fight.

Full of fear, Lilla went closer, so close she could smell its sour hide. The bear was towering, her father stepping in, his face fey as the dawn. She snatched a breath and then buried the spear with all her strength into the bear's side.

The animal roared, twisting in agony, tearing the spear from her hands. Its huge haunches loomed over her. She tried to retreat, vision swimming, but the snow dragged at her. She felt herself toppling, heard her father's yell, saw the hulking beast turning.

And suddenly there was a deadening thud, her head exploded with pain, and she saw nothing but darkness.

'To the hilltop!' cried Erlan. 'Fall back!' There was no one left to hear but Vakur.

The burly warrior yelled in reply, which Erlan took for understanding. The rest lay broken among the wreckage of Vandrung bodies. Dani's dead eyes stared from a bloodless face. Foldurr's throat was leaking blood into the snow like a broken pitcher.

'Back! Back!' he screamed again. Every limb burned with fatigue. He lunged, driving Wrathling through the belly of a Vandrung harrying Vakur.

Vakur cried something and took off uphill.

Whatever chance they stood on the summit, it had to be better than here. After that. . . *a cripple can't run.*

With the Vandrung gurgling at his feet, he had a few moments. He set off, the pain in his ankle dogged as ever. Vakur was halfway to the summit. Ahead, Erlan saw a huge silhouette in the snow. Beside it was the king, screaming like a man who had lost his mind, his face a demon's dance of bloodlust, fever and fear.

Erlan suddenly saw the body was an enormous bear. A sword-tip protruded from its spine, and in its side, a long-spear. Sviggar wrenched free the sword, and without another glance, ran to something smaller lying beside the bear.

543

'Erlan! You're alive!' Erlan turned and saw Kai, hardly recognizable, his tunic a butcher's bib, face a frenzy.

'Get to the summit,' he shouted. 'All of us – now!'

'Help me,' wailed the king. He'd dropped his shield and was pawing at the heap in the snow. Finn was with him.

'Lord, we must go now!' cried Erlan. 'They're coming from the south.'

'My daughter, my daughter.' And Erlan saw her lying there. Her eyes were closed, her honey hair fanned against the snow. Sviggar tugged at her. She flopped over and Erlan saw a dark streak of blood down her face. 'Help me,' Sviggar moaned.

'She's dead, sire,' cried Finn. 'Please – we must fall back.'

'No!' The king was still trying to get hold of her. Erlan saw he wasn't going to leave her, dead or alive. He sheathed his sword and dropped to his knees. 'Take her legs,' he yelled at Finn.

The bowman swore, tossed his shield and scooped up her legs. 'Go – now!'

Erlan needed no second telling. Vakur was already up the gully and atop the stone platform, cursing them to move faster. Jovard was alive, untangling himself from the harvest of bodies. Just ahead of him ran Kai.

Erlan reached the gully. Scrabbling backwards, he could see the others following. The king, full of anguish; Kai, a dozen paces back; then Jovard. Something skittered over the rocks to one side. He looked and saw two shadows scampering down into the enclosure.

'Wolves!' he yelled. 'Kai!' There was nothing he could do. Only watch the boy turn to face them, and Jovard with him.

He heard Kai laughing madly. 'You think you can take me

now I've got me one of these?' yelled the boy, brandishing his sword. The first wolf never broke stride, hitting the ground and bounding straight at him. But what happened then surprised even Erlan. The wolf leaped for Kai's throat, but cool as you like, he stepped aside and whipped down his sword. There was a yelp and the wolf landed in a heap, one ear missing, along with half its head.

Jovard was squared up to the second wolf, which, seeing the other's fate, held back. 'Leave it,' screamed Erlan, reaching the summit.

'Put her down,' said Finn, and they lay her gently on the rocks. The archer had his bow unslung in a second.

Jovard was edging away from the wolf. Kai was yelling, trying to drag him back faster to the gully. The wolf ran at them. Jovard braced his shield, drew back his axe. The wolf took off. There was a streak of darkness. And then it skidded to their feet, dead – an arrow through its gullet.

'Nice,' Erlan muttered.

'Just lucky, I guess,' grinned Finn.

'Reckon we could all use some of that luck.' The king was bent over the princess, looking for signs of life, finding none. Erlan scanned the enclosure. The first of the Vandrung were through the gaps now, north and south. But they weren't running. They stalked over the bodies with an inexorability that was far more menacing, coming on like a black tide. The Sveärs had killed dozens, yet still there were dozens more.

'They're coming now,' he said simply, as Kai arrived gasping at the top, his shield gone, and Jovard leaning heavily on his arm. The king traced a finger down his daughter's face, then stood erect.

'This is a good place to die,' said the old man, nodding grimly. 'A time comes when a man has to look death in the face and say welcome.'

No one said anything. Erlan looked at Kai. The boy returned his gaze but the fear seemed to have gone from his face. He seemed only weary, and old beyond his years. 'No,' said Erlan. 'We're not dying today.'

Finn had a wan smile. 'Sad to say it, but he's right. We might take a few of these handsome bastards with us, but there's no hope for us but Odin's reward. Seems he's come for us after all.'

'No!' Erlan shook his head. 'We are going to live.' And now, above all, he knew he wanted to.

Kai nodded, his long mouth set with determination.

'I always thought you were a pair of madmen,' laughed Finn. 'Now I know it.'

'Make ready,' cried Sviggar. 'All of you die with honour and the Spear-God's blessing.'

And much good would it do them, thought Erlan. The fire was burning low, darkness squeezing back the guttering light. Why, he never knew, but his mind flew back to the sunset lookout over that snowbound wilderness. The beauty of that lonely land where silence reigned like a god.

Maybe silence could be his god. *A god who does not speak cannot lie*. A silent god.

He watched the Vandrung surround the hilltop, watched the circle of monstrous shadows tighten like a noose.

Maybe the silent god would help them now.

▪ ▪ ▪ ▪ ▪ ▪ ▪

She knows that silhouette. The sun is a glimmer through autumn leaves.
She calls for him to wait. That she is coming. He turns.

'Staffen!'

But he turns away at his name and walks on through the trees.
She's running now. Hurrying to him. Closer. Almost with him. A
thrill fills her heart to hold her brother's hand again. To hear his
voice.

But when she can almost touch him, he halts. He turns. He shakes
his head.

'Go back.' His mouth forms the words but there is no sound.

Her heart sinks.

The lips move again. 'Go back.'

She doesn't understand. 'What must I do?' she asks.

He says nothing. Only raises his horn to his lips, and blows and
blows. . .

Lilla's eyes started open. The darkness was heavier than before,
the dawn a long way off. Her body was cold, but her heart was
burning.

She sat up. Men surrounded her. Warriors, their faces just
visible, hard as idols. She looked again. Recognition began to
seep into her mind. *That one is Finn. That one, Kai. That one, the*
stranger.

The night was filled with screaming. But not from these
men. They waited silently. All around her, the screams drew
closer. She saw her father. Saw his bloodied sword, and there
at his belt, his horn.

Suddenly her will was focused, sharp and straight as an
arrow.

She got to her knees. Someone shouted. Her father turned. His face changed. He came towards her, reached for her, but she pushed his hand away, intent only on the horn.

Then she had it, wrenched it from his belt.

'What are you doing?' she heard him ask. But she didn't answer. She put the metal to her lips and blew a note that split the night.

At the first blast, they all turned. But she blew again and again and again, so hard her lungs must burst. Till at last she could blow no more.

For just a moment, the Vandrung's screaming ceased. And in the silence, muffled by the forest and the snow, came a reply.

A sister horn – long and low and steady. And then another.

The men around her stood still as statues, ears cocked. Suddenly, Erlan snatched the horn from her, put it to his lips and fetched a blast loud enough to summon summer.

Then the darkness was a gale of horn-song, sounding ever closer, and with it rose shouts and the thunder of hooves. Fire danced in the forest beyond the circle of rocks. On and on Erlan blew, and it seemed he would never stop. The screams of the Vandrung faltered.

'Odin's Hunt!' cried Finn, laughing.

And all at once through the gaps poured riders bearing fire and steel. The Vandrung quailed and began to fall back. But there was no escape. For the riders came on, lusting for blood and slaughter.

CHAPTER FORTY-ONE

D awn rose thin as gruel.
It revealed a grim sight.

Erlan limped behind the king, moving among the bodies cluttering the hilltop. A pair of fires blazed – one for the Sveär dead, one for the Vandrung – filling the air with their sickly sweet stench. One by one each body was dragged to its pyre.

But the bear carcass lay where it fell. It was strange almost beyond telling. A hulk of twisted limbs and thick hide, but its skull was changed.

The king and his attendants stood over it. Erlan had seen many sights to turn his stomach, but none so weird as the malformed human head sprouting from the haunches of a bear. Or some creature that used to be a bear.

'The wolves were shape-shifters too.' Finn wiped his mouth. 'Seems Prince Staffen is avenged.'

'He is,' said Sviggar. '*He must be.*' He turned away to a Vandrung body. Flipped the head with his boot. 'See how men become what they worship.'

Erlan saw. Certainly there was a cruelty in those lifeless features that no other face he'd ever seen had worn. But was it worship or the demon's seed? He scowled. What did it matter, so long as it burned with the others?

All of this must burn.

In their hour of need, it had not been Odin's Hunt that came to their aid, but the bloodied remnant of Bodvar's two hirds, returned from the pits of Niflagard. Their fury knew no sating: they hadn't stopped till the last Vandrung was slain.

Now morning had come, and when the last body was on the fire, the king took counsel.

'Good fortune brought you back to us, Bodvar.'

'Fortune for some, my lord. By no means all.' The earl's cheek was a maw of torn flesh. Many of his men returned with wounds far worse. Many hadn't returned at all.

'Is Heidrek dead?'

'Not when I left him, though he took hard cuts. He follows behind with the worst of the wounded.'

The king had regained some of his strength. His cough rattled away in his chest, but the worst of the fever seemed passed. 'Tell us what befell you.'

Bodvar took a long breath. 'You and your people are avenged, sire.' And they settled down to listen to Bodvar's account. He began with how they had come to the icefall and almost been confounded.

'Where's that lad of yours?' Bodvar asked Erlan.

Erlan nodded at the summit. 'Up there, mending the princess's head.'

Bodvar grunted. 'Well, he sealed that place tighter than a virgin's cunny.' It took them a day and a night to feed a fire

550

fierce enough, until at last it broke through the ice in a rush of sparks and smoke.

One by one, they clambered into the cavern. Then down they went into the putrid hole, men emptying their bellies, adding to the stench that grew stronger every step. When, by Bodvar's reckoning, they were still some way from the pits Erlan had described, they found a body. The torches revealed horrible wounds in its flesh, one leg ripped almost clean away. 'Seemed he'd crawled there from the deeper caverns, then died alone.'

'Was it like these?' asked the king.

Bodvar shook his head. 'Smaller than these. More like a man. We examined the body. The skin was pale as snow. Filthy – covered in sores and boils. But he had a man's features.'

'A Nefelung,' said Erlan.

'You know what they call themselves, stranger. I just say what we saw. Believe it or not, the sight heartened us. If they had the bodies of men, they could die like men.'

They had journeyed deeper, found more and more corpses – of men and women. All were disfigured by terrible wounds, fallen in pools of blood. And nearing the great chasm of pits, they heard noises, distant at first, which as they approached grew into shouts and shrieks, and the clash of iron. 'I sent two men ahead. They soon returned saying that, though the light was dim, the sounds were clear enough: a battle was raging.'

Bodvar ordered his men to pour into the great chasm and they came upon terrible slaughter. 'Hundreds of the smaller Nefelung set against the larger creatures like these,' he said.

'The Vandrung.'

'If you say so.'

Erlan wondered what had happened after his escape with Lilla and could only imagine the Nefelung thralls had finally turned on their tormentors.

'The pits were a swelter of bodies, tearing each other apart,' went on Bodvar. 'Some of the Nefelung had weapons, most had only their hands. But they had the numbers. Even so, they were taking it hard from these others. We didn't wait to see which would be left standing.' Bodvar had unleashed his men. Many Sveärs fell, but eventually their strength began to tell. They cleared each pit until neither Nefelung nor Vandrung were left alive. And afterwards, they went deeper still to be certain the last of them was slain.

'Did you find more?' asked the king.

'None alive. But the Norns have smiled on you, my lord. We found a chamber filled with gold.'

'Gold?' said Finn.

'Like the sound of that, do you lad?' Bodvar gave a dry chuckle. 'Aye – a hoard of gold such as you could never dream.'

'You don't know my dreams, Lord Bodvar,' laughed Finn. 'They're a place of endless wonder.'

'Doubtless. But the gold is real enough. Every man took as much as he could carry. It's all pledged to you, sire, since we fought in your name.' He nodded back over his shoulder. 'It follows on horseback with Heidrek and his men. Though I carried this as a token for you.'

He produced a thick golden torque necklace from his cloak and handed it to Sviggar, who turned it over in his hand. The great graven orbs of gold at each end shone in the dull morning light.

'It is weighty,' he exclaimed, the torque's yellow glow lighting up his beard. 'And. . . wondrous.'

'The best of the hoard, sire,' said Bodvar. 'The rest comes with Heidrek.'

'What else did you find besides?'

'Much, but all of it foul. Erlan and Princess Aslif were right. It were better left in that place. And now none of this enemy lives to trouble your land again.'

'Did you find a huge body?' asked Erlan. 'Of a man like a giant?'

'We saw many strange things. But not that.'

'Nor a head? A head like a boulder.' Erlan couldn't conceal the urgency in his voice. They must have seen it. It must have been there.

'Not a trace.'

Erlan fell into a brooding silence. *Was he mad?* He looked up to where Kai was tending to the princess. *No, she saw him too.* They had shared those fell visions. Those nightmares. They had been real – real as the black strips of hide swelling the pouch at his belt. That was all the proof he needed.

'How many men did you leave behind?' asked the king.

'When we regained the surface, we had seventy-four missing.'

'Seventy-four,' echoed Sviggar. 'From two hirds?' He shook his old head. 'That's a heavy toll.'

'Shouldn't we be glad for them, sire?' said Finn. 'They sit with the heroes already.'

'Doubtless you'd change places with any one of them,' said Bodvar.

'To be sure,' laughed Finn. 'Wouldn't you?'

Bodvar raised a sardonic eyebrow, but the king answered.

'We will see them honoured, as they should be.' Sviggar gave a bark of laughter and slapped Bodvar's back. 'You've done well, my good earl. Uncommon well!' Abruptly, his cough rattled in his chest. Finn reached for him.

'I'm fine, my boy.' He turned and spat to one side. 'Much better.' Flecks of crimson coloured the crisp white snow. 'We wait here for Heidrek. Send riders to him.'

'Already done,' said Bodvar.

'Excellent!' the king roared. 'Once he arrives, we ride for home. I've been away from my bed too damned long. Aye – and what's waiting for me in it, too!'

They didn't have long to wait. That afternoon, Heidrek and the stragglers caught up. The following morning, the whole company set out for the Uppland halls. Within another two days, they left behind the silent lands of lakes and forests for the hedgerows and fields of the western earls.

Two nights out from home, they even had the comfort of a roof overhead, bringing the king into even better health. And when they rode out on the last day, he was in fine spirits.

A winter sun blazed in the sky. The air was cold and a hoarfrost bejewelled every twig and stem.

Erlan rode a little distance behind the king, Kai alongside him. The boy had seemed distracted these last days. Erlan had often watched his ice-blue eyes gazing into the distance, vacant and dull, his lips moving but saying nothing. When he asked him what he was thinking, Kai would smile slyly and say, 'Oh, nothing.'

As Sviggar's Seat came into view, their pace quickened. The old king pushed on till he was riding at the head of his battered host, noble as any Sveär king had ever seemed. Horns heralded their approach and before long crowds of hall-folk appeared on the road to welcome their returning king.

But as they drew near the Sacred Grove, the king suddenly reined in, slowed to a walk and, abruptly, stopped.

The whole company stopped with him and Erlan saw at once what had brought him to a halt.

There, hanging in the still air from each of the nine boughs of the sacred oak, were the bodies of nine young women, garbed in white shifts, stiff from the frost. Their feet were naked, toes curled into fists. The hoarfrost had settled on their faces, forming glistening white crystals along their eyebrows and eyelashes and on the soft down of their cheeks. Their eyelids were all closed, as if shading nothing more than pale visions in a peaceful dream. Every one of them was beautiful.

'Who ordered this?' Sviggar's voice cut sharp as steel. '*WHO – ORDERED – THIS?*' he cried. But no one answered.

Suddenly there was a wail of despair. Finn leaped from his horse and ran into the grove.

Erlan watched him until figures appearing at the entrance to the hall distracted him. He recognized Prince Sigurd and with him his oathman, Vargalf. Two other men followed behind.

Sigurd raised his arm in welcome. 'Greetings, Father. And my sister too. What happy—'

'What is this?' bellowed Sviggar, pointing at the nine bodies.

Sigurd looked uncomprehending. 'It is a blood worship. You know this, Father.'

'I know *what* it is. *Why* is it? Who ordered it?'

'I did,' Sigurd began haltingly. 'You left me in command.'

'I left you to guard my halls, not to slaughter my people!'

'You were gone so long. You sent no word,' protested Sigurd. 'We knew nothing of whether you were in danger. Whether you would ever return or were already dead.' There was not a trace of contrition in his voice. 'We did what we could to give you victory.'

'Fool!' exclaimed Sviggar. 'We rode to stop more blood being spilled, and here you add nine to those already dead.'

'I consulted with the queen.'

'The queen?' raged Sviggar. 'I left *you* in charge of these halls. Not her!'

'And yet the runes said it must be so,' said a silken voice behind them. Erlan turned with the rest of Sviggar's retinue to see Queen Saldas standing on the edge of the company.

She wore a brilliant fur of the whitest winter fox. Her hair hung loose, gleaming like jetstone, a simple band of silver around her head, her green eyes levelled straight and steady at her husband.

'Saldas.' The name seemed to stick in his throat.

'Welcome home, my lord husband.' She bowed, bathing easily in the gaze of every man present. 'This blood worship was in service to you.'

The old king's glare was hard as flint. 'Did I not order before we departed that there was to be nothing of—'

'Did you not meet with success?' the queen interrupted, her gaze unwavering.

The king snorted. Hesitated. And with that pause, Erlan knew something had been won and something lost. 'This time the Norns wove victory for us. Yes.'

'The Norns?' Her voice bore more than a trace of scorn. 'It was thanks to the High God, whose favour *we* won for you. Your victory is the proof.' Her mouth curled in a most beguiling smile. 'So tell me, my lord – what is your complaint?'

The king glared at her, rage sparking in his face. Then he looked back to the grove. 'I grow weary of death,' he murmured. 'Of these gods who cannot be sated.' He turned to Sigurd. 'Cut them down at once.'

'As you wish.'

Sviggar lifted his voice for all to hear. 'Tonight, good comrades, you must rest. See your wounds are tended. And on the morrow we shall have a feast to remember. My daughter is returned to me and our land is rid of the shadow. We must feast!'

So saying, he rode on, his retinue following behind.

But Erlan couldn't take his eyes from the deathly circle of women. He remembered another group of womenfolk. Bound. Murdered. And for what? Only one answer made any sense. *Because this world is broken*. He felt sick to his bones.

'Erlan.' He turned, recognizing the soft burr of Lilla's voice. But she let her horse walk by, unchecked, only nodding at the sacred oak and its grim ornaments. 'We saved each other from the darkness below.' A sad smile flickered over her lips. 'Who will save us from the darkness within?' She rode on, not waiting for his answer.

'It is a pity.' Erlan looked down and saw Kai peering through his greasy hair at the white women, hanging like ghosts. 'Aye – a real pity.'

'You know any of them?'

'All of 'em,' replied Kai. 'The place will be a deal less pretty without 'em.' He shook his head.

'Well, you'll just have to miss them. . . Or forget about them.'

'Aye, I can forget,' said Kai. 'But he won't.'

Beside the sacred oak, Finn was standing beneath one of the women, hands raised, holding tight to her frosted toes. He was still. Calm. Not raging. No anger on his face beyond a small crease in his brow. Just gazing up at her, as though enchanted – for his wife was certainly beautiful. Erlan watched the clouds of Finn's breath. And just before he kicked on his horse, he saw a splinter of sunlight sparkle on the archer's cheek and fall to the ground.

CHAPTER FORTY-TWO

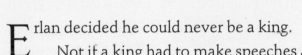

Erlan decided he could never be a king.

Not if a king had to make speeches as long as this one.

Sviggar must be getting tired up there, prating on, he thought. Certainly if Erlan's own body was any marker. He felt stiff as a post and raw as a skinned ox.

Maybe this is how it has to be: the greater the feast, the longer the speech.

And it was an undeniably great feast.

From the rafters hung war-banners with horned beasts and horned men dancing in threads of gold and scarlet. Along the walls were bright-rimmed buckler-shields scattering firelight to every corner of the feast-hall. Smoke billowed through the roof-cuts to the cold stars around burnished cauldrons, swinging like moons above blazing hearths.

When Sviggar had got to his feet, he'd interrupted a Hel of a din. These Sveär folk needed no lessons in carousing. In no time, the faces of men and women had flushed with honey-wine and ale. Horns and beakers were filled and drained, filled and drained. The place was agleam with smiles, awash with the smells of waxed leather; costly perfumes from the south mingled with roasting hogs and hens, honeyed beets and steaming breads, boiling cheeses and barley cakes, smoked fish and sweet-curds.

The noise was overwhelming. Five hundred folk all speaking over one another – loutish shouts, mocking shrieks, belly laughter, bawdy slurs, high-pitched giggles. Dogs barking, tableware rattling, fists crashing, and hall-maids fighting bravely on through the tumult like ships in a storm, to keep the fire of their feasting fuelled.

Somehow, Sviggar had silenced all this. Every ear was given to the king – though Erlan reckoned by now he'd stretched their patience to a thread. He looked splendid enough, with his peculiar stamp of rugged nobility, aged but still commanding respect, the golden torque gleaming round his neck.

Hardly a name went unmentioned – every fallen karl or thane or earl was honoured, as promised. At each, a cheer went up, giving the crowd relief from their enforced silence – steam from a kettle. He'd dragged Bodvar up and they'd drunk him a long toast. Lastly, it was Erlan's turn. The king had done him special honour, seating him on his right beside his daughter. Sviggar waxed long about the service done him, and all the while Erlan stood there, itching to escape the eyes of the crowd.

Despite his discomfort, the revellers had nearly thrown off the roof with their drunken roar of admiration, making him all the more grateful when at last he sat down.

Now Sviggar was assuring his subjects how lucky they were. 'Our markets thrive. Our fields and flocks flourish. Come springtime our harbours will open and we shall become richer still. We have peace! Peace with Autha's heir. Tribute from the Norsk and the Western Gotars.' He glanced down to where Saldas sat, and beside her Sigurd. 'I see a sturdy heir and a beauteous queen. Was there ever a Sveär king so favoured by the gods?' He smiled down at his queen. She returned it briefly, then turned away with cool disinterest. The smile slid from the king's face. He turned back to the crowd. 'Let the feasting thunder this night!' he cried, and a mighty cheer rose from the benches. 'To the War-Father – who has given us victory once more.'

'To the War-Father,' the company resounded. Fists crashed on tables and the feasting resumed with fresh fervour.

As Sviggar was sitting, Sigurd called over the din. 'You're wrong about Autha's heir, Father. The Wartooth hasn't lost his taste for a fight. His sons even less. Their greed will drive them here. They only await their moment.'

'Gods, how you love this tune! Why can you not enjoy this peace?'

'The Wartooth cannot be trusted.'

Bodvar, seated nearby, answered for the king. 'A young man often looks at other men and fears what he sees in himself.'

'Very true, my earl,' chuckled Sviggar. 'Sigurd, I'll leave you a powerful kingdom. Be glad in that. You shouldn't be too swift to see deceit. Trust no one and no one will trust you. A kingdom stands on trust.'

'A kingdom stands on power,' returned Sigurd.

'I'll not trade words with you on how a king should rule. The weights lie even in the scales. Autha's line and my own can live in peace.'

'You dishonour yourself, Father. You cannot love peace and honour both. The Wartooth knows that. That is why he'll come.'

'Harald and I have won enough war-fame for our seat in Valhalla when the time comes. He has no more need to prove himself than I.'

'As you judge, let it be.' Sigurd's tone was biting. 'But when you're gone, war will certainly come. A den of wolves gathers at our borders.'

'Wolves?'

'I've heard Harald's sons are calling warriors to their halls. Ringast hosts the Friesland champion, Ubbi. Grepi and Gamli come from English shores. Others come. Why else would these raven-feeders gather? It isn't to whet their thirst on Ringast's beer!'

'And yet it is a fine brew,' declared Bodvar. 'So they say.'

'If a king rode to war every time one lord feasts another, he'd soon scrape the bottom of his coffers,' said Sviggar. 'Besides, men may be bound by sword or by oath. There are ways of peace as sure as the ways of war.'

'An oath can be broken. Bind a man by the sword, and he'll not trouble you again.'

'Ha! If only that were so,' laughed his father. He sat back, considering his son. 'So, my bold son – what would you have me do?'

'Raise an army. Bring war on Harald before he is ready.'

Sviggar's laugh thundered up the table. 'What is it you really want? A Danish girl to bed? The Wartooth's gold? Another blood worship? Come, tell me!'

'I think only of Sveär glory – and the fate of your kingdom.'

'Aye, it is *my* kingdom. You'd do well to remember it. Perhaps this time in my seat has gone to your head.'

Sigurd looked away with a scowl.

'What think you, Bodvar?'

The earl scratched at his stubble. 'Perhaps send Sigurd to Ringast's hall to see for himself.' Sigurd seemed surprised. Sat a little taller. But then Bodvar added, 'Seems his place is there among the maids of Dannerborg, swooning under Ubbi and those others.'

'Ha!' laughed Sviggar. 'Just so!'

Sigurd's voice turned to ice, a dead smile on his lips. 'I'll not forget your jape, earl. It was one of my father's first lessons – a king's memory is the measure of his wisdom. You shall find me quite wise.'

But Bodvar's face disappeared into his cup, his eyes a little jaded with drink. Erlan wondered whether, sober, he'd make the same joke. Sigurd fell to stabbing at a hunk of pork like it was the earl's throat. But he kept back whatever words he might have spoken as dark thoughts.

'I thought Bodvar wiser than to make an enemy of my brother,' murmured Lilla. The princess was almost unrecognizable from the gaunt spectre that had stumbled out of the darkness of Niflagard. Now, she was undeniably lovely, despite the purple bruise staining one temple. Her hair had been arranged into a lattice of braids, woven through with thin black ribbons and tied up behind her neck, with two loose strands framing her face. Her eyes were lined with coal, making them shine like the surface of a moonlit sea, and she wore a pale yellow gown, fastened with two ornate silver brooches and cinched with a silver-embroidered girdle.

And yet, for all her beauty, she seemed uncomfortable. As if something were making her nervous.

'Bodvar fears no man,' said Erlan. 'He serves the king and Hel take the rest.'

'And you? Do you fear no man?' Her voice was tinged with irony.

'Should I?'

Lilla shrugged. 'You have my father's favour now. But your success will have won you few others' favour.'

'Even if it meant their princess's life?'

She gave a sharp laugh. 'Whether I live or die is of little consequence to most of them, except that it should win them a better name. Now you've taken that.'

'And you?'

'What about me?'

'Do I have your favour?'

She gave him a quizzical smile. 'What do you care about that?'

He shrugged. 'Maybe I don't.'

'Then I won't tell you. I shall keep it secret. Just like you. You like your secrets, don't you?'

He frowned and smiled together, but didn't answer.

'Well then!' She raised her glass. 'Here's to *my* secret thoughts!'

'I guess I'll drink to that.' He chinked her glass and emptied his wine into the back of his throat. He'd never tasted wine until this night, it being the privilege of only the king's household. It went down surprisingly smoothly.

'You're supposed to sip it, you oaf! You'll make yourself dead drunk!' she said, giggling. Then interrupted her own giggles with a loud *hic*.

'I'm not the only one, Princess.'

She palmed her brow, blushing a little. And then she reached out and put her hand on his. '*Please* – call me Lilla. You're always saying, "princess here, princess there". It makes me want to scream!' She laughed, nervously.

'Very well.' He smiled. 'Lilla.'

'Thank you,' she said, heavily. 'You're a very curious man. You know that? I don't understand you, *stranger*.' The edges of her words were slipping. 'Tell me one thing.'

'Well?'

'Just what is it that you want?'

He looked away, picked up the wine pitcher, and slowly refilled their beakers. For a long while, he stared into the dark liquid.

'Vindication,' he said, at last.

'Vindication? For what?'

He lifted his gaze. '*Everything*.'

Maybe it was the wine she'd drunk, but her ocean-blue eyes held his, bold and unblinking. It was he who was first to look away, letting his gaze wander over the curves of her body pressed against the pale cloth.

'You shouldn't look at me like that,' she murmured. 'Not you.'

'Why not *me*?' He leaned closer.

But she didn't give him an answer, didn't look away.

Instead, she lifted her hand, almost in a reverie. It was halfway to his cheek when a voice spoke behind them.

'How charming!' Lilla jerked round, her hand dropping like a stone. Queen Saldas was at their shoulder, a smile playing on her lips. 'Friendship is often born in such terrible trials.'

Lilla looked away, blushing.

'How good to see you safe and happy, daughter.' The queen's face was half-bathed in shadow. She bent down and laid a kiss just below Lilla's ear and then, almost absently, trailed her fingertips across the exposed skin of her shoulders. Lilla trembled.

'How she has suffered! In this awful affair and more. Her poor heart. Love has been such a cruel master.'

Erlan couldn't fail to notice that a strange smallness had come over Lilla. She seemed to shrink under the queen's caresses, her expression suddenly veiled.

Feeling awkward, he fumbled for something to say. 'Princess Aslif is fortunate to have you in her mother's place.'

Lilla shot him a hostile look. Saldas tossed back her head and laughed. Like everything else about her, her laugh somehow lingered in the senses.

'You flatter me that I could replace her in Lilla's affections. Though I do try, my sweet, don't I?' She ran a toying finger along Lilla's jaw. 'But you misunderstand me. The love I spoke of is young love. Isn't it always doomed to sadness? We womenfolk are fated to love men who love war – thus, we are ever weeping.'

Erlan offered Lilla a questioning look but she wouldn't meet his eye.

'Perhaps you know something of this yourself, stranger.'

'Of love?' He snorted. 'I've no answers to that mystery.'

'There are none. We are only to enjoy its pleasures.' Her fingertip trickled over Lilla's skin. 'Or submit to its pain.'

Erlan found the unease between Saldas and Lilla stifling. He got to his feet. 'Pray excuse me, my queen. I hate to think what trouble my servant is getting himself into.'

She scoffed, delicately. 'You'd do well to find some trouble yourself, I think.'

And then, as unexpectedly as she had come, Saldas snatched away her hands and left them.

Erlan didn't linger, hastily taking leave of Lilla, but wondering what had been passing in her mind all that while. Descending the steps, the noise grew to a roar of shrieks and songs and swirling laughter. But the loudest din, of course, came from Kai's bench.

He spotted the familiar flick of his fringe. His face was upturned in riotous laughter. Everyone around him was laughing as hard.

He saw Erlan approaching. 'My brother, my brother! There you are – make way, make way,' he shouted, shoving his neighbours along the bench. 'Erlan, you have to see this. You never saw the like!' He seized Erlan's tunic and yanked him closer. Across from Kai sat Einar the Fat-Bellied – red as a beetroot, beard sticky with mead. Surrounding them was a crowd of men and maids, standing, sitting, legs cocked on benches, girls riding warriors' laps, all yelling at each other, snatching at pitchers of mead, staggering, slurring, sloshing ale.

'Do it again!' cried Kai. 'Go on, you bag of beer – for our hero!'

'What? Again?' roared Einar.

'Come on!'

'Do what?' yelled Erlan.

'He can fart out of his ear – I swear, or I ain't heir to old Askar and his fishy fortune – for all the good it does me! Ha! It's the finest thing! Everyone quiet!' bellowed Kai, drenching Erlan in a shower of spittle.

And many obliged him as Einar seized his nose, gulped down a huge breath, and blew. And then an odd little sound came from his ear – something between the tiniest horn and the smallest fart in the world. The company gawped delightedly as Einar squeezed out a jolly tune. One by one the crowd began thumping the table to the rhythm. Then came a rowdy chorus:

Drink, drink, drink till you drop,
If you can't stand up, you can shove her on top.
Drink, drink, drink to the dawn,
If you can't see straight, she can blow your horn.

They all clashed cups, sank their drink and fell about laughing.

'Quite a trick,' called Erlan when another reveller distracted Kai momentarily. 'Where'd you pick that up?'

'Got in a fight with a fella who bashed my ear with his shield. Ha'n't been able to hear much out of it since.' Einar smacked his fat lips. 'Still, I got a trick that makes folks laugh. He got a bellyful of steel and fast passage to the Heroes' Hall. It's a trade I can live with.'

Someone shoved a frothing horn into Erlan's hand. 'To good trading then.'

'I'll drink to that.'

'You seen Finn?'

'Aye.' Einar's smile curdled some.

'Is he all right?'

'For now.' Einar jabbed his cup up the bench. Further along, in the crook of a pillar, was a man with his back to the wall and a girl moving up and down on his lap. The couple were oblivious to the revelry about them. Erlan recognized the bowman's white-blond hair as the girl moved faster, pulling his head to her breasts.

'Not in mourning then,' said Erlan.

'I guess it's mourning of a sort.' Einar shrugged. 'All I know is the man ain't happy.'

'Well, this is a place to bury your sorrows.'

'So it is,' nodded Einar. 'But then there's tomorrow. . .'

Erlan offered his horn. 'Well, here's to him.'

'Here's to him indeed! We all serve Sviggar, but he actually loves the old bastard.'

And a lot of good it's done him. But they touched cups and Erlan drank off his ale.

'Brother, brother!' Kai was tugging at him excitedly. 'There's someone you must meet.'

'Who is she?'

'Only the love of my life,' he cried, pointing to a group along the table. A girl, head bright with red locks falling to her waist, was rocking with laughter.

Kai gave a piercing whistle. They all turned. 'Bara, come here!' He beckoned wildly. 'Come meet a real live hero.' He was so guileless the king himself wouldn't have hesitated, and she sauntered over.

'Ain't she a peach?' whispered Kai. Certainly there wasn't a thing about this girl that didn't drag a man's thoughts to bed. Everything was round and soft and voluptuous, leaving admiring gazes in her wake. From the spark in her eye, she knew it too.

'A real hero, eh?' she pouted. 'Ain't there a whole hall full of them hereabouts?'

'Not like him,' returned Kai. 'You heard the king – finest bloody warrior in the place.'

'What pleases the king ain't the same as what pleases me.'

Erlan laughed. 'And who are you – that's so hard to please?'

'Ain't he told you?' she cried, sending a quiver through her bosom. 'I'm to be handmaiden to my Lady Saldas. Bara, Baldur's daughter, will be a name to be remembered before long.'

'How could I forget it even now?' drooled Kai. 'You know it was thoughts of you kept me going through those long nights in the snow.'

'Aye, you've told me – and how many times!' She poked Kai in the chest. 'There must be dozens of men who think of me to get 'em through the night – whether they're stuck in a snowdrift or tucked up warm with their wives.' She threw back her curls with a laugh. 'What makes you think I'd spare a thought for you over them, my young pup?'

'Bah! They're mongrels, all of 'em! But I'm pure bred, I am. *And* I got teeth. I know how to bite.'

She sized him up, then gave a coquettish shrug. 'I suppose sometimes a cat likes to play with a pup – but it has to be some kind of animal.'

'Well then!' cried Kai triumphantly. 'You won't never play with a pup like me.'

'So *you* say. But a handmaiden to the queen can have whomever she likes and you ain't impressed me yet. Come back when you're a big dog, eh?' Bara tapped his cheek, and turned to Erlan. 'You should keep your pup on a leash. You don't want him getting scratched now, do you – *hero*?' She drew a provocative nail down his jaw, spun on her heels and disappeared into the throng.

Kai stood staring after her. Erlan slapped his back, laughing. 'Poor Kai! That puss is going to eat you alive.'

'Oh, I hope so.'

'Frey's luck with that one, my friend. You'll need it.'

'You heard what she said. I've just got to impress her and she practically promised herself to me.' Kai looked like he couldn't believe his luck.

'That's not exactly what she said.'

'Nonsense! Now then – got to think. . .'

'Well, I'll leave you to figure it out. I need a leak.'

He left Kai mulling over his problem and went outside.

The night was a brilliant canopy of stars, the air clear and crisp. It was the month of Yule. Close to the winter solstice – the day of his birth. *The longest night.* As he let the night's revelry drain out of him into the snow, he wondered whether his father would be thinking about him. Whether the Vendlagard fires burned a little colder this Yuletide now he was gone.

Now both of us are gone. . .

Suddenly a great sadness brimmed within him. He imagined flying on eagle's wings over these strange lands back to his old home – back to his father's arms.

Tears ran hot down his cheeks.

He snorted, angry with himself. *Enough of this. . . Hakan is dead. He died with his sister.* But the pain in his heart lingered.

He fastened his belt and wiped away his tears.

Suddenly, a brittle voice behind him spoke. 'Something upsetting you, cripple.'

He turned to see Sigurd. The old barb still caught at his pride. He sniffed. 'Many things. And you?'

Sigurd's nostrils tightened, seeming unsure what to say

to this. 'You should be happy,' he grunted eventually. 'This is *your hour*.'

'Not mine alone.'

'Of course,' said Sigurd, impatiently. 'But it was you who saved my sister.' He kicked at the snow. 'I suppose I should be grateful.' His sullen look hardly betrayed much gratitude.

'As should we be to you.'

Sigurd looked up sharply. 'What do you mean?'

'Your part in our victory. It's there, swinging from the sacred oak for all to see. 'Twas bravely done.' Erlan could see the anger pouring into Sigurd's face, but he didn't care.

'You dare make mock of me? You? A cripple!'

The word bit again. Erlan felt his pride pawing at the ground. But he held it in check, saying nothing.

'My father – fool that he is – reckons you a gift from the gods. But every cripple is a throwback of the gods. *Refuse*. Marked with shame.'

'That may be true,' Erlan nodded. 'Yet, though I'm a cripple, your father judged me more of a man than you.'

Sigurd's face curdled in disgust. 'You may have beguiled that old fool, but you never will me.'

'No,' smiled Erlan. 'I shall leave that to others.'

'Don't think yourself superior to me, cripple.'

Erlan leaned in and hissed, 'That's right. I *am* a cripple. But tell me, my lord – what was it crippled you?'

Confusion spread over Sigurd's face and before he could think of an answer, Erlan left him standing there and went to seek more welcome company.

He was soon back amid the roiling revelry, scaling the steps to the high table. He walked along in the shadows behind the high-born guests, passing without their notice, when suddenly – smoothly – a silhouette rose and stepped into his path.

The queen eyed him languidly as she twirled a chalice in her fingers.

'My Lady Saldas.' He tipped his head.

'Our beloved stranger. Tell me, how was your little friend? Is he enjoying our feast and all of its. . . *delights*?' She raised an eyebrow.

Her eyes were still and mysterious as forest pools. If Bara's coquetry called to a man's body, the queen's beauty called to a man's soul.

'The boy's like a cat,' he replied. 'Throw him in anywhere, he'll land on his feet.'

'His master doesn't fare so badly.'

'Perhaps.'

'You turned up here a beggar. Now look at you. You're seated at the right hand of the king.'

'For tonight.'

'You're being modest.' She sighed. 'Don't – it doesn't suit you. Your deeds won the favour of the king.'

'He does me honour.'

'It is your due. Take it for what it is. From what I hear, you proved yourself most able in bringing back our daughter.'

'I'm only glad Princess Lilla is safe.'

'I'm sure you are,' she said, a glimmer of irritation crossing her brow. 'Of course, there are other ways a man must prove himself.' She took a slow sip from her wine-cup, never shifting her eyes from his. 'You went into the wilderness. The unknown. . . and you overcame what lay in the darkness. Tamed what was strange to you.' She dropped her voice. 'A man like

573

you – with your body still so. . .' Her eyes swept over his chest. 'So young. You need a match worthy of you. A different kind of wildness to be tamed.'

Somehow the queen seemed closer now. With each word, he caught a breath of her dusky fragrance – alluring.

Dangerous.

'A different kind?'

'One that has a taste. Once a man tastes this kind, he'll never want another.'

Her lips curved in a beguiling smile, her eyes a cauldron of desire. Heat flooded his loins, as though she'd reached out and caressed him with an invisible hand.

Nearby, a chalice clattered to the floor. He looked round, distracted.

'Think on what I said, stranger,' she murmured when he turned back. 'There are ways to win a king's favour. And there are ways to win the favour of a queen.' She touched his hand. Only for an instant but her fingertips scorched like fire. 'Now I must attend to my husband.'

Erlan watched her go, waiting for the pounding in his chest to subside.

This is a foolish game to play. He shook his head clear and went to resume his seat. Lilla was there, her earlier radiance having returned. But as he sat, she gave him a strange look. Almost reproachful.

He would've asked what she meant by it, but before either spoke, a banging thundered out over the din.

There was a tumult of shouting, a clatter of tableware and the company fell silent, wanting to see what the noise was all about.

Erlan looked with the rest and saw, to his horror, his friend Kai standing alone atop a table, pounding his foot like an angry stallion. Folk around him were trying to pull him down, but he kicked them away, and went on with his stamping.

'What the Hel's he up to now?' murmured Erlan. Lilla couldn't help giggling.

Evidently feeling secure enough, Kai raised his cup. 'My king! My noble king! I appeal to you, my lord!'

At this, everyone let him be and turned to see what the king would do.

And when the whole gathering had been hung in suspense some moments, at last Sviggar spoke. 'Come, young scoundrel. What's this about? You interrupt our feasting – you'd better have good reason.'

'None better, my lord,' crowed Kai. 'I wouldn't dream of troubling you, noble king, were it not to lavish great honour on you.' He gave a slavish bow.

'Lavish, is it?' cried Sviggar, a smile creeping onto his lips. 'Tell me, lad. How does a servant boy mean to lavish honour on a king?'

'Why, with a song, my lord!'

'A song? Nay – you have the wrong king, lad. In all the Nine Worlds, there's nothing so tedious as a skald-singer!'

'I couldn't agree more, good king. A pox on all skaldmen *and* their women, I say. Nevertheless, I have a grand song for you. . . For all this noble company! I swear it's worth the hearing.'

The king shook his head, amused. 'What says my queen to such a thing? Shall we hear him?'

'I confess I am curious,' replied Saldas. 'Let him sing if he wants.'

'Very well,' declared Sviggar, 'for the queen's pleasure then – our ears are yours!'

An exultant smile flashed over Kai's face. And then, suddenly, he fell serious and still, and raising his cup, in a high clear voice, began to sing:

Hark this hall-song Treasure-Giver,
Still the horn-stream brew,
Stories sung of dead men's doings,
None like mine so true.

Wolf's wine soaking Sveär snowdrifts,
Shadows stealing, not a trace,
Black soul spirits, Hel's own children
Murder men of Sviggar's race.
Red-flood rose to Uppland barrow
Sword-wolves sought these wraiths of death,
Swallowed up by silent forest,
Four fine helm-halls bit from breath.

Kai sang on, verse after verse, retelling the whole grisly tale. Erlan let his eyes wander over the benches. A half-smile here, an open mouth there, another with her eyes closed. Listening. Hardly a muscle moved nor a cup lifted. He wondered what places they imagined, what creatures they conjured in their minds, and how different their vision must be from what he, who'd seen it all, remembered.

Kai was nearing the end of his song now. His words recalled the terrible screaming in the darkness, the fear, the stench of battle. . . it was too much. Erlan retreated back to the present.

Back to this place of warm bodies and hot food. Of laughter and song. Of friendship, even. And for the first time, he let an idea linger in his mind that never could have before.

This was now his home.

A smile formed on his lips as Kai finished his song:

Earls and oathmen bravely burrowed,
Red edge roused against the foe,
Found them there in steel and slaughter,
Harvest cut by battle-hoe.
Fey they fell upon the killing,
Brothers bled by Vandrung sword,
Sent them gladly to the Spear-God,
Came back home with shining hoard.

Now with oak-hall rafters ringing,
All shout 'Honoured Sviggar King!'
Stranger sworn a friend and brother,
Worthy earls wear golden ring.
Odin smiles upon his sword-sons,
Men were matched, his favour's won,
Fairest Freya now cries 'Daughters!
Love your lads, ere night is done!'

Kai lifted his cup, drained it to its dregs and smashed it on the floor. The tables erupted in a storm of applause. Kai stood there, overwhelmed, grinning like a crescent moon.

And for a moment Erlan forgot all that had brought him to this faraway hall and beat the table in admiration with all the rest.

577

The king meanwhile rose and waved the crowd to silence. 'So, young Gotar! A king will seldom thank you for proving him wrong, but tonight I'm happy to admit it. We shall not forget the lesson.' He slipped a ring over a worn knuckle. 'Here, lad – treasure from your Treasure-Giver.' He flung it down the hall.

A nimble house-karl plucked it out of the air and flicked it straight up to Kai. The young skald caught it and peered wide-eyed into his hand.

'First time he's been lost for words,' murmured Erlan.

'I doubt for long,' replied Lilla.

Kai dropped to his seat under a shower of backslaps, still gawping at his gold.

'It seems our young skald has inspired me,' cried Sviggar, wiping his beard. 'See this hero of the lad's lay – this Erlan, who came as a stranger. Your servant sang it true. You must now consider us kith and kin.' He looked down on Erlan with a munificent expression. 'Come – stand! Let everyone see you.'

Reluctantly, Erlan stood.

'Two things I have for you. The first is this.' He tugged off the golden torque adorning his neck. 'Take what your courage has won for me. I have enough gold besides.' So saying, he tossed the magnificent torque into Erlan's hands.

'Well? Put it on!'

Erlan did as bid.

'There. It becomes you well.'

'My thanks, my lord.' Erlan bowed his head, adjusting to the new weight around his neck.

'Now for the other,' said the king. 'Perhaps the mead of Odin's tongue is flowing sweet tonight, but it strikes me you can no longer have only this name of "Erlan" – a stranger with your past foresworn. To us you're no longer a stranger. You came as a wanderer – you and your Gotar rascal there. So I give you a new name: "Aurvandil". *Shining Wanderer.* Yes – Erlan Aurvandil is how you shall be known!'

He turned to the benches. 'Come! We drink to this hero of our lay – Erlan Aurvandil!' he cried, and sank back his wine till it ran down his beard like blood.

Erlan looked out over the sea of faces, watching his new name ripple like wind over their lips. He looked to his left and saw the old king's beaming face; to his right, the slender form of Lilla, wearing a smile so faint he thought she might be laughing at him. Perhaps he wanted her to.

He felt the warmth in their looks. *His lord and. . . whatever Lilla must be to him.* But this wasn't all. He glanced along the table into the fathomless eyes of his queen and felt their heat upon him. And beyond her, Sigurd's seething envy.

His gaze travelled further, beyond the table into the shadows. And there, for the first time, he saw the glimmer of two eyes staring out of the darkness. Eyes that he now knew he'd felt on him all night.

Vargalf. The man who moved in shadow. Erlan felt the cold hatred from those eyes and shivered.

All of a sudden a voice cried out his new name over all the others – again and again. 'Aurvandil! *Aur–van–dil!*' And the voice was so filled with wretched despair that it hushed the hall at once. All eyes turned to a man below the platform, kicking and cursing his way free of his seat, clambering over the table and leaping down to the hearth.

It was Finn, drunk as a Dane, his blond hair a dishevelled shag. 'All hail the Aurvandil!' he cried, waving his brimming

579

horn. 'Stranger, see – it is *you* who have the luck you need, not I! The favour of this great house is on you now.' His voice was a rancorous slur, his tongue slowed by drink. 'This house, which rewards faithful service with *murder*! Be on your guard, stranger.' He lurched towards the platform, jabbing an accusing finger at the king. 'I swore an oath to you. As did you to me. Honour. . . protection. . . my blood for yours. . . And what is your word worth, my *lord*?' he snarled. 'Not half a heap of shit!'

The queen leaped to her feet. 'You forget yourself, thrall. You owe your king everything.'

'Aha!' bawled Finn, cackling drunkenly. 'Yes – yes! Our beauteous queen – unrivalled in all the land! All the more so now – would you not agree?' He spun around to stir the approbation of the crowd – but was met only with silence. He turned back to the high table with a scowl. 'A curse on you, damned witch!'

'How dare you,' said Saldas, words sharp as frost. 'I'll see you join your wife in Hel for that.'

'Yes, yes, my lady,' Finn slurred, smiling. 'Plenty of time for that. But first, to the Aurvandil, all hail!' he bellowed, laughing like a madman. 'Hail to his honour! Hail to his fortune! Hail to his fate! *All hail to the Aurvandil!*' And reeling round, he put the horn to his lips and drained it to its last drop.

The company waited in stunned silence. Waited for someone to say something. The king was getting to his feet, but before he said a word, the horn in Finn's hand went spinning away and the archer fell to his knees, choking. Someone screamed. The women nearest him recoiled in disgust. Suddenly he reared up from the floor clutching his neck. Erlan watched, gripped with horror at the dreadful gurgling in his throat. Finn staggered back, smashing into a bench, sending a man careering into the table; pitchers smashed, a hall-maid shrieked, shoving him away from her. He crashed to the floor, tearing at his neck, nails clawing his skin bloody in desperation, his face purpling, his heels scraping frenziedly at the floor. And then. . . the awful gurgling stopped. His limbs stilled. His face turned ashen grey.

He was dead.

A man jumped from his bench, knelt beside Finn and bent over him, sniffing at his gaping mouth. He jerked his head away at once and looked up at the king.

'Poisoned, my lord.'

Sviggar's face was a mask of dismay. Whatever words he had were swallowed up in the babble of voices that erupted. Everyone was shouting.

But Erlan said not a word. He was staring at the ghastly features of the bodyguard, the tumult broiling all around him. And suddenly the torque around his neck felt cold and sinister as a shackle. This prize. This mark of honour.

This gold.

And its touch burned like ice.

HISTORICAL NOTE

A MIGHTY DAWN is not about recreating history. The Scandinavian peoples of the early eighth century were, in the technical sense of the word, pre-historic. They were not recording historical events, as they were elsewhere in Europe and the wider world, where writing and the preservation of written texts had already been going on for centuries.

Thus the only real means available to delve into the shadows of those dark days of northern Europe are the physical traces left behind in the archaeological record, and the echoes of events (which may or may not have happened) in the sagas and poetry passed down the generations by word of mouth, only a small portion of which would ever be captured for posterity in writing, and often centuries after they were first conceived.

Just occasionally those echoes are verifiable.

The *Ragnarök* was a central concept to the Old Norse mind. Fate was unfolding inexorably towards this cataclysmic event, when the whole cosmos would be rent by chaos and conflict, and fall into eventual destruction – the so-called 'doom of the gods' or 'twilight of the gods', depending on which translation one favours.

Our knowledge of the Old Norse beliefs about how these events would one day occur comes from two sources. The '*Völuspá*' (The Vala's Prophecy) is the oldest known poem in Scandinavian literature, part of which scholars date as far back as the sixth century. The other is the later story of 'Gylfaginning', part of Snorri Sturluson's *Prose Edda*, his compilation of Old Norse stories written in the thirteenth century.

Described in these is the *Fimbulvetr* – the 'Great Winter' – that foretells the beginning of the *Ragnarök*. In 'Gylfaginning', one of the gods describes what he knows of the signs of the coming chaos: '*There will then be great frosts and keen winds. The sun will do no good. There will be three of these winters together and no summer between.*'

The '*Völuspá*' is more poetical. It says that the children of the wolf Fenrir will carry off the moon, that they will attack the sun and paint the home of the gods red with their blood. The sun's rays will darken and the stars will no longer be visible in the summers that follow, during which mighty storms will rage.

In other words, they provide quite clear descriptions of specific weather conditions. Norse scholars have suggested that these details might echo an actual event in history – the so-called Dust Veil of AD 536. This was a natural catastrophe, possibly on a global scale, identifiable in the historical sources from other parts of the world. For example, one Roman official in Italy wrote of "something coming at us from the stars" producing a "blue-coloured sun" resulting in "a summer without heat… perpetual frost… unnatural drought." Crops withered in the fields and all the while "the rays of the stars have been darkened."

Other sources from around the Mediterranean and the Near East give similar descriptions of prolonged celestial darkness, unseasonal chill and failed harvests, and all relate how the sun was so obscured in that region that it hardly cast a shadow from the beginning of AD 536 to the end of summer AD 537.

Other scientific data backs up these historical sources, supporting the idea that something drastic occurred in the middle of the sixth century to affect the global environment, which had a particularly severe effect on the region of Scandinavia.

The cause of the Dust Veil is not known for certain. Perhaps a series of massive volcanic eruptions, perhaps an extraterrestrial impact (a comet or meteor of some kind), or else a combination of these. Whatever the cause, the existence of extreme weather phenomena in and after AD 536 is unquestionable and may have had knock-on environmental effects for up to two decades afterwards.

The archaeological record, in Scandinavia at least, shows the result was that large areas of land previously supporting agriculture returned to forestland. This in turn probably triggered a reduction in population. In the area around Uppsala in particular, the majority of villages were abandoned in favour of drastically fewer new settlements set on higher ground, away from rising waters. The collapse must have been sudden and severe. Famine was rife, in turn leading to extreme social unrest and violence. As if this wasn't bad enough, the Dust Veil may also have triggered the outbreak of the Plague of Justinian, which wiped out huge numbers of people in southeastern Europe and may have spread as far north as Scandinavia.

The mid-sixth century also saw a large increase in the number of sacrificial gold hoards deposited across the region. It's easy to imagine that such extreme circumstances might force beleaguered Scandinavians to part with their precious gold in large quantities, in an attempt to appease the gods they believed had brought this devastation upon them.

Whatever the exact explanations, the tumultuous events of the mid-sixth century appear to have left a deep scar on the psyche of the Scandinavian peoples, reflected in the stories they would go on to tell, and preserved in the details of poems like the '*Völuspá*' and stories like '*Gylfaginning*'.

Out of all of this, the central conceit of *A Mighty Dawn* arose.

Suppose that amid all the terror and confusion of this meteorological disaster and the resulting social upheaval, a group of people formed a kind of doomsday cult;

Suppose that, in order to escape the disastrous effects of a dying sun, and perhaps interpreting this phenomenon as a signal of the final doom of the gods and the destruction of the world as they knew it, they went underground;

Suppose that there they stayed, surviving at least, but evolving into an increasingly dehumanised community of earth-dwellers – the *Nefelung*. . .

Of course, my own flights of fancy – that these folk were lured underground under the influence of some kind of demon – spirals these suppositions into the realm of pure fantasy. Archaeologists are unlikely to turn up the remains of one of the shadowy *Vandrung*, however wide or deep they dig.

On the other hand, I'm tempted to say it's not as far-fetched as it first might seem. A cursory look at the doomsday cults of more recent times – Waco, Jonestown, Uganda or the Penza Region in Russia – shows that, whether you believe in the existence of demons or not, the inspiration of evil is as much a part of reality as it is of a fictional novel like this one.

The trick, I suppose, is how to overcome it.

ACKNOWLEDGEMENTS

There are three people without whom I never would have begun to write this book. Two of them would have no idea that this is the case.

I tumbled into the Old Norse world of gods and heroes through the portal of the Ring Cycle, Wagner's series of (some might say interminable) operas. I began listening to these in 2003 at the recommendation of my friend, Richard McElroy, who assured me that, with a bit of perseverance, I would discover in them something extraordinary. He was quite right. But *through* them, I discovered a whole lot more. So I have him to thank for introducing me to the material that forms the seedbed of this novel.

The seed fell much later, during a lecture in the spring of 2009, given by Michael Green, a wise old theologian at Oxford University. This seed would germinate and eventually grow into the narrative that will span the *Mighty Dawn* series. I'm sure Michael would recognize precisely nothing derivative from his lecture in this first book, but it is nevertheless the fact. For this, I am very grateful to him.

Special thanks, though, must go to Tilly Bagshawe, who

met with me when my idea for an epic novel was little more than a pipedream. It was entirely thanks to her prompting that I came up first with a plot and then a proposal, after which there were enough positive noises from her agent in New York to convince me that it wasn't an exercise in total futility to sit down and write the opening pages of *A Mighty Dawn*. That was in June 2012.

The years – just over three of them – between putting pen to paper and being taken on by an agent, were at times arduous and lonely. Stephen King's analogy – that writing a first draft is something akin to rowing across the Atlantic in a tin bath – often felt very apt. Thanks to these people for giving me the encouragement and support I needed to keep paddling: Laura Halonen, Alex Story, Will van der Hart, Rick Buhrman, John O'Loghlen, and my sisters-in-law; and of course, extra special thanks to my beloved parents and my two brothers, Christian and Alexis. I'm particularly grateful to Christian who has read every draft I've written and has never ceased to take both the book and me seriously, even when I wasn't sure that he should.

Will Francis of Janklow and Nesbitt provided further indispensable help. After wading through my thousand-page tome, he passed me on to Helen Francis, his sister. Helen's editorial advice pointed the way out of my literary mire, enabling me to shape my behemoth of a first draft into something publishable. For that, my thanks to both.

I happened to be walking away from a coffee with Charlie Campbell, of Kingsford Campbell literary agency, when the idea that formed the missing piece of the puzzle at last popped into my head. Appropriately enough then, once I had rewritten the book yet again, it was Charlie who offered to take me on, in October 2015. My undying thanks to him and his partner, Julia Kingsford, for believing in *A Mighty Dawn*, for giving it a chance and for setting about finding it a home.

At my first meeting with Sara O'Keeffe, my wonderful editor at Corvus Atlantic, I was thrilled to discover that here was a person who understood my vision, both for this book and for the series to come. Since then, working together with her to ready *A Mighty Dawn* for publication has only reinforced my conviction that the book has found its true home. A thousand thanks to her and the rest of the team at Corvus for their creative input and tireless efforts towards delivering *A Mighty Dawn* to its readers.

A book like this requires a lot of research. Out of the many hundreds, if not thousands, of pages I have read, the work of two scholars in particular stands out. Neil Price's fascinating book, *The Viking Way*, provided a brilliant understanding of the warrior ethic of the Old Norse peoples, and how this interlinks with magic, shamanism and their conception of the supernatural. Additionally, his combined research with Bo Gräslund, about the connection between the Scandinavian concept of the *Ragnarök* and the Dust Veil of AD 536, provided the grounding for the pivotal conceit of this book. I am indebted to them both.

When I started writing *A Mighty Dawn*, I was a bachelor, living alone in a small spider-infested cottage in Norfolk. About halfway through the process, I met and married Natasha, who has now become my inimitable ally in all things. Natasha possesses the most natural instinct for drama of anyone I know – a quality which I, as an author, have learned to appreciate deeply. She also has a finely tuned sensitivity to what does not work – otherwise known as "crap". As a result, there is considerably less nonsense in this story than there would have been had I been left to my own devices. But more than this, she is a creative companion. Whatever I lack, she has in abundance. I cannot express enough my love and gratitude to her for the sacrifices she has made and is prepared to make for the sake of my creative dreams.

When we married, Natasha brought with her my step-daughter, Ella, who in turn insisted on adding a dog to our number. In September, we expect a daughter of our own. Thus, the writing of the rest of this series will be a far noisier experience than the solitary business of bringing this first novel to light.

I'm not complaining.

T.H.R.B.

July 2016